For Lynn, Enjoy.

Best Wishes, Matt

THE AUTHOR

Matt Ritson was born in 1957 and raised on the northeast coast of England. As a youth he studied Art and Architecture at 'A' level, along with Ancient Greek and Roman history, then worked his way through his education, which added to his design skills and instilled in him his entrepreneurial spirit. After gaining a Master's Degree in Industrial Design Engineering at London's Central St. Martin's College, he returned to his native northeast where he spent the first part of his career both as a conceptual design consultant and a prototype manufacturer, before side-stepping into property design and development.

His hobbies include painting and sculpture, travel and hiking and he has a particular passion for the Greek and Caribbean islands. Other hobbies include scuba diving and horology: the collection of time-pieces.

Matt lives on the Northumberland coast.

THE HIPPO-CHRONOS
AKA The Antikythera Key

Book One of the Time-Horse Series

MATT RITSON

Matador
9 Priory Business Park
Kibworth Beauchamp
Leicestershire LE8 0RX, UK
Tel: (+44) 116 279 2299
Fax: (+44) 116 279 2277
Email: books@troubador.co.uk
Web: www.troubador.co.uk/matador

ISBN 978-1848767-317

British Library Cataloguing in Publication Data.
A catalogue record for this book is available from the British Library.

Typeset in Aldine401 BT Roman by Troubador Publishing Ltd, Leicester, UK
Printed and bound in the UK by TJ International, Padstow, Cornwall

Matador is an imprint of Troubador Publishing Ltd

For my lifelong trusted school-friend
and fellow student of Ancient History,
Bernard.
Who urged me to get on with this, the book
that I'd talked about writing for many years,
with the simple, but profound caution:

'You never know what's around the corner!'

CONTENTS

The Atlas Of Poseidonios

Author's Notes:	'On Dreaming'	xiii
	'On Pronunciation'	xv
Prolegomenon:	Part One - The Boy Demon	xix
	Part Two - The Carriage Clock	xxiii

Part I: New Friends   1

Chapter	1	The Wristwatch	3
	2	Boris, The Dog Of Northumberland	15
	3	The Ancient Geek	23
	4	Big Bang Theory	31
	5	Herkoose Odonton	39
	6	Rumours And Lies	47
	7	Daft As A Brush	55

Part II: The Wind Up...   67

Chapter	8	Storytime?	69
	9	The Cassiterides	83
	10	Pirates	90
	11	The Orphan	96
	12	Special Effects	103
	13	Education, Education, Education	108
	14	Zeus!	118
	15	Foreign Muck!	127
	16	Wickedness	137
	17	Ekleipsis	148
	18	Pandemonium	160

Part III: The Legacy Of Alexander And Ptolemy   173

Chapter   19   The 'Deus Ex Macchina'   175
             20   Kyrros   186
             21   'On Time'   193
             22   'On Space'   200
             23   Principles, Design And Development   208
             24   Testing   221
             25   Kyrros' Machine   228

Part IV: Never Look Back   239

Chapter   26   Sensational!   241
             27   A Clean Slate   250
             28   The Night-Mare   259
             29   Sphinxes And Crocodiles   268
             30   The Mouseion   278
             31   The Great Towers   285
             32   The Other 'Time-Machine'   295
             33   The Face Of Ashur   302
             34   Noughts And Crosses   310
             35   Wilful Disobedience   318
             36   The Uninvited Guest   329

Part V: The Exodus   341

Chapter   37   A Scouring Wind Approaches   343
             38   Questions   355

Epilogue: Estam!   361

Acknowledgements   370

... AND SORE FEAR CAME AMONG MEN

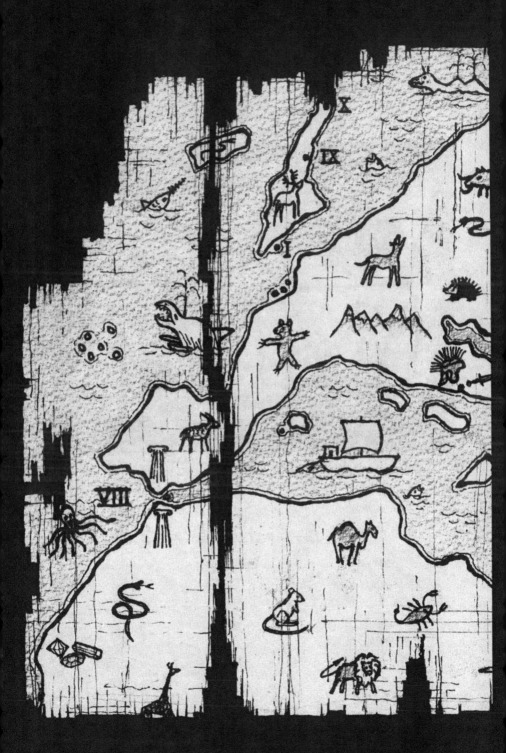

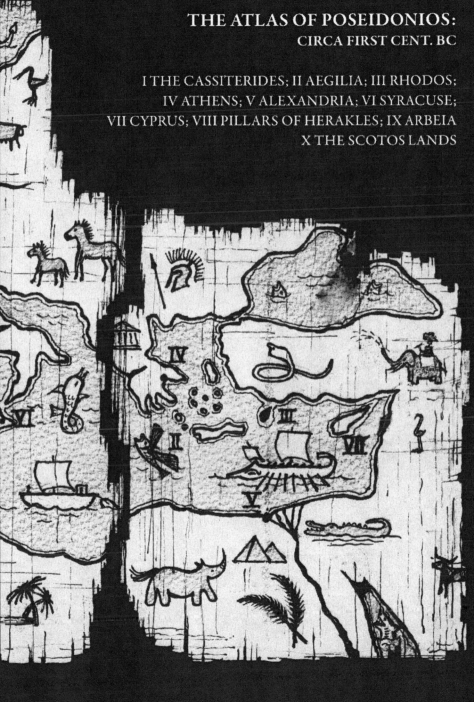

THE ATLAS OF POSEIDONIOS:
CIRCA FIRST CENT. BC

I THE CASSITERIDES; II AEGILIA; III RHODOS;
IV ATHENS; V ALEXANDRIA; VI SYRACUSE;
VII CYPRUS; VIII PILLARS OF HERAKLES; IX ARBEIA
X THE SCOTOS LANDS

AUTHOR'S NOTES:

'ON DREAMING'

One of my earliest childhood memories is of my father telling me bedtime stories of the Greek gods. Alright, I suppose even at five years old or so I must have been a strange child, because, as young as I was, I distinctly recall falling asleep wondering what the *truth* behind those tales might be! What *actual* events might have sparked those legends and beliefs?

Throughout my early school career, I was warned repeatedly to stop looking out of the window, dreaming of such nonsense. Unfortunately, I eventually capitulated: in those days, the cane and the strap were 'healthy' deterrents to anything else!

As I grew into my formative years, I eagerly decided to study ancient history, but I was bitterly disappointed that we would still not even be touching upon these legends; after all, history is about factual accuracy, not wild speculation.

Then, when I entered an adult career of design and engineering, I tried fairly successfully to ignore this former world of fantasy. But ultimately, in this, I thankfully failed.

Now, since the internet came into existence, not so long ago to me, I am amazed that many tiny, hitherto locked away shreds of evidence from across the globe – pieces of a very old jigsaw puzzle – are finally being linked together. This now sheds light on a world hitherto dismissed by experts. I refer especially to the scientific and technological history of society's earliest civilizations.

Over the past decade, at last, this evidence has led me to reconsider some of my first childhood fantasies of technically sophisticated worlds. It might even explain some of those legends, which may not after all have been too far from the truth. Maybe, then, my childhood dreams were not altogether naïve after all?

So now, I urge you, whatever your own wildest ideas:

PLEASE - DARE TO DREAM FOR YOURSELF!

'ON PRONUNCIATION'

Please, don't get too hung-up about pronunciation. After all, this is only an adventure story!

However, for those who insist that it matters, I have listed some of the more potentially awkward words and names together with accepted pronunciations. The words and names are mostly in Greek or Latin. Some other words are in English and other languages. They are **stressed** as written. Most meanings or explanations are offered, but as simple explanations or reminders – not as absolute definitions.

Acropolis [Gk] – Ack-**rop**-olis (the high citadel)
Aphrodite [Gk] – Af-ruh-**dye**-tee (goddess of love)
Ares [Gk] – **Ah**-rez (god of war)
Arsinoë [Gk] – Ah-**sin**-oh-ee (proper name. sister of Cleopatra)
Athena Nike [Gk] – A-**thee**-na **Nee**-kay (all round goddess of wisdom, war and life)
Bucephalus [Gk] – Byoo-**keff**-alus (Alexander the Great's horse and proclaimed god)
Cassiterides [Gk] – Kas-sitter-**ee-**dess (mythical islands of tin)
Chiton [Gk] – **Hee**-ton (short male robe, or kilt)
Chronos [Gk] – **Kro**-noss (time)
Chronology [Lat] – Kro-**nol**-odjy (the study of time)
Cyclades [Gk] **Sik**-lad-eez (group of islands encircling Delos)
Delos [Gk] – **Dee**-loss (sacred island, and supposed birthplace of Apollo)
Deus ex macchina [Lat] - **Day**-uss ex mat-**shee**-nah (Device of the gods)

Diadochi [Gk] - Dia-**dock**-ee (rival successors)

Dizigotic [Eng] – dye-zy-**gottic** (paternal twins – not identical!)

Drodos [Gk] – **Droh**-doss (oak tree, sacred to Zeus)

Druides [Gk] – Droo-**ee**-dess (worshippers of the sacred tree)

Efkaristo [Gk] – Efk-harees-**toh!** (thank you) *spit the last syllable out!*

Ekleipsis [Gk] - Eck-**lip**-sis (eclipse)

Faces [Lat] – **Far**-chez (ceremonial axe surrounded by sticks)

Fascist [Eng] – **Fash**-ist (pertaining to fascism)

Gyrotourbillon [Fr] – Jee-roh-**too**-bee-on (superlative rotating timekeeping mechanism)

Helio – [Gk] – **Hee**-lee-oh (pertaining to the sun)

Helios – [Gk] – **Hee**-lee-oss (one of the elder gods or Titans, and bringer of the sun)

Heliotrope [Eng] **Hee**-lee-oh-trope (sun-worshipper)

Herakles [Gk] – **Herra**- kleez (Greek hero, AKA Hercules [Lat])

Herkoose Odonton [Gk] – Erk-**oos** Oh-don-**ton** (most secret)

Hermes [Gk] – **Her**-mayz, or **Er**-mayz (messenger of the gods)

Himation [Gk] – Him-**matty**-on (ceremonial mantle, worn over the arm or shoulders)

Hippo [Gk] – Hip-oh (horse)

Horologion [Gk] – Or–oh-**lodj**-ee-on (the public time-keeping machine installed in Athens)

Index Librorum Prohibitorum [Lat] – Index Libb-**roar**-um Prohibit-**oar**-umm (library of works declared unsuitable for public eyes)

Keltes [Gk] - **Kel**-tess (cousins)

Klepsydra [Gk] – Klep-**sid**-ra (water clock)

Kronos [Gk] – **Kro**-noss (elder god, or Titan of time)

Kyrros [Gk] – **Kirr**-oss (philosopher, engineer and designer)

Mouseion [Gk] – Moo-**zay**-on - *pucker up!*

Ne [Gk] – Neh! (yes) – *again - spit it out!*

Nemes [Egyptian] – **Neh**-mess (royal striped cloth headdress)

Ohi [Gk] – **Oh**-hee (no)

Parthenos [Gk] – **Par**-theh-noss (virgin)

Peplos [Gk] - **Pep**-lo (heavy, full length dress)

Pleiades [Gk] - **Ply**-add-eez (group of stars, AKA the seven sisters)

Poseidon [Gk] – Poss-**eye**-don (god of the seas)

Poseidonios [Gk] – Poss-id-**oney**-os (philosopher, athlete and noted traveller)

Potamos [Gk] – **Poh**-tammo (place name)

Prolegomenon [Gk] – Pro-leg-**ommen**-on (to say beforehand)

Ptolemy [Gk] – **Tol**-emmy (dynastic name of Greek Kings of Egypt)

Serapeion [Gk] – ser-**app** ay-on (proper name of Alexandrian temple)

Scotos [Gk] – **Sko**-toss (dark)

Steampunk [Eng] Steam-punk (anachronistic, retro-Victorian style)

Strophion [Gk] - **Stro**-fee-on (decorative cloth headband)

Tempus [Lat] – Tempus (time)

Zeus [Gk] – Dzeeooss! *Single syllable – like 'swish!'* (father of the younger, Classical Greek gods)

PROLEGOMENON:

Part One - The Boy-Demon

Midnight: overlooking the Aegean Sea – 585 BC

Flashes of neon pink lit up the carpet of rolling cloud from within. And along with the gentle crackle, the eerie display confirmed that Zeus, 'Father of Gods and Men', had indeed forgiven those below. At least, that was how the new high priest had interpreted the entirely natural event.

Now, on the raised marble square directly in front of the huge temple, the wiry priest flicked his purple cloak behind him and held his arms outstretched – basking in the adoration of his people. A huge crowd, one of the largest that had ever gathered there, had come to watch and take part in the celebration of their salvation. As they did, their roar, and the priest's gold mask, fully concealed his ecstatic laughter. He had duped them all... and spectacularly so!

Here, it was a carnival atmosphere: but a carnival unlike anything ever witnessed before. A troupe of brightly clothed dancers cavorted in and out of the dozens of torches that lined the whole area; and as they romped around, they fuelled the excitement of the crowd. Despite the ample artificial light however, there was a certain darkness about tonight's proceedings. Although they were willing participants, the crowd had, it seemed, allowed itself to be carried along on the thin air of evil that had somehow pervaded the night. Everyone felt it. But, the assembled people told themselves, all of this was necessary. For what else could atone for, or otherwise explain, the terrifying phenomenon they had earlier witnessed.

The greatest possible disaster had been narrowly avoided that day – the new high priest had told them so. Praise the gods that he had been there to intercede on their behalf. Their salvation had been entirely due to the high priest, who had begged Zeus to remove his black shield from the sky; who had implored the god to allow Helios to continue his mission to carry the sun across the heavens in his chariot; and who had identified the young culprit responsible for the near disaster!

The shouting and cheering and general merriment continued. The mood of the crowd was kept to a sustainable level of excitement by mask-wearing players who mimed stories around the altar. These stories about the various clashes of the gods were known to them all: the hero Herakles killing the Gorgon Medusa and riding off on the back of the flying horse Pegasus; and Zeus and the sun in contest to see who could remove the cloak of a pilgrim. All of the stage props were impressively produced – from the golden masks to the wooden framed horse carried now by four of the players. There was more. The crowd waited in eager anticipation to see what entertainment would follow.

The high priest stood dressed in his full regalia. He handed his slim walking stick aside before clapping his hands twice. At the signal, Sirens – more dancing women clad in flowing, trailing layers of the lightest fabrics – entered the stage. They whirled around and around singing out a discordant, ethereal and bewitching tune, interwoven with a weird screeching and howling. It was a most demonic sound that served to astound the crowd, stirring something akin to excitement mixed with fear. The players held the crowd entranced for a long while as drum beats were introduced: quietly at first, then growing to a crescendo. Then, quite suddenly, the noise ceased and the Sirens flittered over to line up in front of the temple – and there was dead silence.

Flanked by two more priests, he walked grandly past the altar to stand on the front step. His arms still outstretched, he looked down at the crowd. Another cheer went up as the man who had saved the day breathed in self-satisfactorily. Slowly, he composed himself, conjuring up an appropriately grave face. Only then did he remove his mask. Now, he turned from them and handed it to the priest nearest to him. The crowds waited with baited breath to see what would come next.

Looking up into the firmament, the priest once again raised his arms and exclaimed, "Oh great god Zeus, we thank you for your forgiveness." Again the crowd gave a cheer. "And now... in return... we will keep to our bargain. BRING OUT THE BOY-DEMON!"

Shuffling through the temple doors and out of the darkness, the ten-year-old boy raised his manacled arms to shield his eyes. The torchlight in front of him was intense. His eyes burned with pain now; his vision so blurred that all he could do was stumble along automatically, prodded painfully forward by two more priests with sticks. The repeated prodding left what appeared to be small red flowers on the back of his off-white robe. He stumbled across the square toward the murmuring crowd, attempting to gauge their mood by the noise alone.

His head was numb with pain. Slowly, he managed to get to the edge of the top step, where he stood wavering, unsupported. His watery eyes blurred the crowd, and noises hissed in his ears. He felt nauseous and started to retch with overwhelming pain from what the young priest had earlier done to his back. And, since his brutal treatment, he was now unable to speak; dark stains surrounded his mouth. One of the other priests hit the back of his legs with another stick so that he crashed painfully forward onto his knees.

The high priest moved in and whispered something to the boy, after which there followed a short commotion among the rest of the priests.

Eventually, turning once again to the people, he called out, "ZEUS!" He stretched out his hands for the third time. "What do you wish to happen to this...? TRAITOR! This... BLASPHEMER!"

He paused for impact before announcing, "For one as wicked as this, surely there can only be one way to deal with him – to take his very life in sacrifice and to beg you never to forsake your people again," The high priest heard only what he wanted to hear from the crowd. The boy could not be allowed to go on causing this terror. And it would be only right and proper if it were true... that through his own selfishness and greed, he had nearly caused the end of the whole world!

Now, looking directly out into the crowd, the priest continued, "I ask all of you assembled here, what is his punishment to be?"

A distant voice in the crowd shouted out the one word that would send shock waves: "DEATH!"

Elsewhere, another lone voice sounded out the same: "DEATH!"

The high priest smirked to himself as he stroked his pock-marked face: what cattle they all were, what fools. What nonsense that still, in this modern day and age, people believed in the gods. Luckily for him they did though – it made them far easier to manipulate. He shushed the crowd again. He had them right where he wanted them now – the whole island was effectively his. He had won. He held out his hand to grasp the boy.

The boy thought his head would burst; there was now a growing pounding in his ears. Hardly conscious of what was now happening around him, he only wished it to end. He heard another long commotion and closed his eyes, unable to take any more pain. Then he felt his hair being grabbed and his head being roughly forced back to expose his throat. It made him choke and gasp for breath. How foolish, he realised, that he had thought to get away with his simple plan against this monster. But still he was not scared; instead he was overwhelmed only by a feeling of deep, deep disappointment. He had failed in his task to stop the priest's wickedness.

He managed to open his eyes one last time, and was able to fuzzily make out another figure. A second priest stepped boldly forward and offered the dish that held the sacrificial knife.

The high priest held the sharpened blade across his captive's throat, and the boy squeezed his eyes tight shut. Then he prepared his soul for its journey to the stars and to his grandfather. He saw a flash of piercing blue-white light that filled up his senses – and then his body became completely weightless...

However, that was only the beginning of his incredible journey!

Part Two - The Carriage Clock

Potamos – on the Greek Island of Antikythera: 1901 AD

The colourful young pelican soared effortlessly in the bright blue sky. Spotting movement below, it jackknifed into the ultramarine depths to re-surface with a single large fish. Jostling its lunch more securely within its beak, it continued on its short journey home, between the twin rock pinnacles and past the tiny ruined temple on the pebble beach. Unwatched, the seabird carried on through the narrow gap in the high promontory and into the concealed island harbour with its wooden dock. It glided over the copper diving helmets that lay beside the steam paddle boat moored there. Then it flapped awkwardly, settling into the nest it had made amongst the group of recovered statues.

The last remnants of what had once clearly been a heavily laden cargo ship had now been fully recovered from the sea bed. Today was the very last day of the difficult, sometimes perilous winter expedition: the first ever proper – that is, paid – underwater archaeological recovery.

Months earlier, the captain and crew of the small sponge-diving vessel that had made the discovery had gratefully accepted the Greek government's offer for the salvage. And, of course, their backing: for what everyone involved saw, for various reasons, as a significant discovery. They were all happy with the outcome. The few 'trinkets' kept back secretly by those personally involved were considered merely pocket money; tokens or keepsakes, part of the finders' retirement funds. Unfortunately, this also included the gold coin that showed the lone profile of Cleopatra: the one coin that could have dated the wreck accurately.

Of course, not everything that had been recovered was

necessarily treasure. There was also a small pile of more modern bits and pieces that had been dumped at the end of the dock. Whilst the group of three international archaeologists stood beside the life sized statues, carefully sketching, photographing and cataloguing the most recent finds, a small child sat alone, cross-legged, in this rare day of winter's heat. Uncharacteristically 'quiet' for him, for the last hour he had been looking from the group to the pelican and the statues while he tapped steadily away with a rock at the heavily marine-encrusted lump in his hands. The thing that he'd earlier decided to rescue from the discarded pile was what he had overheard someone casually describe as part of a modern carriage clock. It had obviously been thrown from the shoreline at some time, and had somehow found its way onto the wreck. Now, he paused in his exploration, and to the relief of at least one of the men, the annoying noise ceased. Despite being chased away several times today, for reasons of his own, the lighthouse keeper's boy from the other side of the island had returned. He looked down at the palm-sized piece of fused green metal plate and gearwheels that he had finally managed to extract from the crud.

The boy's intelligent face, framed by a mop of black hair, studied the fascinating clockwork remnants for a long time. He pondered again over what else it might be: a tin toy perhaps? But this, he knew, was not rusted as tinplate or iron would have been. It was a bit like the roof of the lighthouse – the light-green verdigris-covered copper – though not the same. *No*, he thought, *the darker colour and the pattern best matched the bronze statue of the young man that stood amongst the many damaged and badly sea-scoured marble ones.* Rummaging again in the pile, he found another piece, then another.

Distractedly, he thought of the rambling story with which his father often entertained his family during the long winter nights. *The Tale of Eos* was an island legend: it spoke of ancient pirates and orphans; of wicked high priests and eclipses. It spoke of fantastical ancient machines and philosophers; of Alexander the Great and King Ptolemy of Egypt; and, it spoke of a great tragedy that had begun long ago in Alexandria! What was more, all of it had been passed down over countless generations from memory, just as Homer's tale of Troy had been. The boy recalled a detail from the tale and looked curiously at the bits and pieces, wondering innocently whether it could be true. *If so,* he mused, *perhaps the metal fragments in my hands are connected to the ancient wreck?* It was an inspired guess.

Getting to his bare feet, he decided to ask one of the three experts discussing the latest finds. Crossing over to the small group, in his native tongue he said clearly to the neatly bearded Englishman smoking the pipe, "Excuse me, sir." The man ignored him, so he tugged at his tweed jacket. "Sir, excuse me," he repeated, this time in the reasonable English that he had picked up by listening to them over the past season, "please." He blinked.

"Yes?" The man looked down at the ragged urchin whom he had chased repeatedly. "What is it now?" he asked brusquely.

"Sir," the boy continued politely, "is this part of shipwreck treasure?"

The man looked down at the largest of the pieces, casually taking it from the boy and waving it in front of his Greek colleague's face. Exasperatedly, he turned back to the uneducated boy. "Boy, are you familiar with the word *ana-chron-ism*?" he mouthed needlessly, as if the boy was either hard of hearing or, more likely, stupid.

"No, sir," the boy answered.

"It comes from the ancient Greek, meaning 'in a wrong time' – something that cannot be! The Greeks – or the Romans, whose treasure this was – lived thousands of years ago. This, on the other hand," he looked disdainfully at the green object, "is simply part of an old clock. It is," he smirked across to the only female member of the team, "what we experts call – tosh! Trash! Rubbish! Now... run along." He was about to toss the fragment into the harbour when his young female companion stepped forward to take it from him.

"May I?" she asked.

Her colleague rolled his eyes and breathed deeply. "If you must." *Women!* he thought, turning away to continue his more grown-up conversation with his male colleague.

Behind him, the young woman crouched before the boy who had tirelessly run errands for them for months: delivering messages, bringing in food and supplies from the only island shop or fetching the fresh spring water from the underground cavern up the hill – the well of Andronicus. In a faintly Nordic accent she asked, "And what makes you think it may be part of the treasure, young Mr Galanakis?"

The boy looked up at the pretty lady he had hung around to see all this time, staring again at her deep blue eyes and her straight, fair hair, tied back in a ponytail. Finally, he tried to pluck up the courage to let her know how he felt, before she left his island tomorrow morning to head back to Athens. "Well..." he began, "its colour... It's beautiful – same like you," he gushed.

The charming compliment threw the woman. "You mean like your own eyes?" She smiled at him. *Someday*, she thought, *those young eyes would stop girls in their tracks.* "Go on." She smiled delightedly. "What else?"

"Well, it's not pale green... like lighthouse. It's same..." He struggled to remember the word. "... very green – deep green... and brown, as bronze boy." He pointed at the life-size statue of a wonderful sculpted naked youth: one of the best finds and her personal favourite.

She looked around, checking the boy's accurate observation, and then turned back curiously. "And what else?" she coaxed, settling down on her hunkers, now truly listening to the intuitive child.

"It's heavy," he said. "Not like clock – much heavy," he suggested, weighing the bits in his hand.

She took the other broken fragments from him and looked at the multi-layered patina of greens and browns, deciding that the boy was right. These pieces did match the surface of the corroded statue. *But why*, she thought, *would anyone in the modern world choose to make a clock from beaten bronze and not steel or brass?* The boy had been truly inspired. Not patronisingly at all, she said, "*You* are a very clever boy! Perhaps you're right," she indulged him. "Perhaps it is part of the treasure trove after all. Thank you."

He watched her feel in her purse for a small coin as a reward and as a parting gift before tomorrow, but put his small hand over hers, urging her to put her money away. That was not what he had waited here all this time for.

"Then what else would you like?" she asked.

The boy plucked up his courage and looked into her eyes again, making up his mind. He took a nervous step towards her. To her fascination, he slowly raised his slightly grubby hands to delicately stroke and then hold both sides of her face – all the while retaining her gaze. Then, quickly and without warning, he darted in and kissed her; a short smacker directly on the lips. Immediately, he let go, then fled past her as fast as his legs would carry him, sending the seabird flapping its huge wings as he ran up the hill towards home.

Standing up, the young archaeologist's assistant laughed and watched him disappear as the pelican settled again. Then, as her male Greek colleague approached, she took another look at the fragments, although neither could have guessed the true nature of what they represented.

In fact, what the young woman held in her hands were fragments that had once been part of an ancient machine – the Antikythera Device, as it came to be known – constructed before the birth of Christ. It was a mechanical marvel that would one day finally prove the scientific sophistication and engineering know-how of a world long ago forgotten. Now, at last, it had been rediscovered. Alas, however, it would still be many years before anyone would find out either what it was or how it worked, or even begin to attempt to reconstruct speculative versions of it.

Although even today many experts study it using cutting-edge modern technology, its true design is still not fully understood and its full purpose still not agreed upon. Some say it was a device used to track the stars, others that it was an early ship's navigation device or a device used to calculate eclipses in order to plan the calendar dates of important religious festivals. It has even been suggested that it may have been only a small part of a much larger machine – though who knows what sort of machine that might have been? Not many experts admit to being truly baffled by it, but they do all universally agree that the device is a most intriguing mechanical calculator of some sort – a 'computer' – the oldest known to man.

Perhaps its history and true purpose will never be fully known to the world. But perhaps that truth would be far stranger than fiction – almost unbelievable!

PART I:

NEW FRIENDS

TRUST IN DREAMS,

FOR IN THEM IS HIDDEN

THE GATE TO ETERNITY.

Kahlil Gibran: 20th Cent AD

1

The Wristwatch

The northeast coast of England: today

There was a nip in the air. It was the start of October and the onset of autumn. A chill breeze blew squarely off the North Sea, and along the main village street with its little outdoor cafe. The half-dozen people wearing colourful winter jackets didn't seem to mind the cold as they sat at the little round aluminium tables. They all looked quite happy to continue to tilt their faces upward into the virtually cloudless sky, sunglasses high on heads. Heliotropes: sun-worshippers silently absorbing the last rays of this year's sun whilst squeezing extra warmth from the coffee cups that nestled in their bare hands. More gloomy weather would descend on Tynemouth soon, but for now, the precious sunshine could not be wasted.

In the centre of one of the tables – the nearest to the old brick-built school diagonally opposite – sat a modern still life arrangement: a used white coffee cup and saucer, a cellophane-wrapped biscuit and a mobile phone. They had lain there untouched, beside a pair of pink woollen gloves for the last twenty minutes or so. Now, a solitary wasp, one of the last ones of the season, hovered weakly over the saucer, detecting the sugary dregs, before being casually but gently wafted aside by one of the gloves.

Beneath the table, Boris lay limp on the natural stone pavement, warming himself in the shaft of sunlight that had penetrated the shade. The woolly, blue-grey Bedlington terrier looked for all the

3

world like a discarded fluffy toy. He lay flat-out, forelegs straight in front and rear legs, along with his distinctive shaved rat-tail, sticking straight out behind. Historically, the small dog had been bred just a few miles up the coast in Bedlington town, to catch vermin. As such, he displayed bizarrely supple joints as well as, when required, incredible reflexes. During the past twenty minutes his head had lain flat on his forelegs, almost motionless, painting a picture of sheer boredom as his companion had sat above him. Like her, Boris was content to watch the big, black-painted school gates on the other side of the road. But now the same wasp drifted below the table, just above the dog's nose, momentarily grabbing his attention.

Sniffing the air delicately, the dog shifted his weight from side to side, slowly and carefully bringing each back leg around and forward into the pounce position. Keeping the rest of his body absolutely still, he moved only his eyes, head and slender neck, so that now, bolt upright, his head was held haughtily aloof. His top-knot and his long-tasselled ears hanging down and outward to the sides of his shaven cheeks gave the impression of a headdress of sorts. In total, he bore an uncanny resemblance to the Sphinx. Lazily, he half-heartedly snapped once at the wasp, but as it feebly buzzed off somewhere else Boris' interest in the insect soon waned. His head dropped back down onto his legs. He yawned languidly and stretched, then he gave a long, exaggerated sigh through his nose. He had just started to settle down once more when fresh movement above him signalled something new and possibly exciting. So instantly he sprang onto his four paws and stood, gently wagging his scimitar-curved tail to and fro, ready for the off.

The pleasant-faced young mum who sat with him at the table looked pointedly once more at the big, mannish watch on her wrist and then began to pack up her belongings into the baby-bag that was attached to the back of her pushchair. She stood up and paid the bill to the waitress. Sliding the mobile phone into the rear pocket of her jeans, she put on the gloves. Then, in one flowing move, she swung her jacket from around the back of the chair, pushing her arms through the sleeves. She flicked her black hair out from under her collar and bent down to check that the dog's lead was still firmly fastened to the handle of the pushchair. As she did so a well-wrapped bundle moved inside, briefly sighed, then settled again, safe and warm. Boris gave a woof. She shushed him with a single finger motioned to her lips. Still looking up at her as they moved off, he trotted closely beside the pushchair as they crossed the broad street, passing the spectacular bright red flowerbeds.

The woman continued on her short journey, looking directly across the road at the wooded village green where the life-size seated bronze figure of the Empress of India stood. Verdigris stains discoloured the white marble plinth on which the statue was mounted. Queen Victoria's distinctly unamused expression still had a knack of bringing down the spirits of most who passed her. Not for the first time, the young woman thought idly, *what a way to be remembered.*

Today was what should have been the happy occasion of Alex's fourteenth birthday, but it was also a less happy anniversary. That was why she'd taken the trouble to meet him. The steady stream of smartly uniformed youths who emerged hurriedly through the gates began to wane as his mother spotted him. She beamed as though it was months, not just a few hours, since she'd sent him off through the door of their house after breakfast. At the same instant, Boris began to bark excitedly, keen to see his young owner once again.

As ever one of the last ones out, Alex smiled his easy smile to no one in particular as he sauntered a few steps to the pelican crossing. He looked across the main road at the Gothic church opposite and to his whole family, and pushed the button before waiting dutifully as the light stream of cars swept by. As he did so he juggled a heavy book-satchel that hung diagonally across his shoulders and dropped his quite scruffy black sports bag on the ground. He had just enough time to unravel the dry, mud-encrusted rugby boots that hung around his neck, marking his lapels light brown. Then he combed his fingers through the tousled shock of red hair that now shone orange, red and gold in the sun. From nowhere, a solo cloud dulled his side of the street as the high pitched *beep, beep, beep* from the crossing signalled urgently for him to go! Now!

"Hi, Mam," he called out in his deepening voice, as he picked up his bag again and began to saunter across the road. Most other kids at the school called their mothers 'Mum'; not a local term, but Alex's mother liked it that he chose to call her 'Mam'. It was a small difference but it had always made her feel that she belonged here now. The light changed to flashing amber and he crossed.

The dog, which had been straining at the leash, now stood up on his hind legs and pawed the air. "Boris!" Alex almost shouted. "Come on, boy!" As Alex approached his mum and the dog there was a brief moment when the three narrowly missed entanglement, before the boy dropped his sports bag again to greet the dog with a proper pat and a rub. Taking Boris' woolly head between his hands, Alex stroked his face.

Picking up the bag once more, he stooped slightly to press his face against his mum's in a kind of arms-full hug. One of his passing classmates smirked cheekily and raised his eyebrows as he saw Alex and his mum embrace. "Bye, Alex," he said pointedly as he passed.

"Bye, Jack. See you tomorrow," replied Alex, unabashed.

Immediately, his mum half-whispered in her slight southern American drawl, "You know, Alex, it's okay if you don't do that any more." Then she looked directly at him. "You're quite a young man now, you know."

He looked straight at her. "So? Adults give hugs too, don't they?" he challenged. And with that, he beamed his big smile once again.

Just then, as the cloud drifted on, a shaft of sunshine lit his head from behind as a halo. His mum took a deep, almost sobbing intake of breath. "Gosh... you have beautiful hair, Alex," she said. "Just like your dad when I first met him. You even have his hazel-green eyes." Her own eyes began to fill up but she squeezed back the tears, determined not to let Alex see.

"I know, Mam." He shook his head and pulled a face. "How many times are you going to tell me?" he said cheerily.

And like that, the sombre moment had gone. They both smiled briefly for a moment and then, backing away from him, his mum stood upright and sniffed. Broadening her shoulders exaggeratedly, square on to him, she mimicked, "Here'sh lookin' at you, kid!"

"Humpty Go-cart," retorted Alex, *Casablanca*."

"Very im-press-ive! Two points to you." She smirked at the nickname approvingly, looking down her nose. It was a routine they went through often. His mum – an avid black-and-white film-buff and the writer of film reviews for the local rag – would do one of her usually bad impressions, and Alex, who shared her interest, would guess who'd said the words and in what film, usually correctly. "Come on," she said, "let's go."

Together they turned and walked comfortably back through the town, in the general direction of the twin promontories that each overlooked the Tyne. Their own house was built on the smaller of the two: what was known as the Spanish Battery. Then, as if the thought had just occurred to them both, they took the shortcut under the triple archway and through the alley that led to the grassy bank behind. The chunky tyres on the pushchair took the bumpy, hardened mud track in their stride. Now more exposed to the breeze, which had in fact become more of a direct blast on this windward side of the buildings, the woman's hair blew all around her shoulders and back around her face.

They drew closer to the huge stone monument to Collingwood – Lord Nelson's friend and the northeast's hero of the Battle of Trafalgar. The forty-foot-high memorial statue captured the admiral in his nineteenth-century naval uniform, draped in his ermine-trimmed robe of office. But unlike the rather formal pose that Nelson's column portrayed, Collingwood's likeness stood almost casually, looking out to the river, his left hand leaning on a rope-entwined capstan.

"Let's go up," she suggested, and Alex shrugged his shoulders lightly and stooped to grab the front of the pushchair.

Then he stopped, remembering: "Hang on! I'll let Boris off first." He unclipped Boris' lead from his collar, but instead of climbing the twenty stone steps, the dog bounded across the field toward a rabbit, which darted down a nearby warren at his approach. "Hopeless dog," Alex mumbled. "Some rabbit and ratter he is."

It only took a minute to struggle to the top of the stone-slabbed area. He now stood for a moment remembering the only other time he'd taken the trouble to help her climb up before. That had been when she was still heavily pregnant, expecting his little sister, exactly a year ago. Absent-mindedly, he glanced toward his bedroom window at the back of his house, fifty yards away as the crow flies. Then he tilted his head right back and looked directly up at the stone edifice that was Admiral Lord Collingwood.

Alex's mum chose to sit on the top step, rather than on one of the wooden benches. Lost in thought, she rocked the pushchair behind her whilst looking down at the wide River Tyne below and beyond to the large town on the south side. Her son joined her, sitting at her side, and together they shared the local sights with one another as the boy had often done with his father. Although this time, with his mother, it was as if he was spotting them for the first time.

The tide was coming in. There below, still poking out of the water, were the treacherous Black Middens – the carpet of black rocks that stretched out halfway across the harbour mouth that had been the ruin of many a vessel. Looking east out to sea were the long, inward curving, granite-built north and south piers. Each stretched out a mile, protecting the mouth of the river, and each was punctuated by a tall granite lighthouse. On the far south bank of the river, Alex reminded his mother of the Roman remains and the rebuilt fort of Arbeia concealed behind the houses. Lastly, he pointed west, toward Wallsend – the site of the start of the Roman wall. This point, marking the northernmost border of the ancient Roman Empire, was one of many local sites where his archaeologist

8

dad had worked and where Alex had occasionally been allowed to accompany him at weekends.

Sitting here brought back a flood of memories of his father. The monument had been their place. It was the place where he'd frequently brought Alex to tell him stories of his own career and of his studies of the ancient civilisations of the world. From the earliest age, it had sparked an interest in history that had become Alex's own schoolboy passion and introduced him to Latin and Greek especially. His dad had been very proud of the special gift for these languages that his son had always shown and had personally helped and encouraged him to study them well, in the hope that one day he might wish to follow in his own footsteps. He had even claimed wryly that Alex's way with languages might be genetic, since he himself, and Alex's grandmother before him, shared that particular gift. Alex smiled again, remembering.

The short lull in the conversation signalled to his mum that the time had come to mention what she'd been putting off for months. She looked down at the big watch again. "Alex?"

"Mam?"

"Alex, you've been wonderful about your dad. You do remember it's a year today since he was reported missing?"

"How could I forget?" Alex answered simply.

"Sorry, of course..." she apologised. "Anyway, you do know that I'm very proud to say that you've never really given me anything to worry about since then?" She looked at him with admiration. "I know you were as devastated as I was, probably more so. But when we began to realise he wouldn't be coming back, you seemed to take it all in your stride. Not like me, Alex – I've not really coped, what with the baby and all."

"You've been fine with us: Rachel and me." He nodded toward the pushchair. "I wouldn't go beating yourself up about a freak event that none of us could have predicted."

She took a breath and looked back at him proudly. "Alex, sometimes you've got such a way with words. I'd swear I was talking to... well... a proper adult."

9

He looked directly at her over his right shoulder. "Oh, thanks for that," he laughed.

"Well, you know what I mean," she combed her fingers through his hair.

"Anyway, it's not like I've forgotten about him, you know. I could never do that. It's just that…"

"What is it, Alex?"

"Listen, this might sound weird, but every time I think of him I just can't help smiling." He smiled and continued, "Anyway, I'd rather think of him as living somewhere else, than…" He looked away from her, back out to sea, not finishing the sentence.

"Well, that's good, Alex, and perfectly natural. And I'm sure he'd want you to – up to a certain point, but there comes a time when we both have to let go."

Startled, Alex looked once more at her and said, "No, I didn't mean that, Mam. He's not dead; he's coming back. One day, you'll see – he promised! And dad would never break a promise; you know that."

"Alex, that's all very well," she tried to reason with him, "but sometimes promises get broken…"

Ignoring her gloomy look, he continued, shaking his head confidently, "Not this time, though. If he wasn't coming back, I'd feel it – I'd know inside. Anyway, really, Mam, he'll come back one day – you'll see," he reassured her.

She smiled caringly at his display of unshakeable confidence, not wishing to push him any further for the time being. Instead, looking down, she gently pulled up the sleeve of her jacket and unfastened the chunky leather watch strap. "Alex, Dad always intended for you to have this when you were older, and this is your second year as a teenager now. It was his father's. It's quite old, and…" she stressed impressively, "… quite, quite valuable too!" She removed the watch and held it in her hand, marvelling once again at the intricate workings visible through the glass-backed case. She scanned the double-barrelled Swiss name on the face of the chronometer, *Jaeger-LeCoultre*. "It meant an awful lot to him, Alex."

10

She handed the watch to him and he thumbed the small dent in the case, just beside the winding crown. "Like Rachel, Stan never got to meet his own dad. This watch was all he ever had to prove that his dad before him had ever existed. Look after it well," she cautioned.

He took it and held it tightly in his fist, treasuring it for its family history. Alex often remembered sitting on his dad's knee as a child, asking once again to see the amazing timepiece, the object of his unending fascination. Whenever he did, his dad would always patiently unfasten the strap and flip the watch over to reveal its glass back. Through it, the beautifully intricate jewelled movement could be seen. He recalled his dad's childlike fascination with it as he explained, in simple terms, again and again to his young son how the mechanism worked.

Then one day, just over a year ago – he remembered as if it had been yesterday – his father had looked at the watch and said distantly, 'All of that work, all of that care and invention, all simply to mark the passing of our time in this world.' Then, poignantly, he'd said: 'As you get older, Alex, always remember not to waste the time that is afforded you. It's the one thing we can never get back once we've spent or lost it: no matter whether we're young or old, rich or poor!' Alex clearly remembered wondering what he'd meant at the time, never realising that his time together with his dad was about to come to an abrupt end. 'As for all other advice, sunshine' – he used the name he'd called him since birth – 'take it with a pinch of salt. Your life is your own, not anyone else's, so make your own decisions about what to believe or disbelieve – and do what you know is right.'

Alex looked directly at him. "So, how will I know what's right?" he had asked quizzically.

'Alex,' his father answered into his eyes, 'everyone in the world knows right from wrong – whether or not they choose to admit it. Most people call it conscience. The people that ignore this and shout loudest are usually those who know the least... or have most to gain. Don't let anyone tell you otherwise. The real problems in this world start when we try to find excuses for ignoring what we know to be right.' Alex's dad smiled his usual lop-sided grin at him. 'You'll be grown up soon, and you'll be fine. I know you will.'

He threw an arm around his shoulders; then, suddenly crinkling his hazel eyes curiously, perhaps worriedly, he added: 'Maybe there is one other piece of advice I should give you,' he laughed ironically, 'never make promises lightly. But if you do – always try to keep your word!'

Now, for just a moment, Alex again pondered over that distant conversation. He carefully opened his hand to look once again at the tiny ruby-red jewelled bearings and the delicate gears moving with such precision. All were held constantly in check by the rapidly ticking escapement mechanism and all were powered by the single blue steel coil-spring, set within the manufacturer's delicate rotating orb movement: the *gyrotourbillon*. No quartz and not a battery in sight – sheer mechanical perfection.

"I'm sure you're old enough to look after it now," Alex's mother said comfortably. Then, as an afterthought, she added, "Just don't wear it to school; your teachers will think we've come into money."

"No," Alex agreed, "I'll keep it in my bedroom and just wear it for special occasions. Then he quickly reconsidered: "Well, perhaps I could wear it for a few days – just until the novelty wears off!"

She laughed at his remarkable honesty as he fastened the watch strap around his own wrist now – now only two holes narrower than the indent left by his dad's own, more powerful, wrist. Alex smiled to himself. He wouldn't argue with his mother; *I will just keep it in trust,* he thought, ready for the return of his father.

Then her other words began to sink in and he thought, *if only they had come into money*; then he wouldn't be so concerned about their future. He guessed that things were tight, with the loss of his dad's income. If he'd been on expedition for the University, he'd at least have been insured – but this time he'd been on some sort of private business. "Thanks, Mam." He looked at her. "You know I'll take good care of it."

"I know you will," she said. "Anyway," she abruptly changed the subject, "if your new friends are still coming over, I'll go and get the tea ready. Are you still sure you don't want a party at the weekend?"

Alex nodded. "No thanks."

There was another lull in the conversation, so, taking a deep intake of breath, Alex's mum said finally, "Anyway... time to move on!"

Alex was immediately troubled by her last throwaway remark. *What else might she be talking about?* he thought to himself – not for the first time today. Only this morning, before school, she had made him a breakfast treat of pancakes and syrup – as opposed to anything typically English. When he had questioned her about it, she had mumbled something about having it all the time if they lived in Atlanta. Then, afterward, when he opened the small pile of cards, it was the last handwritten line on the one from his transatlantic grandparents that had set his mind ticking properly:

Happy Birthday, Alex – Looking forward to the pleasure of your company.

That was when he had realised that change looked to be on the horizon, and that was not a happy thought. It was not that he didn't thoroughly enjoy his annual visits to his grandparents' home; they were wonderful. It was just that he couldn't conceive of the prospect of moving away from here, the town where he was born. This was where his friends lived. Mainly, however, it was one sure and single thought that got to him: that one day his father would come home, and when that day came, Alex would be here to greet him.

He hadn't asked his mother what she was planning, knowing it wasn't his decision to make. And although he'd love to know, he was wary in case he got an answer he didn't like. *Best not then,* he thought.

Without speaking further, they simultaneously decided to make a move. Together they picked up the pushchair and went down the steps to find out where Boris had disappeared to. Alex was still deep in thought when his mobile bleeped. He checked the text message and pushed it back into his pocket.

"Alex," his mum said, hanging his sports bag and boots over the handles of the pushchair, "give me a few minutes to settle Rachel then I'll get a few snack things ready – half an hour, okay? We should still mark your birthday some way... even if you do have school tomorrow."

"Okay," he conceded reluctantly.

"And don't be tempted to drag your friends along the shortcut home today; it'll be too windy on the cliff edge."

"Alright," he agreed. Not that he had any intention of taking that route – he wasn't that obtuse. It was only a short slippery drop to the black rocks. Absent-mindedly, he looked around the back of the monument for signs of his friends. Then, from over his shoulder, came a familiar voice, snapping him out of his distant thoughts.

CHAPTER 2:

Boris, The Dog Of Northumberland

"Borrr...iss!" It was Conna, his best friend since they'd started school together.

If Alex was athletically built, Conna was solid. If Alex was inclined to be quiet and more reserved, Conna was outspoken and well... a bit brasher. However, while Alex was perfectly at ease in female company, Conna was inclined to be less... confident. He was yin to Alex's yang, black to his white, but perhaps more applicable to Conna, who was a rugby football fanatic, prop-forward to Alex's winger. But better still, although Alex hadn't thanked him, Conna had been a real friend over the past year. Since nursery days, the two friends had always been, as others had previously remarked, hand in glove.

Conna, wearing a thick tracksuit, ran quickly but heavily up the steep hill, huffing and puffing at the exertion and perspiring slightly at his temples and at the sides of his close-cropped blond hair. As he reached Alex he stooped over, legs apart, holding his knees – head hanging down loosely. He took out his earphones and let them dangle. "Just listening to the start of the Falcons match," he blurted out breathlessly to Alex. His rounded face and slightly ruddy complexion would have made him a target for certain people at his school if he weren't entirely capable of looking after himself. Last year, one of the older boys had even dared to call him *Lardy Boy* to his face – but since then no one had tried it again! It was only, as he himself explained, his frequent sports training that often left him slightly bruised. Unfortunately for Conna, his complexion made him prone to blushing. Whenever this happened, he always became more embarrassed at this than he had been by whatever had triggered the flushed face in the first place.

Between breaths, he asked, "Are they... still... coming over?"

"Yep," Alex replied, "I just got a text – they'll be here soon." At that, Boris, who had been shadowing Conna around the outside of the grassy bank, bounded up the steps and came speeding through his legs from behind. "Whoa! Boris," Conna gasped; but Boris was determined to play now. He circled each of the boys then executed a figure of eight around them, faster and faster, banking right and left into the corners as he did so. Then, quite suddenly, as if someone had flicked a switch, he lay flat out on the stone flags, looking away, doing his impression of the Sphinx. "He's barking mad, that dog," exclaimed Conna.

In truth, Conna loved the dog as much as Alex, maybe because his parents wouldn't allow any pets in their house. (His mother had explained they were far too messy and tying.) So the boys playfully chased the dog around between themselves for a few more minutes, waiting.

Finally, Conna checked his watch. "They're late."

"Only a little," said Alex.

"So you're not nervous then?" he asked.

"Nope." He guessed exactly what Conna meant. "Anyway, they're just friends. And I thought it might help them settle in."

"If you say so," Conna raised an eyebrow.

Alex laughed, knowing his friend was already besotted with one of the new sisters who had joined their school – not that he would admit it.

"Maybe," Conna suggested helpfully, "we should wait for them at the bottom of the hill – just in case they can't find the way?"

"Okay then," agreed Alex.

As they strolled they chatted. "D'you think they're going to be staying in the country for long?" Conna asked.

"I don't know," answered Alex. "Maddie said they'd be here until her mother's treatment was over."

"Right..." Conna's mind was elsewhere.

Together, they plodded the hundred yards down the steep old lifeboat path. Reaching the bottom, there was a distinct pong in the air. A passing trawler on its way to the fish quay must have thrown fish heads and other offal overboard. They had washed up on the semi-exposed black rocks. The sight and smell made Conna slightly queasy, so rather than wait there, they decided to walk further along Hadrian's Way – the riverfront promenade – to seek their guests.

As the pair walked, Boris, who was still trailing behind them off his lead, stopped dead in his tracks. Head held high, he sniffed the air, interested. Then, without warning, he bounded headlong down the granite steps. Alex hadn't spotted the dozen or so rats that were gnawing on the fish heads until Boris bounded into the lot. He grabbed one of them by the tail, flicked it violently into the air, instantly snapping its neck; then, as it came down, he deftly nipped it behind the neck to make sure of it. One rat went for the dog's ear but only bit into the long tassels, at which point he grabbed it and nipped it too. Then he went on to another. After chasing and killing another two in exactly the same way without stopping, he looked around to see where the others had scattered to and decided he couldn't be bothered to follow them, so he promptly returned to Alex's side again. The whole event had lasted no more than thirty seconds.

"Whoa... bloody hell." Conna's jaw dropped as he shouted out loud. "Who taught him to do that?"

Alex was about to answer, "If you think that's fast, you should see the trick he does to Dad." But before he could, a well-spoken girl's voice chirped up with a distinct Caribbean lilt, "Language, Conna!"

Conna and Alex spun around to see Maddie and Bex, the West Indian twins, coming down the grassy bank. Conna's face instantly flushed beetroot red. While he wasn't normally this fazed by girls, there was something about these two that made his tongue seem to stick to the roof of his mouth and that, for the life of him, he couldn't explain.

The girls approached the pair, their attention focused on Boris, who was now at Alex's side. The dog panted slightly but was none the worse for wear for his vermin control. "Hi, Alex. Hi, Boris," Maddie sang to the dog, bending down to stroke him. Alex smiled easily back, returning the greeting to them both, whilst Conna stood agog.

Bex, more stand-offish, stood with her arms folded, slightly behind but still pleasantly self-confident, crinkling her eyes at Conna as he squirmed. All he could muster was a rather weak and croaky, "What language?"

The girls, who were the most unidentical twins imaginable, except perhaps in some mannerisms, now stood closely together. Although at school their uniform made them look more similar, now they were determined not to be taken as twins. Their winter jackets slung casually over their right and left shoulders respectively despite the chill, they now looked at the boys. As always, Maddie, the slighter of the two, was dressed simply: her plain cream dress in sharp contrast to her dark brown skin. Standing beside her, Bex, the taller and more athletic of the two, was more casually dressed in jeans and a loose red jumper. Her lighter skin was dotted with freckles. Maddie's shorter hair hung at her shoulders whilst Bex's longer hair was tied up. The contrast could not have been more apparent. Both, however, wore identical sheepskin 'Ugs' on their feet. The sun may have come out again today, but they were still not properly accustomed to the colder climate. The twins were pretty, not to say intimidatingly so to a couple of boys, and without being conceited they knew it and often used it to great effect. Alex watched, straight-faced, as they immediately slipped into the well-practised double act that he had seen before.

"You shouldn't use language like that, Conna. It's not nice," Maddie chirped up.

"No, Conna, and neither does it make you sound any more attractive," Bex followed on similarly, slightly precociously. "It's the sign of an inarticulate – not to say uncouth – child."

Conna was instantly gutted at the use of the term 'child'. "I only said hell... well... bloody hell," he stammered, wobbling his broad shoulders around exaggeratedly and pulling an innocent face. Then he suddenly added defensively, "I mean... that's all I said. I didn't say..."

Bex cut him off. "Yes, and that's bad enough, thank you. We heard you from up there," she said, nodding behind herself to indicate how loudly he'd shouted.

"It still doesn't make you sound clever or more grown-up, though..." Maddie added to the lecture, following on from her sister's comment.

"...Quite the opposite." Bex finished her sentence.

There, thought Alex, *they're doing it again.*

Not pausing for thought, Conna asked innocently, "Well, what am I supposed to say then?"

Maddie thought for a moment. "How about, wow, that's very impressive!"

"Yes," said Bex, "or how about, gosh, how extraordinary! There are other words in the English dictionary, you know."

"Other than curse words," Maddie ended pointedly.

And even though Alex was now quite sure he was again witnessing the girls' act, neither he nor Conna could quite decide whether the girls were actually complaining about Conna's slight misdemeanour or were just teasing him.

Lamely, Conna said, "Okay then," accepting the challenge. Then, his colour returning to normal, he suddenly made his mind up that they were in fact teasing after all. Swallowing back his sudden bout of nerves, he smiled wryly at both of them and said boldly, triumphantly and sarcastically in his most exaggerated posh voice, "Holy moley, what a clever dog Boris is – whizz-whizz! There, is that better?"

Alex closed his eyes. The girls looked at each other briefly, at

19

first trying to stifle it, but then snorted. "You're mad!" declared Bex, starting to laugh.

Alex shook his head, while the twins decided that they might just finally accept Conna as a friend after all.

"Sorry we're late, Alex," apologised Maddie. "We got lost... somewhere over beside that white tower."

"The High Light?" Alex nodded back along the high bank overlooking the river.

Maddie nodded. "Anyway, what is it?"

"Oh, it's an old Georgian beacon," he answered. "From the open sea if you line it up with the Low Light, the one built down on the quayside – so that they look like one giant tower – they point out a safe path past the rocks."

There, only just visible, was the furthest edge of the Middens. Soon they would be completely submerged. Both sisters leaned over the iron railings to look down at the rocks. They gave a shudder, now appreciating why the towers had been built.

Alex took the opportunity to point toward some of the other historical landmarks, introducing the girls to the river mouth: the Roman remains at Segedunum – fort number one – at Wallsend; and on the south bank, the rebuilt fort of Arbeia.

"Arbeia?" quizzed Maddie,

"Yeah, it's the Latin name for Arabia; the Arabs had a trading post here, long before the Romans came to conquer it. But if you think that's old, they even found the remains of a Bronze Age boat in the river a few years ago."

"Really. This place *is* old," said Maddie.

"Come on," suggested Alex, "let's head to my house." It was the first time he had seen her up this close and he noticed the faintest trace of a scar on her top lip: evidence of some minor cosmetic surgery. He smiled warmly at her; it somehow added to her charm.

As they walked back, Maddie asked casually, "So, Alex, where did the dog's name come from? Boris is such a big dog's name."

Alex raised his eyebrows; it was a question he was well used to.

"It's complicated. Do you want the long version or the short version?"

Maddie looked at him. "How about the short version for now."

"Alright," he began, "once, before we had him, Mam, Dad and I... we were watching an old horror film, *The Mummy*, and out of the blue Dad said that its star, Boris Karloff – the Hollywood actor – used to come to Bedlington to buy terriers to take back to California with him."

"Boris Karloff?"

"As in the original Frankenstein – with the flat head."

"The guy with the bolt through his neck?" joined in Bex.

"Yeah, that's him."

"And did he did he really come all the way here?"

"Sure, and he wasn't the only famous movie star either. Stan Laurel was brought up here too – lived beside the High Light – even went to our school."

"Did he? No one told us." Maddie and Bex looked impressed. "We like Laurel and Hardy films, don't we Bex?"

"Mm-hmm," she agreed readily.

"Anyway, Boris used to breed Bedlington terriers and give them to his Hollywood friends because they're so friendly, so unusual and they made sure there would be no vermin in the houses while they worked away on location. For a while they were a bit of a fashion accessory out there. A lot of Hollywood stars had them."

"Like who?" Bex asked.

"I can't remember," admitted Alex, "but Dad said that there were quite a few. Anyway, when Dad brought the little ball of black fluff in a few weeks later..."

"Black fluff?" Maddie butted in.

"Yep, they're all born like that, then they grow out of it. Anyway, we all thought that the whole thing was such a daft story, there was only one name we could give him – Boris!"

Conna mulled over his own, as he thought, embarrassing full name – deciding to keep the closely guarded secret known only to Alex and himself. Instead, chancing his arm, he attempted to make conversation with the girl walking alongside him. "So, Bex, where did that name come from?"

"It's complicated," she replied. "They're island names – d'you want the long version...?"

"Oh, so it's not because your dad's a football fan then?

"Certainly not, thank you," she snapped, moving off.

Conna saw Alex rolling his eyes at him. *What?* he mouthed silently.

Reaching the bottom of the old lifeboat ramp, Maddie called out, "Last one up's a sissy." She broke into a sprint, closely followed by Alex, Boris and Bex.

"Not again," mumbled Conna under his breath.

CHAPTER 3:

The Ancient Geek

Boris reached the top of the ramp first, followed closely by Bex and then Alex and Maddie more or less together. Conna wasn't that far behind. There the four stopped to take in the whole panorama that continued from Collingwood's monument. It was the view from the promontory, undeniably one of the best on the northeast coast, that gave the place its true appeal.

Within that single sweep stood the south and north piers, between which one of the white Scandinavian ferries was leaving the Tyne, heading out into the steel-blue North Sea. On the distant horizon two RAF training jets chased each other low over the sea, the distant noise of their howling engines unmistakeable. Now that the winter season was on its way, everyone would have to get used to their presence. To the north, a short distance away, was the twin promontory of Pen Bal Crag, with its exposed rock face. On its top stood the skeletal remains of the ruined castle and priory. Alex called out for the dog, which had shot ahead to sniff around the large expanse of grass and the rocks beyond, and then turned to face the ruins. On an evening like this, when the last of the sunlight had started to fade, the silhouette of the priory, with its tall arched windows, seemed to come alive as the golden light picked out the stone tracery. "How old's that place?" Maddie asked conversationally. "It looks like it might be haunted."

Alex raised his eyebrows. "You don't believe in that sort of stuff do you – ghost stories and things?"

"I guess not." She laughed properly for the first time, starting to relax.

Alex couldn't help but smile along with her. "Well... the castle was built in the middle ages, probably from stone re-used from Roman times. Bits of Roman roof tiles and amphorae were even found there. The priory recycled some of the same stone later again."

"Oh," she considered, "clever." Then, quickly turning to the small group of houses behind them, she asked, so which one's yours?"

Behind them, stood the mish-mash of buildings – now all private houses. From the opposite, north end of Spanish Battery Hill there stood four brick-built Edwardian coastguard cottages. The terraced block had been recently bought and refurbished by a local builder. It was probably the high asking prices that explained why they were, after nine months, still empty and up for sale; but for now, Alex and his small family had the area almost to themselves. By contrast to the cottages, the two more individual detached houses that stood in between those and the old watching station were in very much original condition.

"That's where I live," Alex pointed out. "My family's lived there more or less since it was been built. It's a bit on the small side, but we're happy with it."

Alex's dad had always described the house pretty accurately as being from the 'whacko' school of design. It was a whitewashed, pre-war affair with two upper-storey windows and a single round porthole window to the side of the ground floor bay window. It looked directly out to sea. It had a proper garden too – a walled cottage garden complete with a mixture of vegetables and a riot of coloured flowers that brightened the whole of the house from spring to autumn. After that time, nothing of much interest would grow properly on this exposed windy site. The woodwork had always been dutifully repainted every year; the biting winter wind, the salt air and the strong seasonal sunshine made this a must.

There was no garage, but instead an empty, oil-stained drive where his dad's battered Land Rover used to sit.

"So who does that last, big house belong to?" asked Bex, wrinkling her nose.

"Oh... that," Conna butted in dramatically. "That belongs to the Ancient Geek!"

"Who?"

"The Ancient Geek," he repeated clearly.

The old lifeguard's house had been built as a statement of the Victorian's commitment to commerce and safety at sea. But now, nothing had been touched externally for ages. The timber-framed windows that weren't boarded up were in desperate need of repainting, if not replacement. After years of neglect, they were, in fact, almost bare silvered timber. The door too was in need of a protective layer of paint and there now remained only flaky patches over successive traces of previous coats. Again there was no garage, but to its side stood a detached, windowless storehouse – the intriguingly named rocket house. The completely unkempt walled garden was covered in long grass and weeds. Nettles and other ridiculously over-grown leafless bushes almost covered what was just visible of the front door and the ground floor windows. They even partly obscured any views that the upper story French window and balcony might afford. Thankfully, though, the roof was in a good state of repair. Alex wondered about its reclusive, now possibly absentee owner.

"Now *that's* what *I* call haunted looking!" Bex looked at it in astonishment.

Alex shrugged and retold the story of his father speaking about their neighbour a few years ago. "He told me the old man who lives there had always been something of a mystery. All dad knew about him was that he'd come here years ago from Greece – in the sixties. Over all the years he'd lived in the house he'd always avoided contact. But to dad he was never the cantankerous character that everyone else guessed he was, just 'obsessively private', even a 'tad eccentric'. He only got to know him a little, just before..."

25

"So what's his proper name?" Bex cut in, obviously unimpressed by the nickname.

"Haven't a clue," shrugged Alex. "Dad said it was always a bit of a mystery. Anyway, since his retirement he's supposed to be a sculptor of sorts: strange, moving, mechanical sculptures. Apparently, for most of his life he worked at the university – quite the computer whizz kid in his youth – at least that's what *dad* told me." Alex remembered retelling the tale to Conna last year. He also recalled his reaction at the time. Conna had just about choked on the can of Vimto he was drinking. 'Whizz kid,' he'd said, 'you've got to be joking. He must be a hundred years old!' "But now, no one's seen the old man up close for years, or even been near his house. Not since the incident."

"What incident?" prompted Maddie.

Conna butted in again: "The kidnap!" he announced.

Both girls looked shocked.

"Well..." Alex explained, "Dad told me that years ago, just after I was born, the old man caused a bit of an upset."

Conna couldn't resist: "The police were called and everything. His mum and dad caught him wandering off with their new baby – Alex!"

"You! Really... like properly kidnapped?" Maddie gawped.

"Well, not exactly," said Alex, playing it down.

"But he did take you away, didn't he!" Conna knew the tale off by heart. He spun it out: "The old man had picked him up out of his pram and had carried Alex to the edge of the cliff..."

"Well, I think it was more the freaky excuse for his actions that really frightened Mam..." admitted Alex.

"And what was that?" asked Bex.

Conna leered dramatically: "That he was going to offer him to the gods!"

"What?" Maddie gasped. "Sacrifice him?"

Alex shrugged. "Since that day, she refuses to talk to anyone about it. The whole thing completely freaked her out."

"I'm not surprised," said Maddie.

"Anyway," Alex continued, "after a little while, the police let him go free. They told Mam and Dad that he was just under stress – confused. She wouldn't have any of it, though. She was adamant that she didn't want him near the house again. Dad said he even sent her an apology note and some daffodils from his back garden, but since then he's always kept completely out of the way. Dad thought it was a shame really – he always seemed quite lonely."

"Away with the fairies, though," Conna warned.

"Or just a bit sad," said Alex, shrugging.

"So where did you get that name for him?" Bex frowned.

"Well," continued Conna imaginatively – eyes narrowed, "old man... Greek... makes computers... never comes out of his house. That makes him an Ancient Geek, doesn't it?"

Alex winced a little at the retelling of how they'd arrived at the slightly unkind name.

Maddie looked uncomfortably at her sister. She didn't smile.

"It seemed funny at the time," Alex explained, "quite fitting – and as no one knows his proper name, the nickname stuck."

"We don't like name calling," declared Bex shortly. "It's not right – we know about it, don't we, Maddie?"

Maddie looked directly at Alex. He understood – at least in part. "I guess it's hardly the same," he admitted, "but I can't say I like having to pretend to be constantly amused at the same pathetic jokes about ginger hair and pale skin."

"Actually, I quite like it," smiled Maddie. "Few people have got hair that colour in the Caribbean. Instead, they dye it with henna, but it's not the same. It's got no sparkle." Her eyes crinkled.

Alex smiled back at her.

"Well what about getting called Fatty?" Conna asked.

"Stop feeling sorry for yourself – you're just big boned," Bex scolded.

"I am?" Conna clearly hadn't thought of that.

"Well?" The girls raised their eyebrows.

"Okay, maybe it's time we found another name," the boys conceded.

"So does he still live there?" Maddie looked at the house.

Alex turned toward it also. "Well, probably not... at least I don't think so. In fact, I can't remember when I last saw him."

Conna stared. "I think I saw the curtains twitch when we first got here."

"That was probably just a draught. Come to think of it, no one's seen or heard anything for ages, not even the old gramophone records that we used to hear. Mam said she wouldn't be surprised if he was living in a nursing home now."

Conna reconsidered. "Nah. I wouldn't be surprised either," he said, turning around. "Shame, though. I miss him in a weird sort of way. He was kind of spooky, always looking through the window... and a bit crotchety too."

"So what's he look like?" asked Maddie.

Alex looked up at the window, remembering. "Well, we only really ever used to see him when we played on the grass in front of the house – throwing the rugby ball back and forth. The old man used to stand slightly back from the French windows, staring – white as a ghost. He was always dressed the same, in a long night shirt, and always looking a bit bedraggled. And he had a mop of long silver hair and a heavy beard."

"He used to look like a bl...inkin' big dandelion seed-head," Conna almost stumbled, "but whenever we looked up at him he would usually shake his fist at us, so we always kept away. I'm telling you... he's freaky."

There was a short silence and Alex was about to suggest they all went into his house when Conna suddenly blurted out, "He's bloody well there again! I'm sure of it, behind the curtains." Then he adopted his posh voice again and amended, "Sorry, I mean... I say, everyone. I think I saw someone looking from that window... yonder!" He raised a single eyebrow toward the girls, smiling in mock apology. The girls gave him a look of disapproval but didn't bite – this time.

Alex looked briefly. "Conna, that'll just be the wind. He's not there, but even if he was, he's harmless."

"You say that, but you don't know... do you?" replied Conna. "He could still be dangerous."

"Conna," replied Alex pointedly, "he's just an old man now. He's hardly likely to sprint after us and attack us, is he?"

"Well, I'm just saying, that's all. After all, he's still a freaky old far...reigner." He just stopped himself this time.

"What do you mean by that?" enquired Bex.

"Yes, now what are you saying?" repeated Maddie, slipping into their double act again. Alex, now standing by his own front door, grimaced and turned to intervene on Conna's behalf before he had a chance to get himself into trouble again, but Conna was already in hot water. The girls simultaneously pursed their lips, their stone faces levelled at him.

"Not that there's anything wrong with foreigners!" Conna almost shouted, quickly realising his double gaff.

"Actually, we're second generation Caribbean, Conna, born right here on Tyneside," Bex stated matter-of-factly. "Dad's British, he met mum on holiday. Then, he brought her back here. When we were born, they went back; we're not foreign!"

"Really?" Conna swallowed, clearly on the ropes now.

"Yes, Conna," joined in Maddie, looking a little hurt. "But that doesn't excuse you being a xenophobe."

Conna looked pleadingly at Alex for help. "A what?" he looked horrified.

"Someone who hates or mistrusts foreigners," Alex explained in dictionary style as he beckoned them all through the door.

The girls, who were glaring at Conna, butted in: "Yes, really." They looked pointedly back at Conna as they walked up the path.

"I didn't mean it like that. I just mean... well... I wouldn't trust anyone who hides behind the curtains, watching people," he went on, trying to dig himself out of a hole.

"Well, does that mean we shouldn't trust you, Conna?" Maddie casually slung back at him.

"Yes, Conna, does it?" added Bex, raising her eyebrows.

Alex turned back and snorted with laughter to see Conna with the most embarrassed expression across his once more beetroot face. He remembered Conna telling him how, only last week, whilst walking past his house the twins had suddenly looked up together at his bedroom window and waved as he dived out of view onto his bed.

Disappearing through the door, Bex looked down her nose at Conna and smirked cheekily: "Anyways, come along – sissy!"

Without a word, the boy dutifully followed the girls through the passage and into the living room.

"Come on, Boris – now!" Alex beckoned assertively and the dog finally followed them all into the house – clearly not the only one with his tail between his legs.

CHAPTER 4:

Big Bang Theory

Within two minutes, the dog lay asleep in one of his many usual spots, this one under the TV. The four chuckled at the bizarre noises he made; who knows what the dog was dreaming about.

"Alex, you're early," his mother said, greeting them all with a brief hug. "Hi Conna, hi girls, I'm Penny. I guess I was expecting you to be identical," she said, "but you couldn't be more different could you?"

Maddie shook her head proudly to confirm. "We're not monozygotic twins, we're dizygotic."

"Oh," Alex mother sounded impressed. "Good words!" Penny smiled and then excused herself.

As she left the room, Conna grovelled and excused himself once more to Maddie and Bex – just so that they wouldn't get the wrong impression of him. After which, he helped make the girls comfortable in the small but neat family living room. Through the closed glass doors, in the even smaller dining room, Alex's mum started to fill the table, while Alex loped upstairs to get changed.

Feeling comfortably at home, Bex sat cross legged on the floor beside the open hearth.

Sitting on the sofa opposite, Maddie nodded over to the battered old, painted tin rocking horse that stood in the corner. "Where did that come from?" She asked Conna curiously, "it looks like an antique."

Conna went suddenly quiet. Keeping his voice down he said, "It was bought in the sixties – for Alex's dad."

31

"Yeah?"

Conna shrugged. "I liked him."

"What do you mean *liked?* Where is he today – on Alex's birthday – are they separated or something?"

Conna didn't know how to tell them. "Didn't you know? Stan went missing... exactly a year ago." He looked at his watch subconsciously. We were all at Alex's birthday party, waiting for him, when the police arrived instead – some party! He'd gone on an expedition of some sort, to North Africa. It was on the news and everything. All they found was his Land Rover in the desert. But they kept all the details a bit hush-hush!"

"And they've still not found him?" asked Maddie.

Conna shook his head.

"No one told us," said Bex.

"Well, they wouldn't, would they? No one ever talks about it."

"So do you think he's coming back?" asked Maddie.

Conna nodded sheepishly. "I hope so," he tried to keep the faith. "They thought he might've got kidnapped, but when there was no ransom demand... Now just about everybody has given up." He could have said: "except Alex," but didn't.

Even Conna missed Alex's dad, he went on to tell them. Although he was a bit older than his own parents, he'd always had time for Alex and Conna, was always patient with them, always understanding. And, Conna missed the ritual of coming over for one of Stan's Saturday morning bacon sarnies: the thick sandwiches dipped in the frying pan with lashings of brown sauce that he wasn't allowed at home. "Those things," declared Conna, thinking of his own younger, health conscious and more career minded parents, "was the best thing about having a slightly older, more relaxed dad," he was certain. 'You'll do more damage to your heart by worrying about your diet all the time!' That's what *he* used to say."

At that, Alex's mother opened the door. "Tea's ready, come and ged – dit," she sang.

The table was filled with plates full of pizza, hotdogs,

sandwiches and crisps. Alex, now changed into his more usual combat trousers and tee shirt, beckoned them in and seated at the simple round table, they ate. And while they ate, they all chatted about the small differences in their experiences and the language difference between here and the Caribbean: about 'crisps' or 'chips' and 'French-fries'; about 'jam' or 'jelly' and 'jello'; and about 'sausages' or 'hot-dogs' and 'hot dogs'. (And everyone looked at Boris, panting to get in at the food.) After a few more minutes, Alex's mother appeared at the kitchen door carrying a homemade and decorated birthday cake – complete with candles. Even though he hadn't wanted to celebrate the day, Alex appreciated the gesture. "Make a wish," she instructed, and of course, he did. A brief chorus of 'Happy Birthday' later, the cake was cut.

As if it mattered to anyone, at the table Maddie and Bex were equally well mannered, Alex too, whilst Conna scoffed the remaining three pieces of cake with both hands. After twenty minutes or so, the faint, unmistakable sound of a crying baby came from upstairs. Then, shortly afterwards, little Rachel toddled unsteadily into the room, before falling on her bottom. She was closely shadowed by Boris, and then followed Penny. At once the girls came into their own, cooing over Alex's fiery-haired baby sister. "Alex, you didn't tell us," they said as they gently picked her up between them.

"We're lucky to have her, aren't we, Mam" said Alex.

"We certainly are," Penny confirmed. Last year, no doubt due to the stress caused by Alex's dad going missing, she had been rushed into hospital and had nearly lost the baby.

Whilst the girls chatted to Alex's mum about her, Alex took the opportunity to point surreptitiously to Conna's face – to save him further embarrassment. Remnants of raspberry jam and icing were clinging around his mouth and chin, so Alex pointed upstairs. Conna put a hand up to his sticky face, then took the hint and excused himself politely, squeezing past everyone to go up to the bathroom. As he left the room, he suddenly remembered the Falcons match and, checking his watch, retrieved the iPod from his

33

pocket. As he went out of the door, he pushed in his earphones to catch the latest result.

He'd been out of the room for about ten minutes when the girls said they'd have to go before it started to get dark. They stood up to leave. It hadn't been a huge birthday celebration, but it had lifted the curse that had hung over the day.

Alex's mum stood too, holding Rachel in her arms, so the girls thanked her first, then Alex for inviting them over. He was about to suggest doing something else soon, maybe the ice rink or the swimming baths, when suddenly something made everyone stop dead in their tracks.

There was a barely perceptible rumble beneath their feet. Inaudible at first, as it grew, everyone detected it through their feet and bodies. Then, two of the empty glasses that were standing next to each other on the table started to rattle and clink together, slowly to begin with, then more quickly and noisily.

It felt like they were standing near a train line, but they weren't anywhere near one. The ground they were all standing on was rumbling far more now. The rumbling then changed to more of a shaking, as more and more of the room's contents started to vibrate.

They all looked at one another, at first curiously then, as the shaking grew stronger, more worriedly. A faint, high pitched howling, whirring noise came from outside the room and grew in volume and pitch. It sounded like an enormous old steam kettle whistling higher and higher. Maddie became clearly worried. Lips trembling, she suddenly grabbed Alex's hand and looked pleadingly into his eyes.

Boris, whining at first, now began to bark furiously. Then he too began to howl toward the bay window in the living room.

Bex, now unsure herself, grabbed Alex's other arm with both hands. The three huddled together in sudden panic, the girls with their eyes closed tight, squeezing his arms more and more. Now Alex couldn't cover his own ears even if he tried.

The baby, sensing that something was wrong, began to cry as

34

her mother tried to shield her from the noise. Penny covered one of Rachel's ears and the side of her face with one hand, and nestled the other tight against her. Now, Penny closed her own eyes, the deafening noise increasing again until they were all clearly in pain. The dog bayed agitatedly at the window. Alex looked up and into the living room. Blue electrical sparks danced around the window frame like St. Elmo's fire. Maddie half-opened her eyes for a split second and then closed them again. The sparks continued up the lamppost outside, while the noise changed yet again to a screeching. And just then, as Alex thought he couldn't take any more, he saw a piercingly blue-white slow flash of light. It blazed momentarily at the front window and illuminated the whole of the living room for what was perhaps only a second at most. Then there was a clap of thunder directly overhead.

However, as suddenly as it had started, it all faded rapidly away along. Now it became no more than a faint valve-radio whine in their ears.

Nobody spoke. As they continued to listen, a faint clonking sound came from outside in the passage. The girls, still hugging Alex tightly, twisted their heads to squint toward the connecting door. They held their breaths, not daring to speak. Slowly the door opened... and as it did, Conna stopped dead in the doorframe, looking at his feet.

"YES!" He yelled at the top of his voice, punching the air, 'Twenty-one eighteen!' He took out his earphones.

Everyone in the room jumped; Bex screamed. Conna stopped suddenly, gaping open-mouthed, clearly astonished at the sight of Alex and the twins hugging closely, their heads tucked into the side of his face. He let out a faint "Hello, what the blood...inkin' heck's going on here then?" and quickly shut his mouth tightly again before something else had time to slip out of it.

Alex, still visibly shaken, ears still ringing, was the first in the dining room to speak. "What on earth was all that horrendous noise?" he said to no one in particular. But Conna, looking sheepishly around the other faces, gulped, "Well, I'm sorry, but..."

he added, "...I did close the bathroom door first!" Then he went red again.

As Alex watched, Boris looked thoroughly disinterested once again. Now, the dog seemed completely unperturbed. He trotted back over to the TV in the corner and dropped onto the floor. Briefly he assumed his Sphinx position, before he lay flat out as if nothing had happened.

Bex, realising now that the panic had passed, backed away instantly.

Maddie looked up at Alex and smiled politely. Sheepishly, she let go of his hand. "What were those weird sparks?" she asked.

"Beats me," Alex shrugged.

Now having recovered her composure and without waiting any longer or wasting time talking, Bex pushed roughly past Conna to go outside and see if she could see anything or anyone. She was followed more warily by Maddie. Conna, still astounded by the 'group-hug' he'd witnessed in the dining room, muttered to Alex, "What did I miss?"

Alex's mum also began to recover her composure as Rachel stopped sobbing. While the others made to go outside, she stayed to look after the baby. "Maybe it was a plane, one of the training jets," she said, still standing in the dining room.

"What was?" Conna asked, still mystified, obviously unaware of the whole event having been listening to the match in the bathroom. Alex also pushed past him to join the girls outside. By now they had spotted the black cotton curtains flapping out of the broken windowpane of their neighbour's house.

"Do you think there's anyone in there after all?" asked Maddie.

"I don't know, but I think we ought to check, don't you," he advised.

"Yes." They all nodded vigorously in agreement.

Alex and the girls ran out of the gate, around the front garden walls and up to the end house. Judging by the broken glass that lay on the ground directly below the window, Alex guessed that both panes had been blown outwards. He cautiously navigated the glass and the ridiculously overgrown bush that obscured half of the front door and all of the downstairs windows, and reached toward the doorknocker. After knocking a couple of times, he called out, "Hello" and waited a moment for an answer. Then after a couple of moments, he repeated himself, this time through the letterbox in the centre of the door. "Hello – is there anybody home?"

"Well of course there is," said Conna, now standing third in line behind the girls. "I told you I thought I'd just seen him less than an hour ago." The three looked sharply round at him. "Now what have I said...What?" He pleaded, holding up his hands in surrender.

"Check the downstairs windows," said Alex pointedly. So Conna dutifully pushed gingerly past the thorny bushes to check to see if a window was open, while the girls ran around the back to do the same.

After a minute they returned. "Nothing," they said simply.

"Nothing," repeated Conna, "it looks like it's been nailed shut!"

"Is there anybody home? Do you need help?" Alex called again through the letterbox, but there was nothing but dead silence. Then, very faintly, they heard a weak voice calling from inside: "Ne!"

"Nay!" repeated Conna.

"No," Bex stepped forward, realising. "Ne! It's Greek. We were just there this summer, weren't we?" She replayed her holiday Greek in explanation, firstly nodding her head vigorously up and down, 'Ne' then, shaking it from side to side, 'Ohi', finally simply mouthing exaggeratedly 'Efkaristo.' They were the only words I understood for two weeks," she explained.

"Yes, no and thank you," translated Maddie in agreement.

"Pooh any toilettees?" Conna joined in phonetically, triumphantly remembering a gem from his own family's Mediterranean cruise, a year ago. "Where are the..."

"Yes, Conna," Bex cut him off, "we can guess."

There followed a faint tapping from inside the old man's house. "We'll have to go in," said Maddie. "Conna, bash the door open." Conna had his uses.

"Me?" The boy looked flabbergasted.

The three looked him up and down knowingly – by far the stockiest and the strongest of them all. So he shrugged once again, "Okay... I'm not getting the blame for the damage though – promise?"

"Promise," they echoed. And with that, Conna ran at the door with a rugby charge that his games teacher would have applauded.

First contact, the lock was forced to yield and the door flew open sending him straight into the side of the staircase behind. As he crashed to the floor, Bex jumped over him first, then Alex, followed by Maddie. Leaving Conna to pick himself up, they ran in various directions through the bare cracked-plaster walled passage, over its rough floor boards and throughout the rest of the interior, calling out for a sign of life.

CHAPTER 5:

Herkoose Odonton

It was Maddie who found the old man upstairs in the front bedroom, although, in fact, it resembled more of a workshop. Heavy wooden benches lined the plain white walls. All around it was cluttered with all sorts of bizarre mechanical paraphernalia and various tools. Alex got the distinct impression of a room that was somehow a cross between a school woodwork and metalwork shop, and an art and sculpture studio – with bits of jeweller's repair shop thrown in. Strange metal models and gadgets, in something like the style of *steampunk*, but much older, lay around. Cogs and gears were also strewn all over one bench nearest the window. There was a gaping hole in the ceiling, and the entire room was covered in a still settling thin white layer of what was plaster dust. The old man lay semi-conscious in the middle of the floor, wearing what appeared to be a very old-fashioned, ankle-length nightgown. He was covered entirely in the same white dust and rubble from the fallen lath and plaster ceiling which now covered the floor and also covered the overturned and strange looking clockwork mechanisms that lay all around the room. A very large and mangled metal object lay right beside him. Though it was largely covered by a chunk of the ceiling, Alex thought he could make out a sculptured animal of sorts.

Maddie, who had quickly assessed the situation, called for Conna to get help. Then Bex took the initiative to go into the bathroom and find the old man a glass of water. As the girls lifted his head and shoulders up lightly to encourage him to take a drink, Maddie brushed back the full mane of white hair covering his eyes. He held them tight shut to prevent the dust from getting in them. As he sipped at the glass of water, some of it dribbled straight down from each corner of his mouth, leaving clear tracks which disappeared into his thick beard. Lying there, he now resembled a sort of bizarre, not to say macabre, ventriloquist's dummy. A tiny trickle of red showed through the dust inside his right ear as the old man silently rolled his narrowed eyes up at Maddie's face. "My pills," he nodded toward the floor beside an old armchair; he looked in pain. Bex ran over and grabbed the small bottle for him.

While the old man started to come around, Conna ran back upstairs. "Your mum's rung for an ambulance. I told her it would be best just to stay at home with Rachel, 'cos of the dust!"

Gradually the old man blinked, trying unsuccessfully to get his eyes open. Then, starting to come around properly, he again tried unsuccessfully to sit up. He took another sip to clear his throat and at once began to talk animatedly with his right hand. His left hand, covered in thick plaster dust, trailed at a very odd angle on the floor.

He spoke excitedly but unintelligibly in what might have sounded like normal Greek to the others, but what seemed to Alex's slightly more familiar ear, to be not exactly so. Instead, there was the trace of a local Tyneside, *Geordie,* accent and lots of odd sounding words thrown in, not unlike some of the ancient Greek words he'd picked up from being around his dad over the years.

"Please, what time is this?" the old man croaked drily.

Alex looked at his watch, "About eight o'clock."

"No, what month... what year?"

Alex looked at the faces of the girls, worried that the old man was becoming confused. He answered testily.

The old man grimaced. "Ohi!" he said under his breath. "A whole year late." But then, after a short delay, his mood suddenly brightened. "Hah!" he exclaimed. "Hah... hah!" And although Alex couldn't hear him properly, a single word he did clearly recognise –

40

"EUREKA! At least I made it back!" He followed with more of the same short, extraordinarily gleeful ranting. Tears of joy rolled down his face, leaving more tracks.

Conna motioned briefly to Alex, crossing his eyes and tapping a finger at his own skull whilst letting his tongue loll out to the side. "Doo-lally-tap!" he said. "Maybe we should've rung for the nut-house instead."

Bex frowned at him. "Go outside and make yourself useful," she scolded. "Wait for the ambulance." Without answering, Conna shook his head lightly and plodded out of the room. After a few more seconds, whilst the girls continued to hover around him, an odd expression came across the old man's face. He fixed the slits of his eyes suspiciously on Maddie in front of him, "Ashur?" he almost sobbed, followed by another few words in Greek, "...is that you?"

"My name's Maddie," she explained, "you've had an accident."

He looked at Bex silhouetted against the window. "Miriam?" When she didn't answer, he stopped to compose himself, looking back around the room disappointedly. "Not Antikythera then?" he shook his head lamely.

"Auntie who?" asked Maddie.

Alex wondered too. He shrugged.

Ignoring the question, he went on abruptly, "Accident... so I have... I forgot." His head turned slowly again now, squinting at Bex then Alex in turn. Hardly opening his eyes, he nodded lamely at the loft and said unconvincingly, "Water heating... maybe the boiler has burst?" There was no sign of any floodwater.

Maddie and Bex walked toward the window to discuss his state of confusion and other things. Alex heard Maddie say, "I'm telling you, I saw these strange sparks... it was weird..."

"Well what's that got to do with anything?" muttered Bex, as they began to talk the whole thing through.

Fixing next on Alex, the old man beckoned again with his right hand, "Please."

Alex stooped toward the old man who was still covered in

41

rubble, and as he did, he narrowly avoided kneeling on a pair of familiar old-fashioned green sunglasses. The boy picked-up the Ray-Bans and his neighbour took them gently from him. Squeezing his eyes painfully shut, the old man briefly rubbed them, then the dusty glasses, before managing to put them on. Now, waving his hand towards the heavy canvas cover which sat in the opposite corner, he breathlessly indicated for Alex to bring it over. "Please... cover up my sculpture... before it gets damaged."

The old man gestured for him to spread the cover across the tabletop and the tangled heap of metal poking out from beneath it. *It all looks a bit late for that*, thought Alex. Nevertheless, he dutifully and gently covered it all over to his neighbour's apparent satisfaction.

"Efkaristo," he thanked the boy.

Now studying Alex's face and hair more comfortably through the green glasses he said, "I know you..." he coughed weakly, "you are one of the ball players whom I used to beckon to come over," he demonstrated the gesture they had mistaken for fist shaking.

"Yes," agreed Alex, now noticing the slightly lame hand. "I'm sorry, we didn't realise."

"No matter," he peered over the top of his glasses, fixing pointedly on the boy's wristwatch. Alex noticed and for some reason felt compelled to shield it with his other hand.

"You are the boy from next door..." he beamed suddenly. "You are Al-lex!" He pronounced the name thickly.

"Yes," Alex said politely, taken aback that the old man should recognise him, let alone know his name. Suddenly feeling quite foolish at being in the man's house, he said, "Yes, I'm Alex... pleased to meet you."

His neighbour didn't offer his name in reply. Instead, he said vaguely, "Yes... I was about to come looking for you... it has been such a long time since..."

"Looking for me?" Alex was flabbergasted. "Why?"

Switching the subject abruptly the old man said, "You know who these belong to, don't you?" He tapped the glasses with a fingernail. "They are your father's."

Alex frowned. "I thought so."

"He lent them to me," he said honestly. "Don't worry; I intend to give them back."

Alex felt slightly uncomfortable. "He's not around anymore," he managed to explain.

His neighbour beckoned him closer. Tapping the side of his nose with a finger, he whispered, "Never mind, I'm sure he'll return soon. After all, I could never abandon him."

Now what's he talking about, Alex wondered. Maddie and Bex looked out of the window, still deep in discussion about the weird sparks. As the girls waited for signs of the ambulance, the old man beckoned Alex closer still. First checking that he was the only one within earshot, he began: "Your father told me to find you – he said that you would be able to keep a secret – and lend a hand."

"What?" asked Alex. "When?"

"A few minutes ago – or was it last year?" he looked worriedly at the boy.

Obviously he was becoming delirious. Alex listened on placatingly, trying to sound interested. "What do you want *me* help you with?" he asked.

"The thing is, Alex, I do not belong here – I am originally from Greece – many years ago."

"Oh." Alex nodded his understanding of this much. "Yes," He looked at his dad's watch, wondering where the ambulance had got to.

"About my sculpture here," his neighbour began.

"What about it?"

"It has a name," he launched in urgently. "Translating that name from the language of archaic times it was made in, it would today be called – 'The Time – Horse'. However, it is more than just a simple sculpture."

Alex looked quizzically, and a little apprehensively, at him.

"This, the most ingenious machine the world has ever known, was constructed a very long time ago. It is difficult to believe, I know, but as unreliable as it is, this machine was built to exploit the web of fissures which composes the very fabric of the universe. It was built to move across and through both time and distance!"

'Time and distance?' 'Horses?' Alex looked wary, now disturbed about where the conversation was heading.

The old man continued, "For many years, it lay dead – unusable. But eighteen months ago, or is that now six months ago? " he asked the ceiling, "with the help of your small dog, your father and I finally found one of the missing keys that has once more allowed its operation," he spoke into the boy's wide opened eyes.

"Dad and Boris?"

"Yes, that is the dog's name," he beamed. "I remember now."

Alex frowned.

"Unfortunately, I seem to have damaged the machine once more. Al-lex, would you consider helping me repair it. It will take only a few days. I would do it myself but..." he winced painfully in demonstration as he tried to move.

Now the boy looked directly at him, wondering how to get himself out of the situation. "Why ask me?" he quizzed.

"That is a straight forward question that deserves a full answer," said the old man. "But, Alex, let me first caution you. I have only ever told a few people before, and each time trouble followed me. I will tell *you* now, for one last time, because your father said you would not betray me. A short while ago, he assured me that I could rely on you, trust you to 'keep your word of honour!' Is this true?" The boy's face dropped at the repeated mention of his dad. As far as he knew, the two had hardly ever met, and yet he began to recognise the presence of his father's words in those of the old man. "Ye...es," he said warily.

The old man sounded suddenly weary. "Then, Alex, I will tell you. If it is still possible, I wish to return home... to the world and the life I was cheated out of over two thousand years ago!"

Alex looked incredulously at him. "You're saying you're two thousand years old?" he said flatly.

"Certainly not – but I belong back there and then."

"So... you're reincarnated?" Alex raised his eyebrows.

"No!" the old man denied flatly.

The boy struggled to keep up with the conversation.

"Alex, if I can achieve this return," continued his neighbour, "I will finally perhaps be able to try to repair the time-paradox: the chain of enormous damage that was accidentally started in the Great Library of Alexandria."

Alex instantly recognised the name of the ancient wonder which had mysteriously been burned to the ground in ancient times.

"Please Alex, if you will – won't you consider helping me to accomplish this? I must somehow return to my own ancient world: to Egypt in the time you know as 48 BC. And then... we can also rescue your father!"

Alex stood stock still, struggling to take the bizarre claims in.

The old man saw the look of incredulity on the boy's face. Removing the glasses and opening his eyes fully for the first time, he almost pleaded: "Alex, before saying no, at least let me tell you of how the machine came into existence, then you may begin to believe me... without thinking I am insane! Please, find me tomorrow and I will tell you. But for now," he cautioned, "remember, all of this must remain herkoose odonton!' You know this ancient Greek phrase?"

Alex translated in his head. "Something about mouth?" he squinted.

"That's it – a great secret – to be kept strictly behind the row of one's teeth!"

The boy stepped away, intrigued. He said nothing more, whereupon his aged neighbour closed his eyes and sank back down, silent and exhausted, to the floor. The girls moved back over to soothe and pamper him as he drifted in and out of consciousness toward sleep.

A sudden thought occurred to Alex: he recalled a short conversation he'd had with his dad just before he'd left on his expedition to North Africa and he began to stare at the old man. Then he flipped back the canvas and looked more curiously at the

45

weird, dented sculpture lying beneath. The strange shaped and eyeless head of the beast poked up at him, instantly grabbing his imagination. Now Alex began to look with renewed interest at his old neighbour.

In the distance, the rising and falling of a thinly pitched emergency siren could be heard approaching. Through the broken window, Alex sighed deeply as he absent-mindedly watched the flashing blue lights approaching. Conna ran up the narrow drive to meet the ambulance, flagging it to its destination, whilst Boris barked furiously behind.

CHAPTER 6:

Rumours And Lies

The twins' dad, Freddie, as he introduced himself, picked them up around 10.30. He'd been alarmed when they'd first called to tell him why they'd be home late, but then perfectly happy to wait following Alex's mum's intervention and her explanation of the evening's events. Alex had still been washing the plaster dust off in the bathroom, so they never got a chance to meet, but his mum told him afterwards that he'd been very understanding and even impressed by the way everyone had pulled together. When they'd left ten minutes or so after, the twins offered to drop Conna off on the way home, so he went along with them.

Conna lived in one of the biggest houses in the smartest part of village. His parents were already in bed so he let himself in with his latch-key. He went into the voluminous and immaculate kitchen and checked the vast, but mostly empty, American style fridge for something to eat, but nothing had been left prepared for him. Then he went to the freezer compartment.

He had brilliant parents, he told himself. It was just that, as a heart surgeon, his dad worked around the clock. As a result, Conna never really got to see him except for a few brief hours every now and again. His mother, who was a barrister, was hardly around either; she spent most of her time in or around court. Even if she was at home, she could generally be found in dead silence in her own study. Conna spent most of his time in the company of their maid, Sofia, who was a kindly middle-aged sort, but who was under strict instruction to keep the house thoroughly tidy at all times. However, she had gone home to Eastern Europe for a few weeks. It was okay having a few flash cars on the drive and having all the latest computer games he wanted, but sometimes he wished that, like Alex, he could just spend some time with his parents. And, now and again, possibly get a simple hug or even a pat of affection as well.

Never mind, his bedroom was the complete antithesis of his mother's obsessively tidy culture. Once through the door, he climbed over the piles of books, clothes and games and sat on the edge of his bed. There, he watched his own, brand-new flat-screen television and munched on the microwaved pizza he'd made, before climbing into bed for the night. As always, whenever there was no one else around to talk to, he'd sit and watch a documentary – or maybe two.

Back at the Spanish Battery, Alex's house seemed suddenly amazingly quiet. His mother sat on the sofa in silence. "Everything okay, Mam?" he asked casually.

"So, so," she answered. "Alex, I know this might seem a little callous – but don't get too involved over there will you. I still wouldn't trust him if I were you."

Alex looked shocked; it was unlike her. "We're just helping out mam... and it *was* a long time ago... anyway, I am big enough to look after myself now!"

Worriedly, she turned away before heading upstairs. "Okay," she capitulated. "I hope your birthday wish comes true Alex!"

"I hope so too," replied the boy. "I hope so too."

At school the next day, after putting down various circulating rumours that Alex and Conna and the two new girls had broken into and ransacked an old man's house – somewhere, no one was quite sure where – the four planned on going back to see him. This time, no one referred to him as the Ancient Geek. However, after a phone call to the local hospital, they found out that he was being kept in. In that case, they decided, after school they'd meet up at the bus stop and head for the hospital. So duly, by six o'clock, Alex had changed from his school uniform and into his tee shirt and combat trousers. He threw on one of his hooded tops and a parka, and went off to meet his friends.

Twenty minutes later, they walked toward the small room off the main ward. "You must be Alex," the nurse looked at his bright hair. "Go in, you're expected," she said. "He told me he hoped you might be calling. But perhaps it would be best if you go in one at a time."

"Okay," they agreed jointly, "Alex first." Conna and the girls sat in the corridor, while he slipped through the door.

The old man lay propped up silently in bed, his eyes wrapped by a light gauze bandage. He was obviously asleep. Alex took a seat opposite him and settled, looking at the figure that was his mysterious neighbour. Various medical machines surrounded him and tubes of different sorts came from beneath the lightweight tangerine blanket. As the boy studied him where he lay, now a bit more 'cleaned-up', the rather scary ventriloquist's dummy that he'd remembered from the night before didn't look half so bizarre. And neither was he the frail, rather pathetic picture that he looked last night, even though his whole upper body and his shoulders were wrapped in bandages which extended down to his left arm, now held in a sling. The white mane of hair was also strapped down by bandages, which held a wad of padding over his right ear. He had a kind, if not particularly clean face. Odd bits of plaster were still buried in his beard and moustache. Presumably he was still in no fit state to have a proper wash. What was visible of his thin-lipped mouth was closed firmly. Curiously he didn't look half as ancient as he had done covered in the dust. He was old, sure, but maybe just about as old as Alex's dad by the look of him. He reminded him a bit of a younger version of the cheeky photograph that hung in the school physics lab of Albert Einstein – 'The Father of Atomic Science' – the one with his tongue poking out. But the old man didn't have the large nose that often characterised old men. This was a perfectly slim, straight nose. To Alex, he was clearly much younger than they had thought previously, and, he considered, more 'elegant', if that was the word. There was also the trace of an old, deep scar, disappearing from his right temple into the bandage.

Alex watched the old man sleeping silently, his mouth twitching slightly – probably dreaming. Feeling a strange empathy with him, he continued to look at the vaguely familiar face for a few minutes. It was not long before the patient began to awaken; he immediately patted his eye bandage, checking. Instantly delighted to know the boy had come to see him, he did not waste time. Eagerly, he began to relate his bizarre tale in more detail. To Alex's consternation, it was indeed a version of the same story that his dad had told him before he had left on expedition. He also outlined a very dramatic version of what had happened to Alex's father – if Alex chose to believe it – or at least a version of it; although none of these details had been reported by the press, nor previously told to Alex. He also dictated a list of certain proofs, or 'facts', for the boy to write down and check if he wished; so that much, he dutifully did. But, he cautioned the boy, it was all, for now at least, herkoose odonton!

After fifteen minutes, it was a clearly bewildered and subdued Alex who got up to ask all of his three friends in together – the old man insisted. Throughout the meeting, Alex's neighbour was quite charming. He weakly thanked each of them in turn for 'rescuing' him and for visiting him there. But despite asking several times, the old man obstinately avoided giving them his name. Even when Maddie asked directly, he simply proffered the excuse that he had been called by many different names throughout his life. "What did they call you when you worked at the university then?" Alex coaxed, only to be met unhelpfully with: "Professor!" Alex stayed quiet after that. They didn't stay long, he was still clearly tired, but before they left, Alex was again asked to stay behind.

Alex's neighbour sensed the boy's reluctance to believe him. He sighed exasperatedly. "Let me offer one last thing," he urged. "Your father had a very rare and valuable watch."

Alex looked down at it, then to the patient's bandaged eyes. "I'm wearing it now," he advised.

"Good. Then tell me, it has a dent in it... beside the winding crown, has it not?"

"Yes," Alex confirmed that too.

"It was I who caused that – just yesterday."

"What!" Alex said. "Anyway, what's that got to do with anything?"

"The thing is, I have a watch too – exactly the same. I have never seen another one like it. I only bought it a few months ago, because it reminded me of your father's."

"And?"

"Understand," he declared, "it is not one like it, it is the same one, with the same dent, in exactly the same place."

Alex narrowed his eyes. "You're saying the two watches are one and the same! How can that be?" He shook his head.

"I don't know," he admitted. "It is quite a paradox."

That's one way of putting it, thought Alex. "Okay then," he said, seizing on the snippet; this was something that could be easily verified. "So where's yours now?"

The old man sniffed. "Unfortunately," he said stroking the sling that held his left wrist, "it seems that I have mislaid it!"

It was an exasperated Alex who now looked at him.

"But you can still check it out of course," he suggested. "That is not the only odd thing about it. The manufacturer claims to have started making them only since the turn of the new millennium."

The boy scowled. "I'm going," he said flatly, "I'll try and call in to see you sometime next week."

Later, in the cafe opposite the school, Alex sat with his friends, listening while the others talked about the whole experience, especially his reluctance to give them his proper name. He stirred his cappuccino absent-mindedly, wondering about one thing in particular that his neighbour had told him.

"Anyway, I'm not going to call him the Ancient Geek," complained Maddie, "it's just disrespectful."

"And neither am I," concluded her sister. They went back to their latte coffees.

It was Conna who finally settled it. He had sat drinking his hot chocolate from beneath a vast peak of squirty cream and sprinkles, when he suddenly blurted out, "Then how about we call him Tom!"

"Pardon?" the girls asked, jointly.

"Tom," repeated Conna, smiling triumphantly. "*Tee... Oh... Em,*" he pronounced clearly. "The... Old... Man!"

"Oh," they repeated together, "Tom!"

"Yes," agreed Bex, adding, "he can be cleverer than he looks, can't he?" She nodded toward Conna.

Conna tried to work out whether that was a compliment. He frowned.

"It's still not very flattering," Maddie stated flatly, wrinkling her nose.

"It's better than the Ancient Geek..." offered Bex, as she looked accusingly at the boys "...as long as no one tells him where it came from."

"Okay then?" asked Conna.

"Well... yes," said Maddie. "I suppose so."

"That's agreed then, yes?"

"Yes," they repeated, "Tom it is!"

So, while they finished off their drinks, they agreed a rota for visiting Tom over his stay in the ward.

Afterwards, still not quite himself, Alex got up alone to walk the short journey home. Then, before parting company at the cafe door, the girls waited while Conna finished his now cold drink. "See you later," they chimed, then walked arm in arm the opposite way along the street, smirking. After all, it was only a little cruel to let Conna get home before finding the squirty cream and chocolate moustache for himself.

When Alex returned home, his mother asked perfunctorily how the patient was. Alex told her that he was at least conscious, but no more. Then he manipulated the conversation around to the subject of his dad's Land Rover and asked particularly about the condition it had been found in. Warily, she finally admitted that she'd been keeping part of the truth from him. It had indeed been found beside the pyramids at Giza – riddled with bullet holes! Alex's heart sank a little further. However, it confirmed that at least Tom clearly knew something more about the disappearance of his dad than others did. Admittedly though, how, and in what circumstances, were still wide open!

Next day, when Conna paid his usual mid-morning Saturday visit, Alex only partly confided in him with the information that he thought Tom might know something about his dad, but on the strict understanding that, for now, he did not share it with either of the girls. It was too important for anyone to confront his neighbour with it. To do so would be to possibly shut him up before he said more. He left out all of the more outrageous claims. In the meantime, Alex would make it his own task to find out exactly what those circumstances were.

That Sunday evening they all visited the hospital together again. After again avoiding giving them a name, Conna came right out with it. "Why don't we just call you Tom?" he suggested blatantly, despite the still mixed expressions on the faces of the others.

After pursing his lips in consideration, the old man agreed. "Alright... If you wish, it's a no-nonsense name I suppose." So, that was that.

Throughout the following two weeks, the four friends each took it in turns to visit Tom in the local hospital. Alex took in the Ray-Bans that Tom had requested for when they took the bandages off – hospital lights were too bright, he complained. From then on it seemed the sunglasses would never leave his face.

During this same time, Alex was not idle about checking the story out. Since his last conversation, he had spent some considerable time checking some of the given list of 'facts' for himself. During breaks and lunchtimes at school, he had been working in the library until the librarian had 'chased' him out to lock-up each evening. And at home he had taken every opportunity to use his mum's laptop computer to continue with what he described to her as his homework. The disturbing thing was that each of the individual facts that he had been able to check on Google and on Wikipedia had proven true. However, it was the last thing that he found out that especially spooked him.

It was in the form of an answer to his email enquiry, from the watch manufacturers themselves. Oddly, it re-confirmed, albeit rather curtly, the fact that the watch had indeed only been manufactured since 2004 – just as they had repeatedly advised the same home email address last year! And no, they still insisted that there were no earlier similar models or prototypes ever sold before then.

The old watch then, handed down firstly to his father in the 1960s, despite now being on Alex's own wrist, was a mystery – not to say a complete anachronism!

Now he couldn't get Tom's story out of his head. It whirred around and around, even when he was supposed to be busy with other things – at school, with his friends (although they had all been both to the swimming baths and the ice rink together since), and at home. With his mother, Rachel and even poor Boris, he had seemed distant. Conna especially had always been used to spending most of his free time with Alex, but now Alex was always 'busy with other things', staying late in the school library until he was asked to leave. He had appeared intense, even moody on occasions, unusual and uncharacteristic for him, and this change to his character had not gone unnoticed. Even by the end of the first week, questions were being asked about Alex and his behaviour. By the second, people were more concerned. Was it just a perfectly natural growing phase he was going through? Was it because of the anniversary of the disappearance of his dad? Or, was it something to do with his hospitalised neighbour? Certain people began to talk.

But although Alex was conscious of how his routine had changed, he was unaware of any of this 'talk'. That is, until the weekend before Tom was due to return from hospital – the weekend before the half-term holiday.

CHAPTER 7:

Daft As A Brush!

NB a more detailed version of this chapter is posted on the Time-Horse website.

First thing on Saturday morning, Alex lay in bed thinking of his father. But instead of descending into gloom, he recalled again the tale his mother had often told him – the tale of her and his dad's whirlwind romance.

Penny and Stan had met on her solo vacation to Greece when she was still in her early twenties. She was a junior reporter from New York, although, as a fan of the movie industry, she was far more desperate to become a review writer. Resigned to the prejudice of being regarded as too young for the post, she had taken her camera to Greece to see if she could instead begin a new career as a photographer.

His dad had been in his mid-thirties. He recalled her description of him: athletic, six foot tall with a mop of red hair, and ever the archaeologist; he wore khaki shorts, an old peaked cap and his big sunglasses. By chance, they had met on the island of Tinos in the Cyclades islands, where she was taking photographs and he had come to look at an old sundial. Stan described how he'd first heard the story of the device from his mother, and had since read about its importance at home in England.

However, coincidentally, a few days later they had bumped into each other again in Athens, where he was photographing a curious eight sided marble building: the 'Tower of the Winds', also known as the 'Horologion'. That was when they had begun properly chatting about why he was there: on research. The common historical link between the Tinos sundial and the Horologion of Athens, he told her, was that were the supposed work of an ancient philosopher and engineer, Andronicus of Cyrrhus, or, to use the Greek form of his name, Andronikos of Kyrros. Hence the childlike inscription around the cracked rim of the Tinos sundial in particular: simply 'Kyrros'. However, after the completion of the Horologion, Kyrros had mysteriously vanished from the pages of history after a supposed two hundred year career span!

Stan immediately offered to take her to dinner there and then in the nearby Monastiraki area: 'Touristy but good,' he explained. And that had been basically that. She realised that what actually attracted her to him was the confidence his age brought, his lack of pretence, his intelligence and honesty and his mild sense of humour. Although she'd never before been particularly interested in archaeology, it was also the way he could enthuse her, speaking passionately and convincingly about his own subject.

He described the ancient city of Athens around them: from the ruined temple of Athena Parthenos, the Parthenon on top of the Acropolis overlooking the city, to the various other ruins in the area. But in particular, he speculated about Kyrros' Horologion. It was rumoured that it had at one time housed a public water clock – 'an ancient Time-Machine'. Perhaps, he smirked, that might even explain how, if the records of the engineer and philosopher's career were to be believed, he had vanished from the pages of history.

It was only an amusing coincidence to her that being born on Tyneside, the archaeologist was a born Geordie – and she was from Georgia. It was also entirely fortuitous that he had been born and schooled in the very town where one of her all-time comedy heroes had been raised – Stan Laurel. And, he even bore his first name. There seemed to be, if she had been looking, a series of small signs that they had been meant to meet again.

A few weeks later, when he had taken her up on the offer to visit her in New York, he had proven popular enough with most of her friends, though his outlook and fitness had put a few, noses out of joint, especially the younger male ones. On his last night there, over dinner she made up her mind about him and proposed to him there and then. The confirmed bachelor was taken aback by the unusual offer, but given that he had rarely met someone so beautiful, exciting and intelligent, he accepted immediately. Either one knew when one had found the right partner, or one did not. Within the month, Penny and Stan were married quietly and living in his family house in Tynemouth. Shortly after, she was expecting Alex.

Alex smiled again to himself.

The loud knocking and Boris' barking startled him. Then he heard the distinctive voice of Conna in the passage downstairs. He stretched out and looked at his dad's watch, which he now kept by the side of his bed. Eight o'clock – on a weekend! This was a first for Conna. He wondered what had got into him.

"Alex, Conna's here," his mother called up.

"Alright, I'll be down in a moment."

Boris jumped up at him as he walked in the kitchen, and he crouched over to pat him. "Hey, Boris, you've been in the bath – who's a handsome dog this morning?" Standing up again, he said, "Morning, Mam" then he walked over to the sink and gave her a brief hug. "Morning Conna," he called across the table to the figure munching on toast, sitting beside Rachel in her highchair.

"Mummum," came the reply.

"Morning Rachel," the baby, covered in egg yolk, continued to attempt to get the toast soldiers in her mouth. He picked up the frying pan and put in two rashers, ready to make himself a bacon sarnie.

Conna noticed. He coughed politely. As he added another two rashers, Alex couldn't help but smile wryly.

"So what have the two of you got planned for your week off school?" his mother asked.

"Oh, nothing much. Tom gets out of hospital this afternoon and I promised that I'd help Maddie and Bex tidy up his house and help him settle back in this week."

"And me," volunteered Conna.

"So that's his name," she commented.

"Well, not exactly," said Conna, about to explain.

Alex shook his head at him.

"Well that's neighbourly," she said flatly.

There was a silence.

"Fancy taking the dog for a walk?" asked Conna.

"Can do," Alex replied, so with that they walked to the door, grabbing the bacon sandwiches and their coats as they went.

"Klaatu Barada Nikto!" Penny called out after him.

"Eh!" Conna looked back.

"*The Day the Earth Stood Still* – not the giant robot – the other one... can't remember his name."

"Michael Rennie," she replied. "That's one to me."

A few days of autumn sunshine had been forecast for the start of the week – an Indian summer of sorts, before rain and gales later on – but there was still the blast of cold wind to dress for. Typically, the dog was out of the door before either of them.

The boys made their way out along the north pier, heading into the fresh north-westerly wind.

"Come on then, what's wrong?" urged Alex.

"Ohhh... nothing"

"Really?"

Conna looked directly at his friend. "Well, sort of!"

"What's that supposed to mean?"

Conna didn't really know how to broach the subject, so he just came right out with it. "Well... there's a rumour going round in school that the Ancient Geek has convinced you that he's got a Time-Machine. Don't worry," he continued, "I covered for you. I told them Tom was round the bend, you know, froot-loops!"

"What!"

"Well, he must be one short of a full packet of dolly mixtures if he told you that."

Alex couldn't understand how the story had got out. "Where did that rumour start?" he asked.

"I dunno, it's just one of those things I suppose. But yesterday afternoon," he took a deep breath before blurting it all out at once: "Bex and Maddie heard that someone had been waiting outside the headmaster's study and that he heard the head' talking to the librarian – about you being in there all the time and the sorts of books you were reading and the things you were looking up!"

Alex was mortified. So by now, he assumed, everyone in school and the village had heard about the so called 'secret', and the girls, and Conna especially, suspected it to be true. "So it's all down to one person standing outside the head's office is it?" said Alex. "And you believe that!" He tried to introduce an element of doubt into the rumour to cover for Tom.

"Well, is it true?" asked Conna directly.

And Alex heard himself saying, "Well, sort of!"

For the next ten minutes, as they looked out at the icy North Sea, Alex tried to explain to Conna why he couldn't tell him about the conversations he'd had with Tom – because he'd be breaking his word of honour if he did. This, Conna grudgingly, finally accepted. Conna was like that: he could talk and spread rumours as well as anyone, but if you explained to him why he couldn't, or shouldn't, then he wouldn't. Alex however, had tried to lessen the blow, by speaking 'hypothetically' – he explained the meaning as 'possibly but not necessarily true'. If someone had told Conna an outrageous story, any story, would he, Conna, necessarily believe it? No he wouldn't – unless he had checked the facts first – he agreed with Alex. Wouldn't it be wise then, to assume that Alex could be doing just the same? Checking the facts behind an outrageous story, part of which might contain some truth; all theoretically, of course. He did not tell him any more. For now, he especially did not mention his dad's supposed part in things. Furthermore, he assured Conna that he would refuse to believe any such tale himself – unless he found out differently.

"So, the rumour is true then?" concluded Conna, as they walked back along the pier. Alex pretended he couldn't hear for the wind and shouted for Boris each time Conna repeated the question until even he got the message. Not that it shut him up altogether.

"Look," explained Alex, once more in the house, trying to put Conna out of his misery. "I'll show you some of the things I've found so far, but don't tell anyone yet, okay?"

"Okay," Conna agreed.

Alex booted up the lap top and produced the short, hand-written list he had taken down during his earliest conversation with Tom in the hospital:

Antikythera device or mechanism; 585BC; Pindar; Andronicus of Cyrrhus; Tinos sundial; Horologion; Julian calendar; Sosigenes of Alexandria (Soh-sid-jenn-eez); Porphyrusa (paw-firr-oo-sah) – the island of purple; Aegilia (Edj-eel-ee-ah) – its neighbour; and Copernicus (Co-per-nik-us).

There were many more leads.

Within a few moments, after the machine had searched the web, there came snippets of information about the various subjects that he'd typed in. "You see," Alex pointed to the screen. "*Antikythera Device*," he read out to Conna. Conna scrolled down the page and came across an illustration of an oblong box of some sort. It was made of brass and displayed what looked like a twin clock face.

"So," he shrugged. "What is it?"

"It's one of the things Tom told me about. It says here that it's a reconstruction of something believed to be a form of ancient mechanical computer."

"Eh?" Conna wrinkled his nose. "Anyway, what about it?"

"I'm just saying that he's not making everything up – there's at least some truth in it!"

"Oh," said Conna, not understanding a thing. "Really."

"You see," continued Alex. "Two thousand years old – it's amazing, isn't it?"

Conna scratched his head. "If you say so," he accepted.

"It says no one can quite decide what it was used for though, it seems to do loads of stuff. Convert calendars, set religious events and things and even work out exactly where you are, using just the stars!"

Conna looked down the list of FAQ's beside it. "Hang on, have you seen this other stuff – 'Is it proof of Extra-Terrestrial life visiting Earth?' Is this a website for raving loonies or something?"

"Just ignore that, everything else seems sensible," Alex advised. "Look at these other things."

Conna picked a word from the handwritten list at random. "What's this: 'Copper-knickers'!"

"*Co-per-nicus,*" corrected Alex. "Credited with discovering that the world wasn't flat."

"And this, *'Pin-dar'*," Conna mouthed.

Alex typed the name in. "Greek poet and philosopher, 522 – 433 BC."

"Oh," Conna said, not really caring.

Alex read out, "Pindar first voiced the idea that we should be able to explain the origin of the world and everything in it purely scientifically – without relying on myth and superstition, the need for gods and the like – two and a half thousand years before Charles Darwin's theories – evolution and such!"

"Yeah, that's nice," commented Conna, spotting the rugby ball in the corner.

Alex jotted the information down in case it was important, then moved on to *'Sosigenes of Alexandria'*. "And here, look at this."

"Sausagey-knees: 46 BC?" Conna stumbled over the name. "What's this about?"

"I don't know yet, something about calendars, I haven't had time to read it," Alex declared resignedly, ignoring Conna's pronunciation. "I'm just saying that Tom's story has some truthful facts to it. Maybe Tom nows why Dad was on expedition – even if it's not what he'd have us believe. I thought I might find something else to prove Tom right... maybe dad's..." he let the sentence drift.

"What?" Conna's eyes narrowed.

"Well, maybe dad's old watch has something to do with it," Alex almost rescued himself, "I've looked it up myself and it wasn't even made until a few years ago. Both the manufacturer – and the jeweller in the high street told me. He even offered to buy it from me if I ever want to sell – it would be worth an absolute fortune to collectors!"

"Eh?" The idea threw Conna; he wondered what on earth Alex was talking about. "Now you're not making any sense at all."

"I know," agreed Alex, "something's not right!"

"Or someone," mumbled Conna under his breath. He stood behind his seated friend, looking at the screen. "Alex," he said exasperatedly, "don't you think you're getting a bit carried away with it all? Look, me and the girls are thirteen years old now, not seven – and you're fourteen! It makes no difference whether *this* stuff exists; the bottom line is that time-travel is all just made up – kid's stuff, fiction – you know. Like everyone keeps saying, it's time for us to grow up!"

"Yeah, I know – you're probably right. But even some scientists don't agree with that any more. Anyway, it doesn't hurt to read about it, does it? And it is all a bit of a mystery."

Conna shrugged. "Well maybe, and we have got a week's holiday – plenty time to waste. Okay," he offered, "I'll go along with the story for now but I'm not about to believe it unless we get proof – okay?"

"What kind of proof do you want?" asked Alex.

"Anything, all we know so far is that he's either good at fudging things together at best, or he's a fruit cake at worst, and now he's making you act bananas. If I listen to much more I'll end up going completely nutty too."

Alex smirked; he had to admire Conna's inventive use of edible colloquialisms. Still though, what Alex didn't want to admit to anyone just yet, was that in his case, there was a real need to listen to Tom. The same reason that he had tucked it to the back of his mind: maybe somehow, in one way or another, Tom did know something about the disappearance of his dad – whether the time–machine existed or not.

Regardless, Alex rationalised that he could do with putting off the show of proof – or the lack of it – for a little while longer while he struggled to let himself down less abruptly. Perhaps soon this novelty would finally wear off and he would allow himself to come back down to earth, as his mother, Conna, his friends and his school clearly all wanted. In the meantime though, all he could reasonably do was to keep talking to Tom, and keep checking to see for himself. For that reason, he told Conna, "Maybe we'll both get the proof we need soon."

"Okay then," agreed Conna. "Now, can we take the ball out?"

Just after Conna had gone home a couple of hours later, Tom arrived back home in the hospital car. Alex was still waiting with the dog. He tapped his way unsteadily up the path with a hospital walking stick, desperate to get back in his own space. "This modern thing is no good..." he said, "...no spring in it. I used to keep a more comfortable stick for getting around, though goodness knows where it is now. Anyway, I have to get changed," Tom complained agitatedly. "Modern clothes still make me uncomfortable." Within minutes, he had changed into what Alex knew as one of his clean night dresses and he at last began to calm down. "There, I feel better now." Tom saw the boy looking. "It is called a jubbah – still worn in many countries, even after thousands of years," he explained.

Alex shrugged in acceptance. After helping to settle Tom in, he wasted no time in letting him know about the circulating rumours. If he was expecting a vociferous reaction though, it was not what he got. Instead, Tom thanked him for the warning. He was, he suggested, after all this time, too near his goal to risk defeat now. But he also suggested that Alex bring his friends in on the deal. "Perhaps," he added obliquely, "they might be the ones I have been waiting for."

The boy wondered what he meant, but said nothing.

"Yes Al-lex," Tom confirmed, making up his mind. "I will tell the whole story to you all, and maybe then, you will all be able to lend a hand? That way, we might have a result by next weekend."

Yes, thought Alex, *that would indeed be a result* – no more worrying whether Tom knew anything about his dad's disappearance!

Now relieved at not having to keep it all a secret any longer, as soon as he got home, Alex rang Conna and the girls and invited them over on Tuesday – to give him and Tom some time to tidy up first. His friends readily agreed: especially Conna, who declared he couldn't wait to find out how bonkers he was.

So the next day, Sunday, Alex duly helped Tom tidy up the workshop, vacuuming up the thick dust and debris around the room and picking up and cleaning the various gadgetry which had been scattered from the benches. Throughout all of this, Tom's missing wristwatch could not be found anywhere, although he readily dismissed the valuable timepiece. "It'll turn up eventually," he assured. Nevertheless, Tom was still careful not to let Alex see under the dust sheet which covered 'his horse'.

On Monday, Tom's left arm still bandaged and in a sling, Alex provided the necessary hands for him to construct a solid wooden frame – 'to support the damaged machine'. Even then, Tom would still not allow him to stay while he began to examine his horse, ready for a thorough clean and some necessary 'surgery', as he described it. That, he cautioned, would be to strip the machine of its modesty and its mystique. Frustratingly, therefore, to Alex, it remained an anonymous lump.

Alex wasn't used to having many late nights. It had been two o'clock by the time he'd finally got to bed. After studying all sorts of related things on the internet, his head still buzzed as it had all day with the idea that Tom's machine could actually be what he'd told Alex all along.

He rationalised that everything Tom had told him previously tallied almost exactly with what he had now seen for himself. The internet images of the Antikythera device were also similar to the mechanisms in Tom's workshop. And, some of the other types of mechanisms that he'd just identified on his mum's computer might, he reasoned, make some sense in being included in a vehicle of some sort.

However, once again, even on further reflection, Alex still refused to take the leap of faith that told his logical side that time-travel of any sort was anything more than fantasy. As he tried to get to sleep, these thoughts flip-flopped back and forth in his semi-conscious state. The strange, disturbing image of the horse's eyeless head that he'd seen on the night of the accident kept looming in front of him. Every ten minutes or so, Alex would alternatively convince himself 'once and for all' that time travel might be possible, then, that time travel was entirely impossible. Thankfully, after another hour, at three o'clock in the morning, he finally nodded off.

Nevertheless, it would be later that morning that Alex would, with the rest of his friends, finally begin to get to know what all the fuss was about.

PART II:

THE WIND UP...

NOTHING THERE IS BEYOND HOPE,
NOTHING THAT CAN BE SWORN IMPOSSIBLE,
NOTHING WONDERFUL, SINCE ZEUS,
FATHER OF THE OLYMPIANS,
MADE NIGHT FROM MID-DAY,
HIDING THE LIGHT OF THE SHINING SUN
AND SORE FEAR CAME AMONG MEN.

Antilochus: 7th Cent BC

CHAPTER 8:

Storytime?

Tuesday: Day One of Tom's story

Helios cracked his long whip and began his steady chariot journey across the sky, carrying with him the sun. It made for a beautiful sunrise, and Tom stood back in his old spot at the French window gazing out to sea. He watched the sun turn the sky from gold, to pink and even tinges of green, before it turned red for a full ten minutes. Finally, it turned to the clearest blue.

Alone, Tom recalled the incidents from his youth that had led both directly and indirectly to him being here and now. It had been years since he'd actually opened the window, a mixture of his unwillingness to take further part in this world – here, where he did, yet didn't belong – and his own built up resignation that he had trapped himself in the wrong time and place. However, this morning, Tom had oiled their hinges. He wiggled the doors back and forth further and further, each time working the oil deeper into them. Now, the sun still cool, he stood watching it rise without the virtually ever present sunglasses.

A while later, a knock at the door snapped him out of his distant thoughts. "Alex," Tom called down enthusiastically from the landing, "come up. Look at this marvellous sight." Alex opened the unlocked door and climbed up the stairs, Boris trailing silently behind The boy had expected him to be talking about his machine, but instead it was still covered. Seeing him standing there, he joined Tom at the French windows.

"Boris, my little friend, welcome." Tom patted the dog briefly. Together, man and boy watched the scene, while the dog sniffed around the whole room. "Help me," he eventually turned to the boy. So Alex took the left-hand door handle while Tom opened the catch on the right. Together, ceremoniously they opened them and stepped out onto the small balcony beyond. Tom breathed in deeply, filling his lungs with the still crisp salt air, silently sharing the majestic dawn with Alex – free from his shackles again! Together, they watched as the grey and white gulls and a few black cormorants followed in the wake of a solitary trawler, darting into the sea to pick up the discarded slops, their distant cries carried on the wind. "In a way," said Tom, "this always reminds me of my childhood home."

After what must have been ten full minutes of a very comfortable silence, Alex looked back into the room to see what time it was. Tom knew instinctively what he was looking for. "About eight-thirty," he said to Alex. "That reminds me, I still haven't found my watch. I think I may have thrown it out yesterday with the rubbish. There again, I might have picked it up and put it somewhere safe," he sounded unconcerned. I found this though," he handed Alex what looked to be a genuine enough gold coin – Roman. "Take it... take it with you and check the date of it if you like; when you have, I'll tell you where I found it. However, you might not believe me," he looked down his nose at the boy.

Alex again ignored Tom's excuse for still not producing the mystical twin watch. He grinned anyway though. "How did you know?" he asked as he weighed the coin and put it in his pocket, to check it against his father's books.

"Know what?" Tom quizzed, "what is the time of day, or that you were looking for a clock?"

"Both."

"Firstly, I am used to looking out of my window – I know exactly where the sun is in the sky; that is all."

Alex accepted his expertise.

"But secondly," Tom complained, "today's society is completely obsessed with dividing the day up into smaller and smaller parts. 'What time is it?'" he mimicked, wrinkling-up his face. "No one takes the 'time' to just enjoy the 'time' we have. Instead, people in this world run around like headless chickens one minute, in fear of being 'late', then they sit around, waiting for the right time to arrive before they get on with something that has to be done regardless. They race to work in cars and trains, never walking; they overeat and then spend the saved time exercising off excess weight in gymnasia – or simply in watching other bogus lives on TV. Or even playing electronic games – mostly games of pretend violence;" he twiddled the thumb of his good hand energetically, "instead of playing real sports. Few people in this world use time positively anymore; to think, or talk to each other properly, or be creative; learn to play a musical instrument, draw or paint. They just waste time..."

Alex followed his drift and nodded but didn't speak, finding Tom's condemnation of modern life harsh... if perhaps true.

"And another thing," he continued the line of his rant, "no one in the developed world uses the time they have available to learn anything new. Education has become such an ugly word these days, such an undervalued topic! It is taken for granted at best, or strenuously avoided at worst. Whilst in the developing world, small children who know better crave for the benefits it may bring. And all of this is what passes for a life philosophy these days." He saw the look on Alex's face and began to calm down. "Still, I suppose," he offered grudgingly, "enjoying an easy life is a philosophy of sorts."

"Philosophy?" Alex wrinkled his nose at the word.

"Alright, so it's a big word," Tom shrugged, "but everyone in the world has a philosophy, whether they know it or not. It is simply what you think about your life and how you will live it. Example: yesterday we cleared up everything, yes? We started in the morning and finished at night. We worked through – stopping only when it was appropriate; and not because a 'time piece' told us to. Your own senses are what count Alex. When the sun comes up, get up and enjoy the day – or stay in bed if you wish. But let it be a conscious decision. When it goes down, go back to bed – or stay and watch the moon and stars. Eat when you are hungry..." he continued the moral lecture.

"...and drink when you are dry." Alex completed the saying.

"Exactly – this is only one example of a simple philosophy. But take my advice: please, don't rely on a mechanical contraption to make those decisions for you – I certainly won't have one on the wall of my house!"

Alex couldn't help smiling to himself, surrounded as they were now by all-sorts of clockwork and other mechanical mechanisms, at the notion that Tom was so vehement about the perils of clock-watching.

Without further ado, Tom turned back to Alex, "Nearly time for your friends to arrive?"

"Almost." Alex checked his dad's watch.

Within minutes, dead on cue, they heard the knock – no doubt that would be at Conna's insistence.

Boris began to bark. While Tom went to the bathroom, Alex ran downstairs and half opened the door. Determined to lighten up the proceedings from the very start, looking again at his dad's watch, he asked, "Yes?" Conna stood on the step in front of Maddie and Bex. "Erm?" he answered, looking confusedly at his own watch and reverting back to his more bashful state now once again alone in the presence of the girls.

"Very funny," Maddie smiled warmly at Alex, knowing full well that they'd arrived at the right time.

Grinning from ear to ear, Alex opened the door wide and stepped back from it. He beckoned them into the hall, delighted to see that they'd kept their promise to come over and at least listen. "Go on up then," he said.

One by one they passed him, Bex rolling her eyes up as she did. They rattled straight up the bare wooden stairway. "Go in, I'll just fetch Tom," he called after them.

Conna was last in. "Har – har," he said flatly, pulling a silly face at Alex.

Upstairs, they walked into the now cleaned up and transformed 'laboratory'. They passed the tidied benches, now draped with dust covers. Presumably, beneath them were the strange machines and other paraphernalia they'd seen on their first, now somehow distant visit. However, the gaping hole in the centre of the ceiling was still obvious enough. Conna stared straight up through it, at the glass roof-light above.

Rather than get drawn straight back into a conversation about what had happened that night, everyone, it seemed, was determined to avoid the whole subject. Until such time as Tom brought it up of course. Where there had been only rubble before, there were now neatly stacked piles of books keeping down a dust sheet which covered the huge lump that occupied the centre of the floor. Obviously this was the mysterious machine. Tactfully however, although they guessed perfectly well what it was, no one mentioned the bulky object – no one so much as looked at it. It was as if it wasn't there.

Conna and Maddie especially were delighted to see, and now hear, Boris waiting upstairs. The dog barked excitedly and pawed the air, first at Maddie, who stroked his face and head in greeting, after which Conna playfully teased him as usual. After a short while, Conna began to 'mooch around', as he called it, nosing under the dust covers on the bench. He could see what looked like old, even antique mechanical toys, although he didn't recognise any of them.

Maddie wandered over to the far end of the room. Dotted around there were a few other items of note that no one had even begun to notice on their last visit. Now cleaned up, some of them were surprisingly unmissable. Firstly, standing in the far left corner of the floor was a huge archaic skeletal globe of some sort. It was made up of a series of interconnecting hoops and spheres and fabricated from what appeared to be brass. Maddie and Conna went to look at it more closely. Conna trailed a finger across a small engraved brass plate on it, trying to decipher the words. "The Arm-ill-ary of..." he struggled to pronounce the name, "Gali-leo. Anno Domini 1564-1642," he mumbled under his breath, wondering where he'd heard the name before. Maddie stood closer. The top of it reached as high as her shoulders. In a way, she thought she recognised the device somehow – though not quite. It was, she decided, a bit like the representation of an atom that she'd seen at school. Looking at it casually up and down, she finally realised what it was: a model of the solar system – but with only six planets? That was odd.

"I know!" exclaimed Conna suddenly. "He was in that song," he mimicked in an alternately falsetto, then a strained but deep voice: "*Galileo – Galileo, Galileo – Galileo, Galileo Figaro... I'm just a poor boy no-body loves me!*"

"If you say so, Conna," Maddie smirked. Then she turned her attention to the other smaller objects in the opposite, right, hand corner. A fruit bowl, full to the brim sat on one end of a small hand-built driftwood table. On the other sat an old-fashioned wind up gramophone with its big, worn papier-mâché trumpet. It was complete with a tin of needles and had a short pile of the old heavy and brittle twelve inch records beside it. Curiously, or at least unexpectedly, in the middle of the table lay two sets of what Bex thought she recognised as Northumbrian bagpipes. One set looked like Scottish bagpipes but smaller and more delicate; the other was much more crude and simple, with a plain, well worn leather bag. She hadn't imagined Tom as the musical sort.

Bex headed straight past the now scrubbed-up old brown leather sofa and stood beside the French windows, still open despite the chilly breeze. "Wow, what an amazing view!" She looked directly outside to the edge of the cliff. "I love to see the sea," she sighed, absent-mindedly thinking of faraway places. "I loved it when we could swim at the beach every day."

Maddie and Conna sauntered over to join her. "Mmm, not as warm as the sea outside our last house though," she commented ruefully. "There's a bit of a difference in temperature between the North Sea and the Caribbean."

"I wish it was time to go back." Bex said to no one in particular.

She went on gazing out of the window, while Maddie explained: "When mum took ill last year, dad's company transferred him back here temporarily – until she gets through her treatment. That's why we're all here now," she said resignedly.

Concerned, but trying not to express too much overt interest, Conna said, "Good, I mean..." Then more tentatively added: "So how long do you think you'll be here then?"

"Oh, at least till we finish eleventh grade, I should think. The doctors have said it might be a long haul."

"Right," said Conna, nodding his head at the floor, two years. Not wishing to ask any further details, and giving only a hint of anything away whilst trying desperately not to blush, he said honestly "I'm glad you came."

The sisters smiled almost imperceptibly at each other, silently noting the first genuine compliment Conna had paid either of them. Neither of the girls looked directly at him though, this time deciding not to tease.

Together they all looked steadfastly out to sea, comfortable in each other's presence, waiting patiently for Alex and Tom to arrive.

Alex greeted the others again before Tom had a chance to join them. "Listen," he kept his voice down, "thanks for coming, I know you're all sceptical – I know I would be if I was in your shoes. But I really think you should listen to the full story before you make any rash judgements about Tom's sanity." The look on each of their respective faces left him in little doubt however, that it was his own judgement, not to say sanity, that was also being held to question. "Please, just listen to him, and give him a fair hearing before you make up your mind."

It was Maddie who spoke first. "Alex," she asked conspiratorially, "what if we do listen to him and we all think that he's... well..."

"Mad?" Conna finished off tactlessly.

Maddie took a sharp intake of breath. Ignoring Conna's outburst, she said caringly "...in need of help."

Alex considered the request carefully. "I suppose," he thought aloud, "that would depend on two things. Firstly, that after listening to him, we still can't agree that we believe his story."

"And secondly?"

"That we think, because of that, he may be a danger to himself – that is, if we don't think he can cope on his own," he shrugged.

"Err, and 'C'," Conna wobbled his face exaggeratedly toward them, "that he may be a danger to others!" The silence that followed the remark told Conna what they all still thought of that likelihood.

"Alex," Maddie continued, "promise us that if we're worried, we'll contact someone about him – no more putting off. We don't want him having another accident!"

Alex thought long and hard. He'd promised Tom that he'd help him, given him his word of honour. He had admitted to himself that the whole thing was about as far-fetched as it could get, even that he was possibly allowing himself to get carried away with the whole idea for the most obvious of reasons. But, if he was wrong in believing Tom, at least there was no real harm done – other than the fact that he would have to start letting go of the prospect of his dad ever coming home. Even then, he was sure Tom wasn't being malicious. Although he still only half believed him, Alex would still admittedly be disappointed, not to say devastated, if he was wrong to place even his limited trust him. However, to report Tom to any of the authorities because he was 'a tad eccentric' was surely beyond the pale. Although he had to admit that if they jointly couldn't accept the story, surely it would be cause for concern, and perhaps that in itself was enough of a reason to break his promise – maybe?

"Alex?" prompted Maddie.

Alex looked at the others, and at the look of concern in their eyes.

"Are we agreed?"

He made up his mind, "okay."

"Sure?"

"Sure." He reluctantly repeated his agreement. "I think it would be best not to challenge Tom directly though," he declared. "Let him do the talking."

Everyone nodded in agreement. Everyone, that is, apart from

Conna, who was teasing the corner of the dust sheet up. He had just about managed to glimpse a rough wooden frame below, when Tom's voice interrupted him. He dropped the sheet immediately.

"Welcome, welcome to my house." The simple greeting sounded genuine enough. Almost as if he had heard the previous conversation, Tom limped heavily into the room wearing the Ray-Bans. He was now almost fully spruced up, still fastening the top button of a clean cotton jubbah with his good hand. Through the glasses, he looked straight at the four. Holding out his good arm to 'hug' the girls, he leaned forward and kissed them each politely but formally, first on one, then the other side of their faces, as if they were civic dignitaries, rather than friends or family. Then he turned to Conna and kissed him just the same on each cheek.

Conna, frozen in his tracks at this unnecessary and most un-British of greetings, fought briefly but unsuccessfully to stop himself from going cherry red. In an effort to cover his embarrassment, he automatically grasped the one uncovered brass box on the bench. "What's this?" He almost shouted at Tom, though he was certain he already recognised what it was supposed to be from looking at Alex's lap top. "Did you really make it?" he almost accused.

Tom's face froze in deathly silence. Worry lines now showed at the corners of his eyes: signs of his own doubt about giving the four any potential evidence that might be used against him. It was a risk he needed to take though. Surely, this time they must be the ones he had been waiting for. Taken aback at the directness of the challenge, he said simply, "Well yes, of course I did Conna, I'm not making this up. But this is only one of many failed attempts to recreate the so called Antikythera device. 'Nearly right', but you know what the definition of nearly right is, don't you? 'Wrong!'" Tom took it from him and replaced it on the bench.

"Sure, Tom," Alex and the girls agreed. Bex gave Conna a withering glance as his normal colour returned.

Turning back to face the girls and Conna, Tom said a little abruptly, "So... you have all come here to help me? Or to be my judge, jury and executioner, perhaps?"

Without hesitation, Maddie said straightforwardly, "Well it was you who invited us, but no, Tom, it's not like that, we're just here to listen. After all, the whole idea is pretty difficult to believe."

Tom snorted, admitting to himself, "It is... certainly. I will grant you that. Alright," he accepted, "then let us at least promise to be honest with one another." With that, some of the tension evaporated. "I like your honesty," Tom continued, "and you're caring, visiting me like that. For what it is worth, I think that I will be able to trust you – all of you. You are young enough to be open-minded and old enough to be..." he searched for an appropriate word... "discriminating – you can sift through all of the evidence for truth – hopefully without feeling the need to stick to accepted 'wisdom'." With that, Tom limped to his armchair and turned to sit. "Let's not attempt to fool each other though, you know that I am talking to you for one reason only," he raised his eyebrows above his sunglasses. "I really have no choice anymore, do I!" He sat down heavily in his armchair, giving out a grunt.

Inhaling painfully and deeply, he chose his words very carefully. "I am getting older and the life I have lived is not the one I would have chosen... but that is matterless. Now there are other things far more important at stake, and you may be the last generation, the last chance to avert self-made catastrophe! Whilst it may be too late for me, your generation will inherit this Earth soon enough, as it has been passed down for countless centuries. Then it will be you who will have to decide how it will be run. What will be the rules and who will be allowed to make them? Have you ever wondered where this world is headed and at what breakneck speed? Where we will all end up unless we finally begin to learn from the mistakes of the past? Mankind, and its various forms of government, have over many thousands of years learned various ways to manipulate the surface population – not always for the good of all. The key to this all, lies in education: the education of everyone on the planet. Perhaps if the world's population realised how they were constantly being manipulated, they would not be so quick to take arms against one another." His face turned to each in turn, then toward the ceiling in thought. The four friends looked at each other's faces and a gloomy silence suddenly started to descend on the small group.

Trying to lift the mood, Maddie approached Tom. She produced a small gift carrier-bag, which she'd tastefully decorated with ribbons, curled spirally and hanging down its side. "Tom, this is for you," she offered.

"For me... why?" The expression on Tom's face changed gradually from confusion to acceptance. Stock-still at first, his eyes narrowed behind the shade of his glasses. He seemed taken aback at the small gesture of kindness.

"Because we're all trying to be friends?" Alex suggested simply. "Give you the benefit of the doubt, so to speak. It's from all of us – Conna chose it."

"We thought it might cheer you up" Maddie said, her sister Bex adding cheekily, "Maybe even put a smile on your face."

The look on his face, which had now changed from acceptance to delight, seemed ridiculously disproportionate to the gift. It was as if no one had given him a gift for years. Visibly shaken, almost dazed, he dropped absent-mindedly into his native tongue. "Efkaristo – thank you everyone. Thank you for your kindness." He got up to thank each in turn. Conna moved behind the sofa before he could even think of kissing him again. Instead, he nodded and put his hand up.

Tom looked inside the bag. In it was a CD: 'Holidays in the Sun – Greek Bouzouki hits.' Although the music choice symbolised everything that epitomised his own sorrow for what had become of his beloved homeland, now known in the main as a place only for sunny tourism, he appreciated the well meaning gesture for what it was – even though he didn't possess a CD player. It was a simple token of friendship. Now, he felt that he really might begin to trust that the small band of young but real friends who had gathered around to 'save' him. In an attempt to hide his small weakness, Tom promptly got out of his chair and made his way silently to the bathroom, removing the sunglasses and wiping his eyes with the back of his hand as he did so. He disappeared around the doorframe.

No one spoke much when he left the room, and when they did it was only to whisper concern at the way he'd taken their gift.

A few minutes later, he returned. Once again wearing the ever-present glasses, he entered the room. Still visibly subdued and shaking his head disbelievingly, he sat down once again. He looked pensively down at the gift for a while, then, as if finally deciding, he looked at the four, each in turn. At last he spoke. "Forgive me," he begged, "it has been a long time since I trusted anyone – it always goes wrong when I do. Though perhaps this time... just perhaps... finally it will be different!"

Suddenly deciding, Tom sat back in his chair. "Yes," he said, finally making up his mind, "I will tell you everything I can," he said simply. "Alex has told me of the rumours circulating the town, so you already know something of my predicament. Well, alright, so be it. But just in case you cannot believe, or refuse to, and this causes you concern – to doubt my sanity for instance –" he raised his eyebrows and looked at the four faces, "I will tell you in the form of a story. Let us call it *The Tale of Eos.*"

"The tale of what?" Alex mumbled.

"Its name will become clear in the fullness of time," assured Tom.

"Just a story?" Bex probed. "Meaning what, exactly?"

"Let us say that it will protect us all."

"What!" Conna sounded already astonished. "Protect us, from what?"

"Wait, I get it," Maddie spoke up. "You're saying that this is only a hypothetical story – about your sculpture and where it *might* have come from – without confirming or denying that it's true..." she nodded toward him, "so that if we don't believe you, and, let's say, we thought it was so..."

"Far-fetched?" Tom helped out. "Go-on."

"...That we might consider informing... 'someone more'!"

"Let us say at the hospital?" Tom smiled.

"That you would simply deny that it was anything other than..."

80

"A story," completed Tom. "Correct!"

Silence followed as they looked at one another.

"Well that's as clear as mud." Conna looked directly at Alex for an explanation. Alex didn't speak though, waiting to hear all of their reactions.

Instead Bex explained, paraphrasing Maddie – but still fixing her gaze on Tom. "So, Tom here's going to tell us this 'secret', but if anyone splits on him, he'll tell them it's just a story, okay?"

"Well put," said Tom.

"Ohhh... clever," the penny eventually dropped with Conna, "and then no one can accuse him of being a nutcase!"

"If that's how you'd like to put it. Is that a deal?" smiled Tom.

"I suppose so," said Conna. "It's only ancient history anyway. It's not like it's important these days, is it?"

Tom pursed his lips; he didn't comment.

"Okay," they agreed one by one, "it's a deal," Maddie offered first, then Bex, then Conna and finally, Alex.

"But before we start, please, close the window, pull up the sofa and make yourselves as comfortable as you can. This is certainly not a short story. The full story will take at least few days to tell."

With that, Alex beckoned to Conna to help him shove the sofa from its home beside the window, over to Tom's armchair. Once in place, they offered a seat to each of the two girls, Conna naturally taking up the seat he was used to at home – cross-legged on the floor beside the sofa. Alex took the last seat beside Maddie, after reaching into his pocket to bring out a small notebook and pencil that he'd brought for the purpose. As he placed it on the arm of the sofa, Boris, without invitation, immediately jumped onto his lap and curled up like a cat.

"Come on then, Tom," said Alex on behalf of them all, "we're all ears."

The four waited patiently as Tom also settled comfortably into his own armchair. "I'll try not to get too technical – stop me if I do – but I need to set both the background scene and the time frame if you are expected to follow the whole series of complicated events.

But," he reminded them, "don't forget, I am telling you this as just a 'story'.

Firstly, closing his eyes in concentration, he then took off his sunglasses. And this time, he passionately began to recount every detail of the tale that he'd never before shared with a single soul, not even Alex, now beginning to perhaps trust that he was at last in safe hands.

CHAPTER 9:

The Cassiterides

"Try to take yourself back in time: many thousands of years ago," Tom began softly, "to a world which centred then on the Mediterranean and the Aegean Seas. A world in which there were many fundamental mysteries. Obviously, the earth was flat; otherwise everyone would have fallen off. And, it was reasoned, it all probably floated on the sea, especially islands, which many seafarers swore moved around!

The golden disc of the sun circled the earth, rising in the east and setting in the west, bringing light, warmth and life. Though quite how it moved, no one knew. The moon – the white disc that changed shape and illuminated the night sky – was a similar mystery. The stars shone down from their constellations, moving slowly through the blackness along with the known planets. And the changes in the weather, especially storms and other natural phenomena, gripped mankind's imagination. Inevitably, in ignorance and fear of these mysterious events and of how the whole world worked, man himself created many belief systems. How all of these amazing things had been created and, more specifically, who had created it.

Thus, the various creation myths of the gods were born to 'explain' everything – and they continued to be developed all across the world. Even today, the names of these various European deities are etched on our subconscious, in the names of the planets, the days of the week, or months of the year."

Everyone settled into the story as Tom continued. "Gradually, over many millennia, early mankind began to realise that the changes in seasons and the movement patterns of all of these heavenly bodies were linked. What was more important, they were, in the main, entirely predictable!

As man moved away from being a hunter-gatherer and toward an easier life, that of crop and animal farmer, accuracy of predicting the various seasons – the best time to sow, the best time to reap – became more and more vital. To get it wrong could be catastrophic: sow too early and the crop might by ruined by frost – too late and it might not ripen at all. Harvest too late and the crop might die in the fields. Crop failure for any reason could mean the difference between life and death! Tribal chiefs and rulers of at first cities, then what later became states or countries, knew that their safety and prosperity depended on the accuracy of these predictions. And so those rulers encouraged the various self-made religious leaders and priests – who had from the earliest time generally involved themselves in 'stargazing' – to make these predictions on their behalf. They had noticed, for instance, that when certain stars reappeared in the sky, the seasons were about to change – although this expert knowledge was valuable and therefore closely guarded. The various 'belief systems', or religions, and stargazing: what much later became separated into astronomy and astrology had become inextricably linked.

There was of course good and bad in this. On the one hand, the priests became experts and proposed various mechanisms that could explain the workings of the universe and the seasons more and more accurately. On the other hand, whilst this was indeed desirable, these mechanisms could not be seen or heard to conflict with the previously established religious beliefs. The various gods that had been proposed by man were the creators of the world and everything in it; the penalties for suggesting anything else in any society or country, usually judged by the same priests or rulers who relied on them, were harsh – if not fatal! However, this fundamental conflict of interests would continue to plague mankind indefinitely. It became the single most valuable tool of manipulation.

In time, various calendars were proposed to keep track of the seasons and the year – in various countries and regions – and of course with varying accuracy: calendars such as the Babylonian calendar, the Sumerian calendar and the Egyptian or 'Sothic' calendar and so forth – named after the 'dog star' Sothis, or Sirius, whose seasonal appearance in the southern skies heralded the annual flooding of the river Nile, making it fertile once again.

However, as each society had to work with the others, it became necessary to convert the same date in any calendar. For instance, to take a simple example, how would you even arrange to meet someone if everyone used a different calendar – if your twenty-eighth day of the fifth month became the second day of the sixth month to someone else? Strange to us now, but a big problem then. All caused by the lack of understanding of how exactly it was that we now know the universe works."

Tom squinted at the faces to check that he hadn't bored them with the mini lecture. No, it seemed he hadn't. In many ways, he knew from experience, younger people could be cleverer, more inquisitive and receptive than adults. Once again he closed his eyes and began to relate the story. "Over my own time, I have learned to refer to the date in terms of BC – Before Christ – and AD – Anno Domini or After Christ. The dates I use are simply more universal – and now," he smiled, "it will make the following story easier to follow.

Many years ago, in the year we would now call 595 BC – what is known as the pre-Classical Greek age – it was an ancient world. More than six hundred years after the fall of the great city of Homer's Troy, but before the Classical age of Greece, of the great city states of Athens, Corinth and Sparta. It was two hundred and fifty years before the time in which Alexander the Great conquered the world. And, it was also far earlier than the time that a small town in Italy would rise up to dominate both the affairs and the history of most of the world known to them, a world which would eventually become the Empire of Rome!

The place of the story then, begins in the eastern Mediterranean, just off the most beautiful sun-drenched and fertile island, reputedly occupied by the descendants of the hero Herakles, AKA Hercules himself. The island rose majestically from what Homer himself had described as 'the wine dark sea'. It was an already well established seafaring nation. An island and a city-state called Rhodos – or Rhodes, as it is more widely known today. The names of many, many places constantly change."

"We've been," exclaimed Maddie, "that's where we were just on holiday before we came here, weren't we, Bex?"

"Yeah, so have I, last year," Conna sounded equally astonished at the coincidence. "Well, at least just for one day. We called at the island on a cruise ship, 'course I was the only one that got off, mum and dad were in the ship's health spa. I wanted to see the big statue: the Colossus of Rhodes – one of the ancient wonders of the world – but it's gone now, a bit disappointing really. But blood... I mean, good grief was the sun hot!"

"Shhh... don't butt in," cautioned Bex.

"No, that's alright," continued Tom. "It may help you understand. The island was the supposed birthplace of at least one of the gods, and as such, as Conna says, it was blessed by the sun. The population even at that early time thrived not only on its abundance of crops of all sorts, corn, fruit and vegetables, olives for cooking, washing and lamp-fuel and grapes to make wine, but also, like many other islands, Rhodos began to thrive on the tourism industry..."

Everyone looked astounded. "Tourism?"

"Certainly... except that they were then known as 'pilgrims'," continued Tom. "At that time, the 'Chora' of Rhodos, its capital, had a vast and beautiful Acropolis – the high citadel overlooking the sea" (Tom pronounced it ack-**ropp**-oll-ee). "A hill on which stood many of the most amazing, mainly painted wooden temples, dedicated to a myriad of the most diverse gods imaginable, all representing their various creation myths. Some were built in honour of the Greek gods, Zeus, Apollo, Athena, Poseidon, Helios and many more. Some were built in honour of the Egyptian gods,

Ra, Osiris, Anubis, etcetera and yet more temples were built in honour of the Persian gods, Zarathustra, Sibele and the like. All, however, lived in peaceful co-operation and co-existence on this luscious island in the sun.

According to many legends, to the eager agreement of the priests, the gods had brought the world into being here in the Aegean Sea – the sea of Greece. And as such, pilgrims from all over the known world travelled to this place – 'The Cradle of the Gods' – to see for themselves the many spectacles, or to give thanks to the gods for a good event in their lives. Maybe wealth had come their way, perhaps it was the successful birth of a baby. Most people though, came to ask the gods a favour: something that could be brought about only by their direct intercession. Because of this, the island had gradually become a huge mixture of races, religions and cultures from all over the world. As a result, this 'melting pot' had also started to become a 'pot of gold'.

As Rhodos' reputation for splendour grew, more and more pilgrims flocked to visit. These pilgrims provided wealth. This wealth allowed new attractions to be provided. In turn, these new attractions brought more pilgrims who brought more wealth and thus paid for greater attractions. And so, the cycle of wealth continued; it all worked very well. Pilgrimage thrived, and, as the pilgrims were encouraged to pay for the gods' help, the priests and ruling classes of the island especially prospered. To-date, everyone was happy – at least, those on the surface were!

However, as in many civilisations, there was a sub-class which was not intended to benefit: the untouchable class, a whole sub-culture which toiled sometimes literally below the streets and even in and below the temples. It was they who kept the town clean and carried out the many other services that the industrious island required. Not that the vast majority above knew or would have cared about their situation, they were too busy having a good time – business, as they say, was booming."

Finishing the background story, Tom paused for thought and only now began *The Tale of Eos* proper:

"Off the western coast of the island of Rhodos, a few miles out to sea, a small-ish rather ordinary looking single-masted cargo boat – a lugger – slowly approached with perhaps ten or so crew and another handful of pilgrims.

The early morning sunlight danced and sparkled like a million stars on the bow wave as the ample, cooling breeze pushed the vessel toward the plain natural harbour. At that time – in the days before the Colossus – the harbour was flanked only by two short piers and marked by two painted poles, topped by fire baskets, or beacons. It was filled with many boats, mostly pilgrim vessels, but it also held the vast island navy: one hundred or so 'penteconters' – the double-masted rowing ships with the painted eyes that had not changed since the time of the Trojan wars. Such was the wealth and power of this place.

Traditionally, this was the part of the journey that the pilgrims loved. Their excitement mounted as, after a lifetime of work, they had finally made it here, their dream destination and home of the gods. As they approached, the outline of the temples on the Acropolis could be seen on the promontory way above the port, gold details and attachments glistening in the sun. This sight, together with the clamouring sound of celebration reaching out to sea like the voices of the Sirens, conspired to beckon the pilgrims and their money closer to the island. Even before the pilgrims had landed, guesthouse owners lined the harbour, shouting out invitations of bargains and 'discounted' places to visit. It was always the same here, on one of the very first 'themed holiday' destinations.

However, the mood on this particular vessel was very different, it was far more sombre. The Phoenician master and vessel owner, a small round man with mahogany skin, stood to the fore of his ship, still clearly saddened and shocked at the recent loss of his lifetime friend. A man whom, to be fair, he only met annually on his long voyage to the Cassiterides islands at the western limit of the world; the legendary Islands of Tin. 'Legendary', of course, only because the dangerous route to their location – through the pillars of Herakles and far to the north – was a closely guarded trade secret. It was known for a thousand years, only to a few Phoenicians and fewer Greeks. Although the age of bronze weaponry had largely been superseded since the discovery of iron and even primitive steel, there was still a very great demand for bronze, not only for weapons but for cookware, sculptures and many other everyday items. Bronze was made from a mixture of two metals: copper and tin. And though copper was found all over the area, tin was always in very short supply. Therefore it was a much prized cargo.

On his annual journey to the largest of the Cassiterides, the master had once again met with his friend the trader, whom he had come to rely on to stockpile the tin he had journeyed to purchase. Not that he hadn't tried to find an alternative supply of other profitable goods – he had. He was a businessman, was he not? Like many forgotten others, hundreds of years before him, he had asked the 'Druides', worshippers of the sacred tree of Zeus, the Oak tree – the 'Drodos'. He had followed the island coastline north, as far as the 'Scotos Lands' – the 'Dark Lands' – but to no avail. Eventually, like others, he had come to the conclusion that the 'Keltes' – the people known to the Greeks as their 'Cousins' could always be trusted to keep a bargain and deliver the goods to him.

Over many long and dangerous return journeys, the man had made friends with the villagers whom he came to visit and purchase the precious tin from, and now he was back on the tiny but well guarded islet off the southwest coast of the main island. This was where the tin was collected together. And this was where his friend the trader had assembled the annual cargo, ready for him to collect."

CHAPTER 10:

Pirates

"As usual, after their good-natured bartering process, the business friends had spent the evening at the trader's roundhouse, but this time the trader was uncharacteristically down at the mouth. The trader, a tall middle-aged man with long grey hair hanging down to his broad shoulders and a neatly bearded intelligent face, was both physically strong and used to wielding weapons to fend off any would-be robbers. He commanded great loyalty and respect from his village, although he was not himself the chieftain; that title belonged to the father of the trader's beautiful white-skinned and blonde-haired wife. However, it was the trader's eyes that seemed to have the desired effect on most people, including the Phoenician.

They were of the most extraordinary pale but somehow bright green colour. They seemed to have the effect of burning into one's very soul, so that even the master, who was extremely skilled at bargaining, found it difficult to lie or even exaggerate to him, even to increase his share of the profits. The master's respect though, was returned equally. This much travelled man of the world had taken the great effort to learn the trader's native tongue. He would each night entertain the entire village, especially the children, often with grossly exaggerated tales of the strange lands and people – sometimes even sea monsters – that he'd encountered. For this reason, the man was highly regarded in the encampment. Now the master enquired politely as to the source of the trader's trouble. And so the trader told him of the worry he had for his wife.

Just after the master had left them last year, the baby his wife had been expecting at the time had been delivered prematurely. As a result, his wife had nearly died in labour, and the girl-child had been stillborn. Now she was with child again, and his desire above everything was to at last have a child of his own, either boy or girl – each was equally valued and respected in his culture. But the thought of losing his wife preyed heavily on his mind. He had thought of taking the long cart journey with her to the fabled ring of tall ancient stones to the east. He remembered the magic of the smaller blue stones from his last journey there as a youth; but the baby had not many weeks left to come now, and because of the hard winter, they'd lost the opportunity to travel there earlier to pray for a safe birth.

The master pondered a while. He knew of an island, he told the trader, a very special island which the greatest of all of the gods was said to inhabit. A real god. The very god who brought the sun across the sky each and every day, and that without whom, life across the earth itself would not be possible. Sometimes on his voyage home, the master would pick up a few passengers, pilgrims, and deliver them safely there – for a fee of course. However, as it was not more than a few days detour from his destination in North Africa, even if he did intend to pick up other pilgrims this time, the master offered to take them there as a token of friendship – at no extra charge.

The trader thanked him for the generous offer, and next morning, after consulting his wife and the chieftain, agreed to take the long but absolutely necessary journey. After which, they would stay on the island until the boat returned the next year, for their journey back to the Cassiterides.

And so it had been. The master's long voyage home southward to the Pillars of Herakles – the first stage of the journey – had been extremely smooth for that time of year. Usually it was much rougher across the vast dark blue bay. Carefully they picked their way through the huge grey sea monsters which spurted water into the sky. But this was still safer than hugging the coast, where they may be prone to robbery or piracy, especially with this rich cargo. Even when the boat turned due east and passed from the 'Great Sea' through the narrow strait that the master called the Pillars of Herakles and into the 'Middle Sea' – the Mediterranean – the journey had been uneventful. It had been almost pleasurable for the trader's wife, who had never before travelled more than one day away from her home. Onward, the boat continued, stopping only once to take on a few fresh provisions at the main port on the island of Sicilia, the Greek settlement of Syracuse. It was there that he had also picked up the few paying pilgrims, before leaving hurriedly after much curiosity had been displayed toward his extraordinary looking guests. To have skin as white as theirs marked them out; they were either from very far to the north or were very rich – clearly they did not have to work outside in the sun. Either way, they were a target. Day by day then, they continued on to Rhodos.

The trader and his wife had been at sea for almost three weeks now and had travelled hundreds of leagues. A league was an approximate measure of the distance that could be travelled comfortably in an hour. Not to be confused with the much later Roman league of a set one and a half miles. The weather had been kind to them; they had enough wind to fill the square sail, but not a sight of storm clouds. Another few days and they would approach Rhodos, and in record time too!

The master, the trader and his wife sat in the stern of the boat as they passed between two rugged islands.

Porphyrusa, on the larboard side, was named after the Greek word for 'purple', and was the place where the precious dye was produced from murex shells, the only way that the colour could be produced. Thousands of sea-creatures, which were found only in the most extreme depths, were required to make a tiny amount of the dye. The dye was then fixed into the fabric using ammonia, distilled from boiling human and animal urine. The strong and peculiar stench of the process drifted out to sea, making the woman gag.

On the starboard side the Phoenician pointed out the smaller island of Aegilia. A temple with a pitched roof – like the one they'd marvelled at when they'd called in at the port in Sicilia – appeared almost hidden. It lay in a small cove, protected by two tall rock pinnacles near its mouth. The whole area really was a most beautiful and fascinating part of the world. Away from their own cold land, the trader only hoped that the heat of the sun wouldn't burn his wife's milk-white skin. It was for that reason that she kept herself covered.

As the islands seemed to pass by, another boat emerged from what was obviously a naturally concealed harbour right beside the first cove, coincidentally, the vessel headed the same way as themselves. The master beckoned to one of his crew to keep watch on it – 'may the gods forbid' it from being a pirate vessel. They were notorious in this part of the sea, constantly on the lookout for vessels that were unlikely to be able to defend themselves. On the other occasions when he'd encountered them, his boat, the lugger, which was not really built for speed but more to cope with the rough seas, had been either empty or carrying a lighter cargo. This day though, with the heavy cargo of tin weighing the draft of the boat down, he couldn't hope to outrun the bigger vessel gaining on them. As the wind and oar powered vessel sped across the sea, it wasn't long before the crew of his own ship had begun to pick up their bronze short-swords from where they'd been stashed on board.

The trader from the Cassiterides calmly and purposefully removed his upper clothing. He unwrapped his own much longer beaten iron sword from the oiled rag that protected it from losing its razor's edge. Keeping it in his left hand, all the time he looked vigilantly toward the rapidly approaching boat. He called to his wife to stay down and close to the mast, which she did. Then he took the tiny soft leather bag that he wore on a cord around his neck, the bag he had worn since his initiation into manhood at thirteen summers old. He opened it and purposefully dipped the middle and forefinger of his right hand into the blue ceremonial pigment that it contained. He streaked it directly onto his glistening, sweat-covered body, around and around in swirls, then finished-off his face almost entirely in blue. The crew and the other passengers watched open-mouthed as he did so, never having witnessed a spectacle so ungodly, so terrifying to behold. The crew were instantly buoyed up at the sight and gave a cheering yell of bravado.

The pirate vessel drew alongside and got closer and closer to them, forty men or more standing there quietly but menacingly. They stared at the blue painted figure in the stern of the cargo boat. The cheery shout from its captain that was supposed to disguise his true intentions didn't work on the Phoenician. He shouted back in the strange Greek tongue that the same painted warrior had not heard for a long time. The pirate captain seemed to understand him however, and pointed to the warrior. He shouted something, asking about him. The Phoenician shouted back his own warning and kept to his original direction of travel.

Then suddenly, without further warning, the pirate vessel shipped oars and launched itself toward them. It crashed directly into their side. Grappling hooks were thrown toward them, two finding their mark, as the two crews ran to the sides of their own ships. The two vessels were heaved closer together by the pirate crew. The ensuing violent battle was, however, mercifully short and sweet.

Even though the pirates got more hooks onto their prey, the cargo ship crew successfully repelled their would-be boarders. But this was largely as a result of the terrifying display of rage shown by the blue 'devil-warrior'. The man ran back and forth slashing wildly with his own longer sword at any pirate who attempted to board, or otherwise endanger his wife. Within moments, the ropes from the grappling hooks had been cut and the pirate vessel had called off the attack and turned for home. The strange blue being was taken as too great a risk to their own safety.

During the fight, a single, rather wiry pirate had managed to get to them but had been instantly cut down where he lay still – not far from the trader's wife. Three of the master's crew were injured, one had lost three fingers from one hand, but the master and crew would be forever grateful to their friend for saving their lives, the boat and their cargo.

They cheered each other in relief at their escape from near death. And as they did, the trader walked quietly to his wife's side and crouched to lay down his sword, so that he could comfort her after the fright of it all. Unseen by him, however, as he did so, the pirate 'corpse' at his side took one last opportunity to make his selfish mark on the world. He grabbed the sword and with a single stabbing motion into his back, mortally wounded the warrior.

On the remainder of the long sea journey, the few people who had never before met, but who had now formed a strong bond by virtue of being reliant on one another in the face of death, were devastated at the sudden change of circumstances. In the following two days after the attack, the health of the warrior slowly deteriorated. Nursed by his grieving wife and the other pilgrims, sadly, before they could reach the island, before the gods could be called upon to intercede on his behalf, on their last evening at sea, the warrior had passed on peacefully.

As was customary in these hot lands, his body, laid out immediately in his best clothes by his wife, was wrapped in a shroud. The master weighted the body with some of the tin ingots to take with him to his own afterlife – wherever that may be. Then, the man's long grey hair tied behind his head, his eyelids closed, beard combed and forehead freshly anointed with the little bag of blue pigment, the small pouch was returned to its place around his neck. His sword was placed in his hands and his body was finally ceremoniously cast overboard, leaving his wife to carry on their pilgrimage alone."

CHAPTER 11:

The Orphan

"It was because of all these events," continued Tom, "that when this particular boat finally docked at Rhodos, it was with a mixture of elation and sadness. The woman had changed especially into her high status white robe, trimmed at the edge in purple. She was shrouded lightly with her white headscarf and veil to shade her from the already blistering sun, and helped by the others onto the short boat-landing. It was to the repeated protestations of the other pilgrims, and more especially the master, that she insisted she must make the journey alone and on foot to the Acropolis.

An hour later, through the growing crowds, she headed steadily for the high citadel. As she did, she was jostled from side to side. On she went, through the swelling mass of visitors to the island, all making their way slowly and merrily through the market stalls. She passed the hundreds of stallholders selling 'lucky' trinkets, 'sacred' water, and exotic 'bargain' fabrics. As she passed through the troupes of brightly clothed exotic temple dancers advertising their own offers, she began to slow down. Now the woman stopped more and more frequently to stand and rest.

Eventually she reached the bottom of the steep hill and the long zigzag ramp that climbed to the top of the hill of the Acropolis and its row of temples. For a moment, she sat on a short wall beside it, catching her breath. She watched tiredly as a pair of small lizards skipped across the rough, hard, sponge-like stone at the bottom of the wall. She smiled briefly as one of them nodded its head rapidly up and down. The other, standing on a large fossilised seashell whose memory remained preserved in the stone, produced a red 'flag' from its throat. Then, unsure of whether or not they were dangerous, she stood up and moved on.

Sternly, she pushed herself forward onto the ramp and shuffled with them into the writhing noisy mass of visitors to the island. Then at the top she sank to her knees with exhaustion, slowly trying to catch her now heaving breath. Eventually, after a short while, she began to recover and look around, now trying to get her bearings. Each temple, each building, was starkly different to its neighbour, but as yet she had not spotted what she was looking for. She glimpsed the various amazing temples, each one a marvel in its own right. In her own land nothing like this existed. By contrast, almost everything was naturally coloured in dull shades. Yes, perhaps there were timber and stone circles, man-made hills – the henges and barrows – but nothing – nothing at all like this. She was filled with awe and bewilderment at the sight of this amazing place. Surely they had been right to attempt the long journey; this child must, she prayed, be born healthily. Unlike the daughter that she'd borne only a year ago, this child must live. And, she willed, it must be a boy – to carry on his father's line!

A small Temple, square-ish with chunky, rather crude columns that the Phoenician had described to them, appeared as the crowd surged forward in a wave, carrying her briefly with it. A brightly painted blue and gold headdress could be seen on the head of a huge black statue of a man with the head of a dog. There was another with an ugly green coloured animal head which had an elongated many toothed snout, then another with the recognisable head of a hawk. There were many, many more. They all frightened her. She looked away, stumbling forward, arm in front to protect her unborn baby. Another temple, more like one of those she'd seen on their voyage here, an oblong building surrounded by columns and – a roof! In fact, the whole building, now up close, looked as if it was covered by a roof. But this was not a straw roof like those in her own encampment; this was an amazing solid, pitched roof of some sort. The red painted triangle to the front of it had within it a huge mask. The head of a horrific sabre-toothed woman with snakes for hair, stared down through cats eyes, from above the huge doors. A loud, ghastly moaning noise came from her gaping mouth. Not that she understood what it was saying. One of the temple priests stepped forward and offered: 'Curses... curses on your enemies... from one obol, guaranteed to work! Buy curses here, from the gods themselves!' Again she looked down and hurried away back along with the crowd that now approached the top of the hill.

A bronze statue of another of the gods, a boy holding a bow and arrow in one hand, gazed amorously down at her from a marble pedestal as she made her way steadily past. Again the priests offered, 'Find love... Find the woman or the man of your dreams. Two obols! Two obols only! Special today!' This time she looked curiously at the statue as she passed, but then she carried on. However, movement behind her told her to look around. When she did, she saw the whole statue was turning toward her. Then its hands moved, beckoning to her. Her head went down as she broke into a stumbling run. Suddenly, after the loss of her husband and the stress of walking up this hill, she felt the unmistakeable sensation: birth pangs. But it was too soon, the baby was not due for another week or two!

The crowd marched on, relentlessly sweeping her along with it. Another priest also tried to get her to visit his own temple, where a huge statue of a bearded god pointed at her with an odd, three-pronged golden fishing spear. No, she wouldn't go in, this was not the god she had heard about, the god who would save her son. She would recognise him from the description the Phoenician had given, she knew she would.

She passed by another statue standing outside the greatest of the temples, immediately recognising this god from the bolt of lightning he held in his right hand – Zeus. This was supposedly the most powerful of the Greek gods. Huge man-beasts and horses were carved into the same triangle above the doors. As she looked up, it felt like all of the carvings on the Temple of Zeus began to look back at her; they were so lifelike. Then even this statue seemed to move, its feet and head turning towards her also. This really was a strange and terrifying place.

Seeing the purple trim of her robes, a priest stepped toward her smiling and speaking in the tongue that she still couldn't understand. When she clutched the neckline of her dress tightly and signalled that she had no money to give him, the false smile dropped and he quickly flagged her on her way past. Instead, he eyed another rich looking pilgrim in her wake. The pain in her abdomen grew as she passed each of the great temples before going on her way.

The next temple was similar to the last, but this time much smaller, and in a way friendlier. Real fear began to grip her as she staggered painfully on. *Not now, she thought. Not before I can speak to the god, plead with him to let our child live, especially if he resembled our last stillborn child. Surely, he would look after him.* She thought of the sacrifice her husband had made – and the long journey. *Please, please let it not have all been in vain.* She began to panic.

Then, miraculously, above the heads of the crowds she saw what had been described to her. Catching the sunlight in the white marble triangle above the door, she saw the four white horses. And there behind them, standing resolutely in the same carriage that carried the golden sun across the sky, was the white marble figure of Helios. His hair was made from beaten gold and sunbeams radiated from his head in the form of a flattened crown. As she watched, sunlight sparkled in the two huge embedded emeralds that were the pupils of his eyes and he seemed to smile beneficently down on her. She was nearly trodden on by the following crowd. But then she was helped gently to the temple steps by a woman's outstretched hand. Although the trader's wife was completely exhausted, she gazed, smiling up at the god – just as he had been described. Yes, she thought finally, she knew they had done the right thing by coming to seek his help.

Taking a deep breath, she walked weakly but freely, past the few people standing on the top step of the Temple of Helios. An old, kindly looking priest in rough, natural vestments held out his hand to take her arm as she nearly stumbled again. Mistaking the gesture, she reached beneath the neck of her robe. The chieftain's daughter took off the heavy knotted gold rope 'torc' or collar – her father's precious wedding gift to her that she'd kept hidden at her neck throughout the voyage. She pressed it into the priest's hand. Similarly mistaking her gesture, the priest accepted the rich gift. To 'buy the temple' for oneself all day was expensive and rarely done, but she had offered payment freely after all and the priest could sell it and do many good works with this amount of gold.

He looked curiously at the bump at her abdomen and, without speaking, smiled knowingly into her eyes, nodding to her. He would still let her in, even though it was frowned upon by the other temples. He led her by the arm through the huge temple doors and gently forward into the dark, silent temple itself. He beckoned her to walk further inside, and toward the golden doors of its inner sanctum which he opened for her. Then, alone, she walked forward into the now empty space, while the priest returned to close the main doors behind the last exiting pilgrim. The woman knelt in front of the life-sized statue of the god who carried a wide bowl on his head – containing the golden sun. She gathered her thoughts and prepared herself for what she now knew was the imminent birth. Although the priest was aware that anyone or anything that might sully the sparkling surroundings of the temple, or in fact anything even remotely unclean was strictly forbidden on pain of death, he decided that this was clearly an exceptional circumstance. So he stood guard while the natural phenomenon of childbirth was allowed to take place in his temple.

But he could not – he must not – intervene directly with the process of childbirth itself. It was one of the most 'unclean' acts. Instead, he watched in empathy from the distant shadows as the delicate-skinned woman silently gave birth to a tiny child.

It was only when the ivory-skinned baby gave a single cry as it emerged from her womb, to be immediately cradled in her hands, that the priest stepped forward. Rather than allow her to struggle with the connecting cord, he took out the small sacrificial knife that hung at his side and cut through it himself. The woman smiled in satisfaction and warmth into the perfectly healthy baby's face – a boy! Then, knowingly, she weakly offered him to the priest. Sensing the full situation, he nodded to her in trepidation, but just the same, he bent to take the baby from her where she now sat cross-legged on the floor. Looking directly up at the statue, she mumbled something in her own tongue. Then she turned her face lovingly toward her son, now safely delivered into the priest's arms. Still smiling serenely, the boy's mother closed her eyes for the last time and slumped gently forward, quite still.

The priest realised at once what had happened. *Now what can I do with the baby?* he wondered patiently. He walked out of the inner sanctum, to the back of the temple and scooped up a handful of the sacred water from the huge bowl and washed the baby's face and hair. Then he gently patted it dry with his clothes. Facing the statue in prayer himself, he murmured some words of his own.

After a moment, he pushed open one of the doors and walked out into the sun, now directly overhead. He crossed the temple square and made his way through the unseeing crowd, toward the edge of the cliff. He looked down over the marketplace and at the sea beyond, reflecting the golden sun, and said aloud into the sky, 'Helios, most bounteous of all the gods, without whose precious gift of sunlight, nothing on earth can survive, if it is your will, please tell me – what it is your wish for this boy?'

There were no witnesses as the priest cradled the boy in the crook of his arm. But, whilst he shaded his eyes with the other hand, the warm air quickly and gently dried the baby's face and head.

The old priest's caring face cracked into a broad, ironic smile. The naturally intelligent man, who had lived long and had seen many things, good and bad, had for lots of reasons begun to doubt everything he had previously believed in. Recently, even in his faith in the gods. Perhaps he was now getting carried away with the tragedy of the situation. Nevertheless, it was the strongest portent he had ever seen or known. Perhaps it was indeed a sign from Helios. But surely, this time, nothing less than a miracle had just occurred in front of his own eyes.

Bathed in the hot midday breeze, as it dried, the boy's hair seemed to change colour from black through brown and now it shone orange, red and gold – the colour of the sun itself. Now the priest looked more closely at the baby's face. His tiny eyelids fluttered open once, unfocused in the sunshine for the briefest of moments, but in that short time they revealed the brightest of green eyes.

Overwhelmed with pride, that fate itself seemed to have chosen him for this duty, the priest quickly made his way back to the temple and stepped back through the doors. He himself would keep the boy and raise him as the son he had never had – on behalf of the god, of course! He would serve with him in the temple. Helios had chosen, he decided to believe again; so be it."

CHAPTER 12:

Special Effects

Tom paused for a moment, letting the start of his long story sink in. Temporarily he perched the sunglasses on his nose, and through thin slits scanned the four faces opposite him for clues as to its reception. Alex added another word to the short list he had previously started writing in his notebook: *Cassiterides; Pillars of Herakles; Syracuse; Murex shells* and now, *Helios*.

It was Maddie who spoke. "Tom, what did you mean about the moving statues, and moaning temple masks?"

"Ah," said Tom. "As the poet and philosopher Pindar said even one hundred years later about Rhodos:

'The animated figures stand
Adorning every street
And seem to breathe in stone,
or move their marble feet.'

At that time, many of the temples had started to resort to what we might now consider 'dirty tricks', in an effort to boost their popularity."

"And their treasure chests, no doubt," added Alex sceptically.

"Very true," agreed Tom. "But let me explain:

From the earliest times on the island, there had been natural caves scattered throughout the area of what had become the Acropolis. Doubtless the people who had lived on the island in antiquity were 'troglodytes', or cave dwellers, and no doubt they had felt the extraordinary experience that it is to be deep underground. To hear the deep booming echoes of their own amplified sounds and movements, feel the claustrophobic damp and smell the very earth itself. It was an eerie experience that aroused in them deep primeval feelings and excited them.

Eventually they were prompted to carve out the relatively soft, porous marble and enlarge the caves into caverns for ritualistic use. No doubt also, around that very time, the opportunity was spotted by someone to make a profit from those places. Even in the old priest's time, one of the earliest underground caverns – forerunners of the temples – 'the Nymphaion' still existed and was still in use. Again, no doubt in part, because it held the added attraction of having the trickling sound effect and the practicality of having its own highly saleable 'sacred water spring'. Gradually, over time, the marble blocks that had been cut out of these caverns were used to build other places. Over more time they were shaped into regular blocks, which in turn made it easier to build rectangular shelters.

Over many generations, as the people became more sophisticated, it was only natural that this should be reflected in their architecture. Until eventually, one day, they would reach what many people across the world still regard as the epitome of architecture – the Classical Greek temple. As a result of this natural progression, many of the temples on the Acropolis had been built directly on the land that the priests already owned, over the original caverns, which now became underground basements.

Now these foundations and the basements of many temples were being converted, tunnelled out into dark labyrinths. This allowed concealed access to the new 'special effects': the moving statues, hollowed out to allow a child to operate them either from inside or via a set of levers and pulleys. These small, often *silenced* orphans and slaves scurried around the dark passages like rats. It was also their task to climb up ladders built into hollowed-out pillars and creep into the roof space, to operate the special effects up there. For instance, the moaning tubes: tubes which led to the mouths of the temple masks or to other statues to make them appear to speak. There were also many other special effects that kept the paying audiences convinced of the existence of the gods.

In these cavernous roof-spaces, the children operated 'bull-roarers': diamond-shaped boards attached to ropes that when swung around faster and faster, made a loud moaning, roaring sound. Or thunder machines: long wooden boxes that in the temple below, sounded like the scariest of all natural phenomena when a studded iron ball was rolled back and forth inside it. Not unlike that one," Tom pointed to the long box that stood partly covered beside the table. "Please fetch it to me and I will demonstrate."

Alex brought it over and Tom tipped it back and forth, while they closed their eyes, imagining the full effect. "Of course, the real ones were much larger, much deeper and noisier and fixed onto the ceiling, which itself acted as a giant diaphragm or speaker. Those made a far more convincing sound."

"It's like the sound effects in a theatre," said Maddie.

Conna, ever the sceptic, snorted at the idea. "And these thunder machines and stuff were supposed to scare the..." he faltered, "...shekels out of the pilgrims, were they!" He checked Bex's face.

Tom shrugged his shoulders. "Easy to mock now, from the perspective of this technological world, where light floods a room at the flick of a switch, music – even from a full orchestra – is on demand and scientific discovery dictates that there are few things left to believe in. But try sitting alone in a vast darkened temple, home of the god of thunder and lightning, with howling, moving statues surrounding you and the booming CRASH of thunder coming from above, before you criticise these ancient peoples."

Alex couldn't help smirking at the way Conna had suddenly been shut up.

Tom got slowly to his feet and crossed to the bench. He went onto another model, a one metre tall wooden wheel of sorts. The others watched from where they were, as he continued, "Those were not the only special effects known to the ancients; there was also this!" Around the wheel's ten centimetre wide circumference was a fine cloth band – silk as Tom pointed out. A spring-loaded arm stood in front of it, holding a piece of amber in contact with the silk. A long, coiled length of copper wire was wrapped around the amber. The bulk of it rested on the table, while the end dangled a short distance from the floor. He began to spin the wheel slowly and as he did, a steady stream of thin blue sparks of static electricity began to leap across the short gap. With a distinct 'crack', this tiny 'bolt of lightning' discharged itself to earth.

"You do know that the ancients knew of this process many, many thousands of years ago don't you;" he addressed them all. "The lightning in the sky wasn't the only form of electricity known to them. And you do know what the Greek name for 'Amber' is, don't you? 'Elektra'."

"As in electricity!" Alex pondered aloud.

"Of course," advised Tom, "the bolt that could be sent from the hand of a statue was much larger."

Alex frowned. "But isn't it dangerous?"

"That depends on the size of the charge," answered Tom, "and whether or not the equipment is earthed. At this small size, it is not particularly so!"

The four began to let their fascination grow as Tom explained more and more about these and other long lost discoveries dotted around them. "If these are accurate," said Maddie, "the ancients must have been very clever."

"Very," agreed Tom. "Not at all the near cavemen that modern society seems to want to believe. It may well have been over two and a half thousand years ago, but those times were not as primitive as many people think. In truth, these men and women – these boys and girls – were just the same as you..." he said poignantly "...and I!"

Maddie spoke up. "And all of these special effects were operated by slave children! Wasn't it dangerous for children to be crawling around in those tight spaces?"

"Absolutely," Tom answered. "Accidents were certainly not unheard of, but the spaces were too tight for anyone over the age of eight or ten; and unwanted children have unfortunately never been in shortage in this world. They were therefore quite expendable."

The shocked looks especially on the girls' faces, prompted Tom to add quickly, "I do not condone it, I merely pass this knowledge on. There were many unwanted children in those times. As cruel as their labour and conditions were though, at least their treatment was better than the much later Romans' heartless and instant solution to unwanted childbirth."

No one asked; they didn't want to know. But each could guess at what that solution might be.

After a few seconds of silence, it was Bex who next spoke. "Tom, what did you mean by *silenced* children?"

Tom looked down at his hands. "For quite obvious reasons, the pilgrims – and the general population of the island – could not be allowed to know of these deceptions. It was for that reason that many of these children were..." he struggled to find an acceptable way to put it, "prevented from speaking... physically."

Bex absent-mindedly closed her mouth tightly, her tongue pressed to the roof of her mouth.

Bit by bit, the casual heartlessness of the age dawned on them all.

Shrugging away these uneasy thoughts, Alex asked, "So what happened to the baby?"

In reply, Tom answered softly, "Let me continue." He closed his eyes and removed the sunglasses once again.

CHAPTER 13:

Education, Education, Education.

"The Temple of Helios was one of the few that had converted the cavern below it into living quarters, if only reasonably comfortably. There, as he grew, the baby's presence was at first concealed by the priest, but it became obvious to him and others that this admittedly quiet child's existence could not be hushed up any further – rumours had started on hearing at least the occasional cry in the temple. The priest began to re-tell the tale proudly, of the 'miracle' of the boy's birth, arguing that because of the precise circumstances, there had been no sacrilege committed in his temple. As for keeping a child in the temple, that, as I have just said, was already well established practice. Also, because there had been no immediate clamour for action to be taken against him – the tale was very popular and the legend grew – it was thought better to leave them in peace.

Not that the priest would have any talk about the boy being a god – he was categorically not! As proof, he would tell people openly that he himself had buried the remains of his mortal mother.

As for his father, nearly a year later, a Phoenician mariner had turned up enquiring about the child. After briefly exchanging with the priest, the tragic circumstances of the boy's parents' journey, and their death – but steadfastly refusing to confirm their country of origin – the mariner vanished again, safe in the knowledge that the boy was now being properly taken care of in his own country of birth.

No, whilst the priest had been happy enough to give the boy an appropriate name, 'Helio', in celebration of his miraculous birth – later shortened to Lio – he was nevertheless a mortal boy and he would be given no favours. Well, perhaps just a few. And so, the boy grew up in the loving care of the priest, whom he called his 'grandfather' and he lived in the surroundings of the temple.

Their living quarters in the temple were modest. The reasonably small set of rooms that were part of the basement allowed them to live and work in the same place, which in turn added to the priest's popularity, as he was on hand to minister to the temple followers in the case of emergencies. In addition to the common living room where they jointly prepared meals, ate and talked together, each of them had an another small room or cell for sleeping and privacy. The rooms were plain and tidy and sufficient for their needs. The lifestyle that the boy enjoyed then was not extravagant but neither was it too frugal.

Not that they worked alone; there were plenty of other priests and helpers, unusually both male and female, who all had their tasks to perform, such as ushering the crowds or collecting the freely given offerings from the pilgrims. However, they did not live in the temple; they were day workers and volunteers.

From the earliest age, the boy had discipline instilled in him. Each morning, he was encouraged to rise from his bed just before sunrise – to greet the dawn in a short prayer of thanks, even if he did sometimes return to bed straight after. Then, similarly, to give thanks at dusk for the gift of each day's natural sunlight.

He had his own duties too: helping clean and tidy at the end of the day; helping his grandfather to purchase the necessary temple supplies and even in infancy, starting to be familiar with the 'business' of the temple and how it ran. For instance, he learned to count the offerings of money into the temples own distinctive yellow-ochre coloured leather pouches.

By the age of five, he frequently ran errands through the

bustling streets, where to many of the locals he became a true delight to meet. He had none of the arrogance that any other 'special' child might have had. The boy grew up with a sense of real values, for real things, taught to him by the priest. But most of all, he knew that he was truly loved.

The old priest himself had many varied interests which expanded Lio's holistic education. Firstly, the priest's charitable work took up a lot of his time. Since 'finding' Lio, he had set up a small orphanage on the other side of the island. Lio often visited. Further to this, he was trying to raise enough money to purchase a small plot of land on which to put together a community of those individuals unfortunate enough to have contracted leprosy. He was one of only a few who was convinced that it was not a curse visited on these people as a punishment for some imagined 'sin'. Although whatever the cause, he reasoned, it certainly seemed to be contagious and Lio was not encouraged to come with him on his visits to the sufferers. However, he did explain many of his thoughts to the young boy.

Although these and other ridiculous superstitions sometimes made him irritated, in all the time the boy lived with him, he only once heard his grandfather lose his temper. And that eventual event would mark a tragic turning point for them both. Long ago, he once confided in the boy, he had made a vow of non-violence that he never intended to break. As he grew, Lio had occasionally heard the persistent rumour that supposedly in the man's youth, before turning to the priesthood, he had once killed another man in an argument over a young woman, though neither man nor boy ever mentioned it.

He taught the boy the principles of making medicines from the many imported herbs and spices that he bought in the main marketplace, some of which the priest sometimes took himself to relieve the occasional tingling sensations in his left arm and the slight pains deep within his chest.

Together, they shared the priest's curiosity in stargazing: watching the sun, the moon and the stars, the priest pointing out their constellations. He even had a favourite: the constellation today known as 'the great bear', 'the big dipper' or 'the plough', amongst others. He knew the names of the two pointing stars: Merak and Dubhe, that showed the way to Polaris. This, the Pole star, hovered over the centre of the earth and around it the world turned. It was also the star where the priest often joked that he would most like to spend eternity, explaining his belief that somehow, in some form, we would each in turn join the stars – at least in thought. Lio also learned the names of other stars:

There was Sirius – the 'Dog Star' – the brightest star in the sky, that once spotted returning from its absence in the sky during winter, heralded the flooding of the River Nile in Egypt, which would then fertilise the farmland with its rich mud and silt. And then there were the Pleiades or seven sisters, the oldest recorded stars known to man. Although through Lio's younger, better eyes, he could see at least nine! The boy learned these and many more, along with the positions of the other thousand or so stars visible to the naked eye, not forgetting the five known planets of course: Hermes, Aphrodite, Ares, Kronos and Zeus. Later, in Roman times, these names would be directly translated as Mercury, Venus, Mars, Saturn and Jupiter, the only planets visible to the naked eye.

Lio learned also, at the earliest age, how to tell the time; to accurately use the sundial the old priest himself had designed and built. It was a solid marble block which had a quarter hemisphere dished in its top surface. It sat at the front of the square outside of the temple. The priest taught the boy how to check its alignment to Polaris in the night sky – true north – and then showed him by day how to read the time precisely. This was done by closely watching the sun's shadow – cast from the bronze style, or 'gnomon', as it later became reinvented – while it moved in degrees past the hour and minute lines marked inside the dish.

Of course, he also learned to read and write, although not many other people at the time could, but his real education though – his education for life – had often been in the form of short stories, fables and parables told to him in the evenings over their main meal of the day. He remembered well an early fable, told by Aesop, a slave who had lived many years before and whose stories had so amused his master that he had eventually freed him. This was a much repeated favourite of his:

Helios and Zeus argued one day: which god was the greatest. 'I am of course,' boomed Zeus, 'I can summon any of the gods and men to do my bidding; I can make anyone bend to my will.'

'Then prove it' challenged Helios, pointing to an old pilgrim walking on a hill below – 'make him remove his cloak.'

Zeus boomed his thunder and sent thunderbolts while the Furies blew the winds around him. But all the time, the pilgrim wrapped his cloak tighter around his body. Zeus was enraged, but could do nothing more.

Then Helios rose up high in the sky, carrying the sun. Gentle warmth bathed the man, who after a short while removed his cloak to bask in its gentle radiance.

The clear moral of the story, that gentle persuasion could often succeed where threats and bullying could not, were fully accepted and adopted by Lio as one of the basic tenets of his life. It is perhaps sad, however, that the priest himself did not perhaps fully appreciate this, nevertheless, Zeus and those who adopt his ways do not always quit as easily.

It was a happy and learned young childhood then, and Lio enjoyed mixing with the many visiting foreigners. Also, with the help of his grandfather, who had himself been born in Sumaria, to the east, he learned the many tongues of the pilgrims. In fact, the boy was extremely gifted in this respect.

He had a few young friends, not many; the whole temple area was not a proper residential area. The High Priest of the Temple of Zeus, who was generally a humourless man, occasionally let him visit the children who worked the machines in his temple – though only after work. So Lio would go over and play outdoor games with Marduk, the barefoot slave boy of his own age, although sometimes, to his slight annoyance, his older sister Ashur would tag along.

They were Nubians, Lio's grandfather supposed, or possibly from even further afield, judging by their blue-black skin, their tight black curled hair and handsome features. Though, they were themselves unsure where they were from. They had travelled there as toddlers with their parents, but as inevitable with some people, their money ran out after too long a stay. It was then that, trusting they would have a better life there, and to get the money to return home, their parents had sold them into slavery – to the High Priest of Zeus. They were far from the only ones though, it happened all too often. Such were the values of that time. Yet despite his lot in life, Marduk always seemed happy; at least, enough for him to wear a permanent smile. Most times they were not allowed to stray out of doors, they were only slaves after all, but when Lio visited, they would always find a new game to play.

A favourite game of theirs was making shadow plays in the dark temple corridors. Using one of the oil lamps, they would use their hands to make the shadows of animals and birds, giggling and making up stories of the many beasts that both Marduk and Ashur distantly remembered seeing in their own country: lions and zebra, crocodiles and unicorns – big fat grey horses that roamed the plains wearing a single horn on their snouts. Animals, the like of which Lio had only ever known from their skins – the skins that were sometimes sold in the markets in the agora. Even Ashur was good at the shadow game and could often make better animal voices than the two boys. In general she always looked and behaved more remotely toward Lio, not shy exactly and still happy to have the occasional company of another child a little below her own age, but somehow different toward him than to her brother – in a way that Lio didn't understand. He even attempted to teach Marduk and Ashur to write a few things: their names; the names of a few animals; yes, no and thank you, but still she remained slightly aloof, always keeping her distance.

Their master, however, never let them overstep the mark and was eager to let them know their place. Once, Lio's grandfather made the mistake of giving him two toys to take with him for his friends: a small painted clay horse that could be pushed around on its four wheels, and a carved wooden doll with moving limbs, but they were returned next day by the slaves' owner. The High Priest of Zeus did not want them distracted from their important work in the temple.

Occasionally though, when the temple was closed, which was very rare, they would be allowed to go down and skinny-dip, splashing and swimming in the harbour as nature intended. They jumped and dived in from the surrounding walls to swim, if a little dangerously, between the cargo ships or haulers. Something intimidating about the low-swept warships led them never to swim amongst the penteconters though; the painted eye on each of them seemed to warn them away. Nevertheless, it was always to both of the boys' slight annoyance that whenever they did go swimming, Ashur could out-swim and out-run them both. Although, unlike the boys, she would never attempt to copy the actions of 'Pelos', the traditional name for the island mascot, a pelican, which was often found in the harbour. The sea-bird could often be found plummeting beak first into the harbour to fish, or more often, be found gorging itself on its catch, only to laze around afterwards. The boys, however, would often dive in, just to show each other they could!

Lio's two friends particularly enjoyed those rare sunny moments in their otherwise hard lives, and it was always difficult for them to return home, but the thought of escaping never entered their minds. The penalty for attempted escape was not worth considering. However, whilst their own high priest did not share the same enlightened view of individual freedom as Lio's master, he did feed them properly, if not appetisingly, and he did not beat them much. Neither had he removed their tongues – though in truth, that was perhaps because they were required to take it in turns to beckon to the pilgrims intelligibly through the speaking tubes of the statues. And that was all the slaves could reasonably expect. In any case, their friend Lio would often smuggle in a treat from his own table and this would at least make them happier for a short while – until work began again.

As the years passed peacefully, Lio's friendship with the two grew stronger, and the Temple of Helios grew in popularity as people came to listen to the priest's advice as much as make offerings to the god. So, too, grew the popularity of the boy, who was well known and liked, especially by the stallholders and traders in the agora, not least because by touching his extraordinary hair, they themselves had decided, much to the annoyance of his grandfather, that the boy could bring them good luck.

By the age of ten, Lio and his grandfather shared a most extraordinary bond. The boy and the high priest often discussed many subjects that Lio had expressed his own curiosity in, and the boy did not usually mince words.

One day, they were walking past the Egyptian temple, when a slight earth tremor – they were relatively frequent in this part of the world – caused the collapse of one of the corners. With it, the speaking statues of 'Anubis' and 'Sobek' – the dog and the crocodile headed gods were toppled. While the crowds screamed and fled in panic as they always did after this most powerful sign from one of the gods, the old priest told Lio to wait where he was, whilst he himself ran toward the choking cries of a small child who had been trapped deep in the earth below the rubble. After a few minutes, the still body of a soil covered child of about seven years of age was recovered too late, whereupon one of the Egyptians came over to the priest, shouting at him to drop the boy before someone saw, shooing him away as he did. Two of the temple servants then picked up the still warm body and, before anyone else had time to see, threw it quickly over the wall into a heap of assorted rubbish that had accumulated there.

It was an ugly incident that demonstrated to Lio the full callousness of what went on in some of the temples and in the name of the gods. The old priest took the boy quickly home and, on request, explained briefly how and why the child had been killed. Thus the priest broke one of the most solemn secrets on the island!

115

That evening, after watching the priest scribble down more astronomical observations on a sheet of new and expensively imported papyrus, Lio asked: 'Grandfather, why do all of these pilgrims come to us and give us money to seek the advice of a god?'

The old priest explained sympathetically, 'Lio,' if you were a poor farmer or shepherd and you needed something, you would seek the advice or help of your father or grandfather, wouldn't you?'

'Yes,' the boy readily accepted.

'Then, for those of us without anyone else to ask, it is only natural, necessary, to look to someone higher, isn't it?'

'I suppose so,' Lio accepted. Then, hardly stopping for thought, he asked, 'But why do the other Temples employ such trickery toward the pilgrims?'

'Lio, this is something of which we never speak. Only the temple workers know of it – it is dangerous to speak of,' he held his forefinger to his lips. Charitably, though not necessarily believing his own explanation, the priest suggested, 'These simple people, most of whom have never seen a proper house let alone one of these majestic temples,' he beckoned around him, 'wish to see a sign. Any sign that the gods have heard their prayers – even though sometimes they may not be graced with the answer they prayed for. But often their faith is what keeps them going in their lives. Sometimes it can even keep them alive through illness or hardship – I have seen this! Consider then, does it really matter if some of the temples grace them with a sign to help them?'

The boy considered this for a moment. 'Even if they pray for a curse on someone, like the people who visit the Temple of Zeus?'

'No!' the priest answered bluntly, 'that is a *dis*-grace; to encourage anyone to hurt or show malice to another has nothing to do with the gods, of that I am certain. That is one of the worst treacheries to the gods themselves – it is only man who is responsible for deliberate harm.' In conclusion, he offered the boy an open question: 'Consider, Lio... if Zeus, or any of the gods, are the epitome of goodness and all that is wise and right in the world,

116

and they are all powerful, how could it follow then that these same gods would want or need to encourage mere mortals to hate and even kill one another on their behalf? Is that the request of a god – or a demon?'

The boy nodded his head sagely – it was a lesson he would never forget.

That night, even though Lio's question had been a fair one, the priest was nevertheless upset enough to have to take his chest pain medicine.

And so, in time, Lio grew both in stature and in knowledge, and both he and his grandfather were truly happy with their simple lives. Unbeknown to either of them though, storm clouds were gathering on the island that would devastate their peace and happiness and change the whole course of not only their lives, but of all history itself!"

CHAPTER 14:

Zeus!

"The Temple of Zeus was the largest and grandest of all the temples on the island. However, for the past two pilgrim seasons, it had slipped down not only in the popularity ratings, but more importantly, in the revenue stakes. In the centre of the inner sanctum, a colossal statue of Zeus reached up to the roof. The statue, the largest on the island, had been carved from the local porous marble, then filled with stucco – a kind of smooth plaster – and painted in bright colours. The statue was clad with beaten, solid gold clothing, reaching halfway up its body.

Its purpose was twofold: firstly to inspire and fill with awe anyone who saw it, not least to intimidate any pilgrim to give generously to the temple; secondly, not just a statue, it was in fact also a reserve of wealth, a 'bank' for the island. As money was required from time to time, for example, to renew the island's defensive warships, part of the clothing was removed and melted down to be struck into coins. Once the gold clothing had reached all the way up to the shoulders of Zeus, but now he was half naked. The bank was running low.

Zeus was supposed to be the Father of Gods and Men: Ruler of Mount Olympus, home of the gods; King of the Skies; and King of Thunder and Lightning. Hitherto, it was always the temple to take the most money on the island by far. However, now the temple took less than half of the reputed funds than did the neighbouring Temple of Helios. Revenue counted on by the government was being diverted away without their control or approval and channelled into more charitable causes.

This evening's assembly now met in secret in the inner sanctum. In theory it was headed by the High Priest of Zeus: titular most powerful religious leader on the island. However, it was also attended by many representatives of the ruling classes who owned a large stake in the temple. They had met on four occasions now to discuss ways to stop the rot, 'before they were penniless' and the position of the High Priest of Zeus threatened to become a laughing stock. The situation could not – would not be tolerated further! The high priest, however, was at a loss to devise a way to bring about this desired upturn in their mutual fortunes.

The chairman of the assembly sat at the low altar table which held a stack of empty offering bowls. 'Tell me, Priest,' he boomed, 'what factors exist that have brought this dire situation about?'

The high priest reflected; knowing he would be asked the same question as before, he had already rehearsed his answer. 'Firstly, there are a number of factors,' he coughed for emphasis. 'The smaller temples have re-invested *their* funds heavily into rebuilding and redecorating.' He left unsaid, the implied accusation that this assembly had divided the Temple of Zeus' funds amongst themselves.

The chairman gritted his teeth, taking the explanation like a slap in the face. He had often been accused of corruption himself. Slipping his gold armbands below his robes, he said, 'Go on.'

'Secondly, many of the temples employ more attractions. Moving statues, crying statues that produce tears of wine – and now one of them is trying to devise a machine that can send a bolt of lightning – from the finger of their god. They do not come cheap but they do bring in vast revenues. Gone are the days when a rumble from the thunder machine inside the temple roof will alone suffice. The pilgrims donate far more money when they have seen an unmistakable sign for themselves: a readily identifiable omen or portent.'

The chairman butted in. 'But not all the temples use this

trickery; next door, the Temple of Helios has none – and look how it prospers,' his gruff voice accused.

This was the crux of the matter, the high priest knew. This was the real reason for the meeting. Resignedly the high priest admitted, 'They have one reason that cannot be denied,' he sighed deeply. 'The sun-haired boy is a greater natural gift for the Temple of Helios than anything that we could devise.' He ended weakly, 'Perhaps he is indeed beloved of the gods?' The question floated out.

The chairman suddenly lost his temper. He swept the copper bowls onto the floor with an echoing crash. 'Pah! You're not telling us you actually believe in any of this nonsense?' He waved his hands around at his surroundings. The gods are for those who cannot understand any different! Only fear of what will befall them if they do not believe makes them controllable!'

'And profitable,' a voice from the back shouted.

'Quite right,' agreed the chairman. 'A boy is allowed to be born – sacrilegiously within the temple – and because he is a freak of nature and has not only red hair but white skin and green eyes, he is proclaimed as a hero...' then he added sarcastically, '...a *favoured* one to the gods – this is madness! It *has* to stop,' he shouted, 'before all is lost.'

The high priest wasn't too shocked at the outburst. While he himself still believed in the gods, he knew that there were many amongst the ruling classes who did not. But until now, no one would have dared to suggest, especially to the high priest himself, that this – the temple and the gods – were all 'nonsense'. He continued, 'Also, it seems, that the high priest of Helios does not pay formally for his staff, people work for him free of charge – women too.'

The chairman growled again, 'could we not charge him with this further sacrilege then.'

'Sadly not,' someone behind him called. 'The laws state only that women cannot be *paid* to work in temples.'

'Nevertheless,' the high priest continued calmly, 'it is a

combination of all those factors that has caused this regrettable situation.'

From the darkened main body of the temple, outside the open doors of the inner sanctum, a silky voice hissed from the shadows. 'Then I suggest we deal with it swiftly, before it is too late.' A short, slightly-built man with sallow skin and a heavily pock-marked face walked toward the assembly. He was followed by the tallest, most muscle-bound Egyptian manservant that the chairman had ever seen. The shorter of the two limped into the centre of the sanctum, holding an unusually slim, carved ivory walking stick in his right hand. Dressed in fine clothes, on his back he also wore a heavy cloak of purple which drew the desired murmur of respect that he had intended, although no one knew him. The stranger knew how to dress to impress.

'And what would your course of action be?' the chairman asked the new face, assuming such an importantly dressed person must have been invited to attend.

The newcomer had travelled a long way from Sicilia to this island, sensing an opportunity to increase both his status and his wealth. According to his expert and most secret sources in Syracuse, he had only a few days left to make his mark here. It would not be long before the opportunity would be gone again – for precisely another eighteen years, eleven days and eight hours – but he had chosen his target well. Turning to face those assembled, he said, 'It will be painful, but necessary.' Then he paused dramatically.

'Yes, go on?' the chairman said encouragingly.

'The first problem is "ours", we re-invest massively if that's what it takes: renew this temple fully, repair and repaint it to the same standard as our competitors,' he stated simply.

There was a murmur from the others.

'To do this, we must simply invest more money.' The murmur grew to a grumble of disapproval.

The chairman held up his hand to shush the grumblers, and then nodded grudgingly. 'What else?'

The stranger inhaled dramatically. 'The boy! The boy is the real

121

problem.' Not only does he recruit more pilgrims openly, and in the most disgraceful way – allowing them to touch his hair – but he mingles with the slave children right under your noses. Who knows what secrets are betrayed.'

There was another mumble of disapproval. He paused, considering whether to speak the thought they'd all had throughout the past season but didn't dare voice. 'But even if Zeus himself was to act on our behalf and the boy was to... disappear, no one could predict what might happen as a result.' He tapped the stick lightly in open palm of his hand. The assembly members shifted uncomfortably, murmuring again.

'If that happened' he patted his curly black hair into place, 'it might even worsen the situation. Who knows' he raised his eyebrows, 'we might even be blamed ourselves.' He sneered, what was to become an almost permanent sneer.

The chairman leaned forward. 'Then what would you suggest?'

Theatrically stepping into the centre and turning his back to the high priest – in itself an act of gross disrespect – the stranger turned his face to the assembly and said: 'I have a suggestion.'

Again there was a murmur.

'If a situation was engineered whereby the boy... shall we say... falls from grace,' he tapped the stick lightly in his hand again for emphasis. 'Then, it would be more than acceptable to take action against him, and perhaps against the Temple of Helios even,' he casually suggested, 'confiscate their own vast funds – to rightly pay us back for putting us into a situation where we are now forced to refurbish our own temple,' he sniffed. 'It is only a suggestion.'

The changing murmur took on a different note.

'Tell us more,' urged the chairman, clearly very interested in the prospect of not having to put his hand into his own purse after all.

'Of course, certain changes would have to be made first.' The stranger turned and looked the high priest pointedly up and down. 'We can have no more weakness or charity shown: free admissions, free "sacred water" for the washing of hands... very amateur,' he shook his head pitifully. Turning back to the assembly, he said, 'Perhaps it is simply time for the high priest to retire early.'

The high priest's face dropped. 'But that has never happened before – the high priest's position is given unto death!'

The stranger looked deep into the priest's eyes without having to voice the obvious threat. The sly, cruel look on his face said it all. But then he voiced it all the same: 'Take your well earned retirement old man,' he growled through his gritted teeth, 'leave the situation to me.'

The noise of approval boomed around the Temple; clearly it was time for the Greek ways of enlightenment and understanding to make way for a more robust Sicilian regime. Collusion between state and the gods was reaffirmed.

The new High Priest of Zeus did not waste any time. Next evening he called unannounced at the Temple of Helios. The old priest greeted him open-mindedly, and led him limping along with his stick. He was shadowed by his silent and straight-faced manservant to the private chamber below. The bench in the centre of the room was littered with the priest's stargazing equipment: fine sets of callipers, scribes and an abacus, along with numerous papyrus scrolls – or more correctly, papyri. Quickly, almost secretively, the boy's grandfather moved the scrolls to the corner of the room before welcoming them in. Lio sat on a stool against the far wall; he smiled politely at their guests.

'I'm Zeus now,' the Sicilian introduced himself grandly, claiming the self-styled title. Not waiting for the old priest's reply, he added. 'I'm in charge of this island's affairs.'

The old priest raised an eyebrow at the grandiose claim, but said nothing.

'So this is the red-haired wonder boy that is the talk of the town,' the Sicilian sneered at Lio.

'Greetings, sir,' Lio said respectfully.

'I gave you no leave to speak to me!' he snapped.

'I beg a pardon for the boy; he is encouraged to speak his mind here,' stated the old priest simply. 'This is Helio.'

The younger 'priest' nodded to him and sat down. 'All servants should be seen and not heard, should they not?' He nodded back toward his own servant, who made a short, odd barking noise in reply. 'None of my servants will ever embarrass me – or betray any secrets – the Egyptian slave markets have a way of making certain.' He made a silent gesture of holding his own tongue between the thumb and forefinger of one hand, while with the other he mimed snipping it off.

Ignoring the distasteful performance, the old man asked, 'May I offer you something? A cup of water or wine, perhaps fruit of some variety?' He beckoned the boy to pick up the full fruit bowl and offer it to their guest.

'No!... Thank you,' the Sicilian grudgingly remembered to keep his manners. Getting quickly to the point, he said, 'I hear the fortunes of your temple are thriving.'

'Yes, many prayers have been answered,' confirmed the old, proper priest.

'I was referring to your revenue – your share of the pilgrimage money!' The young, false priest snapped again impatiently.

'Oh, that,' the old priest continued shrewdly; he'd understood very well what he'd meant.

'I'm told you're the richest temple on the Acropolis now.'

'I'm not sure, if you say so,' the old priest agreed amicably. 'Anyway, it's sufficient for our needs. It allows us to do much more each year.'

The High Priest of Zeus narrowed his eyes. 'And what needs might they be?'

'Oh, we fund an abandoned children's camp on the other side of the island.'

The young priest's expression changed. Intrigued, he narrowed his eyes even more, and asked, 'a factory?'

'No, a refuge: somewhere to grow up in peace. And then we have the leper village, of course.'

The young priest didn't quite understand the concept.

'For what purpose?' he probed. 'For future slaves? No one would take lepers... unless they were put into mines...?'

The old priest changed the subject deliberately, knowing his guest did not share his own altruistic ambitions. 'I've been told you're from Sicilia, is that so?' In truth the old priest had already been tipped-off about the newcomer's presence on the island; nothing much happened here that didn't reach his ears sooner or later.

'Yes,' the Sicilian said absent-mindedly, still trying to figure out the scam.

'Was it a large temple – your last post?'

'Temple?' the young priest spat out. 'Certainly not, I was assistant to the governor.'

'But then you found the gods?' the old priest intoned meekly.

Suddenly, dropping any pretence, the young priest narrowed his eyes menacingly. 'This, old man, is simply a business opportunity. And I've been in business too long to be taken for a fool – the grain stores were doubled in Sicilia due to me.'

The old priest turned his back to him. 'As, I believe, were the number of people taken into slavery... and,' he added, 'were the number of deaths from starvation'.

Zeus glared at him. 'Listen you old fool,' he growled threateningly, 'If I were you I wouldn't lock horns with me.' He got up suddenly to go. 'I'm glad you've made "sufficient for your needs" but your greed must stop! There are those of us who have greater needs. I for one have no intention of living in the pigsty you would live in,' he glanced around him. I have a modest villa to build.'

'Mmm,' said the old man, 'and I suppose that palace you're already planning to build overlooking the sea isn't going to be cheap.'

Snarling, the Sicilian returned, 'The high priest of the most powerful god on this island – Zeus! cannot and will not be made to suffer the indignities of living in a lesser house than anyone else on the island. I will be... "stepping-up our offer..."'he smiled self-satisfactorily, '...to the pilgrims as soon as possible. I hope you will be able to cope with the increased competition.' Turning to leave, he warned, 'and rest assured, I will not be tolerating any more of this boy's blasphemous behaviour. I would keep him under close scrutiny if I were you! In future there will be no more mixing with my slaves – and I'll make personally sure that there will be no more whispering between them and this – freak!' He finished off the rant by clicking his fingers for his manservant to follow him to the door.

'I'm certain that Helios will guide us,' said the old priest, getting up to say a goodbye to his guest but by the time he'd got to his feet the young priest had already stormed out, his manservant in tow.

'Something tells me that we haven't heard the last of this "Zeus",' he smiled ruefully at the boy. 'What do you think, Lio?' He rubbed the inside of his left arm. 'Fetch my medicine, there's a good boy.'

The boy had never seen his grandfather so obviously concerned like this and he wondered what was to become of this new situation."

CHAPTER 15:

Foreign Muck!

Tom continued the tale. "It was the end of the following afternoon and Lio was returning from an errand. Since he had been very young, he had always been a fast and reliable runner for the old priest. On this particular day though, although he was happy to have the half day off from his many tasks in the temple, he was saddened that he would not be allowed to see his friend, Marduk – or his sister for the matter of that. Although he didn't want to think about it, he was also very concerned for their safety.

A short while after the new high priest's outburst on the previous night, Lio had clearly heard the unmistakeable sound of the children next door taking a beating. He'd heard it before, several times, when the other priest had lived there, but this time it sounded entirely different. Instead of the short cries of tolerable pain, there had been the continued ungodly screams of real pain, horrible pain. Even now, in his mind he could hear the guttural sounds that continued into the night, preventing him from getting to sleep. The noises even led him to go into his grandfather's room to ask him to intervene – which, much to his grandfather's own shame, he realised that he could not! As a result of his lack of sleep, Lio was now tired, desperate to get home, and eager to find out what he could about his young friend and his sister.

The normally confident, plain sandaled young boy walked heavily, dressed in the same unbleached rough white vestments as his grandfather. As always, his head was hooded against the heat of the sun. He made his way along the main thoroughfare in the agora, between the temples and shops, across the dusty marble-slabbed square, and past the various arcades selling all sorts of things. There were copper cooking pots and utensils, spices and cloths of various sorts. The experience of all of the exciting things before him temporarily distracted him from his worries. As always, he was in awe of the sights and smells of the 'big market' as he knew it. A donkey cart full of earthenware pots and vessels stood blocking the crowd. Without hesitation, the boy ducked under it. Crawling on his hands and knees, he slipped once more into the moving stream of clamouring pilgrims who had come to marvel at the sights.

At this time in the afternoon, the temples and shops assumed a carnival-like atmosphere. The area was, to him, a fairground, where if he was lucky he might be given a 'token', a small gift of food perhaps from one of the many food stallholders. There were many such places, but the one that the boy loved best was the Persian food stand. The exotic spiced food that he smelled as he passed it always made him crave the taste again. And there, just in front of him, beside the bottom of the zigzag ramp, stood the familiar stall again, its owner wearing his outlandishly colourful clothing and silk headdress. The boy pushed through the dense crowd to get a better look at it before going home.

Standing on the ramp, his head just above the top of the bench, he held his eyes closed, inhaling the many varied and wonderful smells: aniseed; nutmeg; cinnamon and cloves; and all sorts of herbs. They all conspired to make the most mouth-watering food he'd ever known. He opened his eyes to see it all laid out in front of him in baskets, bowls and plates: reds; yellows; greens and browns. There were also cooked dishes of all sorts: meats; vegetables; aromatic rice and pulses; beans and lentils. All brought here by the traders from foreign lands – some from the edges of the known world. The sight and the aroma of it all were incredible. His piercing green eyes opened wide with delight.

'Hah,' came the familiar high pitched voice of the stallholder as he noticed the boy, 'My little friend Lio,' he shouted toward the crowd, 'come, look. It is my lucky boy!' The stallholder grinned to see Lio again. Beckoning the boy to him, he stooped to pick up his lightweight carcass as he had often done before. One of his assistants roughly cleared a space for him, then he stood the boy on his bench.

Part of the crowd filing past the stall to go on to the temples stopped to look at him. 'Look' the stallholder continued. 'A most beautiful and wondrous boy is amongst us; come!' The crowd gathered as it always did. 'See, not only does he have lucky green eyes, but he has the hair of Helios himself.' The boy, who had learnt to trust the stallholder, didn't attempt to resist as the trader gently removed his hood, letting it fall free to his shoulders. As always there came the sound of sudden astonishment as the sun lit up the boy's head, framing his milk-white face with the golden hues of his bright mop of red hair. 'See!' the stallholder exclaimed. 'Is this not a lucky omen for you all?' The crowd surged forward, clamouring to touch the boy's head for luck, then gently stroke his hair as he stood there innocently on the bench top. Of course, Lio realised that this was a little mischievous; his grandfather had told him so. 'You shouldn't let people use you like that, it could cause us trouble,' he had warned him. But what harm could it do really? he wondered. This was no less honest than the tricks practiced by most of the temples.

As always, after they had touched his hair, the crowd inevitably turned its attention to the stallholder's foods. And, as always, the assistants rapidly took advantage of the renewed interest in their stall, selling out as fast as they could. After a short while, the stallholder lifted the boy down to the ground on his own side of the bench. Crouching down, his face level to the boy's, the trader spoke gently to him. 'Well Helio, my lucky boy, what is it that I can pay you for the good fortune you have brought me today?' The boy looked around the food and at all of those exotic cooked dishes; his eyes flitted from one large pot to another. 'That please,' he pointed directly to one of the smaller pots of meat cooked in a sauce.

'No! Not that, it's not for one so young. It has a very rare spice, from many sea-leagues to the east – black pepper; it's very spicy – hot!'

The boy nodded. 'Yes, that,' he repeated.

The stallholder laughed. 'Then try some first.' He delicately picked out a small morsel between his thumb and forefinger and popped it into the boy's open mouth. He waited for a reaction. 'Well?' The boy rolled the meat around his mouth, savouring the taste, the like of which he'd never known before. Then, after a moment came the heat. It was wonderful, numbing his tongue and mouth, the vapour travelling up into his nose. He gasped, sucking in the air to cool him down, as the small mouthful slid down toward his stomach. The stallholder's eyes crinkled mischievously, waiting for the boy's reaction, but he didn't expect this one.

'More,' said the boy. 'If it pleases you!'

'More?' the stallholder giggled delightedly, shaking his head in amazement. Standing upright again, he reached for one of the small flatbreads and cut it in half, forming two pockets with a deft flick of his small knife. Filling firstly one half, he handed it to the boy, then, judging the boy's reaction, he generously filled the other half. 'There...one for each hand.'

The boy flashed his eyes once more as he was patted on the head – by the stallholder this time. He thanked the man, then he turned to run up the ramp and past the slow moving crowd, toward his own temple.

Reaching it, instead of going home, he slipped down the side. He shot all the way around the back and into the gap between the Temple of Helios and the Temple of Zeus. Then he made his way through the secret door, low down in the wall of the Temple of Zeus. Via the labyrinth of oppressively warm and stuffy tunnels, he was finally delivered into the inner sanctum of the Temple upstairs.

'Pssst,' he called out into the vast dark empty space, the sound echoing around it. 'Pssst! Marduk, Ashur.' He searched for the voice of his friends but no reply came, except that he thought that he might have heard a faint sobbing from below the temple floor.

As silently and as respectfully as he could, the boy tiptoed across the polished white marble floor toward the altar – the long black marble table, now lined with empty copper offering bowls. Checking around him once more, he crept toward it, head lowered so as not to look directly at the gargantuan statue of the god who sat on his throne behind it.

Deferentially, he placed both halves of his greatly prized meal into two of the bowls, bowing low as he did so. He backed away and then lay prostrate on the marble floor – arms outstretched as the priests did. 'Father, Zeus,' he whispered under his breath, 'Ruler of Mount Olympus and of all the heavens, hear me. If you will, please speak to your new high priest and tell him to stop mistreating your servants here in the temple. In return, I will promise never to speak against you in favour of our own god Helios – this I will solemnly swear to you.' Silently, he got to his feet and, still careful to avoid the gaze of the enormous figure of Zeus, he crept back through the temple and into the basement then back toward the door. As he went toward it, he heard the sobbing again, so he turned to follow the source of the noise.

In the light of the single oil lamp, at the end of a dark corridor Lio could just about make out the face of his friend Marduk huddled close to Ashur. His spindly arms hugged her body close to him as they crouched together in the corner. They looked dreadful. Her face was buried in his chest, the back of her head still trickling with blood where her hair had been roughly hacked off. She sobbed as her little brother tried to comfort her. Lio started toward them but stopped when Marduk signalled with his open palm for him to back away. It was too dangerous! The friends looked once more at each other and, for all the pain that he had undergone, Marduk still managed a tired, limp smile from his blood stained mouth. A distant noise sounded elsewhere in the basement, causing the little girl once more to sob uncontrollably. So, with a last look and a tentative wave to his friend, Lio turned and ran quickly – breaking into tears as he burst out of the temple.

From the shadows of the temple above, the boy had been

watched throughout. The new high priest limped over to the offering table. Reaching casually into one of the bowls, he took out one of the 'offerings' that he was in no doubt had been placed there for the temple slaves. Lifting it disdainfully to his nose, he sniffed at it, then tossed it casually to the floor and stood on it. 'Foreign muck,' he said under his breath. He'd like to see them attempt to eat spiced food now!

That afternoon, returning directly to his own room, Lio fell asleep crying. It was dark by the time his grandfather finished work in the temple, and for once he did not join him outside in the dusk prayer. Later, the priest awakened him to have something to eat. Yawning, he lay there a few minutes thinking about the plight of his friends, saddened dreadfully by their situation. After a while, he got up and stumbled into the room, still half-asleep.

Now entering through the outside door, the old priest tried to comfort his boy gently. 'Ah there you are Lio, are you hungry? Give me a moment and we'll prepare a meal together.'

'Where were you just now?' asked the boy, hoping for news of his friends.

'Oh...' the priest answered, 'checking the sundial – making sure that it is aligned absolutely precisely with Polaris.' He scribbled something on an old sheet of papyrus that lay on the table in front of him. Tomorrow is a most important day for me.'

'Why is that?' The boy asked, trying to take his mind off the plight of his friends.

'This is my father's old chart,' answered the old man importantly. 'It is most confidential,' he continued conspiratorially, 'but I have a theory – and I am not alone.

When I was just a small boy of ten years old – as you are now – living with my family in the easternmost part of Sumeria, far to the east of here, one day, the sun was suddenly blotted out. The Greeks call this an "ekleipsis" – because for a short while, the sun literally "ceases to exist", causing great panic. When I was a boy, because nobody knew what had caused it, my own father encouraged me to make my very first heavenly observation and record the date and time on this, the calendar kept by him. Here it is,' he pointed to the quite shaky ancient and now fading figures and writing. Lio listened on. 'He asked me to promise to watch and listen for the next one that he'd calculated would happen. It was eighteen years later that the event happened again. In fact, it was six thousand, five hundred and eighty-five – and one third days to be exact: eighteen years, eleven days and eight hours precisely.'

Grateful as he was for this distraction from his other thoughts, Lio was at first only mildly interested by the story. But now that his attention was captured, the boy sat down and listened intently.

'What,' asked his grandfather, 'do you think happened six thousand, five hundred and eighty-five – and one third days after that?'

'It happened again?' Lio guessed.

'Exactly! The first gap between the first two events was measured precisely. The second – the same as the first – may have been coincidence. But if it happens again tomorrow for the third time, it will prove that this is a perfectly natural series of events. Perhaps it is a dangerous idea, but I think it is caused by the path of the moon crossing the face of the sun, temporarily causing this "eclipse". Not as some would have it, an evil omen visited upon us by the gods. If I am right, it should occur at precisely the fourth hour after midday tomorrow, give or take a few minutes either way. We can measure it on the sundial together.'

Their conversation continued for a great deal longer, while the priest shared the secret theory that he had worked on for most of his life: that the sun was possibly a sphere. It was, he thought, a ball of fire of some sort, and therefore like the stars, it somehow produced its own light. The moon, he deduced, was also a sphere. He demonstrated this by moving an oil lamp around a hand sized ball, while the boy stood on a fixed spot and observed the changing shape of the shadow that fell across it. It produced all of the moon's phases, from full, to half, then crescent and back again. The moon, his grandfather explained, was a kind of smaller planet, but instead of orbiting the sun, as by observation the others did (moving regularly, but never straying more than the same distance from the sun, first to one side, then the other), the moon orbited the Earth. Sometimes, very occasionally but always the same time apart, the orbits of the two would coincide and for the briefest of moments the moon would visibly cover the path of the sun, and the earth would fall into its shadow.

Instinctively sensing that Lio had reached the right moment in his own life, for the first time the old priest decided to share his own private philosophy with his boy.

He sat down on his chair and said earnestly and truthfully, 'Lio, whilst I am myself still, perhaps illogically, inclined to believe in the power of Helios, or at least in the certain knowledge that all life on earth relies on the existence of the sun, it has occurred to me often that the mechanics of the universe are quite logical – but are not yet understood. The knowledge of this can either be used to educate people for the common good, or to hoodwink them into false beliefs. I would prefer to take the former option. However, there are those who would jealously guard this knowledge in order to manipulate and exploit mankind. To some, knowledge brings enlightenment, to others – knowledge is power! Perhaps one day, man will discover the workings of the universe and act wisely upon it – sadly, it seems, in my lifetime he will not. Maybe one day, Lio, a man may even stand upon the moon's surface?'

Lio listened intently, understanding well but struggling to believe the last absurdity. Then, as soon as his grandfather had stopped speaking, his gaze shifted and the sad expression returned.

Realising that the boy's mind had wandered elsewhere, the old man stopped trying to distract them both. Lio's grandfather put his arms around his boy and hugged him tightly.

From somewhere outside there came the muffled noise of a short single cry and a soft thud, followed by urgent whispering. Distantly, a dog began to bark; then, after a while, it stopped again. Probably just an argument; they decided to ignore it. Best keep away, it could be trouble.

Whilst Lio did share the interest of his grandfather regarding this ekleipsis, he could not take his mind off the more important worries he had. Washing his hands thoroughly in the bowl of water kept on the stand in the corner, the boy came back to sit at the table. After his grandfather had offered thanks to the sun for their meal, Lio suddenly spoke up.

'Grandfather,' he asked, 'why can't we stop the new priest's cruelty toward his slaves?'

The old priest looked at his son and explained, 'Lio, you are young; there are many wrongs that men visit upon each other that we are powerless to change.'

Not satisfied with the answer, the boy went on, 'But, Grandfather, why do they not know that they are doing wrong?'

'My son,' he said, 'Everyone in the whole world knows when they are doing wrong. Never believe anyone who tells you differently, they are either bad, mad or both: wicked! The fact that they do wrong is entirely because they wish to. In my years at this temple I have many times tried to dissuade people from doing wrong, but they know this for themselves already and yet they do it anyway. The only reason they ask me first is that they are trying to find an excuse to do what they want, but what their conscience is already telling them not to do: take what is not theirs; hurt someone; force someone to do their work for them; even kill each other and still blame it on me or one of the gods. Inevitably, when I refuse to bless their actions or intentions, they simply find another god to ask permission of – then they do it anyway. All I can do is remind them that we are all here on the earth to enjoy *equally* the life that is given to us. I hope and pray that they'll listen.'

The boy picked at his meal. More directly he said, 'Then why is it alright for some people – even children – to be enslaved, used to do work then beaten or even killed, and yet we do nothing?'

'It is not right,' answered the priest, 'but sometimes the laws made on this earth are made by men who would justify these rules to excuse their own selfish reasons. Sometimes they even claim that these rules were made by their gods. Regardless, according to most of these laws, slaves are considered property. Even if they are killed, that is up to their masters. It is no one else's business.'

Frustrated at this iniquity, Lio spoke up: 'Then the law is wrong!'

'Yes,' agreed the priest.

'Then we should say this!'

'We should,' his grandfather capitulated.

'Then I will!' Lio decided rather angrily. 'Tomorrow!'

Wondering what he might be planning, the boy's grandfather smiled worriedly and clasped his boy's hand, nodding his approval. For the first time, the master could not argue with the pupil, even though the thought of what might become of it frightened him – for his own sake and for the sake of his boy! That evening, the pains in the old priest's chest grew suddenly fierce."

CHAPTER 16:

Wickedness

"Later that night, before retiring to bed, Lio made his way quietly outside into the cool midnight air. He stood forlorn at the top of the steps, beside the wide corner column of his own temple. After his long afternoon nap, he was now far from tired. He looked worriedly over at the Temple of Zeus, wondering what evils had gone on there. Often the space between the temples was pitch black, but tonight's full moon shone from directly ahead, bathing the gap in blue-white light. The light picked out the accumulated rubbish that pilgrims and others had thrown away that day: discarded rags, uneaten food and other filth. Thinking of his conversation with his grandfather and determined to help his friends, he turned and walked around the other side of the column and looked up to marvel at the moon. Something was desperately wrong; he could feel it. And in turn, that made him feel helpless. Powerless to get involved, he could only hope and pray that Marduk and Ashur would be alright – but that was not what he feared would be the case. Deep down in the pit of his stomach, he was filled with dread for what might have already happened to them.

Lio stood there, silently gazing at the moon and the heavens, remembering where as a child, his grandfather had pointed out the stars and Polaris in particular – Lio's favourite – if there was such a thing. Behind him, the secret door to the Temple of Zeus opened. Unnoticed by Lio, a pair of huge hands shoved the little girl roughly outside into the gap. It was the rattling of the chains that made the boy turn to look.

What he saw sickened him to the core. There, manacled by the ankles, wrists and neck by short chains, was Ashur. She could not stand upright, all she could do was scurry around like a rat, her feet shuffling as she was forced to pick up and attempt to eat the discarded scraps of food. Not that it seemed she could; she gagged every time she was forced, moaning – an awful, unnatural moan – as she did. The priest, who had emerged from the door to stand over her, lashed her back and shoulders repeatedly with his stick as he growled at her. 'Make the most of it,' he warned. 'In future this is all you will get from me.'

Ashur squatted close to the ground as a crumpled heap of soiled rags. She sobbed miserably to herself, while the priest beckoned to his servant to reach back through the door. Not straining at all, he dragged another, slightly smaller bundle of rags out into the moonlight, dropping it where it lay, before the priest kicked it roughly to one side so that the door could be closed. The girl began to sob uncontrollably. Her body convulsed and shook. 'And this,' Zeus gritted his teeth and continued in his silky voice, 'is what will happen to you, if you continue to attempt to communicate with my enemies.' He laughed once: a short, cruel snort. 'Oh, I forgot, you can't speak now, can you! Never mind, you won't need your tongue anymore. You can just grunt approval when you're given a command.'

Lio was filled with dread, not wanting to watch or believe his own eyes. He had never seen such wickedness. He stood stock still, too frightened to move – for both their sakes. As he watched, the little girl eventually quietened. Then suddenly, perhaps feeling his presence, she turned her face toward Lio. She looked directly into the face of her only remaining friend in the world. It was a look of utter despair, silently pleading with him for help. Shocked, the boy looked down at her with pity – only a few yards, but a thousand miles away from him, and now all alone in the world. Lio was devastated.

Incredibly, despite the terrible state Ashur was in; despite the filth and dirt that covered her thin body and limbs and the torn, discoloured rags that now only half covered her back; despite the roughly shaven and matted black hair that covered the many visible cuts and gashes to her head and a long cut in her top lip, Lio felt the most curious sensation, the like of which he had never felt before. As her huge ebony eyes looked up at him, the boy seemed to truly see her for the first time. At that moment, lit by the moonlight, it appeared to him the most beautiful face he had ever seen in his life.

His mouth opened to speak to her but he dared not even whisper. All he could do was nod weakly at her in an attempt to signal to her that he cared. Her bottom lip quivered as the white moonlight revealed the glistening traces of dried tears on her face. Then, without warning, the concealed door was opened by her owner and, on command, the huge servant grabbed the chain at her neck and pulled her roughly inside.

'In! Leave him,' the voice shouted unnecessarily. 'His body will serve as a warning that I mean business!' And with a last glance over her shoulder, first at her brother, then once more to Lio, Ashur was gone.

Immediately, Lio clambered down the steps and crept uneasily toward to the discarded pile of rags that had once been his friend. Gently, he uncovered the boy's face and head. Still warm, though obviously lifeless, Marduk's body lay twisted and broken in a heap, his face streaked in dried blood. Even in death though, somehow, pitifully, the little slave boy had managed to retain his fixed smile. Lio looked briefly at the marks on his body, heavy wealds where he had been lashed repeatedly, presumably with the stick. What savagery!

Surely, he thought, *people will act now*. He would tell his grandfather about what he had witnessed immediately.

Weeping for his friend, he bent down to look again at his face, then he whispered a solemn oath into his ear. 'No matter what it takes, I will take your place – I will take care of your sister for you'. With that, he covered Marduk respectfully again and made his way back to his own temple. From the top step he looked back – curiously, somehow expecting to see the girl again. Then, catching his breath, he continued inside.

Within moments, the concealed door in the Temple of Zeus opened and closed once more. It seemed that the wonder-boy had taken the bait.

Lio racked his brain all night, thinking of how best he could deliver his plea to anyone who might be able to help. He realised, of course, that no one of high standing would be prepared to give him – a mere child – an audience. It seemed to him, then, that the best option he had was to address the crowds directly. He would do it by himself, just as his grandfather and the market-traders did, and implore them to take pity on Ashur and have her released. It was a simple enough and altogether innocent plan, which might seem obvious to most young people. However, it is unfortunate that whilst youngsters are often blessed with the gift of being able to look clearly into their own conscience and believe that if they act on it, others will inevitably follow, adults are far more adept at guile and often seize on this innocence as a point of attack.

That night, after telling his grandfather what he'd witnessed, Lio went back with him to the gap to collect the lightweight body of Marduk. The old priest then picked up the dead child and carried him heavily to his temple.

Washing and preparing the child for burial, the priest started to clean in and around the boy's battered face and mouth. Suddenly, for the first time in his life, Lio witnessed his grandfather lose both his control and his temper. 'THIS WICKEDNESS CANNOT GO ON!' he shouted to himself, banging his fist on the bench top. *Tomorrow*, the priest thought to himself, *I will speak to the High Priest of Zeus*. And, if necessary, he would purchase the girl from him. No matter what the cost, he would at least save her from further harm.

It was perhaps unfortunate though, that in trying to protect each other, neither Lio nor his grandfather confided in one another what their plans might actually involve in combating this most horrible state of affairs. Not, sadly, that it would have affected the outcome.

At first light of dawn, after they had stood with one another, as they had each and every morning, in silent contemplation of the sun's great gift of life, Lio and his grandfather took Marduk's shrouded body to the burial ground just out of town. The old priest reverently placed the body into the prepared deep round grave, taking care to tuck the boy's knees beneath his chin so that he now finally looked at rest in the foetal position. Now, from beneath his robes, the man produced a pair of new clay shoes and placed them in the grave. While others often placed ritual clay clothes in graves in order to accompany them to the afterlife, the priest simply wished to give the boy one modest gift that he had never possessed in life. Likewise, Lio produced a familiar toy: the wheeled, clay horse that Marduk had not been able to take home in infancy. Now he could at last keep it with him. He placed it beside the body and looked for one last time at his smiling, sleeping friend before tucking him in with the shroud. Although Lio was saddened, he did not weep. He had decided to store this emotion for later use in addressing the crowd. Lio then said a last goodbye.

Throughout this time, the Temple of Helios remained closed, Lio's grandfather preferring not to leave the other priests in charge. He and Lio were aware of an important foreign delegation that had been sent by the King of Lydia, especially to speak to the old priest. It seemed that his reputation had now spread as far as the lands of his childhood.

Because it was closed, no doubt much to the satisfaction of the High Priest of Zeus, a huge crowd had started to gather at the Temple of Zeus. As Lio and his grandfather arrived to open the doors of their own temple though, at least half of the crowd immediately diverted to form a queue outside the Temple of Helios. As they went into their temple, the old priest looked down curiously at a streak of green running through the white marble paving directly beneath the portico, and another in pink. In all of his years, he had never noticed them before; all of the other streaks in the marble floor slabs were grey-blue. He wondered again about his eyesight. His eyes were beginning to grow dim now, he knew. He had always been proud of his eyes, but last night had been proof enough for him that it was finally beginning to fade. It had taken him over an hour to verify the position of Polaris accurately against his instruments and fix the exact position of the sundial. By the time he had gone below to his charts, his eyes were swimming, making it difficult to write everything down fully. They had recovered enough by first light this morning though; at least enough to write down what he intended to say later.

One by one the people filed in, some speaking to the old High Priest of Helios himself whose reputation had prompted them to travel from lands afar. Amongst the crowd was the delegation from the Lydian king, wishing to speak privately about a matter of state, a matter of great urgency. The old priest's opinion was needed, as a most respected representative of the foreign gods, as to whether it would be wise to still continue to prosecute their fifteen year war against the Medes or whether, as they had been already advised by the high priests of their own gods, they should cease hostilities.

Of course, all the advice the priest could ever offer was on spiritual matters. He was not permitted to get dragged into a political situation – matters of state, which this clearly was. But sometimes, when he could, he would couch his words so that they might make maximum impact. Seizing this opportunity to act, he said, 'No good can come from continuing the bloodshed; perhaps Helios himself will confirm it this day.'

Reluctantly perhaps, the advice was accepted and would be relayed to the king. 'Let us hope that the Medan king has been advised the same,' cautioned the delegate to the furiously scribbling scribe.

As the steady stream continued into the temple, the old priest beckoned to the boy to join him outside. The shadow had passed eleven hours of the clock on the temple sundial. Taking the boy by the arm, his grandfather walked unsteadily to the sundial, breathing

142

not so deeply that his boy might notice, then he asked Lio to fetch him some water. While he was away, the old priest swallowed another of his potions; the pains that had lasted all night were not subsiding this time as they always had. He was aware of their potential seriousness, but tried to put the matter out of his mind.

When Lio returned, his grandfather took the small copper bowl from him and took a drink. Pointing to the thin shadow on the sundial, he said, 'Stand watch. Between four hours precisely and ten minutes after four, this afternoon – that is when it should happen,' he nodded.

In order to reassure his grandfather, the boy turned and looked directly at him. Using his own bright green eyes for the first time to great effect, he said, 'When the time comes, I will not lie grandfather. I will simply convince them that we are worthy of their trust, then perhaps they will listen to our plea – for justice!'

'Lio,' replied the old man proudly, 'I am happy that you will do your best, no one can ask anything more. Therefore, I will leave this in your own capable hands and stand behind you as you speak.' He went on, 'My son, throughout our time together, you have listened to me and learned well. For my part it has been a great honour and a privilege to have been chosen as your grandfather – and, I hope, your friend. These are dangerous times Lio; who knows what will become of all this turmoil, but last night you taught me a lesson that I had either forgotten or abandoned over the years. You are right. We *will* make a stand against this child slavery – together. It is a great evil and a mark of damnation against all humanity. For now though, I have my own task. Now, before this afternoon, while I attend to some other things, run along and check the sundial one last time. Make sure that the wax seal is intact and it has not been accidently bumped – you know what these crowds can be like!'

'Of course,' agreed Lio. The boy walked toward the sundial. Then, distracted by the call of the familiar voice of the Persian trader, he walked over to speak to him.

Now that the boy was out of the way, the High Priest of Helios turned toward the Temple of Zeus. It was time for him to intervene directly on the girl's behalf. Taking the steps unsteadily down from his own temple, then painfully back up to the front of the Temple of Zeus, he opened the heavy front door and went inside.

Once in the darkened interior, there was no need to ask the whereabouts of the High Priest of Zeus. The huge manservant beckoned him through the Temple and into the grandly decorated chamber that was Zeus' office. Obviously, his visit had been anticipated – the manservant disappeared quickly without a word from his master.

Zeus, the young high priest, stood behind his workbench. 'Yes, what do you want?' he asked rudely. 'I'm in a hurry.'

'Let us not quarrel,' the old priest offered. 'I've come to purchase the slave girl, Ashur.'

'Hmm...' Zeus considered, 'Is that what she's called? However, she is not for sale.' He smiled thinly, 'goodbye!'

The old man had anticipated this hostile reception. In order not to provoke further unpleasantness, he reached inside his robes and threw a small ochre coloured pouch of gold coins onto the desk.

The young priest looked at it and plucked it up in his hand, weighing it. 'You – or is it the boy? – must prize the girl greatly. How would you like her, alive or dead?' he asked, smirking.

The old priest threw down the other pouch he'd been concealing.

'That's more like it,' Zeus said. 'Though, sadly, still not enough. She is fast approaching a more... "useful" age.'

The old priest threw down the last bag. 'That is my final offer, it is all I have, but the girl leaves now!'

'Well, well, you are impatient, old man.' Zeus clicked his fingers and the servant came back around the door. 'Unchain the girl and bring her straight in.' He smirked to himself, weighing the gold. 'It seems she is beyond compare to the followers of Helios. Thirty times more than I would have paid for her – still, not a bad profit for one night's handiwork.' He tossed the bags carelessly onto the corner of his desk.

The old priest did not take the bait: the girl was not safe yet. Instead he said, 'Then I offer my hand, opened in peace upon the deal.' He held out his right hand.

The young priest snorted. 'I'm surprised you'd take my hand on a deal. Still, I am a man of my word – as much as most men. You really are an extraordinarily stupid old man, aren't you! You're so weak. I don't know what anyone sees in you. And yet, you take more money than most people I've ever known. Tell me old man, what is it, what have you got that people should flock to you for guidance?'

The old priest considered the question. 'I have been blessed,' he answered simply, 'to listen to, and follow, the same conscience that is born to all men – and my own heart.'

Zeus glared at him in reply – clearly irritated by what he took as an insult.

Just then the young girl came in through the door. She hesitated briefly, then immediately ran to the old priest, knowing inside that he'd come to take her. She threw her arms around him for protection. The old priest lightly stroked her shaven head as the Egyptian followed her into the room and stood in front of the corner of the desk, at his master's side.

'Run along, girl...' the old priest advised. 'Go and find Lio.'

Ignoring the short sentimental exchange between them, still seething, the young priest said, 'Wait, I'm afraid I'm beginning to have second thoughts about this... No, I'm afraid that the deal won't work for me after all... but I'll keep the gold all the same if you don't mind.'

The girl paused just outside the doorway and turned to wait.

'Come back here you,' warned Zeus, 'NOW!'

Ashur shook her head wildly as the old man barged across the room and blocked the doorway with his body, his hands against its frame. His conscience and his vow of non-violence would at least permit this.

'What do you think you're doing?' Zeus laughed openly at him.

'I'm saving her from you! Run, Ashur, go now, while you have the chance.'

'Stop her!' the young priest growled as she ran out of sight.

The old man tried to stand his ground as the Egyptian approached, only to be pushed easily aside.

'Go and bring her back, fool!' Zeus warned through the doorway. 'Or don't dare come back at all! And as for you, your days are numbered old man.' He turned, walking back to his desk. 'But all in good time,' he added, glaring at the old priest.

The old priest, guessing that the girl had by now escaped, made his way exhaustedly back through temple, out through its doorway and into the light. He felt relieved and, if the truth be known, a little pleased with himself for standing up to the other, much younger man and his huge servant. He paused to catch his breath. Then, light-headed, he crossed the sparsely populated square and almost stumbled down the steps. There was a commotion coming from the crowd on the square outside of the Temple of Helios.

Lio was approaching, laughing and smiling. 'You did it! You did it, she's here; she's inside our Temple.' He congratulated his grandfather gleefully as he climbed breathlessly up the steps toward the boy.

'Good, I'm glad,' his grandfather said. A tired smile showed on his face. 'He didn't want to let her go, but we won, didn't we!' Relieved, but clearly out of breath, suddenly clutching his chest, he fell onto his knees and into the boy's outstretched arms.

Within minutes, everyone knew what had happened: the old priest had had some sort of argument with the new High Priest of Zeus about a little slave girl. The strain of it all had been too much for their beloved Priest of Helios. But where was the new priest? Surely he must come to help, or at least explain! And yet he was nowhere to be seen.

Lio nursed his grandfather's head in his arms where he lay in the middle of the square. He tried not to cry, being brave for his grandfather's sake. The other priests held back the gathering crowd. The old man looked up into the boy's green eyes. 'Lio, it seems I have to go... It's alright; I've just run out of time,' he smiled, 'no one's fault!'

'But I don't want you to go!' Lio managed to croak.

'No, this is a *good* time to leave here. I have finally managed to do a good deed against all the odds. I have saved the life of a child in place of the life that I selfishly took many years ago,' he finally confessed to the boy. 'I have finally bought back my own integrity – my dignity! What is more, I have you here with me and I have the blessed sunshine. What more can a man ask for to make a fitting departure? No Lio, it will be fine – and you will be fine.'

The boy breathed deeply, choking back his emotion.

The old priest's pains increased. Sensing that he didn't have much time left, he whispered urgently, 'Lio, I took the liberty of writing down a few words that you might consider using when you speak later. You will find these written words at my bench.'

'But... I can't do it... not now,' Lio stammered 'not after this.'

'But you must,' insisted the old priest. 'Ashur is not the only child to be affected. You must at least try. When you say my words, I will be standing behind you.' A sudden pain caused him to hold his breath tight, then, when it had passed, he smiled. It was the rarest of deeply satisfied smiles. 'Though,' he joked, 'I would have liked to find out whether I was right about this afternoon's ekleipsis. Perhaps I will be able to watch it from up there – from Polaris!'

With that, Lio's grandfather closed his eyes and his consciousness passed peacefully into the stars, leaving only the worn out body he had occupied here on Earth."

CHAPTER 17:

Ekleipsis

Maddie's lip quivered as she watched Tom reach into his the folds of his jubbah and bring out a tissue to wipe his nose. Bex watched his face as he sniffed before returning it. Conna looked on curiously, mouth opened slightly, whilst Alex jotted down another note before looking up. Nobody spoke for a long time. It was Tom who eventually broke the silence. "However..." he emphasised, "those things all happened a long time ago." He sighed deeply.

"Where were the police?" asked Conna. "How could anyone do that and just dump the body in plain view?" It was more of a statement of disbelief in Tom's story, than shock at what might have actually happened.

Bex answered for Tom. "You weren't listening, were you? Marduk was a slave: a possession. The priest, Zeus – or any slave owner could do what he liked with him – anything at all – completely lawfully!"

"Remember," Tom pointed out helpfully in answer to Conna's question, "that the police are a very modern concept in society, only a couple of centuries old. Before that there may have been soldiers or militia, volunteers from the local community who would keep safe watch over property in the town, but no police."

"And no decent laws either!" Maddie almost spat out emotionally, upset at both the concept and the story. She wiped her eyes with a tissue.

As if to emphasise the point, Boris sat bolt upright and began to bark, until she patted his head, then the dog sat looking at Tom.

"Indeed..." Tom accepted the meaning of her criticism. "But the process of developing the rules of society had to start somewhere, and this was arguably the very beginning of a more 'democratic way' – a way for the people to govern themselves. To do this, each society has firstly to determine its own laws. As for child slavery, even today it continues; despite being declared illegal throughout the world. Are there still not 'sweat-shops' in many of the poorer countries? Surely this is just the same!" Tom let the accusation towards modern civilisation hang in the air.

"Yes, we know," answered the girls in unison.

Changing tack, Alex asked for the first time since Tom had started the story. "Tom, is that true, I mean about the timing of the solar eclipse?"

"Basically, yes," he answered, "and the old priest had accurately predicted the date. In our modern calendar it would be 28th May 585 BC. So, certainly, he had himself observed the principle that is still in use in calculating modern eclipses, now known as the 'Saros cycle'. Though perhaps it was not altogether as accurate as the boy's grandfather had thought. Anyway," he inhaled deeply, "ironically, the main problem was not in accurately predicting the eclipse, but in accurately telling the time!" Tom raised his eyebrows visibly above his sunglasses.

Alex underlined the figures in his notebook and then put down his pen before looking up.

"Now, may I continue?" Tom asked politely.

The four faces nodded back; now, clearly hooked.

Boris looked up at Maddie's face and, deciding that she was once again alright, settled down on Alex's knee.

Tom closed his eyes to continue. "Despite his deep trauma, Lio felt compelled, for all of the right reasons, to go on with his plan – such as it was – and speak to the crowds before the expected event. So, even as the priest's body was being prepared for burial, the boy found his grandfather's notes and carefully cut off the corner from the sheet of papyrus that they were written on. Folding it tightly,

Lio pushed it absent-mindedly into his robe. It would be difficult without his grandfather's support, but he hoped that by reading the speech aloud, he would be able to do him justice.

In the temple across the way, the mood was not as one might have expected. Yes, it was true that the man who had caused the downturn in the fortunes of Zeus' own Temple was now out of the way, but it didn't take a genius to work out that the consequences could be disastrous for the Temple of Zeus, especially if the full truth of what had happened somehow got out. The old man could become a martyr. Even in death, he might become more popular than ever! And, what was more, in the eyes of the crowds, the villain of the piece could easily become the High Priest of Zeus. *Entirely undeserved,* he thought!

The Egyptian had been despatched to retrieve the only witness, the girl, over two hours ago but he had still not yet returned. Not that she would be in a position to speak out against him. Nevertheless, Zeus still had his own plans to attend to. And, critically, time was running out. For now, he would lie low; stay out of the way till the last minute. If the Egyptian didn't bring the girl back soon though, he would make him regret it!

Little did Zeus know that on realising what was happening around him, the Egyptian had sensed an opportunity to grasp his own freedom. He had watched and tasted his master's vicious cruelty many times over the years, but this time he would not take it any longer. Torturing children was beyond the pale, and he cursed the Sicilian to Sobek for it. Regardless of the whereabouts of the girl, he was not about to assist in the search for her as he was not going to risk his own life chasing her in this crowd. Anyway, Egypt was not such a long way from Rhodos, and even a small ochre bag, such as the one he had in his fist, held far more gold than it would take to get him there and live out his life in peace.

By three hours after midday, the news had spread around the island: the Priest of Helios had died, and in mysterious circumstances. Crowds larger than anyone had ever known had gathered to mourn their tragic loss and to show their support to his adopted grandson, Helio. Despite his own numbness, the time was rapidly approaching when Lio would have to make a decision as to whether to go ahead with the plan or whether to abandon it forever. Yet, deep down, he knew what that decision must be. At the allotted time, at twenty minutes to the fourth hour after midday, giving him twenty minutes clear, the hooded young boy made his way out through the temple doors and through the crowds that had assembled all around. The murmuring crowd was ushered back off the square by the male and female priests and helpers, so that as he stood on the top step, Lio looked down and across at them all.

Some recognised him. 'Look, that's the sun-haired boy, isn't it?' they said. 'It's the priest's boy. What's he doing? What's he up to?'

Taking down his hood to reveal his face and head, Lio said nervously: 'Pilgrims, people of Rhodos, you know me!'

The crowd looked up to him, still wondering what the young boy would tell them.

'Please, listen to me, you know who I am. My name – given to me by my grandfather, is Helio. I was born here in this temple.' He pointed behind him with his hand. 'You all know me,' he croaked, his mouth dry. 'Listen to me, I beg you!' One of the temple helpers handed him a drink. Gradually, the commotion died down. 'I wish to speak to you, on behalf of my grandfather and my friend Marduk... I need to talk to you about something, a great wrong which has been done – and continues to be done.'

There was a murmur in the crowd. 'Scandal!' There was the hint of scandal about this. The crowd began to listen intently. Taking a deep breath, the boy continued, now more confidently, 'This morning, my grandfather, the High Priest of the Temple of Helios and myself buried the broken body of my friend Marduk. He was just a boy of my own age, a slave boy who had been beaten to death by his master for speaking to me and for being my friend.'

The crowd stood open mouthed, wondering where the tale was going; was it about the new High Priest of Zeus? There was already a rumour that that was what all this was about.

'Afterwards, my grandfather went to speak to Marduk's master, to buy my friend's sister, Ashur, and save her from the same fate. She was savagely beaten too.'

There was a growing murmur from the crowd; a young boy and his sister, both slaves! That narrowed it down.

Lio shushed them. 'My grandfather managed to save her, but not before her tongue was cut out.'

There was an 'Oooh!' of distaste in the crowd: only barbarians did this, surely not the Greeks!

'But she is only one of many who work in these other Temples!' He pointed to his right, at the Great Temple.

There was a hush in reaction to the statement, so it *was* about the new High Priest of Zeus after all!

'My grandfather was so upset by this situation that he was going to help me speak to you all, but this afternoon he died, here at his temple.'

Someone in the crowd shouted out: 'Tell us who killed him – they must be brought to justice!'

'No, no one killed him, at least not physically,' admitted Lio readily. 'Perhaps the whole situation broke his heart – perhaps it was the result of the argument to free the girl. Who knows? But no one actually killed him.'

Then what is the problem, thought most of the crowd in silence? *Nobody killed the priest and the life of a slave belongs to his master anyway!*

'I am here to beg you to consider the lives of the temple children, the slaves who work here in terrible conditions. It is they who make the statues move, the gods moan and the thunder roar.'

Wait! Everyone knew that it was the gods who brought the statues to life, was it not?

'It is these children who sit in the narrow tunnels' Lio went on, 'crawl beneath the temples to speak into the moaning tubes and operate the thunder machines inside the temple roofs. They are beaten or killed at their masters' will.'

Throughout the speech, the crowd stood as silent as the grave, unable to believe these revelations. These things were all tricks? Surely not! But that would mean that all of the other priests were

152

lying... and, if they were lying about this... what else were they lying about? Still coming to terms with this accusation, nobody shouted out in protest. A few of the priests from the other temples were in the crowd. They moved off nervously, sensing potential hostility. Lio had done the worst thing imaginable – he had just broken the strict vow not to tell of these secret things – surely it was all over. This could spark a riot – a revolution!

The crowd looked around at each other in disbelief. The gods' voices were none other than the voices of children? And they themselves had willingly paid the temples for these services! Gradually the noise grew, until it eventually reached a clamour. The gods were nothing but tricks to make money and to persuade them that all was well in the world, while no doubt, the ruling classes laughed and took their money. This was outrageous!

As the truth began to sink in – although there were many who struggled to believe any of it, and still a sizeable minority were vociferously offended at the possibility – Lio had to shout to remind them of why he was telling them all this: that whilst he thought it to be wrong to use trickery in the temples, it was the plight of the slave workers, the children, that was the real issue. However, the crowd was now far more interested in seeking retribution, not to say revenge on those temples that were the chief suspects of these shameful practises – those with the biggest or most displays!

'My grandfather was an intelligent man.' Lio called out, 'he was a good man who cared about many things.' Few were listening – he had to shout. 'He cared about stargazing, how the world worked: the sun, the moon, the stars and planets – in a natural world, with a natural god – the sun. The god Helios was for my grandfather a symbol of the natural workings of the world, not a real person. Open your eyes like my grandfather, you do not need these gods to worship, and neither do you need child slaves to work all of these illusions. In fact, you should not hold child slaves at all. It is a great wrong!'

The crowd was listening again, openly shocked by him and not all convinced, but at least listening. *Perhaps,* thought a few, *the boy could be right*. The old priest had, after all, guided most of their lives with similar thoughts. That part about the child slaves was not right though, surely. Many were purchased lawfully, and what would happen if they were not purchased anyway? Surely they would starve or would have to be kept in gaol – for life?

Lio would have to hurry now, he knew, before time ran out. 'Today my grandfather foretold a very special event, an "ekleipsis",' he spoke truthfully. 'As a boy, my grandfather saw the sky darken as the daylight was blotted out, but this did not frighten him as it did the other boys. Instead, he recorded the exact time and place and waited many years for it to happen again. When it eventually did, he wrote the details down again. Many years later, when it happened for the third time – exactly the same time apart – he knew what had caused it. It was not, as the other priests will tell you, "the gods threatening us all to behave ourselves like frightened children". It was simply the natural path of the moon crossing that of the sun, and for a few minutes casting a shadow over the earth, just as we cast shadows on the wall with our hands by the light that shines from an oil lamp.'

The crowd began to stir again, thoroughly unsure of this latest revelation. It was stretching their understanding to take in these further fanciful tales. Not many were educated people and so they misunderstood – the moon passing in front of the sun? Even if this was possible, surely it had to do so at the command of the gods. Yes, many of the people had experienced an ekleipsis before, and it was a terrifying thing to behold. Surely then, that could not be a trick. Doubt began to set in, but the boy continued, unaware that he was losing them.

He stood at the dish of the sundial, looking intently at the thin shadow. It slowly crept past each of the minute lines, five minutes to the fourth hour. 'Any moment now,' he announced boldly, 'the moon will pass across the sun, and the earth will fall into its shadow, causing it to become dark and cool. Sensing this, the birds will stop singing and the animals will fall quiet,' he cautioned. 'But do not be afraid – this is a "natural phenomenon". It will not harm

154

you and it will last only a few minutes.' Despite his reassurance, the many faces of the crowd told a different story. Superstition dictated that it was unwise to speak of these things; it was courting disaster!

'Please remember, this will not harm you!' he repeated earnestly. He patted his robe, searching for the scrap of papyrus, about to deliver his grandfather's speech. Where was it? He looked but he couldn't find it. Surely he hadn't lost it. Again he searched in vain. It was important. His grandfather's words were meant to help the crowd realise who they all were, take stock of themselves and defend the values that his grandfather knew they jointly held – without the need to blindly follow superstition. Lio couldn't remember it all though. Reluctantly he decided that he would have to deliver the speech another time.

While he finished his search, the crowd started to mumble. Fear grew as people strained their eyes toward the blistering sun, but, *thank the gods*, the crowd thought, nothing happened. Masking the sun's full strength with his hand, Lio looked up patiently, straight at its surface. His eyes could see nothing but the intense white light; there was still no sign. Where was it? He strained his eyes, watching. Panic began to spread in waves across the crowd. One or two loud moans came as some of the priests returned – the Priests of Zeus. The boy spotted one or two of them whispering to those around them. What was going on?

Still no sign. Then Lio himself began to worry; something was not right. Perhaps his grandfather's calculations were not as accurate as he'd hoped. He waited in anticipation and in deathly silence for another two minutes, staring directly at the face of the sun. Screams went up from the priests, orchestrating fear, which in turn led to more moaning and screaming. Now beginning to fear that it might not happen at all, Lio again checked the sundial to see if he had made a mistake. No, surely he had pinpointed the shadow accurately, the style had not been bent or damaged, the time was as it said. He placed his hands on two sides of the corner and as he did so the sundial wobbled slightly, a tiny pebble caught beneath its corner. Slowly, looking curiously beneath the huge block of marble, he saw that the wax joint between it and the paving slab had been accidently broken; but how? Only a giant could have moved such a huge stone. Lio was confused; what could have gone wrong? Then it began to dawn on him – this as was no accident!

Sensing growing hostility, a dog began to bark, setting more off around the edge of the town. The priests had by now whipped the crowd into a screaming frenzy. Despite their previous doubts about the gods, fear made them believe again. *Doubts*, they thought collectively, *raised by this young boy – this child! Why have we even listened?*

Lio's heart sank. He had begun to figure it all out. Last night, after his grandfather had checked the alignment of the sundial, someone must have moved it. And the only candidate that he could think of for that task was the huge Egyptian. But that in turn meant only one thing. He must have been commanded to do it. He looked over at the Temple of Zeus, but there was no one to be seen.

A dozen people, all men, dotted carefully throughout the crowd fell to the ground, now foaming at the mouth. As the sickening realisation of what had happened set in his stomach, Lio glared up once more toward the sun, willing the event to begin, but there was still no sign. Then, from his right, he heard a voice. He turned to see, but was almost blinded by the sun. Now he realised the consequences of his mistake in failing to check the sundial.

From the square at the front of the Temple of Zeus, a silky voice called out. It was chillingly unmistakable to Lio. 'STOP THIS AT ONCE!' the high priest screamed, playing to the crowd.

The crowd, now in complete disarray, seized on his words. 'Yes, let it all stop,' they pleaded aloud, looking toward the priest.

'In my short time at this temple I have witnessed many things. Much wickedness and BLASPHEMY!' Zeus yelled, 'especially at the hands of this boy.' He pointed accusingly with his stick. The crowd began to settle, listening to this new voice. Perhaps they had been too hasty; perhaps there was another side to the story.

'This boy,' continued the priest, 'born SACRILEGIOUSLY in the temple behind him, and protected by the High Priest of Helios himself, has at long last been found out – by me!' The crowd stirred at this new accusation; more scandal.

Lio listened on incredulously, now dizzy and feeling nauseous after staring repeatedly and directly at the blinding sun, unable to see as the priest lied shamelessly.

'Two days ago, I caught my own slave boy hiding this bag of gold,' Zeus went on, holding one of the two remaining ochre pouches aloft. 'Naturally, when he would not tell me where he got them, I was forced to beat him until he did. Unfortunately, he died later; but this was only what he deserved. This money was stolen from the High Priest of Helios – see! These are his money bags, are they not?' Keeping up the pace, conscious of the real time, he went on. 'And how did he get them? I hear you ask. From none other than that BLASPHEMER, the supposed son of the temple, who thought he could deceive the old priest about these and other things. Only a few hours ago, his own supposed grandfather came to plead with me for help in dealing with his wayward grandson. But I would not help him; it was his own naïvety in tolerating such a wicked boy for all these years that had brought this situation about. It was they, not the other temples who have been deluding you all these years, encouraging you to believe in the 'natural powers of the sun' and to turn your back to the gods.'

A mysterious, lone "heckler" called out right on cue, 'Show us the proof of all this!'

'Proof... you require more proof... even though he has BLASPHEMED this day again; even though he has promised you a "natural" miracle, which has not come to pass; even though I have in my hand the very bag of gold; even though the high priest died of shame in front of you all...' He paused dramatically. 'Alright, then bring the boy to me!'

At first, reluctant to force him to do so openly, a small group of men were cajoled up from the crowd to take Lio, his head still reeling, from where he stood propped up by the sundial. They escorted him down and back up the steps to the hastily transported altar, where the high priest now stood. Slowly, the crowd turned to follow. He had them in the palm of his hand. It wasn't going exactly to plan perhaps, but adaptation to present circumstances was at the heart of manipulation, and, after all, he was, he congratulated himself, very good at it.

The boy stood dazed at Zeus' side, his arms held behind him by one of the priests, while another grabbed him by the hair, forcing his face toward the sun. Now in clear distress, he continued to glare at its surface, burning his eyes and damaging his eyesight permanently. He squeezed his eyes almost shut, then tried unsuccessfully to look out at the crowd. Lio didn't know what to do or say, it seemed as though everyone had deserted him. Suddenly, the boy felt completely alone for the first time in his life – like Ashur. He thought fleetingly of his friend's sister.

Time was marching on. The priest began. 'You wanted proof – then you shall have it. Demonstrating clearly to the crowd that he had nothing in his left hand, he slipped it into the boy's robe and pulled out the remaining ochre pouch. Whispering into Lio's ear, he boasted, 'That was a little trick I learned in Sicilia.' Standing upright again, he called out, 'Do you wish to know why the priest died of shame? It was because of these...' Theatrically opening the bag in front of the crowd, he pulled out two huge precious stones: two emeralds.

Lio strained his watery eyes to look at them as they sparkled out of focus. 'They are not mine,' he said in confusion.

'Oh really? They are not yours,' the priest confirmed. 'What an admission... then would you like to tell everyone where they came from? No matter,' he continued quickly, 'I will.' Now he was revelling in his own performance. 'Last night, while everyone was in their beds, this THEIF crept onto the temple roof and prized them from the eyes of his very own god, LOOK!' He pointed to the golden haired statue of Helios standing in the chariot. Manhandling the boy's head around by the hair, he made him look for himself towards it. Lio shook his head blankly, not able to grasp the enormity of the deception of the priest. The crowd gasped. It was true. At first glance everything looked alright, but now, on examination, those closest to the statue could clearly see that the precious eyes of Helios were indeed missing. Instead, green pigment had been daubed childishly onto pebbles and shoved roughly into what would have been the empty irises of each eye. It was absolute sacrilege. A shout went up, 'Sacrilege, flog him!' Then another, 'Flog the little thief' but no one could identify where the shouts were coming from.

A single high-pitched voice of support sounded out. 'Prove that it was the boy that took them then!'

There was a distinct chill in the air. The priest felt it. Nothing visible yet, but any minute now... 'Oh!' The priest feigned shock. 'Still you doubt my word! Then let the gods themselves decide!

Helios, carrier of the sun across the sky, if the boy is innocent, defend him now, let the light of the sun shine down on him. But!' he mocked, 'if he is guilty, let Zeus, Father of Gods and Men, Ruler of Mount Olympus and King of the Skies, blot out the light of the sun with his great shield and prove to these,' he screamed, 'DOUBTERS AND BLASPHEMERS once and for all, who is the most powerful of all the gods.'

With that, unheard by the crowd, the priest began to tap the stick against the marble step, a regular 'ticking' sound, as he began to count to himself."

CHAPTER 18:

Pandemonium

"As Zeus spoke, almost exactly on cue the earth started to turn unmistakeably cool. At that, just as Lio had predicted, the birds stopped singing and the dogs stopped barking. And slowly, the rim of the black disc that was the shield of Zeus began to eclipse the sun. At first, it seemed to gently kiss the extreme edge of it from below and to its left. Then surprisingly rapidly, it encroached more heavily. Now it started to gradually block out the sunlight.

Within moments, the event had the desired effect. From the middle of the crowd, a woman screamed. A few shouts of consternation followed; then pandemonium – 'all demons' were set loose. People began to panic, screaming and begging for all of it to stop. But the god's shield moved further across the sun's surface, blackening half of it now, turning the day into night. People tore at their hair and clothes, and dropped to their knees in individual pleading, begging both Zeus and the high priest to forgive them for listening to the boy. Surely everything the high priest said was true after all – the boy had been born sacrilegiously in the Temple! He did have the eyes and hair of a demon! He must have been tricking the pilgrims all this time. And, there was the final proof – the stolen emeralds – the very eyes of the god he was supposed to have served but had now even denied the existence of! 'Zeus, please do not abandon us,' the crowd began to cry hysterically. 'Zeus, forgive us.' The high priest relished every moment, concentrating on his counting. He watched the moon take up its full position, now covering almost the entire face of the sun, leaving only the flaming corona – the crown of it visible. This really was quite spectacular, Zeus had to admit... and entirely natural to boot.

Then the tapping stopped: the moon had reached the exact centre of the sun – the halfway point. By Zeus' reckoning it had taken two hundred, and twenty-five seconds – give or take. Just as had been calculated by his paid sources – the visiting priests from Miletus whom he had bribed back in Sicilia. They had said it would be seven minutes and thirty seconds for the whole event. Now he would have two hundred and twenty-five seconds more to make his mark on them all.

'It is you who have abandoned Zeus,' the priest cried out to the crowd. 'It was you who ran to Helios – and now you ask for the help of Zeus,' he accused.

The crowd pleaded and begged as he milked every last drop from the event. *Better not mis-time it though*, he thought, *especially now that it was all going so well – so very much back on course.*

'Those of you who worship Zeus – get down on your knees and beg forgiveness!' Immediately most of the crowd dropped, dragging the others beside them down with them. Shouts of abuse were being levelled at those who remained standing. Even those who were still inclined to believe the boy's account of this being an entirely natural phenomenon were starting to worry. Until, for their own safety, they were forced to capitulate.

'Now,' called the priest, 'Zeus, King of the Skies, your people have seen the error of their ways. Please, I beseech you, remove your shield, and let Helios continue on his journey. Let the sun shine down on them once again!'

Within moments it began to get visibly lighter. His timing had been flawless – the past two days of tediously practising tapping out the seconds had been well worth the effort. 'Seize the boy,' he called over his shoulder. 'We will deal with him later.' Lio was led roughly away by the upper arms, head bowed in blindness toward the crowd. 'All of you who are now faithful to Zeus assemble here tonight,' the priest called out. 'We will celebrate his forgiveness in spectacular fashion!' *And then we will also decide how to deal with the boy,* he thought – now that he held his life in the palm of his hand. But before that, he wondered, *shall I cut out his tongue, to prevent him giving evidence. Or is that a little too obvious?* Maybe he should give it some further thought.

With that, Lio was whisked away into the Temple of Zeus as the priest checked the emeralds in the bag and tucked it into the folds of his robe. 'Morons!' he said contemptuously under his breath and went inside. At least that thieving Egyptian hadn't got his hands on those before he'd disappeared.

On the square outside of the Temple of Helios, the crowd slowly began to disperse. A single ragged figure had crept unnoticed from the door of the temple, scurrying through the feet of the crowd to find the one face she had seen Lio talking to earlier. Spotting his distinctive headdress, Ashur crouched behind the Persian trader and tugged at the hem of his colourful garments. At first annoyed at the distraction, he realised that she could not talk. Then, looking at her shaved head, he realised that she was the girl that the old priest had rescued.

Beckoning him to follow, she slipped up the steps and into the square, then hid behind the sundial. The trader approached her curiously, as she signalled him to stoop to her own eye level. Ashur pointed to the marble base and at the disturbed wax. The trader didn't understand, so she tried to move it, but it was too heavy for her. He was struggling to comprehend. 'What is it?' he whispered. She took both of his hands by the wrists and placed them on the base, shaking them lightly. Still he didn't understand. 'Like this?' he moved his hands. She nodded. He moved them again, 'like this!' She nodded vigorously. He pushed a little harder still not understanding – but this time it moved.

The trader was no genius, but he immediately understood: the sundial had been knocked out of true! It could not possibly show the time correctly if that was so. Realisation of the truth gradually began to dawn on him. The boy had been right all along about the 'natural event'. It was just that someone had tampered with the sundial. He guessed quickly who was behind it.

Clearly though, this was not the time to bring it to the attention of the crowd: their blood was still up. And they were racked with fear. The trader knew how to read the crowds, that was his own accomplished personal skill. Later, when sanity had returned, that would be the time to take this evidence before them. He stroked the girl's head gently and nodded to her. 'I understand,' he whispered, 'but not now,' he cautioned, 'later.'

Noticing a folded piece of papyrus, he bent down and picked it up. The trader read it through carefully, folded it back up, then slipped it into his money pouch."

"How could that happen," asked Maddie, "how could they turn on him, just because he was a bit late with his prediction?"

"Yeah, why did everyone believe the high priest?" added Conna.

Tom held up his hand to field the questions. "Fear!" He said simply. "In any world where superstition and misinformation go hand in hand, it is difficult for one to know the effect of quite a dramatic and seemingly most 'unnatural' event such as a total eclipse. The crowd," he went on, "simply panicked, as we are all wont to do sometimes. Of course, it didn't help that the boy had inadvertently lost the patience of the crowd just beforehand – by telling them that they were doing wrong in keeping slaves."

"But they were," pleaded Maddie.

Tom breathed in deeply, considering his words well.

"Sometimes, to achieve a desired result, it is wiser to bring people onto your side first – persuade them, not alienate them. This is of necessity a slow process of education and consideration.

"Even though he was right?" argued Bex.

"Even though he was right. That is simply the way of the world – that is the true art of politics."

"But that would take ages to change something," said Maddie.

"Yes," declared Tom, "but better than risk change not happening at all."

"Maybe," suggested Alex, "Lio should have remembered the fable of the sun and the wind – Helios and Zeus."

"Indeed," concluded Tom in consideration. "Indeed he should."

"So then what happened?" prompted Conna.

"What was the outcome? Before I tell you, you tell me: so far, what do you think of this story?" Tom asked.

Conna shrugged. "I dunno, it's just a story, isn't it? I suppose it makes some sense."

Maddie backed him up. "Yes, Tom, so far there's nothing to disbelieve – as a story."

"And you?" Tom quizzed Bex.

"Sounds alright to me," she shrugged. "I wouldn't know anything about the history of it though – whether those things were true or not."

"A fair point," he admitted, "but, for what it is worth, that is all entirely true – I promise you."

Alex wasn't going to be drawn – yet. He would check his facts first.

Tom took a deep breath. "So far so good then? However, the reason I ask is that if you are struggling to believe the story so far, I will guarantee to you that you will struggle much more to believe what happened next.

The full scene outside of the Temple of Zeus that evening was indescribable; although midnight, a rumbling electrical storm illuminated the entire scene. Dozens of torches burned around the edges of the square. A huge crowd had come to watch and take part in the celebration of their salvation, and to witness what would happen to the boy they knew well. Brightly coloured dancers cavorted in and out of the torches, whirling around and fuelling the excitement of the crowd. It was a carnival atmosphere, but it was a carnival unlike anything witnessed before. Tonight there was a certain darkness about the proceedings. Although they were willing participants, the crowd had, it seemed, allowed themselves to be carried along on the thin air of evil that had somehow pervaded the night. Everyone felt it. However, they told themselves, this was, after all, at least meant to be a celebration of the avoidance of a near disaster... wasn't it? Zeus drank in every moment.

Whilst the shouting and cheering and general merriment continued, the mood of the crowd was kept to a high level of excitement. Mask-wearing players silently mimed stories at the altar. The stories were all known to the crowd, the various clashes of the gods, the hero Herakles killing the Gorgon Medusa and riding off on the back of the flying horse Pegasus. All of the stage props were impressively pre-produced, from the golden masks to the wooden framed horse, carried by four of the players.

Lastly of course, came the parable of Zeus and Helios. How the winds had blown, but the pilgrim had pulled his cloak tight around him, only to remove it when Helios brought out the sun. However, now the end had been changed; it had been adapted to reflect the current circumstances. In this version, Zeus himself had intervened personally, covering the sun with his enormous shield, until the shivering pilgrim fell to his knees. Now he covered himself in the cloak again. Only when Zeus had removed the shield was it possible for the pilgrim to remove his cloak permanently. Thus proving that Zeus was, after all, the most powerful of all the gods! The crowd waited in eager anticipation to see what entertainment would come next.

The High Priest of Zeus stood in his full regalia, wearing a gold mask, black robes and his purple cloak. He stood in front of the crowd and clapped his hands twice. Sirens, dancing women clad in flowing, trailing layers of the lightest fabrics, entered the stage. They whirled around and around singing out a discordant, ethereal and bewitching tune, interspersed with a weird screeching and howling; a most demonic sound which served to whip up the crowd.

The dancers kept the throng entranced for a long while as the drums grew to a crescendo. Then they suddenly ceased and the Sirens flittered over to line up in front of the temple. Suddenly there was silence. Only the distant crackling of thunder could now be heard.

The high priest, flanked by two bearded priests to each side of him, walked grandly past the altar and stood on the front step. He looked down toward the crowd – his arms outstretched. A cheer went up as the man who had saved the day removed his golden mask. He turned from them and handed it to the priest nearest him. The crowds waited with baited breath, eager to see what would come next. More celebration of life, they supposed.

Looking up into the sky, the priest raised his arms to the heavens and exclaimed, 'Oh great god Zeus, we thank you for your forgiveness.' Again the crowd gave a cheer. 'And now in return we will keep to our bargain – BRING OUT THE BOY DEMON!'

A few people cheered drunkenly, not fully realising what was going on, but that was all. The majority fell silent. It was not what they had expected. Neither was it what they wanted, they were not at all used to this.

Shuffling through the temple doors and out of the darkness, the boy raised his manacled arms to shield his eyes against what to him was the intense torchlight in front of him. His eyes burned with pain now, his vision so blurred that all he could do was stumble along blindly, prodded painfully forward by two more priests who walked behind him wielding sticks. The prodding left what appeared to be small red flowers on the back of his off-white robe. He stumbled across the square to the grumbling crowd, gauging their mood by the noise alone. For the first time in his life he felt hated. Worse, he felt stupid. Stupid to have thought that he, a young boy, could have addressed the crowd as his grandfather the priest had done. It had been a disaster, and now he was going to have to pay for allowing himself to fall into the trap that had been sprung on him by the most wicked man that he had ever encountered.

Just before he had left the temple, Lio had had his mouth forced open by one of the priests, while the high priest tried to hurriedly grasp his tongue. However, unable to hold the slippery thing as the boy struggled, Zeus had in frustration punched the boy in the mouth instead. Then, using the bronze handle of his ivory stick, he had carefully targeted a single agonising blow to the back of Lio's head. The pain was excruciating; it left him both dizzy and deafened. Slowly, he managed to get to the edge of the top step, where he stood wavering around unsupported. His watery eyes blurred the crowd and noises hissed in his ears. But that had that not been the worst pain that he had encountered since he had been taken into the temple that afternoon; not that he'd seen the thin pointed steel rod when the ivory sheath was removed. Suddenly he felt nauseous, starting to wretch with the overwhelming pain from the lashing he had taken on his back.

One of the priests hit the back of his legs with a stick so that he crashed forward painfully onto his knees. The high priest moved in front of him. With his back to the crowd, he stooped to whisper closely into Lio's face. 'Now we'll see how popular you are.' He spoke viciously from between his clenched teeth. 'What have you got to say to that?'

Completely innocently, without guile or even control, the boy vomited directly into the priest's face. Seeing this, one of the priests grabbed the ceremonial bronze bowl of sacred water and tried to throw the contents into the face of the priest. However, the bowl slipped from his hands and the edge of it delivered a sharp blow, leaving a neat gash across the high priest's forehead before tumbling noisily down the steps. Trying to retrieve the situation, another priest ran over with the drying cloth, before starting off to pick up the bowl. 'Leave it,' hissed the high priest, trying to control his temper.

Regaining his composure, now turning once again to the people, he called out: 'ZEUS.' He held up his hands. 'What do you wish to happen to this traitor, this... BLASPHEMER, who gouged the very eyes from your servant, who caused the death of one of the young "helpers" in your own house and called your reputation as the greatest of all the gods into question? For one as wicked as this, surely there can only be one way to deal with him, by taking his very life in sacrifice and to beg you never to forsake your people again.'

There was a shocked reaction from the crowd, a mixed rumble from everyone. Human sacrifice, surely not! This was Rhodos, the heart of civilisation. The ultimate sacrifice was an ancient ritual that had not been performed for years, at least not in the lifetime of anyone gathered here. But then, some began to consider, he *had* nearly brought about the end of the world after all. He could not be allowed to go on causing this terror and it would be only right and proper if it was true... that he had indeed stolen the very eyes of Helios himself.

Now, looking directly out into the crowd, the priest continued. 'I ask all of you assembled here, what is the punishment to be?'

For the third time today, recognising the carefully planned prompt, a distant voice in the crowd shouted out the one word that he'd been told to deliver: 'DEATH!'

Another lone voice repeated the same: 'DEATH!'

It was such a stark word, an ugly word that had not been heard called out like this in living memory. At first silent, there was now a rumbling from the main body of the crowd, but if the priest had expected the call to be taken up by them, this time he was wholly mistaken.

The crowd stirred uneasily, unsure of this leap toward a quick, almost snap decision. It had been a day fraught with mixed emotions. They had expected some form of retribution or justice to be eventually taken against the boy of course, even, possibly, his execution – if that was the decision of all of the people. But surely there would be some consideration given to the boy's story first. Whatever society's judgement though, it should not happen now. Not in the dead of night – this really was beginning to look like nothing more than a barbaric human sacrifice. It was not something that was considered civilised, acceptable or part of the Greek way of life.

A few locals in the crowd were now crying – openly weeping for the boy who they had known for years, now kneeling forlorn in front of them. The temporary insanity that had gripped them this afternoon now left them to question the way things were being handled by the new priest. They were certain that the old priest, Lio's grandfather, would not have perpetrated this act, and never in this fashion. He preached forgiveness, not vengeance!

'Spare him,' a few people suggested tentatively.

The high priest ignored the calls and shushed the crowd again.

Then, a lone foreigner's voice shouted out, 'Let him go, I know this boy, he wouldn't have done these things.'

A small contingent in the crowd rallied around and picked up the cry. 'Let him go!'

This wasn't going as planned. A few other well orchestrated calls echoed each other in retaliation: 'No, the boy must die... he is guilty, he must die!'

'Release him!' The voices of the crowd were thoroughly divided.

'I cannot,' declared the priest impatiently, 'the gods will not permit it.' And, he added another lie, 'he has now freely admitted it himself!'

'Why? What have you done to him?' called out the high pitched voice.

The crowd was in danger of turning against him. *Better get on with it now before things worsen.* He turned to the priest who had thrown the bowl at him, consciously remembering his face for later. 'Bring the boy here.'

Lio, now half unconscious, was picked up roughly and thrown down onto the altar that had been brought out for the occasion. He lay momentarily stretched out. The red flowers had almost joined into one now, wetness soaking rapidly through the back of the boy's robe, spreading ever larger and wider. The noises continued in the boy's head as he was now forced to kneel up on the altar. Then he fell forward exhausted onto all fours, the top half of his torn and loosened robe sliding from his shoulders to reveal his back, now slashed wide open. It was crisscrossed with deep lacerations and oozing blood, causing the crowd to shudder at the state he was in.

Then, from the opposite direction, the direction of the Temple of Helios, there appeared a face that was familiar to all of them.

The Persian trader stood rigidly at the sundial, looking directly across at the priest. He called out clearly, 'The boy is innocent...' Then holding out his hand to take the small hand of the figure behind him, he led her gently to stand at his side. 'This girl will tell you herself!'

If the priest had been initially startled by the appearance of the single figure, it did not last long. The market trader and the mute, this he had to see!

The trader walked comfortably toward the edge of the square to address the crowd. The girl stood slightly behind him, less comfortably, clinging to his hand for comfort.

'This man,' he pointed to the priest, committing himself from the start, 'is a liar and a cheat!' The crowd fell deathly silent – aghast at the direct accusation of such an important person. 'He has manipulated you all from the start, and you have allowed him to. How else would he know in advance to have all of these theatrical props prepared? These players have been practising for days!' The absolute silence continued as the crowd considered the implication of his accusation. 'You have allowed a complete stranger, a man you know nothing about, to come here with his barbaric ways and low morals and within a single day, destroy the reputations of your own much loved priest and his boy Helio. And how? By astounding you with superstition: by cheap trickery and by forcing children to do his bidding!'

Zeus wasn't impressed. If nothing else, he had this ignorant crowd's fear on his side. He had proven it once, he could do it again.

'Did not the boy forewarn you all?' the trader continued. 'Even after the death of his grandfather, a learned man who educated his grandson in many things. The boy told you not to be afraid of the ekleipsis that was going to happen, I heard him with my own ears. And simply because it was a few minutes late, you fell into the trap that this evil man had set. Look! Come and look for yourselves at the sundial,' he pointed over his shoulder at it. 'This cheat, this charlatan moved it away from true north, just enough to fool you

170

all – or was it your bodyguard?' he accused. 'Where is he now, has even he had enough and deserted you?'

The trader was getting a little too near the truth. The priest was getting aggravated.

'And the emeralds, who has them now, you?' The trader challenged.

'I have them in place of the slave boy that I lost because of this devil.' By his level tone, he seemed to think it entirely fair.

'And who stole them for you? Who climbed up there to replace them with the painted stones? It was the dead brother of the girl here, wasn't it! You tried to stop her from telling anyone but she didn't have to speak to bear witness against you. She has simply pointed at your handiwork: the broken wax seal on the sundial; the paint that you forced her to clean up where the boy, her own brother fell to his death whilst switching the emeralds. She has even pointed out the blood stains in the marble that remain from where he fell.'

Ashur glared angrily at the priest.

Now the trader was getting annoying. The priest would make sure he had him taken care of after this was over.

'What did you do to her brother to force him to risk his life so? Flog him with that stick of yours? Or was it this girl you flogged instead? Or both!' Softly, the trader asked the girl to turn around. Gently, he removed the rags from her back. The flesh was just starting to heal, but the mess still drew a new gasp of horror from the crowd as they saw the visibly pink gashes across her black skin. The trader stroked her face and took off his own colourful outer robe to cover her. 'And what about the boy, Lio? Is that why you have now done the same to him – to get your false confession?'

That was enough! 'DO NOT LISTEN...' the priest spat out 'to this... FORIEGNER any longer! I warn you all, Zeus has saved you once today, I ...' he slipped up, *'He* ... will not let it happen again!'

'Release the boy!' A shout went up.

'NO! I WILL NOT, THE BOY'S BLASPHEMY AND GREED WILL BE PUNISHED.'

'RELEASE HIM...' the clamour started to grow. Now, the crowd was beginning to see clearly again.

The trader let go of the girl's hand and began to walk down the steps, past the crowd, then back up toward the boy on the altar.

Now, beginning to sense possible defeat, the high priest handed his stick to one of the other priests and grabbed the boy by his hair, forcing his head back to expose his throat. He had to prevent him from speaking the truth. Another priest stepped boldly forward and offered the dish that held the sacrificial knife.

Lio was in a complete daze now, not knowing where he was or quite what was happening to him anymore. His eyes were closed and there was a growing deafening pounding in his ears. He thought his head would burst.

As the trader approached the top step, he cried out, 'If you dare touch that boy, then may your gods curse you throughout eternity! Let Zeus himself visit you – if that's what you wish to believe – but let him come to protect this boy, before visiting justice upon you!'

The boy felt sick again, the noises in his ears getting louder and louder. His head now pulled back from behind, he tried to focus on the crowd, but couldn't.

'Release him!' The crowd surged forward, moving up the steps.

The other priests and the dancers moved back in trepidation. The people would not allow any more of this. Zeus held the sharpened blade to Lio's throat, ready to dispatch him.

But it was then that the 'miracle' happened!"

PART III:

THE LEGACY OF ALEXANDER AND PTOLEMY

KNOWLEDGE EXISTS IN TWO FORMS –
LIFELESS, STORED IN BOOKS,
AND ALIVE, IN THE CONSCIOUSNESS OF MEN.
THE SECOND FORM OF EXISTENCE
IS AFTER ALL THE ESSENTIAL ONE;
THE FIRST, INDISPENSABLE AS IT MAY BE,
OCCUPIES ONLY AN INFERIOR POSITION.

Albert Einstein, 20th Cent AD

CHAPTER 19:

The 'Deus Ex Macchina'

In turn, Tom looked at each of the faces of his guests, then he continued the tale.

"As the crowds in front of the temple stared in horror, Zeus, the high priest, refused to let go of the boy's hair. He was determined to go through with it now – no one could stop him.

Then, the earth began to shake: slowly at first, then more violently – a tremor perhaps. But next came the noise – a rising, deafening roar along with a high-pitched screaming and hissing sound. Without warning, a ball of pure blue-white light appeared in the dead centre of the square. It hovered over the marble briefly, before seeming to kiss it delicately.

At first only a few metres in diameter, it grew slowly, as if moving at a time much slower than theirs. Then, as it reached its full five metre diameter, a puff of noise like a controlled explosion sounded. It was a combined noise, in total – something akin to thunder – but a layered noise unlike that of any other. The weird sound was accompanied by a blast of warm wind that suddenly emanated from the centre of the light. It knocked over those nearest to the ground, and sent all others scurrying to safety. Tiny crackles of blue lightening appeared to dance across the marble around the temple portico. They skipped out safely over the heads of the surrounding open-mouthed crowd, stopping them in their tracks before each crackle fizzled out into the night.

Watching the faces of the crowd and then feeling the blast, the priest turned around slowly. Finally letting go of the handful of red hair, he stumbled back from the source of the blinding light himself and fell screaming silently to the ground, covering his own eyes and face with his arm, the back of his head hitting the altar. He cowered as there appeared, hazily at first, the image of a heavily bearded older man. It was not the ghost of Lio's grandfather though; this figure was younger, taller and fully fit. He sat astride a gleaming horse, his white robe billowing out around him. Warm breath streamed from the horse's nostrils into the evening air, before it settled steadily to the ground.

Lio was dying – weakening by the moment – even though the priest had not managed to use the sacrificial knife. The carefully delivered blow to the back of his head had fractured his skull and, unbeknown to him, his body was beginning to overproduce fluid around his brain, causing him to witness hallucinations. It had also produced the severe pounding in his head, effectively deafening him. All he could hear was his own heartbeat. In addition to this, his body was both dehydrated from him having been given no water throughout his incarceration in the corridor beneath the temple. And, of course, there was his severe blood loss. He would not last much longer. Through his blurred, dying eyes and their severely burned retinas, he witnessed the true Zeus himself. In his right hand he carried his rod of office, a zigzag bolt of lightning, as he dismounted Pegasus. Lio watched the figure stride toward him, glaring around him at the spectacle he had invaded. Then, with a silent swoop, the boy was picked up and carried back to the waiting horse.

Carefully placing Lio on it first, the figure climbed on behind him, and the horse reared its front legs into the air. In front of the crowd, the great god Zeus held the lightning bolt aloft, threatening retribution on them all for their mistreatment of one of the immortals – Helio! And to the astonishment of all – not least the market trader, who'd been about to risk making a grab for the boy, and the little girl who stood beside the sundial – the father of the gods himself vanished into thin air, just as miraculously as he had arrived!"

As Tom sat back, the four faces that looked back at him represented four entirely different variations on incredulity:

Conna, being the most obviously sceptical because of his wide open mouth and entirely blank expression had followed the story well enough. For what it was worth, since Tom had begun the tale, he hadn't purposely challenged his word directly at any time so far, although he was obviously one of the most cynical. To him, it was the kind of adventure story that he liked and would have readily accepted as such. That there was meant to be some kind of truth behind it however was, as far as he was concerned, nonsense – except perhaps in a historical sense. And in that respect, he did not care particularly for ancient history. And so he had no opinion on any of the historical references Tom had made throughout. It was, as Tom had forewarned them all – a struggle to believe. But to Conna, this miraculous ending was patently both fictional and unbelievable. It was a shame too, because he'd enjoyed the story so far. That truth was – as he understood it – that Lio had been literally rescued by Zeus on a flying horse. And that had now sealed his level of scepticism – absolute disbelief! Thus it confirmed his diagnosis of Tom as an 'utter nutter'.

Maddie's face, on the other hand, showed more tolerance. She had listened intently and sometimes emotionally to Tom's tragic tale and was less sceptical. As an avid reader herself and therefore used to a good plot, she had accepted the story entirely differently from the start. She had been far more willing to listen politely. Not that she was naïve – she certainly was not – but she had herself partly witnessed the noise and commotion that Conna had missed on that distant day of Tom's accident: or, at least, the weird sparks afterward. Because of that, she wondered if she recognised in his story part of the description of Lio's 'Deus Ex Macchina'. This now made her more curious than accepting. The story had struck a chord within her though; it had roused within her a deep compassion for the children depicted throughout. Furthermore, this child slavery, as Tom had previously pointed out, even today, continued unchanged – except for the name of course. It was now euphemistically known across the world only as 'child labour'. In fact, half of her mind had been elsewhere since his mention of the barbaric treatment of the child slaves in ancient times. She had empathised especially deeply with that particular injustice, given the likely genealogy of her own Caribbean roots. Even as Tom continued, she had found her attention wandering toward finding new ways of bringing attention to the current situation worldwide! She was then, unconvinced but still open-minded toward Tom.

Bex was an entirely different kettle of fish. Deliberately holding herself more remote from Tom from the start, though not unfriendly, she had hardly spoken throughout. She was in her own way analysing him for herself. She wondered why he felt the need to drag them all into this wildly fictional account of what had caused the noises and the accident that Sunday. What was he hiding, she wondered? Bex was not convinced at all about Tom and she was quite willing to tell him so – call his bluff, so to speak – if she thought it would shock the others into making up their minds. Her face reflected this attitude in its rather aloof, poker faced expression.

Alex sat in the background, desperately hoping that he would believe Tom now that he had decided to flesh out the brief account he had already given Alex privately. This, even though he knew where the story was going and had guessed at what the figure of Pegasus might be. However, as he listened intently, taking down notes every now and again, he did this for one reason and one reason only. Not out of interest, not as an 'aide memoire', but to try to verify the snippets of information later. As to whether he actually believed what he had been listening to so far, like Maddie, he was himself still unconvinced – and this saddened him. Whilst to the others this was just a story of little consequence, if it was true, and he was the only one of the four who presently knew more or less where it would eventually lead, to Alex, whether the story was true or not would have a massive impact on him and his future happiness. Therefore, he hoped desperately that Tom was both sane and somehow telling the truth, even though at this moment he was still deeply undecided. The pensive, more than slightly concerned look that had appeared on his face, had registered uneasily with Tom.

Tom coughed. "Could someone refill my glass please?" he asked. "All of this talking has made me a little dry."

"Sure," said Conna, painfully getting to his feet, "I'll get it – ouch, I've got pins and needles from sitting so long." He took Tom's glass and limped to the bathroom, happy to say or do anything to break the uneasy silence that had now descended on the room.

As soon as Conna returned, Maddie finally spoke. "Tom," she began lightly, "you know this story?"

"Yes," he answered.

"Well," she coaxed gently, "I know we all agreed that this was all a sort of hypothetical case, you know, everything you've told us so far."

"Yes?"

"Are you saying that because the boy – Lio – was hallucinating at the time:" she wrinkled her nose, "that he was the only one to see these things? Or are you in fact saying that everyone else in the crowd saw the same things happen?"

"Yes," he repeated levelly, taking the glass of water from Conna to sip from it.

"Well... which is it?" she prompted.

Tom thought for a moment then said unclearly, "Both."

But that was nonsense surely. If he couldn't decide that, then this must all indeed be just 'guff', as Conna had previously suggested. There was no point in beating about the bush, so Conna came straight out with it... in a manner of speaking... trying not to be too rude! "Err... Tom, how come one of these gods just suddenly appeared out of nowhere... 'whizz-bang-flash'..." he indicated the quotation marks with his fingers in the air, "and carried him off to the heavens or whatever. You're not telling us that Zeus and Helios and all that stuff really exists are you? "Cos if you are," he shook his head, "I'm going home now."

A frustrated Bex echoed Conna's comments – more rudely

179

than she meant it to sound – "Look, I'm sorry Tom, but this is not so much a *story* now, as much as it's becoming a complete *fantasy*."

Feeling Tom's hurt, Alex spoke up in his defence. "Hang on, that's not what he's saying, is it Tom?" He hoped against hope that it wasn't. *Tom*, thought Alex, *was simply being a bit too subtle for his own good.*

"Yes, alright then," agreed Tom. "I suppose what I should have said was: from Lio's point of view and in his weakened state, it appeared at that moment that an actual god – Zeus – had literally come to his rescue – not that he had ever been brought up to believe in their literal existence as such. So, from that point of view he was confused. And no, Conna, he was not taken up to 'Mount Olympus' to live with the gods. Neither was he delivered to 'Hades' to live with the other departed souls. In fact – he lived on!"

"Oh!" exclaimed the three principal objectors; Alex remained silent.

"No, it was not the gods, but an entirely different and very human rescuer that had arrived to take him away; quite coincidentally, looking very similar to the many depictions of the god Zeus, and therefore confusing both the boy and everyone else who witnessed the spectacle." Tom looked around, not quite accusingly. "Does that answer your question more fully?" The objectors kept quiet. Placatingly, he continued, "Let me explain. The date was now 50 BC."

He held up his hand before anyone could call out, but Maddie asked anyway. "Tom, this is the same story isn't it?"

"Indeed it is," he assured them all, "don't worry."

Still with the initial look of confusion on their faces, everyone nevertheless settled down to continue to listen to Tom's astounding story.

"As I said, the date was now 50 BC: over five hundred years after the boy had been rescued – five hundred and thirty-five to be exact. The island of Rhodos had changed a great deal during those years – though it still attracted very many visitors. There were now many more archaic temples on the island, though not exactly the same ones in which Lio and his grandfather had served. All of the original crude, locally quarried porous marble temples had long been rebuilt. In their place, now stood exquisitely carved, imported marble temples. All of their spectacularly painted friezes glistened in the strong sunlight. All, that is, except one, and ironically that one was the great Temple of Zeus – although it had now been re-named and re-dedicated as the Temple of Apollo, after the favoured son of Zeus. In the aftermath of the events I have just spoken to you about, many people turned from the worship of Zeus and toward Helios. Indeed, a huge statue of Helios was built to straddle the harbour, but had long since fallen into the sea. There it lay, still part submerged.

Elsewhere in Greece, during the intervening five hundred years, the Greeks had reached that cultural plateau – the pinnacle of which I spoke earlier – as illustrated especially by the 'Epitome of Architecture', which we still recognise and readily value even today.

They had surpassed even themselves throughout their Golden Age in many respects. The first true democracies had been formed. Athens especially experimented with many ways of attempting to govern their own affairs, systems whereby *every* man played a part in direct government, not just kings and tyrants.

The arts: playwriting and the theatre – entertaining and imaginative tragedy and comedy, written to uplift the human spirit, had been developed in works that we still study today. Fine art – sculpture and ceramics had been developed through many distinctive phases. Now honed to perfection, they had been, and would be forever held aloft as the zenith of Greek artistic endeavour.

Philosophy was also developed: how and why we exist in this world and how it all works. The subject encompassed the many sciences, including, mathematics, engineering, physics, chemistry, medicine, astronomy and biology.

There were also the technologies. These technologies were the results of the sum total of scientific knowledge and experience, put to practical use in the many inventions of their world.

All of these things and more were extremely well developed in that age, establishing many of the basic principles that hold sway even now. Far more than, in this day and age, we have come to give them credit. The pace at which the Greeks had moved world civilisation forward in such a short time frame would not be rivalled again until the end of the thirteenth century, which saw 'The Renaissance', or 'The Rebirth', of civilisation.

Sadly though, most of the records of the advances made in the sciences and technologies in particular were lost to us over the years, mainly in one tragic and unexplained incident – in Alexandria! However, we will return to that particular incident another time. At the time of this part of our story, the golden age of the many separate Greek city states had now passed: Athens, Sparta, Corinth etcetera. Also passed was the time of Alexander the Great: son of King Philip II of Macedon.

From the start, Alexander had been raised for greatness. His bloodline, it was claimed, could be traced back to that of Achilles, the Greek hero of the battle of Troy. Even on the night of his conception, his mother, a priestess of a secret religious cult, had claimed that his true father was Zeus himself. Accordingly, throughout his short life he publicly claimed to be a deity – which he claimed also for his horse Bucephalus. Although I am absolutely certain that, in truth, he understood and used this act merely as a device to unite the Greek speaking populace behind him. After all, he was educated by none other than the great philosopher Aristotle – who later became infamous for his disbelief in the gods! Under Alexander's leadership, the united Greek city states had conquered the known world. By treaty, he had then allowed many of the rulers of the conquered countries to remain in power. But he had also, into the bargain, renamed many previously established great cities after himself: 'Alexandropoulos', or 'Alexandria' – there were many of them.

For a short while, the world became united. However, because of his 'sudden and mysterious death' at the age of thirty-two, having left no clear line of succession, his empire had just as quickly dissolved into disarray and fragmentation. Many of his generals and friends fought to take control of the various parts of it. But... as I have said, all of that brief period in itself was now long ago. Now command of the world had passed firmly into the hands of a new culture.

The Romans, who had succeeded the Etruscans in their own country, had now established themselves throughout every known country – not by treaty, but by armed invasion and suppression. Bullying and swaggering around the known world, the Romans took from everywhere they could! Yes, it can be easily argued that they made great benefits throughout this world, but at what cost?

The countries they overtook were often destroyed or at least looted to excess. They did not take mere tokens – their looting was on a grand scale, most of it ending up in their capital: Rome – 'The Eternal city'. While they professed to emulate the Greeks, more simply put, they robbed, plagiarised – or copied them directly. They even took and renamed their gods. For instance Zeus now became Jupiter, Father of Gods and Men, ruler of the world etcetera. And, in their quest for power, they brought with them an entirely new and opposing set of values. Far from trying to assimilate or absorb foreign culture into their own – to learn from it – they were determined to crush it out if it was not to their own taste or liking. In place of learning and understanding came might; and might became right!

All conquered countries were 're-educated' to the Roman way, and anything not of the Roman way had to be eliminated for fear it would foment rebellion. Where the Greeks had taken prisoners in battle as slaves, rather than slaughter or imprison them, the Romans had a belligerent and cruel streak, and an insatiable lust for blood. Before slaughtering their captured enemies, they ritually humiliated them – men, women and children – and by the most barbaric methods imaginable – or rather, unimaginable! They captured wild beasts, not for their own fascination, nor for their education, nor even to use their skins out of practicality; but simply to slaughter them in their various arenas for the satisfaction of their citizens, purely for their own crass and ignorant tastes in 'entertainment'.

Even the largest of the islands that had been known in ancient times as one of the Cassiterides had not escaped their attention. Although not as yet part of the Roman Empire, only a few years previously it had been invaded by the leader of the great power of Rome himself. The soon to become great dictator, Gaius Julius Caesar, had invaded the island and had officially named it Britannia after the people he had found now living there: the Britons.

Rhodos had also inevitably changed in attitude; not only the temples but the morals of the island were now almost entirely corrupted. The island was now no more than a vast fairground for adults. The revenues of Rhodian society prospered as never before. The Romans came to revel on their island as the world's first true 'tourists'. The Temples were huge and although not now filled with slave-powered devices, there were nevertheless devices there in abundance.

A huge demand had opened up for mechanical devices, 'automata', of ever increasing ingenuity. They had been developed gradually throughout the past half millennium right there on the island. Now, on top of the electrical devices and others that I have already shown you, there were also many more mechanical devices and machines that did various things. Most, of course, were for either amusement or for use in the temples." Tom described an automatic door opener which was powered by prayer – in so far as when the pilgrim purchased a sacred log from the priest and then lit it in a basket outside of the doors of the inner sanctum, the flames would cause a vacuum to draw air through a concealed tube running beneath the floor. This would trigger a locking device and the counterbalanced doors would open, to the amazement of the crowds. There was even a coin operated vending machine, for the dispensing of 'sacred water'! But there were also very practical machines. One machine even demonstrated how various calendars throughout the world might be converted automatically!

The four began to let their fascination grow again as Tom explained the technicalities of these and other long lost discoveries.

After a short while, Alex asked innocently, "Tom, didn't the ancients have mechanical weapons, I mean apart from swords and spears and bows – machine weapons?"

Tom was taken aback by the directness of the boy's curiosity. After a distinct pause and in an altogether more subdued tone he acknowledged him. "Man has always made weapons – from the first battles fought with sticks and stones. Doubtless, until the time we have finally learned better ways to run the affairs of our 'civilization', we always will – though for how much longer?"

Alex didn't ask what he had been going to, but his neighbour answered all the same.

"Technically fascinating though they were, I only ever made a model of one 'weapon', the rest are best forgotten."

Tom's mood had changed. They all returned to their chairs, before he despondently considered whether to continue.

CHAPTER 20:

Kyrros

A few moments later, on reflection, Tom apologised. "I am sorry, Alex – and everyone – yours is a perfectly natural curiosity. It is just that in this modern world we seem to forget that the purpose of even a modern sporting weapon like an arrow was originally to take life. Please bear that in mind."

"Sorry, Tom, I didn't think," apologised Alex in return.

The old man shrugged before going on.

"It was, then, a world of wonder on the island of Rhodos. Truly, at that time, the island was one of only a few legendary places to be. It really had become a magnet for many great and learned scholars over the years who now either lived, studied or had visited the place. And, since the time of one such scholar, Hipparchos, it became quite literally the centre of the world! But more of that later."

Tom inhaled, allowing his mood to pick up. Smiling proudly, he announced, "I would like to introduce you all to the name of one more scholar at this precise time in our story, for me, the greatest of all time. Unfortunately for some, the great man was known by various names. This single fact would cause much confusion and irritation to modern day scholars. 'Professionally' he was known as Andronicus of Cyrrhus, after the town of his birth in Syria, which was founded by Seleucus Nicator, one of Alexander the Great's generals. In Greek he was known as Andronikos. Privately though, he was known by his colleagues and friends more simply as 'Kyrros'."

Alex immediately recognised the name from the story of how his parents met. *Was it just another coincidence,* he wondered?

"To add to this confusion, throughout his extraordinarily long career, he moved around constantly: from his country of birth, to Alexandria, Athens and many of the Greek islands, including Rhodos.

Kyrros was a tall, broad-shouldered, middle-aged man of great personal charisma. His rather lived-in face was thickly bearded and he had thick, rather unkempt hair. Something about him, not only his distinctive, virtually colourless eyes, and booming voice always commanded respect. Though, in truth, both of these were helpful factors which he often used to his benefit. Up to the point at which we join him, his public career had not been particularly noteworthy, although his work to date showed, above all, a great understanding of design principles. Nor had it produced for him what anyone might call a particularly comfortable lifestyle or existence. However, that was often the case with these scholars and philosophers. Amassing great wealth was frowned upon by them, as they knew it had little to do with providing a happy or fulfilling lifestyle. In fact, all the majority of these men required was enough money to allow themselves and their families to live 'in dignity'. Being able to pay one's own way in the world – without having to beg, borrow or steal – was a perfectly acceptable, not to say laudable, goal. Amassing great wealth was for fools. Having the opportunity to indulge themselves in their pet subjects was often payment enough and greatly respected by society. Also, possibly even because of this, many lived to a great age. Ninety or even one hundred years old and beyond was not that uncommon. But the world was not so polluted then.

The veil of Kyrros' public obscurity would one day be lifted though. One day, en route to Athens, he would visit the island of Tinos. There, the Roman governor would see him looking closely at and criticising the rather damaged and inaccurate old sundial that stood in the agora of the small seaside port. After a short conversation, during which Kyrros would assure him that he himself could do much better, the governor would then invite him to design and build a suitable replacement.

As a direct result of the design of this public sundial, he would then immediately be given a healthy commission by the Roman governor of Athens to build a public timepiece in that great city. In itself, that device – the Tower of the Winds, or, the Horologion – would become a marvel of antiquity so intricate that, over two millennia after it was built, the modern world is still loath to accept the level of sophistication achieved in its design. Although his new contract would eventually catapult him to fame and posterity, for now, this fame was still a while away.

However, Kyrros' sudden and mysterious disappearance from history only a few months after the tower's inauguration, still baffles modern scholars. But that would have more to do with his other private, that is to say, entirely secret identity, than that of his public profession."

Tom gazed around the four faces, before continuing solemnly. "As a man of truly exceptional genius, Kyrros had been singled out in Alexandria some time ago by the most exclusive and secret organisation of philosophers that the world has ever known: the intriguingly named, 'Chronology Society'. They wished him to head an ancient and ongoing experimental research project, a project which had, to date, taken over two centuries of dedication and experimentation. With his help, they would at long last bring it to its successful fruition. It was a project of such potential importance that if anyone other than the trustees became aware of it, it would either bring instant ridicule on their professional standing or worse, great danger to them all. The project, if their theory proved correct, had the potential to change man's perception of the universe for all time, his understanding of time and space, and indeed the very sequence of time itself. It was for these reasons, then, considered herkoose odonton – most secret!"

"What was it?" asked Alex, suddenly animated. "What was the project?"

Tom looked at each of the four faces in turn and declared flatly, "Why, to build a Time-Machine of course!"

And although each of them had already guessed what he was going to say, still everyone looked amazed. Now, no one spoke another word as Tom began to describe the whole technical process from start to finish.

"Kyrros had, as I have said, spent most of his known career occupied in what could be considered by some as mundane enough tasks. In the year 50 BC, by the time he had reached the relatively middle age of fifty-eight years old, there were not many of the machines – the temple automata on the island of Rhodos – which he was not familiar with. In fact, many of those machines represented his own improvements on previous designs. In his earlier years, he had written many papers on these and on many other subjects. The common thread though, was that the subjects were all somehow connected with various mechanical devices and applications he had encountered throughout the life he had lived, sometimes on Rhodos but also from the times he visited other important centres of learning. He had, for instance, visited Persia often, where he saw and wrote about the many forms of water pumps that were used to irrigate the fields and make them more productive. In Athens he wrote about and discussed the many diverse mechanical devices he had seen in windmills and the like, but of all the places he had visited, only Alexandria of Egypt captured his imagination as much as Rhodos.

He had lived in the city of Alexandria for a period of ten years in his youth, in the paid employ of King Ptolemy XII 'Auletes', or, 'the flute player', patron of the arts: a king who, although not a man of great intellect, was both hungry for knowledge and fame. Under the mantle of Ptolemy then, Kyrros had been able to indulge his own great passion for learning within the most famous seat of learning of all time, the Mouseion of Alexandria, and within it, the Great Library of Alexandria."

"I've heard of that," said Maddie impressively. "That was one of the wonders of the ancient world, wasn't it?"

"Strictly speaking, no," answered Tom, "although it should have been. However, that issue is perhaps not worth arguing about. Sadly, the library did not survive the ravages of time. I should explain," he went on.

"Historically, after the mysterious death of Alexander the Great, while still campaigning abroad, Ptolemy I Soter – meaning saviour – the boyhood friend of Alexander, a man educated by the same teachers as Alexander himself, assumed one third of his conquered territories and replaced the Egyptian Pharaohs, who had become a pale shadow of their ancient forebears. Making Alexandria his new capital, Ptolemy had then established an 'invited' community to live within the palace grounds – for the expressed purpose of furthering the understanding of mankind. In fact, he had initiated a law: that any vessel or traveller visiting Alexandria could be searched to see if it was carrying 'books' or scrolls on board. Anything of interest would then be confiscated, copied but then returned. The copy was then deposited in his Royal Library. Of course, the community was also always open to new 'thinkers' or 'philosophers' – on any subject whatsoever. And to these philosophers, many of whom had been persecuted for their free thinking over many centuries, this sanctuary of learning had become a breath of fresh air. It should also be understood that although the common language of the country remained Egyptian, from that day forward, the official language of the royal court – including that of the places of learning – became Greek.

In our story, the present Greek speaking king, Ptolemy XII, following in the direct line of descent from his Greek ancestor Ptolemy Soter, upheld all of these traditions. However, the Mouseion did not include the kind of library that we would think of today. Far from the often sterile or boring places we now think of solely for the purposes of borrowing books, it was much, much more. To begin with, the Mouseion was divided into two linked parts. Firstly, the library proper: this was where over five hundred thousand 'books' were stored – half a million! They were books which contained the majority of all known things, though in the form of scrolled papyri to be exact. By no means coincidentally, this, the forerunner of paper – which took its own name from the processed papyrus reeds it was made from – was made right there in Alexandria. These works were stored here for the reference of scholars or philosophers, to read and learn from. They were held there so that they could in turn be used to expand the sum total of universal knowledge. In this respect the Great Library was a forerunner of every school, college and university across the whole of the modern world!

The second part was the store, what might be more properly called the museum; not like a modern museum mind you, not one of those other stuffy places where one may find collected objects and curiosities, although there were of course all of those other things that one might still find in a museum today. This museum was built as a place of wonder, a place to 'muse' or think over and openly discuss great ideas, and develop these thoughts. It had within it many workshops and other places where scholars could develop new technologies or artists could learn their craft.

In the time of Kyrros, however, the Great Library was not open to the public. Ptolemy himself was not about to let members of the ordinary classes know what he sometimes struggled to understand himself. Although from the little he did know, he did grasp the fact that knowledge was power – and power in the wrong hands was dangerous! Of course, by inviting new thinkers, scholars and philosophers to Alexandria, he was also keeping abreast of any new ideas that might be 'useful' – to him or his country.

As I have previously said, in many countries, 'thinking' was dangerous – no matter how open to new ideas they professed to be. There was almost always the inevitable block or impasse when these 'free thinkers' got too close to the truth for comfort. At that time still, anyone who might inadvertently question the authority of the many and varied religions – especially the state sponsored religions – did so bravely. By suggesting an alternative theory to the commonly held beliefs of how the world worked or had come into existence, they automatically came under direct scrutiny themselves,

191

almost always at their own peril – one way or another.

Still some philosophers were openly ridiculed, some criticised directly and ostracised or banished from their country, some were even imprisoned – or worse! And works that had brought about their derision or peril were almost always removed entirely from the pages of history itself. By contrast, in the Mouseion of Ptolemy, the opposite reigned true. Free and radical thinking was positively encouraged – it was the only way that mankind could move forward, wasn't it? How could it follow that to stifle thinking could ever be good for man? This was always assuming that these secrets were not openly discussed. Some men could comprehend the universe in its entirety – others could not handle the truth of that knowledge; better to be cautious about who these theories were discussed with then."

Tom strained his eyes over the top of his glasses and emphasised, "Just as on that fateful day of the eclipse, five hundred years earlier on Rhodos, if certain people in the uneducated population learned these things, panic might have ensued. Then civil unrest, for no real reason, might follow. Ptolemy XII knew this."

CHAPTER 21:

'On Time'

"It was into this radical world then, that Kyrros had stumbled and later found himself invited to stay. At first, it was his own improvements on existing devices that brought him to the attention of the Mouseion, his fascination for methods and mechanisms and his understanding of how things had previously worked. He was able to improve these things vastly. In this respect therefore, he had become one of the world's first accepted practical 'designers'."

Smiling, Tom mimicked Conna's earlier inverted commas with the fingers of his good hand, "eventually, he was also given the title of: 'King's Engineer', although oddly, he only ever met the king on a few occasions, and his son, the king in waiting, only once.

It was, however, his fascination for one subject in particular that would mark him out from the other scholars. A subject that many others had mused over in passing, and that in some respects many, many had spent their lives studying, at least in its division. A subject which was as invisible as it was unfathomable. Kyrros was a man absolutely gripped by the entire subject of 'time'.

Time, not just as in how best to divide it into years, months, days, hours and minutes, as the earliest Babylonian culture had originally devised – the twenty-four hour day being agreed the most divisible number – but in the very essence and definition of time! What was 'time'? he asked. It was the question that had fascinated him ever since he was a small child. He had asked his father at an early age to explain what it was, only to be disappointed by his and others' replies. Almost always, those who took the question seriously at all, which were few, would compare time to something else entirely unrelated. 'Time is a flowing stream – it cannot flow back in the opposite direction!' they might venture, or 'Time is like the passing of the sun – it cannot be turned back!'

Although well meant, the young Kyrros was never remotely satisfied by these respective metaphors and similes. From the age of fourteen years old, not unlike the boy Lio, five hundred years earlier, he had already learned much about astronomy and how to tell the time precisely, using the many and various types of sundials that were now in existence. At an early age he had even begun to think of how they might be improved, not only in precision but in ease of readability. Some of them were still incredibly difficult to decode or read, without being given expert instruction on how to do so! But as for the very essence of what 'time' was, until he had reached Alexandria, he never did formulate a conclusion as to how it might be explained.

In this respect, after a few casual conversations over the duration of his initial stay at the Mouseion, a number of people directed him toward the works of several philosophers who had had their papers deposited at the library. Handwritten, learned works by previous geniuses centuries earlier who had 'hypothesized' or mused over what time might in fact be, and even as to what form it may take. It was even guessed that time might in fact all be experienced or observed relative to the observer, in so far as it appeared to pass more quickly the older a person got!

There were of course several obscure, not to say bizarre theories, but nearly all could be divided into three main principles:

Firstly, there was the 'Straight Line' or 'Cause and Effect Principle', by which it was proposed, apparently quite logically, that any series of events which might happen would cause another series of events to occur once, never to be repeated. Imagine, if you will, a short scene..." Tom made up his own light-hearted but outrageously chauvinist example, in order to try to explain to the four sitting in front of him.

"The observer and hapless main character in this scene, a

194

woman in ancient Alexandria cleaning her doorstep, has left a bucket of water in a doorway, causing her husband to trip and fall over it. Time then moves on. If she moves the bucket afterward, it will not change the outcome, and she would still no doubt end up with a beating. Therefore, by this principle, it was impossible to turn back, or otherwise manipulate time! Though quite where the straight line began and ended could not be logically explained.

Secondly, there was the 'Spherical Principle', by which time itself might be considered spherical in form – just as the Earth and the ancient Greeks' solar system appeared to be to them. Even, perhaps, layered like an onion skin, with even the stars being studded on the inside of the outermost layer."

"What!" interjected Alex, "the Greeks knew that their world wasn't flat?"

"Of course," answered Tom unequivocally. Not wishing to get off the subject of time, he offered, before continuing, "if you wish, I will explain that later.

By this spherical principle, it was proposed that time may be a series of events that inevitably rotated around and around and therefore might repeat itself eventually – just as certain 'stars', now known as comets, were observed to return over great periods of time. Around that, time and matter was simply space, nothingness, although how far that extended, and into what, was never properly explained either. In our short scene then, if time constantly revolved, our unfortunate observer, the woman with her bucket, might end up with several beatings for the same mistake!"

Tom continued, "It was, however, another obscure writing that contained a principle that caught the attention of Kyrros: a spinning 'toroidal', or doughnut shaped universe, without beginning or end. In it, everything moved in a perpetually flowing stream. A stream in which 'bubbles', or pockets, of time and space were intricately related to each other in a kind of 'cosmic sponge' of time, space and all life itself.

It was this Toroidal Principle, where everything turned itself over and through constantly, that caused Kyrros to take note and develop the theory further. The principle occupied him almost to the point of total obsession. If it was true – that time and space were interrelated – then surely, he argued, though only to a few of the more receptive minds in the Mouseion, it might even be theoretically possible to alter or manipulate the structure of time itself. Even, perhaps, somehow move through it, or pass across it in a shortcut, from one side of the doughnut to another as it inevitably returned around a central void; again, always quite theoretically, of course!" Tom looked squarely at each of the four. "Though today, this principle of moving through time and space via a 'wormhole' is surprisingly well known and accepted. In our example then, by moving and manipulating time itself, our now fortunate observer, the woman, might finally get a chance to move the bucket before her husband trips and thus finally avoid the beating!"

Each time he mentioned the woman taking a beating, Tom noted the look of disapproval on the faces of the girls. "Lastly, to quite literally add a twist to this theory:" Tom suddenly produced a roll of gummed paper from beside his chair. He tore off a short strip and began to form it into a loop. "If I twist one end of this paper through one hundred and eighty degrees," he licked the end of it delicately, "before sticking both gummed sides together – like this," he held up the finished result, "I end up with something that looks like a horizontal twisted figure of eight. Today, this is called a 'mobius strip', or the figure 'lemniscate' – the mathematical symbol of infinity. The result demonstrates a never ending, solid, two-dimensional object."

"What?" asked Alex, looking up from his notes – "not three?"

"No, two!" Tom handed the loop to Maddie, along with a marker pen. "Please would you be so kind as to take this and draw a line along the centre of its plain side."

Maddie wrinkled her nose. "Okay," she agreed. Placing it on her knee, she carefully started to draw the line. As it got to what should have been the end, the surface continued onto the gummed side and around for another full loop before reaching the start of the line. Bex and Alex looked curiously on at the demonstration. The line appeared to run around both sides, and yet was only one.

"I don't get it," said Conna, "what does that prove?"

"That logically, the loop in front of you has effectively only one width and one single, never ending side – as the line occupies one side only, the theoretical thickness of the paper is immaterial – although the whole of the flattened, twisted 'doughnut' appears to occupy another measurable depth," he said simply, indicating its top to its bottom.

Conna scratched his head.

"Of course there is also at least one other dimension considered by most," Tom went on. "It all exists in time!" He looked at the clearly baffled faces. *No*, he thought, *perhaps that had taxed their minds too far for just now; best not to get too ahead of himself... well, maybe.*

"There is one other thing," he suggested, handing Bex a pair of scissors. "If you carefully cut around the pencil mark, you will notice something else."

While she did this, Tom completed Kyrros' thoughts on the subject. "Maybe, the philosopher reasoned, if time and space did continue to spin around forever, eventually all problems would be solved as everything was updated, although the players in each scene would of course only be aware of their own reality, and not conscious of the changed scene before or since. However," he conceded readily, "this is all difficult stuff to get one's head around."

Bex completed the task he'd given her. As she snipped the last bit, the whole thing sprang into one, larger, continuous loop – bizarre!

"And one final thing, if you cut it again around its whole length, it demonstrates something else," Tom instructed Conna to take over with the scissors and after a minute or so, the loop was predictably separated into two, each one the same size but half the width of the previous one. However, each loop was now interlinked with its other half, like the tangled start of a chain.

"Now *I* don't get it," confessed Alex. "What does that prove?"

"I haven't a clue," sniffed Tom: "other than that the subject of the linkage of time and space are unbelievably baffling!"

All four now smirked curiously at the enigma.

Up to this point they had sat and listened patiently, but now that Tom had stopped for a breath and to take a drink from the ever present glass of water, Bex, who had pursed her lips several times throughout, finally spoke up. "Tom?"

"Yes?" he answered.

"How come it's only the men that get a mention in this tale – and not the women – except as objects of fun? How come you keep saying that it was the 'men' who helped make the machine?" She really had become quite agitated by the constant references.

"Yes," he considered, "for all its enlightenment, Greek society at that time was entirely convinced, at least on the surface, that it was only men who mattered. Girls were not schooled or educated then. But frankly, few boys were either. No, privately some of the philosophers may have spoken to their wives to use them as 'sounding boards', to see if the women might be able to follow some of their ideas, but even if a woman did bring an idea forward, it could not be presented in public. That would bring scorn on men and would inevitably lead to the rejection of the idea being presented."

"Just because it came from a woman?" asked Maddie.

"Yes, better to let her husband explain and take the credit publicly."

Bex was fizzing. "But that's so... unfair, so..."

"Patronising!" finished Maddie.

Tom smiled ruefully at them both as he said, "It was a hard truth of that time, but all one could do was learn to live with it. Some attitudes take a long time to change."

Both Maddie and Bex glanced from Tom to Alex and Conna, nostrils flared but saying nothing more.

Boris sat up roughly and, detecting the chill, barked once at Tom and once at Alex and then lay down again.

Then Bex almost spat out, "Only primitive societies treat women as lesser mortals."

"Agreed – absolutely," Tom nodded, "and sadly it was often on the pretext that it was on the command of one god or another."

"Maybe that's because these commands were always written into books by men," suggested Alex helpfully.

"EXACTLY!" chorused both girls.

"Perhaps," finished Tom, sensing uneasy territory, "but rest assured, at least one woman played a part in all this design and development work, and incidentally brought herself to the attention of the great man himself!"

CHAPTER 22:

'On Space'

"Come on then, spill the beans," Conna almost smirked, "What's this about the ancient Greeks knowing that the Earth was round all those years ago?"

"Yes, Tom," Maddie spoke up, "we remember from primary school that it was only supposed to be at the time Columbus discovered the Americas, 1492 AD, that the idea of a round Earth instead of a flat Earth, came about. Don't we Bex?"

Her sister nodded "You're saying that two thousand years ago, the Greeks knew that the Earth was round?" She twisted her face.

Tom considered this. "Actually it was the astronomer Copernicus – earlier in the same century – who is commonly credited with this discovery. But yes," said Tom confidently, sitting suddenly upright, "yes the Greeks did. It was quite obvious to many by then. Simple observation told them it was round. Being a nation of seafarers, it was only natural that one would watch boats, trading vessels, set off from the harbour to 'disappear' over the horizon. These vessels did not fade into a distant dot, getting smaller and smaller until they vanished. Instead, they appeared to reach a certain point then 'sink', leaving only the top of a sailing mast in sight. Obviously then, the ships had gone over a curve in the Earth – in any direction – therefore quite clearly, the Earth must have been spherical. Heavenly observations also confirmed this. The only weakness to counter this early theory was that no one could properly explain how anyone fell off the earth and why the water in the seas did not pour away.

One possible way of explaining this away, however, was that

relative to its surface, the centre of a sphere was always 'downward' from any direction *around* its surface. Therefore, everyone and everything in the world was constantly, effectively 'falling down'. Otherwise, perhaps, they reasoned, the earth might be a magnet of some kind – like the curious metallic rocks, magnetite, which had long ago been discovered. And of course," he slipped in casually, "the Greeks also knew about the 'magnetic' pull exerted by the moon on the seas, causing the tides. Through this, some hypothesised that the Earth might also be magnetic."

Now everyone struggled with Tom's alternative history of discovery.

"They were not the best theories and they did not scientifically and mathematically explain the theory of gravity as did the English gentleman philosopher Sir Isaac Newton in the eighteenth century. However, they did serve as at least a possibility to the Greeks as to how our own continued presence on the Earth might be explained."

Maddie frowned, clearly thrown. "So you at least agree that it was Isaac Newton that discovered the law of gravity in the seventeen hundreds!"

"Perhaps," conceded Tom.

"How do you mean, *perhaps*?" she asked frustratedly.

"Just perhaps," repeated Tom. "But it was in the way I have just described, first theorised by the Greeks, then sadly 'forgotten' again. That is, until 'coincidentally', just before the beginning of the Renaissance of thirteenth century Europe." He was having fun with these finger indicated inverted commas. "It was then that an ancient book by the great philosopher and engineer 'Heron of Alexandria' was finally found in a private collection in Arabia and translated into Latin. These things were rediscovered since! As even Newton almost admitted to plagiarism," Tom quoted:

"'If I have seen farther, it is by standing on the shoulders of giants.'"

The four looked at each other, wondering if this part of the tale could be true.

"Just a minute..." Conna again butted in. "What do you mean 'rediscovered.' How did it all go missing to start with?"

"Is this important?" prompted Alex, now desperate only to get on with the main story.

"Well I just want to know... that's all," Conna answered, looking pointedly at Alex."

Maddie and Bex were also curious now.

Tom looked at the consternation on the faces of his audience. Not wishing to get further off the subject or cause offence, he inhaled, knowing he would have to explain.

"Alright, briefly, since the birth of Christianity, the Church argued about the construction of the world. Not unsurprisingly, it preferred to stick the Bible's Old Testament account of creation: that God himself made everything within six days. In time, the Christian Church became divided and the main parts of it, especially the Roman Catholic Church, took the view that it would be best, 'for the good of the people', to abandon the difficult to understand spherical Earth principle, which said that the Earth and the known planets revolved around the sun. Instead, the Church decided to return to the flat Earth principle – with the sun revolving around the Earth!

It was happier with this, as, apart from all else, it was easy to paint or illustrate a geographical location for Heaven – above the clouds – and a place for what was re-invented by them as Hell – below the ground. These places of eternal reward or damnation were critical both to their belief and their operation. You understand?" Tom looked pointedly down at his hands. "It is 'unfortunate' that the Church then decided, perhaps for the best of reasons," Tom conceded, "in their opinion, to save souls, that it had a duty to systematically eradicate any works that disagreed with their preferred account. As a result, many learned scientific works were destroyed, or at the least seized by the Church and locked away in its library of banned or prohibited works – the 'Index Librorum Prohibitorum'.

By contrast, Arabic beliefs were not offended by these alternative views – even much later than the ancient Greek times, when Islam came into being. Enlightened Arab collectors of these works hid them from harm and there they remained for many years – even many hundreds of years."

No one spoke up, and Tom was glad to have avoided causing offence to any of the youths. It was not his purpose or desire to cast doubt on any personal faith each might or might not have – only enlightenment as to what had *actually* been done in the past. He quickly got off the subject and back onto the point he was originally trying to make.

"As I began to say, Heron of Alexandria in the years ten to seventy AD lived much later than the time in which this story is set but he had made a career and his fortune from collecting and writing down the many ideas that he saw around him. Some, even at that time, extending back as far as five hundred years – his own 'ancient' world. He published many books, especially concerning these ingenious mechanisms; of course, along with his own inventions. Some, including Kyrros' own accounts, may even have found their way into Heron of Alexandria's later compilations.

Though at the point in time when this translation was printed and distributed around the whole of the Latin speaking world – the Renaissance – these expensive hand printed books were affordable to only a few aristocratic philosophers and wealthy patrons. It was because of this, that interest was rekindled in what else the ancients had already discovered. Other forgotten manuscripts now also came to light; things that had been held under lock and key in several places for many centuries – largely, as I have said, in Arabic collections. Perhaps, in the light of all this," Tom considered aloud, "it might be worth asking what truly sparked the apparently sudden rush of brilliant ideas during Europe's Renaissance – 'rebirth' or simply 'rediscovery'."

Still lagging behind in the conversation a little, Conna expressed his own thoughts more succinctly on the one matter that he understood. "Anyone could say that the Greeks knew that the world was round – where's the proof?"

"Quite right, Conna, and I'm sorry but I cannot provide scientific proof that the ancient Greeks positively knew. However, surely you've seen many representations of the Greek god Atlas: sculptures and mosaics etcetera, carrying the world on his shoulders, yes?"

"Yeah?"

"Well... wasn't the world he carried nearly always depicted as a sphere, or at least round?"

Conna considered for a few moments. "Come to think of it, yeah," he agreed, turning to the others. "It always was, wasn't it?"

"Anyway," Tom cut the conversation short, "we digress. What I should have said was that there had been plenty of real discoveries in those fields of the sciences. And those discoveries were 'coincidentally' closely linked to this story." Tom stopped to ponder this, his eyes closed behind his sunglasses.

Just as he opened his mouth to speak, Conna butted in frustratingly: "Who actually discovered it all in the first place then, which Greeks?" He didn't actually say 'prove it'.

Alex and the girls glowered at Conna.

Tom sighed, stroking his hair back. "Perhaps it would be easier to give you a short list of these great minds, do you think?"

"Okay then," Alex accepted.

"Alright," followed Maddie and Bex.

"Yes, I think that would be wise..." Tom settled back into his chair. "Please note these names down ... then, if you wish, you may check them later.

To begin with, there was Aristotle, 'panepistemon'," Tom pronounced this pan-**eppis**-temon. "All round speaker and writer who lived between the years 384 and 322 BC. He was an Athenian philosopher, a student of Plato and founder of much established thought. Aristotle was also the teacher of Alexander the Great and Ptolemy. He wrote many books including a book on the scientific workings of the universe entitled '*On the Heavens*'. As usual at that time, because he seemed to be questioning the way the gods ordered the world – not to say their very existence – he was widely criticised for his blasphemous views and, after the unexpected death of Alexander, had to flee.

Then, around 322 to 250 BC lived a philosopher by the name of Aristarchos of Samos, who was the first man to put forward the heliocentric principle: that it is the sun which sits at the centre of our solar system and not, as people previously believed, the Earth. He also believed that the stars were stationary and a great distance away from us. This was based on much tireless observation of the stars and planets but it was in direct contrast to the earlier and well established teachings of Aristotle. His work was considered dangerous to society and was therefore 'lost'.

At the same time, from 276 to 195 years BC there lived Eratosthenes of Cyrene." Tom pronounced the name, Erra-**toss**-then-eez. "This man would go on to become the head librarian of the Great Library of Alexandria. An all round scholar, he heard a lecture by Aristarchos and throughout his own life developed the idea further. In later life he even built a precise model of the universe showing the five other known planets. An 'armillary', not unlike the one standing in the corner of this very room," Tom pointed to the corner. "It was made to help explain the principle to his many students.

There was also Hipparchos of Rhodos. Hipparchos lived from 190 years, to 120 years BC. He remarkably accurately calculated the circumference of the earth – within twenty-six miles of its true 24,902miles – around one tenth of one percent error. He devised the system of latitude and longitude we still use today. Except his meridian line of zero degrees longitude was placed through Rhodos and not as today: Greenwich, England, where Sir Isaac Newton lived and worked. He also accurately calculated the distance from the earth to the sun, and even the tilt of the earth's axis. And, he was a good friend of Archimedes, the great engineer mathematician and inventor – the philosopher who famously coined the phrase 'Eureka', when he stumbled upon an unrelated scientific principle of his own.

Finally, there was Seleucus of Seleucia who lived between 190

205

and 150 BC. He was born five years after the death of Eratosthenes, and forty years after the death of Aristarchos. He also came to the conclusion that the sun was at the centre of the universe and that, furthermore, the moon not only revolved around the Earth, but, also attracted the tides of the sea which were consequently moved by it. He knew that the height of the tides depended directly on the moon's position in conjunction with that of the sun. From this, he compiled the world's first 'tide-table'! This also led quite logically to the idea that the planets might themselves be magnetic – and thus toward the idea of gravity.

Between these five philosophers alone, and there were many more, over a span of around two hundred and fifty years, they had laid the foundations for others to develop their ideas further. Ideas of how the universe in all its complexity could be demonstrated to work, by perhaps a fairly simple scientific model." Tom again pointed directly to the corner containing his own armillary. "At last, the motion of the world could be explained by simple mechanics and without having to cling to the ancient superstitions and beliefs that it was the gods who made and quite literally moved and guided it all!"

"Now," Tom re-started, "Can we move the story forward?"

"Yes please!" Alex fixed Conna with a stare.

"Alright," confirmed the twins.

Conna opened his mouth to say something, but then looked at the other expressions in the room. Instead, he shrugged. "Uh-huh."

"Thank you! Then to get back to the story, the subject of Kyrros' strange conversations was evidently, though quite innocently, communicated through the Mouseion. Even to King Ptolemy himself. His own fascination with the subject briefly ignited to the point of actually coming all the way to the Mouseion itself – from his palace two hundred paces away – within the same grounds! to speak personally to Kyrros.

But more significantly though, Kyrros' earliest ravings had also come to the attention of a very select few of the older members of the Chronology Society. Fascinated with Kyrros' ideas, they decided to get closer to him, in order to both befriend, and genuinely listen to what he had to say.

Although they would themselves remain obscure, these older members represented in one way or another, the interests of many previous philosophers who had not only mused the same or similar principles, but had also expostulated or proposed ways to actually manipulate the joint fabric of space and time. Even, if you will – move bodily through time and space itself, just as Kyrros dreamed!"

CHAPTER 23:

Principles, Design And Development

NB a more detailed version of this chapter is posted on the Time-Horse website.

Once again they settled as Tom began. "I have so far spoken of how, many years ago, the principles of time and of space were grappled with, in an effort to understand them both. In the many years since these principles were first introduced, many more philosophers tried, with varying degrees of success, to move this knowledge forward, almost entirely in secret – for the many reasons I have already touched upon. By the time Kyrros was accepted by this secret society – the Chronology Society – all of this knowledge was in one way or another already there. But it needed the incisive mind of a much superior intellect to sieve through it all in order to begin to compile all of the pieces and then formulate a way to manipulate the very fabric of time and space itself and not least, begin to design a Time-Machine. In great secrecy then, helped only by a sworn few members of the society, Kyrros began to do just that.

To return to our story, a sensible vehicle was required. But it had not yet been decided whether the vehicle should be something to be travelled in, on or through. Perhaps the best solution, it was reasoned, was not to move a vehicle at all but to accelerate atomic particles of matter around in a portal, or doorway, in order to allow the chosen traveller to step through. However, this presupposed, of course, that the time and space which the traveller wished to visit would not have access to the same portal and that once the time-traveller had gone. Either he would have to stay permanently in his destination, thus no one would know if the experiment had worked, or he would have to transport with him another portal – to effect his return – thus setting up a means of travel between two fixed points in time only. Of course, each time he travelled somewhere else, he would have to transport another portal. This concept was deemed unacceptable for many reasons."

Through the dark lenses of his glasses, Tom noted the look of complete and utter disbelief on all four faces at the mention of 'atomic particles'.

"In truth, that word was taken from the Greek, *Atomos,* meaning 'the smallest part'." He held his hand up – "Yes, I'm afraid that that too was hypothesized by ancient Greek philosophers: Demokritos and Leukippos, much, much earlier, in the time of Plato, who lived between 428 and 427 BC. It was they who first proposed that everything in the world might be made up of tiny particles too small to see. Look it up," he challenged before anyone could speak. "Though little of their works still exist; it seems that the great philosopher Plato himself had them destroyed, presumably because he himself opposed their dangerously radical theories.

By using some of the basic principles I have demonstrated already," Tom beckoned them to look around the bench-tops, "Kyrros then led a team of dedicated philosophers, engineers and technicians to build the machine that would be required to manipulate, or travel through, time and space.

It was comprised of three key parts:

Firstly, the main body of the machine, which incorporated a clock of sorts and something Kyrros named the *Power Condensing-key,* or motor – what became known as the *Power-key.* This, in itself, incorporated a massive flywheel, in the form of an Elektra Wheel – as I earlier demonstrated. The heavy wheel both generated its power and acted as a kinetic energy store. The Power-key also had two powerful springs – one for the outward journey and one for the return – which had to be wound up with foot pedals. It also held what Kyrros referred to as a *Burst Initiator*, something designed to convert this electricity to negative energy – to allow the machine to exploit the fissures of time and space. The secret of the Burst Initiator's construction was for security reasons known only to Kyrros himself and his most trusted technician.

Secondly, the machine had a *Chronology*, or *Time-key* – what became known as the *Chrono-key*. This was a sophisticated mechanical computer which used the stars to navigate: a kind of satellite navigation system." The four sat up and began to pay attention as they each recognised the oblong box he went on to describe in detail.

"And thirdly, there was the *Cosmology*, or *Distance-key* – what became known as the *Cosmos-Key*. It was an armillary sphere, a miniature of the much larger one standing in the corner of this room, but enclosed in a thin, spherical shell, studded precisely with holes – to represent the stars." Everyone turned their heads to see the representation of the planets. "This controlled where the machine went.

As well as being key parts to the machine's operation, both the Chrono-key and the Cosmos-key had important secondary roles. Both parts were removable. Both were literal keys to preventing the machine's unauthorised use. Without the Chrono-key – the computer – the machine could only move forward in time, never backwards. Anyone taking the machine without permission would simply disappear into the future, never to return. Without the Cosmos-key – the armillary – the machine could not move from the spot it presently occupied in space. You understand this?"

"Yes," Alex and the girls nodded.

"Not space, space – outer space – you mean it couldn't move around the world?" Conna checked.

"That is correct, Conna, whether in the present, the future or the past, it would always remain in the same physical position relative to its surroundings," confirmed Tom. He moved swiftly on.

"As the years passed, there were of course many other, more technical difficulties to be overcome in this lengthy design and development process. However, Kyrros quickly got right behind many of the thorny issues. Many, many versions of different key parts were tried, tested and in turn failed, but curiously no one ever took this badly. It was frustrating, yes, but these failures merely served to teach the respective teams where they'd gone wrong, and as a result, it caused them to redouble their efforts. Many experts in their own specified area of interest, 'boffins', if you like, just as today you have computer..."

"Geeks!" Conna completed the sentence self-satisfactorily. He smiled conspiratorially around the room. No one smiled back.

"Indeed!" Tom continued enthusiastically, "there were at that time also, people who could hardly dress or feed themselves but in other ways their genius was so great..." He left the sentence unfinished. "These people worked tirelessly for decades to move the project forward. And slowly, bit by bit, it did.

By the time Kyrros was fifty-five years old, both the Cosmology-key – the Cosmos-key – and the Chronology-key – the Chrono-key – were almost perfected. In time, they also proved extremely accurate instruments.

"How accurate?" asked Alex, for no particular reason but out of interest. "How many decimal places were they accurate to, Tom?"

Tom closed his eyes, took off his glasses and pinched his nose in concentration. "That is difficult to answer. Firstly, Kyrros developed his own, unique, system of counting and recording numbers: the prevailing Roman numeral system was far too difficult to programme – but, if we are to move the story on, I would prefer to explain how he did that later. However, for now, if the Greeks were to have used the same decimal system as we do today, I believe that the Cosmos-key would have been accurate to about 10,000 decimal places."

"What!" everyone gasped.

"But," Tom protested, misinterpreting their look of disbelief, "it did not have to be more accurate because the detailed extent of the 'known world' was much smaller then, basically Mediterranean and coastal Europe, North Africa, Persia and India. One or two decimal places out might make the error of, for instance, ending up next door instead of the desired location, that was all – and hopefully not too important. The Chrono-key, however, had, of course, to be much more accurate. Time being infinite, even the error of one or two decimal places could result in the traveller ending up a day, a week, a month or even a year earlier or later. This then, was accurate I believe to at least 100,000 decimal places!"

All jaws had dropped. That was absolutely and utterly unbelievable!

"Ah, now I know what you're thinking," Tom guessed correctly. "How could they calculate that so accurately? How could they work out anything that precisely without having access to a computer to perform those calculations to begin with? Well, they did have one..."

All eyes were raised and mouths opened again.

Tom explained, "They had a very special computer, known to them all simply as 'Pelos', after the pelicans that used to fly into the grounds. They would gobble up and store food in their beaks, then carry it off to regurgitate it for their later satisfaction; likewise with Pelos and numbers. But this Pelos was not a gadget – instead, he was the rarest of all human beings. He was totally blind, almost deaf, his cranium oversized and his body small, round and terribly deformed. He could not hold a proper conversation with anyone – his mind did not work that way. He would only repeat whatever he heard. But, given a mathematical problem, he could regurgitate the answer faster than it could be written down. He was, in fact, the lynchpin of the whole project."

"I've seen that!" blurted out Conna again. "I saw a programme on telly – 'savants' they're called – there's one in America who can work out the correct value of pi to one million places, just off the top of his head – whatever pi is?"

"Perhaps," agreed Tom, "and there have been many who have been institutionalised because of this *madness,* but this most rare talent was used by the Greeks, for everyone's benefit."

"Wasn't that just exploitation?" asked Bex acidly.

"I don't believe it was," answered Tom. "The others knew how privileged they were to have the benefit of Pelos, and in return, they always cared for him and his mother – looked out for them both. In some ways, I am sure, he must have known he was truly appreciated and valued as a member of society. He was always fully 'protected' within the team and without hint of scorn from anyone – until his tragic loss much later..." He looked at Bex, "Is that exploitation or integration?"

"I don't know," she said simply, considering the question.

"Anyway, Pelos' head became the computer that helped to build the mechanical computers used in their own machine.

There were of course other problems which arose and which were addressed as they came along. Not least, the development of special materials: for instance, a grade of steel which had sufficient spring in it to allow the wheel to be wound up like a clockwork motor, yes?"

They nodded again.

"And which, incidentally, was the thing finally discovered by a woman cleaner – a woman whose father had recently been killed in a so-called 'honour dispute', and who had recently had to fend for herself. It was she who stumbled upon the principles of heat treatment: hardening and tempering, whilst cleaning the workshops, by accidentally knocking a hot metal coil into a bucket of oil. And this is also what brought the young-ish, not unattractive woman to the personal attention of the great man himself."

Tom took another sip of water, and returned to the story. "Her name was Miriam, and part accidentally, but mostly intuitively, she had made the breakthrough that they'd all been waiting for. She was of course rewarded for this." Tom looked impishly at the satisfied faces of Bex and Maddie... considering. "As a result, from that moment forward," Tom spoke directly to the girls, "it was decided that she would be allowed to continue alone with her experiments from first thing each and every morning to late afternoon. And afterwards, she could begin the cleaning in the evenings, so that she would not get too exhausted working into the early hours of the morning. Such was the appreciation and magnanimity of ancient male society."

The girls looked aghast. "You've got to be joking..." growled Bex. "She still had to go on cleaning after work?"

Taking off his glasses, Tom squinted directly at her and permitted his face to show a rare smirk. "Yes, I am," he admitted, "I made that bit up – I believe it is called a wind up. But I just had to see your faces."

He giggled suddenly, a high, gleeful laugh that did not suit him in the slightest, until the laughing made him start to cough and clutch his chest in pain.

Alex and Conna both looked to see Maddie's and especially Bex's face. Judging by their reactions and their crinkling eyes though, they took it in fun. Thankfully they joined in with Tom's laughter, but not before Bex let off steam by pulling a face and playfully punching Conna on the shoulder. It had been a small joke, but the first time anyone had said anything remotely humorous all day, and in that moment, it brought the party of five still more closely together.

"No, in truth, Miriam's mind and interests lay elsewhere. With everyone's blessing, and especially the thanks and financial support of Kyrros, she began to study the subject she found closer to her heart – medicine. But more about Miriam later," he smiled at the thought of her.

"Eventually, as the various parts of the project finally began to be progressed, it became time for the form of the vehicle to be decided. A simple, wheeled vehicle was considered, then rejected when someone asked, 'What if it lands on a slope and rolls out of control?' Then 'What about a small building or box,' someone suggested, 'something which may be carved to represent how it effortlessly it might move on the winds. Kyrros even drew it out properly, taking many days. It was a tall, elegant, octagonal timber box with a pitched roof and a door. But then it was decided that it would be difficult for the traveller to see where he had landed, and that that might lead to problems. The inclusion of small glass panels, a *window* – was discussed but then rejected as it might easily be broken, possibly dangerously."

"Glass!" Alex looked up from his notepad.

"Certainly," Tom looked astonished. "After all, the stuff had been around since the time of Sumerians – 3000 BC."

Tom went straight on. "Regardless, the idea of a wooden box moving through time and space seemed absolutely preposterous, so this idea was also shelved. Finally, the one form everyone agreed on was one nearest to the Greek's own hearts, and, in the modern tradition, its form became dictated by its function – a horse!"

Tom smiled to himself. "While Kyrros was still in his forties, he roughly sketched out the design on a small sheet of papyrus. The diagrammatical representation showed both its outline and some of its internal details. He then re-drew the whole machine in just ten days – and several nights. It was a much stylised horse, of course, and strictly speaking only the size of a small pony, although its body was elongated for stability. Four, shortened and slightly splayed legs – still relatively slender – carried the mass of not only the machine but its rider. A deep chest, extending toward the ground, encased the Power-key and flywheel. The rounded buttocks of the horse provided a perfect position for the Cosmos-key. The structural body was itself the frame, the exo-skeleton delicately pierced throughout in a stylistically designed interpretation of the imagined web of time and space fissures that it would be built to travel through. It would also both reduce the machine's weight and allow visual inspection and cooling of its working parts without necessarily having to open the various assembly hatches and inspection panels, although there were still several of those incorporated into the design. Also, into the main assembly hatch on top of its back was incorporated a quilted saddle. Thoughtfully, it was made from only the softest hide.

And finally came the stylised head and neck containing the Chrono-key, complete with more controls and mechanical indicators. Regarding Aesthetics, Kyrros styled its head on the many tiny ancient horse sculptures found throughout Greece. They all had a common feature – long trumpet shaped muzzles. It also had two matching features for pure decoration: on the top of its head sat a neatly clipped tuft of red bristle – its mane – and trailing from its rounded back end was a short, plaited red tail.

A handsome, or rather ugly beast – depending on the eye of the beholder – it was to be sculpted entirely in bronze, as were many of the gear wheels and other working parts. Only the various springs and the gear spindles and axles were to be fabricated, or made, in blue steel, as were the many long 'tendons' that were the internal linkages – designed to connect the working parts of the whole machine. These would ensure that everything would work together in perfect mechanical precision and sequence." Tom paused, wondering whether to share a last snippet of information. *Should he...?*

"Actually," Tom pursed his lips exaggeratedly, "come to think of it, there was one other mobility feature that the engineer had designed-in. Each of the horse's hooves contained a retractable castor so that it could be manoeuvred easily. They were deployed via a single lever that hung down from the animal's underside..." he coughed delicately "...between its rear legs. "Kyrros cleverly incorporated the design of this lever into what used to be known as its *pizzle!* For safety, a spherical shaped lock kept it up in place with a deft twist of the wrist." He demonstrated – his hand outstretched in the air. The boys' hands subconsciously dropped to their laps, while the girls smirked. Tom's face did not betray a thing. No one but he spoke. "It was, after all, a perfectly sensible place to keep the delicate instrument – out of harm's way.

Nearly two hundred years after its possibility was first imagined, and after being developed by all of those generations of experts, the machine began to be manufactured and assembled – still, incredibly, in complete sworn secrecy. The head librarian, being one of the leading 'theoretical' Chronology Society members, ensured that every part of that secret was kept. What was more, he always provided a plausible excuse for any of the Royal Family, or anyone else for that matter, as to what the actual work in the workshops represented. 'Time keeping and astronomical devices,' became the stock excuse.

In fact, following one particular close shave, in Kyrros' absence, when the king's son – who would one day become Ptolemy XIII – had dropped in suddenly one day, the librarian even authorised an extra armillary and time-computer to be made, though they were similar, but rudimentary versions. They were confidentially given directly to the boy himself just to back up the story; not that the librarian ever told Kyrros about the incident – he was not about to admit to the engineer that his security measures had very nearly been breached!

Then, as the machine came together, other conversations that had been held centuries earlier began to resurface."

Tom looked at the now fully attentive faces, wondering whether to risk boring them with this new detail. "Stop me if this becomes too tedious," he warned, "but I would also like to tell you about some of these... worries." He continued simply, "Yes? It is important!"

No one registered a complaint.

"From the earliest time, the 'moral and ethical' debate surrounding any question of changing the sequence of time, either deliberately or accidentally, had been conducted with some vigour. Usually, this happened late in the evenings around the dinner table. Whether or not it would be right to change the past was one question often revisited. No matter how well intentioned, by doing so, future 'history' might be changed – possibly cataclysmically. Firstly, in this respect, and possibly for the first time ever, the 'Autonomy Principle', or what has how become known as the 'Grandfather Paradox' was voiced. "I will explain:

Say a man travelled to the past and for some reason, possibly accidentally, met his grandfather and told him that he was his grandson who had travelled through time to see him. Say also that this grandfather spoke to his fiancé at the time, who would eventually be the grandmother of the boy and he told her the tale.

Say then, because she feared for the sanity of her betrothed, that she refused to marry him and bare his children – the traveller's own mother or father. As a result, if the traveller could therefore not be born, would he cease to exist now or in the future? Would he 'fade away'? And if so, how could any of these scenarios then have taken place to begin with? It would be a paradox!

Secondly, following on from this, what if the traveller accidentally changed a detail that could result in a change of history? saved the life, for example of a small, perhaps drowning child, who might grow up to become the one person who could change the tide of a world event – say an established and past battle.

Thirdly, say someone journeyed to the past and met himself. Two versions of the same person could not exist surely. What then might happen, how would that situation resolve itself? No one knew and no one could know; except if it ever happened and that would potentially be too late.

These dangers were all too obvious! Strict rules would have to be set to ensure this could never happen. It was as a result of these discussions that precautions and rules were agreed and put in place:

Firstly, it was solemnly agreed that the device could never be used for personal gain of any description. No one would ever visit the future and be able to bring back advanced knowledge, or anything else, to their own time.

But then, stealth being the most obvious precaution, the second rule was never, never be seen either 'entering' or 'leaving' a time and place.

Thirdly, never, never, never intervene in anything witnessed.

And fourthly, no matter what, never, never, never, never get personally involved in any way, shape or form and therefore risk causing any form of the paradoxes already mentioned. In short, always keep a very low profile, don't interfere, and bring back nothing! You understand this, yes?"

Everyone nodded. "Yeah," "yes," "mmm," "sure," they variously agreed.

"As these rules were developed, someone later suggested that,

218

as a fifth rule and a further precaution, no date should ever be revisited twice. The traveller's accidental meeting with himself could prove too complicated to ever unravel. A banned period of twenty-four hours either side of any date previously visited must therefore always be strictly adhered to. These sensible precautions were intended for the good of all.

The rules agreed, the completion of the project took a further three years from the time that Kyrros had first drawn the design of the horse, during which he journeyed back and forth to Alexandria, though only when necessary – he was a very bad sea traveller. Usually, this was to visit his beloved Rhodos, or Athens, or to discuss the supposed progress of his other work, which, to be fair, had begun to suffer badly – especially toward the very end of the secret project. In fact, despite being given the commission on the Tinos sundial over a year ago, he had not even started it. Diplomatically however, he persuaded even the Roman governor of Tinos that both 'time and tide' would indeed have to wait for this man. What choice did the governor have? After all, the wait, they were certain, would be worth it. Such was the charisma of the great philosopher and genius.

During these absences, Kyrros' place was usually taken by another quite senior and quite literally colourful philosopher who had shared many of the same interests throughout his own career. Once nicknamed 'the athlete', Poseidonios of Rhodos claimed that in his youth he had explored most of the world. Certainly, his dress reflected this. He frequently wore the longest, brightest coloured wraps across his back, though, eccentrically covering both shoulders. This 'kilt' as he called it was then pulled between his legs and looped through a belt. It was an affectation he had picked up in cold places of the globe. He further claimed to have mapped most of the world. However, it was now because of his advancing age that he was desperate to see the machine work before his own time had a chance to run out. As the various key parts came into being, it was he who personally tested each individually, going to great lengths to prove their accuracy. Despite now having a personal

phobia of sea travel, it was he who took it upon himself to travel –
on land, wherever possible – to the furthest parts of the
Mediterranean and beyond, to test both the prototype Cosmos-key,
and the prototype Chrono-key, before they could be copied into
the final or 'production versions'.

However, this testing was not without real risk; the seas were
not always safe. In fact on one obscure but treacherously rocky
island to the south of Porphyrusa – the island of purple – as they
struggled to find a place to land safely, the ship he'd been travelling
on had been chased and almost captured by pirates. It was only the
philosopher's expert knowledge of the area that saved them; he
insisted that the master beach the vessel in a hidden pebbled cove,
beside a tiny temple!

Eventually however, the testing complete, final assembly took
place and the finished machine stood in the place to where it had
been especially brought: the small, concealed inner chamber of the
Great Library itself."

Alex smiled to himself, relieved. They were finally getting
somewhere. This had been a long and sometimes tedious part of
the story. But now, all of that detail had, by the expressions around
the room, managed to persuade the others to believe or at least
consider believing that Tom really did know what he was talking
about. The explanation of the event that he had been leading up to
was not going to be explained by 'magic', neither was it a spiritual
event – a 'miracle' etc. The machine, and therefore the whole story,
was indeed based on ancient principles known to the Greeks.

All of the sciences and technologies described so far had, for
hundreds or thousands of years, been lost to man. But now, finally,
in the twenty-first century AD, and with the introduction of the
World Wide Web in particular, these pieces of ancient knowledge
were beginning to be rediscovered.

CHAPTER 24:

Testing

Tom breathed deeply before going on. "For a full week, everything had been prepared: all moving parts oiled where necessary and all linkages adjusted. The spring motors had been wound fully, taking an hour's hard work to push the retractable foot pedals around and around. The target place and time had been set almost on a whim. But Kyrros, knowing the island from his youth, knew that the marble square outside the Temple of Helios on the island of Rhodos had been there for many hundreds of years. It would therefore provide a good flat 'landing' place for him and the machine. As for the timing – the night before the legendary eclipse – it was simply something he'd always been curious about and keen to prove, and now he had an opportunity to witness it for himself. Although he would only leave the present time-zone for one hour, he would, according to his own theory, be in the other time zone for a full day.

He would land, everyone agreed, completely silently and in the dead of night. At that time no one would be around in this ancient non-residential area. He would then have time to deploy the internal castors and push the time-machine somewhere under cover. He would watch and take note, without interference, for a twenty-four hour period. Then, precisely an hour from the time he'd originally left, he would return home to give his report. How much more complicated could it possibly be?

The mood in the hidden chamber that late morning was electric.

Oil lamps had been lit and placed in the many niches around the room, not only to allow any last minute adjustments to be made, but also to increase, in a small way, the sense of occasion. Though the great majority of the people who had worked on various parts of the machine had been and would remain unaware of the true nature of the project, there were ten people – all men – who did know. That morning, all ten, including Kyrros' most trusted technician, were assembled around the room, waiting in eager anticipation of the moment they had worked steadily toward all their lives. In addition to the ten, there was of course one other person: the project leader's personally invited guest, Miriam. All, except Kyrros – who had specifically asked them not to draw attention to themselves by wearing anything unusual – wore their best ceremonial gowns.

Miriam in particular had raised the eyebrows of many of them when she arrived elegantly dressed in her best *peplos* – a heavy, full length dress – and her hair tied up with a thin hair band – a *strophion*. They had always been used to seeing her dressed only in her rather masculine library uniform of unbleached white cotton – the same as their own. None had ever seen her properly dressed in any of her own clothes. It was a revelation to them, how their former colleague could look when the occasion permitted.

'Kyrros,' it was Miriam who spoke to him as he climbed onto the prototype machine, watchful not to trip on his own long robes. 'Be careful,' she said cautiously, perhaps with a hint of something more than just friendship. 'Don't forget your way back.' She smiled directly at him for the first time.

The ever so slightly worried look on his face told the real story of what he was thinking about the adventure. Nevertheless, he said, 'Don't worry; I will be back in precisely one hour, as arranged.'

'Kyrros,' one of the older men who had collected around the horse spoke up. 'If we don't see you again, what shall we give as the name of the horse you rode away on?' he joked. 'You never did give him a proper name.'

'Is it Bucephalus?' someone suggested referring to the famous horse of Alexander the Great. Meaning 'beautiful-head', it was hardly appropriate.

'My horse already has a name,' he replied: 'The Chrono-Cosmological-Fissure-Tracking-Machine,' he said straight-faced.

'But that's not a name, it's a title,' objected Miriam, 'and everyone must have a name.'

'Every *thing*,' he corrected, looking down at her. He really hadn't thought of her before now as, well...?

'Then what about Pegasus?' someone shouted.

'Certainly not! I will have no gods taking the credit for this work of man. Alright then,' he conceded, 'if you must have a name,' he selected the two appropriate Greek words, 'call it the "Hippo-Chronos",' the Time-Horse!

'Call *him*,' corrected Miriam. 'Although it is still not a proper name.'

Kyrros smiled at her persistence, now wishing to see her again when he returned. Butterflies gathered in his stomach as he neared the point of no return.

'Wait!' another said, coming forward. 'You've missed a bit,' he stood at the head and pretended to polish it, while the others chuckled – as if it wasn't already gleaming like a mirror.

Now the most senior man of all: Poseidonios, walked steadily toward Kyrros. 'Take care,' he said seriously, 'the world can be a dangerous place.' Then, handing him what appeared to be a long spiralling walking stick, he cautioned Kyrros: 'Here, take this, it is surprisingly useful. It has accompanied me all around the globe. Carry it in case you are attacked. It has a stout, bronze ball on the end – but don't lose it, it belonged to my prize bull.'

Smiling, touched by these last minute demonstrations of care from people he had long ago realised were not just work colleagues but true friends, Kyrros took the bull's pizzle in his right hand and sat up in the saddle. 'I will look after it,' he said. 'Thank you.' The time was moving on. It was almost exactly midday. 'I will see you all soon, in one hour – no more.'

With that, everyone stood back in a rough circle around the

newly named Hippo-Chronos that stood in the centre of the chamber. Then Kyrros pushed one of the two motor-release levers that controlled the machine's stored kinetic energy. The culmination of his life's work was about to be put to the test.

Very, very gradually, almost imperceptibly at first, one of the great blue coil springs was released from the locking mechanism and allowed to begin to unwind. This caused a few of the gears nearest to it to move around slowly and silently. Within moments, other, bigger wheels moved, powering the single, heavy flywheel within the Hippo-Chronos' chest. In turn, this crawled, before slowly picking up speed. As it did, a band of silk cloth which was bound around its rim rubbed against the hundreds of short bars of amber. A bright ring of blue sparks flowed steadily around the wheel until the ring of static electricity built up more and more. Soft whirring sounds began as other mechanisms began to move. Then, before long, those sounds became louder as they changed into a steady drone.

The machine began to vibrate steadily as its internal mechanisms began to accelerate. Now the noise was incredible. Wind from the whirring gears began to channel through the twin vents on opposite sides of its muzzle – its nostrils. As it did, the machine began to rock from side to side. Worried looks from the small assembly around the Hippo-Chronos grew as it lifted briefly. The machine wobbled unsteadily onto its rear legs, causing Kyrros to shift his weight forward in an attempt to balance it. If something began to go seriously wrong, he could always abort the test by pulling back the control lever. But this would undoubtedly cause untold damage at this stage. *No, better to ride out the discomfort*, he thought. When the motor reached its full power, the full charge of static energy would automatically be distributed through the Power-key and straight into the Burst Initiator to produce this long mused over negative energy. Only then, after generations of speculation – and forty of his own fifty-eight years – would everyone finally know if it had all been worthwhile.

The whirring grew and the draught caused by it pushed through the web-like structure of the frame, blowing Kyrros' white garments around him. The noise was growing louder by the second. It was now almost deafening as he looked around. His friends covered their ears in pain. It was a whine the like of which no one had ever heard before; the scream of a tortured metal animal – the scream of the Hippo-Chronos itself.

A thousand gears and drive-wheels all began to whir around faster and faster. Then, mysteriously, Kyrros ceased to hear anything at all. For a brief moment he existed in a world of complete silence. He looked around himself as a breeze seemed to blow into the faces of the others. Then there was a sudden, silent gust of wind that seemed to simultaneously blow out all but a few of the fluttering lamps. It knocked everyone slowly backwards and over to the ground. Next, as he struggled to hold onto the lever with his left hand, still gripping the spiral stick in his right, he was enveloped totally, silently, in an intense blue-white light. He seemed to hover slightly off the ground, but not for long, perhaps only a few seconds. Finally, the light was dimmed and he felt the bump of the machine coming back into contact with the solid earth.

As the horse touched down, Kyrros looked at the back of its head and to the etched thumb wheels – the succession of barrels which were the only visible indication that the machine's journey through time and distance was complete. But there was still a screaming in his ears; though not mechanical, this time, it was human!

He looked up and around him, astonished. It had obviously worked in regard to location: he was in Rhodos – he recognised the Temple of Apollo – the old Temple of Zeus – behind him. But that was not where he was supposed to be. He was supposed to be to his left-hand side, outside the old wooden Temple of Helios. However, that was not the major problem. For some reason, instead of a deserted and pitch black square, he found himself in a torch-lit square, surrounded by one of the biggest crowds he'd ever seen in his life. Screaming faces stared back at him as if he was in a dream. They backed away from him in horror.

He looked all around now, starting to panic, wondering what to do. Should he throw the second control lever and release the second, return spring immediately? Or should he attempt to dismount and explain who he was and where he'd come from. Obviously, he could not just sit there.

Everything seemed to move so slowly around him, as if his own body was still moving at an accelerated pace to his surroundings. None of this had been part of his expectation. Then, directly in front of him, he saw a priest. At least he assumed he was a priest from his archaic and ostentatious garb of gold and purple. It was certainly someone of high standing; only fabulously rich or well connected Romans could afford to wear the colour in his own time. But it was what the priest was doing that caused his immediate horror and disgust. He had by the hair a badly beaten and blood soaked boy. The boy was obviously about to be sacrificed by having his throat cut at the altar of Zeus. What barbarians his ancestors were; no one had remembered or heard of this before.

With one glance, Kyrros took immediate stock of the situation and decided exactly what to do. Climbing down slowly, in case anyone was thinking of coming near him, he wielded the spiral stick about his head. He seemed to float slowly across the square toward the pair. As the wiry priest recoiled from him at the sight of his approach, letting go of the boy on the altar, Kyrros swooped to pick him up. He stared the priest down, who now fell to his knees and scrabbled behind the altar. Then the rescuer turned and walked calmly back to the Hippo-Chronos with the boy.

With a last, withering look of admonishment to the entire crowd, he climbed up onto the machine and released the return lever. The same sequence that he'd experienced earlier began again, taking a minute to build up the speed of the machine. But this time, with the boy in front and he at the back, the load shifted rearwards.

For a moment, the front of the machine lifted high in the air, balancing precariously on its back legs. This caused Kyrros to thrust his free hand – the hand that held the spiral stick – forward into the air, to balance the horse before it settled again. As he looked around him and across at the square in front of the Temple of Helios, the last thing Kyrros saw before the light enveloped him, were two clearly delighted faces.

One was the cheering face of a colourfully dressed and stockily built man who was standing on the corner of the square. And across the way, beside a curiously dished block of marble, there was a young black girl wrapped loosely in a similarly colourful gown. She was jumping up and down in celebration. Then the horse disappeared from view."

Tom looked around him. "All of the cautions and promises – the need to keep a low profile – to never interfere – no matter what – all of those well considered plans were trashed in what was only a few minutes to Kyrros, but a full day to his friends in Alexandria. And for one of the most laudable and valuable reasons in the world – the preservation of human life – the delicate structure and the sequences of time had been inadvertently but permanently altered, triggering important time-paradoxes that could never, ever be undone. Not even with all the time in the world at the engineer's command!"

CHAPTER 25:

Kyrros' Machine

Slowly the mid-afternoon sunshine crept through the roof-light of Tom's house and began to pass through the gaping hole above the dustsheet covered lump. As if by design, the patch of light began to highlight it, now drawing attention to it. Alex didn't seem to notice; he continued to scribble down his notes.

Tom picked up his glass and took a long drink. Still clutching it, he looked lost, forlorn, in a world of his own, as if the retelling of the story had reopened an old wound.

Maddie felt suddenly quite sorry for him, though she wasn't sure exactly why. Clearly, at least he believed his own story and it had begun to have an effect on his mood. She glanced at the dustsheet, wondering.

Bex twisted around to look first at Maddie, then followed her sister's eyes to the lump. She stared long and hard, longing to take a look beneath the dust cover.

Conna looked around at the others, trying to judge by their expressions whether they believed this part of the story; for the first time wanting to believe Tom himself. Not knowing what was beneath the cover was beginning to frustrate him.

Neither Alex nor anyone else spoke.

Tom saw each of them looking. Maybe it *was* time to give them something to grasp physically. After all, it might help. Regardless, it was time for him to now take a leap of faith and trust his invited guests. When the boy had finished taking notes,

Tom offered, "Al-lex, perhaps it is time for you and your friends to take a look at the machine we have been discussing all this time."

Alex's eyes lit up.

Still no one else spoke.

"Of course," Tom offered, "I understand your reticence to believe all of what I have told you – in fact any of it for that matter." He looked around again at the expressionless faces, "But now I will show you the vehicle that made this all possible: Kyrros' Hippo-Chronos." He got up carefully and walked to the head of the covered machine. "Please... Alex, might you lend me a hand?"

"Sure, Tom," Alex readily agreed, as he stood up, longing to see for himself. Boris hopped down to let him stand, and, one by one, each of them stood to gather around the lump.

"Conna... Maddie... Bex," asked Tom, "please could you move the piles of books for me?" *This is it*, thought everyone in the room. *At long last they would all get to see what the fuss was about. The object that Tom claimed the ancients had designed and built two thousand years ago!*

Conna and the three girls stood together in a row. Then, trying not to be too theatrical, Tom and Alex ceremoniously flipped back the cover with a flourish. Along with it, a thick pall of dust flew into the air. Everyone stepped back automatically, choking briefly. After a few moments, as the dust began to clear, all eyes quickly scanned the mysterious lump. Whatever each had imagined – a polished, perhaps even a frightening horse-shaped machine – maybe looking somewhat ancient, this was not it. Instead, what each of them saw could only be described as a complete anticlimax.

Alex and his friends' first impression was of a rather small, broken animal, covered all over with thick plaster dust. Perhaps a horse – but if it was, it was a much stylised horse. Its strange, balding head was more or less as described: heavily sculpted into a kind of trumpet-shaped muzzle; on top of its cranium, pink bristles jutted up in a sad tuft which looked like a well worn broom – the remnant of its mane? It looked thick with dandruff. The black holes that were it eyes looked dead. Bizarrely, as Tom smoothed the dust away from the end of its flattened muzzle, he revealed a comic smile daubed on it in thick white paint.

The battered body was indeed peppered with holes, arranged in the web-like pattern that Tom had described. But the most striking feature was that it did not have legs. Instead, they had been roughly sawn off at the knees, and the whole external skeleton lay within the crude wooden chassis that Alex had helped Tom to make, the two main horizontal timbers of which lay to either side, sticking out in front and behind like collapsed legs. There was only a wispy looking pink rope where a tail should be.

The look of bitter disappointment on Alex's face could not have been more apparent. His friends were equally devastated after the whole, incredible build up.

Tom smiled triumphantly at them all as he wiped his hand over the back of the sculpture, scattering more dust. "Well, what do you think?" He asked proudly.

Alex was devastated – dumbstruck!

Bex was similarly silent.

Maddie tried to be positive. "It's smaller than I thought," she offered.

"Perhaps," conceded Tom.

Conna twisted his mouth. "Where are its legs?" he asked.

Tom coughed, clearing his throat. "Unfortunately, although the Hippo-Chronos has been used only a handful of times before – three of those being return journeys – over the years, its shapely legs became increasingly more damaged. Sadly, I had no choice other than to remove them," he explained. "But anyway, now it is more stable – and that was always a previous design fault." Tom saw the look on Alex's face. He smiled again, knowing what was going through his mind. "Don't worry, Alex, come closer; give it a chance." With that, he beckoned them all closer to examine the specimen in detail.

The bright sunlight that streamed in through the hole in the floor above, now strained through the thinning cloud of airborne dust which hung in the room as a fog. As they looked on, shafts of filtered light played weakly over the back of the machine and its dried, cracked leather saddle. Sunlight occasionally darted inside it through its perforated, almost rust-coloured frame, and as Tom smoothed-off more of the dust, the object's complexity became clearer and clearer to them. Again, each noticed, there was something of the steampunk style about it in the tiny working details. Alex had never seen the like of it before; *ancient technopunk* is how he now began to think of it. He looked at Tom's face and back down at the object. For all the dishevelled state it was in, it was nevertheless, he had to admit, a remarkable sight. He looked again. Then, one at a time, they all began to pace around it in silence, looking for clues to what it *really* was.

The small dust clouds slowly continued to settle, allowing occasional stronger shafts of light to pierce the horse's form. With it, delicate hand-scrolled patterns covering the whole surface were revealed; the carved indentations began to glitter as the sunlight flitted over the surface. However, it was now what had suddenly become visible through the 'rib-cage' that began to fascinate them. A single, flickering shaft of pure white light had managed to penetrate deep inside the machine for a moment, arbitrarily highlighting what were clearly highly intricate gears. There were also springs and other purposeful looking engineering mechanisms jam-packed throughout the whole body of the horse. But it was one thing in particular that really grabbed Alex's attention; his jaw now dropped and his eyes became alive as the light reached the chest of 'the beast', as he had begun to think of it.

There, amongst the other gadgetry, but still clearly visible beneath the 'breast-bone', lying vertically in line with its 'spine' was the reflected glint from a massive flywheel, its circumference surrounded by bars of amber. On each side of it was a closely coiled blue steel 'watch-spring'. Also dotted throughout the rest of the body, what were obviously small but bright ruby-red jewelled-bearings. Alex began to get goose bumps. He could feel the hairs on the back of his neck actually begin to stand up, a sensation he had only heard of before now. On closer examination, to him, this battered, horse-shaped machine was nothing less than the most fantastical clockwork mechanism that he could have imagined in his wildest dreams. Slowly he began to concede that this might be the machine in Tom's story – exactly as described.

At the same time, Conna narrowed his eyes and walked slowly around to the horse's side then its head. Its dead 'eyes' began to draw his imagination. He certainly couldn't stop looking at the strange object and especially the bejewelled bits around it. It reminded him of something... What was it?... Suddenly – it struck him; that was it, it was like a massive version of Alex dad's watch!

Looking through the latticed sides of the horse's buttocks, Maddie could clearly see a perforated ball, in what appeared to be the now familiar metal representation of the universe. The whole machine also reminded her of something, but what?...

Lastly, Bex, arms folded, looked curiously at the strange eyes and muzzle, but she more closely examined the expressions on the faces surrounding her.

Now, in turn, each truly began to appreciate the mechanical marvel in front of them. However, the true purpose of the machine, in the absence of any visual clues, would have been quite obscure had Tom not already suggested it.

Tom stood proudly upright, his hand white with dust. He stroked the remaining bristles of the horse's head and repeated his earlier question to Alex in particular. "So, what do you think?" He grinned broadly, now completely relaxed for the first time that Alex had ever witnessed. The boy was truly dumbfounded. He stood back from both the machine and Tom, trying to think of something to say that wasn't the obvious question. "Come along, Alex, tell me – what *do* you think?" Tom pushed.

Trying hard not to give up his scepticism just yet and looking for something which might betray another purpose, Alex returned to the head of the machine. Through the black eye-sockets, the boy glimpsed the outline of something he thought he recognised: one of Tom's experimental gadgets. He raised his eyes at the others, before peering inside to check, cupping his hands tight around his eyes. Where a brain should be, he saw... what was it? a dial with several hands... a carriage clock? His face dropped. Surely it wasn't what he thought. He might be able to identify it, if only he could just make out more of the detail.

As the sunlight continued to dart across the machine, the inside of the cranium was suddenly illuminated. It was just for a split second, but it had been long enough for him to see it properly! Alex stepped back, startled. He confirmed what it was immediately from the replica that sat on the bench... the Antikythera Device! He was immediately filled with a mixture of both panic and excitement, not knowing whether to believe his own eyes.

His friends looked on, equally fascinated, though in contrast to Alex, seeing only a vastly complex machine. All over it they could make out small dents and scratches – perhaps scars from its history – evidence of where it might have fallen or been mistreated. And, looking inside it, just as described were all sorts of complicated workings that none of them actually – that is to say really – understood. Except, that is, that they closely resembled some of the demonstration mechanisms they'd already been shown at Tom's bench!

Alex glanced at each of his friends in turn, trying not to get carried away. *What was the purpose of the beast?* he wondered still, *if it was not what Tom had told them.* Was it all just a larger version of one of the mechanical computers Tom had mentioned? Surely not. Why would anyone make a whole computer in the shape of a horse? It didn't make sense. Some bizarre form of transport then – possibly! A clockwork horse: an automaton. But as Alex studied it, it was clear that there were no obvious major moving parts. The head, neck, body and what were left of the legs were all part of the same skeletal fretwork. He looked back at Tom, his own mouth still open. Tom still wore his grin, delighted now to see the look of awe and wonderment on the boy's face.

Alex gave up. "What is it?" he gasped through the dust, realising that he already knew. Surely it couldn't really be... Tom couldn't have been telling the truth all along, could he? Not wanting Tom to answer – in case he told him it was all an elaborate hoax – he heard himself say, "What does it really do, Tom?"

The old man spoke gently: "But you all *know* what it does," he nodded his head gravely, "don't you!" He walked over to where Alex stood and placed his hand directly on his shoulder. "Now do you believe me?"

As if Tom's touch had been the cause of it, the boy seemed to crumple onto the sofa, too traumatised to speak. Now, as if Alex could ever forget the name, Tom introduced everyone in the room formally. Warmly he announced, "Alex... Conna... Maddie... Bex – this is the machine which Kyrros built in ancient Alexandria. Please, help me, so that between us," he said enigmatically, "we can avert the great catastrophe which was caused in the past – *before* it has time to happen!"

Pausing briefly to let the thought sink in, he inhaled dramatically. Focussing once again on Alex, he smiled. "*This,* is the most incredible machine that has ever been created by man. This, Alex... is the Hippo-Chronos!"

The four friends looked at Tom in dead silence, before eventually, Alex spoke. "What exactly do you want us to do, Tom?"

Tom looked at them all. "Sadly, as you can all see, the whole machine needs to be stripped down, cleaned and rebuilt if it is ever to work again. It must be cleared of any contamination that might clog its delicate workings; that happened once before – disastrously! Quite evidently, it will be very difficult for me do it all alone, with only one uninjured arm. I propose instead that over the next few days we all work jointly on the task – don't worry, I will instruct and guide you."

Alex spoke for them all. "We can do that, can't we?"

"Abso-flippin-lutely," smirked Conna, finally mastering the art of not swearing.

"Okay," agreed Maddie simply.

"Well… alright," Bex went along with the rest of them.

At that, Boris, now bored, trotted over and lay stretched out full length in front of the machine, his upright head facing in the same direction. "That's it," cried Maddie, looking at the trumpet-shaped muzzle and the wooden carrying handles sticking out in front and behind. "That's what it reminds me of – Boris!"

Nervously, they gave a short laugh, smiling curiously at the quite correct parallel. It did indeed resemble the Bedlington Terrier lying beside it.

Tom smiled again and gave them a few more minutes to explore the machine, then suggested, "Now, perhaps we'd better make a start." Slowly and methodically, the task began.

By mid-evening, the whole thing was stripped down, the various complicated components laid out neatly across the blanket placed on the floor for the purpose. Tom saw Conna's head nod as the boy waited for the next task. "That," declared the taskmaster, "is enough for today. It's getting late and I'm sure your parents will wonder when you are coming home."

Conna's eyes opened wide, blinking. "No, that's okay, we're fine," he declared, looking google-eyed around him.

Maddie had started to yawn and even Alex was beginning to flag.

"No," said Tom, "I think it would be best to stop now. We will continue in the morning – if you wish. You can help me clean the individual parts tomorrow; we'll take a midday break from the rest of the tale. A couple of hours each day should do it."

Maddie looked at her watch. Tom was right, it was nine o'clock and their dad would be there any moment to pick them up. "Perhaps it would be best if we come back tomorrow then?" she suggested.

"Yes," agreed the others, even though they were quite enjoying the task so far after all.

"Ten o'clock then, after breakfast," suggested Tom. "It will give us all time to reflect."

"Okay," they all agreed jointly. "Then ten o'clock tomorrow it is!"

Time to reflect was one way of putting it. Individually, each of them now planned to check or at least discuss this as much as they could before coming back. Even if it meant getting out of bed very early in the morning, holiday or not.

That night, Alex assumed correctly that his mum had decided to have an early night. He and Boris crept in the back door so as not to disturb either her or Rachel. The dog immediately wolfed down the contents of his bowl, while Alex grabbed an apple for supper instead of warming up the meal his mother had left for him. Once again he borrowed his mum's laptop from the table and went straight to his room.

Admittedly, the story he wanted to believe was the literal one that Tom was busy telling them all now, though now alone again, he still couldn't commit himself. He booted up the laptop and 'Googled' his way, in no particular order, through the list of key words and phrases he'd collected from Tom's story, intending to tick them off as he went. Instantly, the results started to come back. Starting with *'solar eclipse of 585 BC... predicted by Thales of Miletus... interrupted battle between Lydians and Medes... visible throughout the eastern Mediterranean...* it was all there – four key points at once! It wasn't absolute proof that Tom was telling the truth of course, but there were a lot of verifiable facts that proved that at least the story had some historical substance. Alex could at least hope, couldn't he?

In their own home, the girls talked to their parents about their concerns. Their mother listened attentively from her wheelchair as they recalled some of the day's events which involved Tom. Neither one wished to drop Tom in it, nor did they – now instinctively protective of the old man – but each was concerned about him. After saying as much, between them, they then dutifully checked their assigned portion of Alex's list. Alarmingly, it seemed like Tom's detailed historical version of events seemed most probable – and that, in turn, was most disconcerting.

In bed that night, Tom dreamed the same dream he'd had for

the past year. He lay motionless in the dark as a leaping bronze horse and rider – a small boy – seemed to hover silently past him. Reluctantly, he watched it float into the distance.

Time, it seemed, was passing him by. He turned painfully onto his side and slept only fleetingly, until dawn.

PART IV:

NEVER LOOK BACK

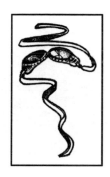

LET'S NOT BURDEN OUR REMEMBRANCE

WITH A HEAVINESS THAT'S GONE

William Shakespeare 16th Cent AD

CHAPTER 26:

Sensational!

Day Two of Tom's story

Just as they had arranged outside Tom's house the night before, now at nine-thirty the next morning, Maddie and Bex knocked at the back door of Alex's house to meet there for breakfast. Alex's mum, busying herself with the baby, called out her hellos to them from the lounge as they arrived. In the kitchen Alex prepared a simple breakfast, a huge pile of toasted teacakes and a similarly huge jug of fresh orange juice.

Alex poured them all a glass of juice while they chatted, waiting for Conna. It was unusual of him to be late, he was normally the most punctual of all of them, but at twenty to ten they were still waiting. Then at last there was the knock, and Alex opened the front door to him. No doubt Tom would now guess that they were having a 'secret meeting' before going into his house. *Too late now*, Alex thought, so saying nothing, he led Conna into the kitchen. "You might want to pop up and wash your ear first," said Alex, "it's black with dirt."

Conna reached up and touched it gingerly. "Nah, it's just a bruise." He winced. "I must've caught it – probably when we were practicing with the ball, remember?"

Alex frowned but didn't reply.

"Whoa! Frank Cooper's Marmalade – just like mum's," Conna almost shouted.

"So what do we think?" asked Maddie, as Conna sat down with them.

"Well," began Alex, "I've checked loads of stuff that he told us yesterday," he said pulling out his own part of the list that last night they'd divided it into three.

"Sho've I," mumbled Conna through a mouthful of toast, reaching for his pocket.

"Conna please!" Bex complained, pulling a face and flicking off the bits that he'd sprayed at her clean tee shirt.

"Shorry," he sprayed again.

Alex looked sternly around the table. "Well the stuff I've checked certainly seems okay – in detail! Everything, from the date and exact time of the eclipse, the battle between the Lydians and the Medes; did you know that the battle was called off because of the eclipse? They both thought it was a sign from their various gods! And then there were the other things," he said enthusiastically. "The accounts of the temple machines," although, he conceded, "they were thought to be from a period much later."

"Yep," Maddie agreed. "Same with our part of the list: Murex shells – did you know that purple dye came only from the island of Porphyrusa – Aegilia's neighbouring island? And that the islands were renamed? They're called Kythera and Antikythera now!"

Conna finished swallowing and looked over to the others. "Well the bits I've checked out certainly seem to check out: Alexander and Ptolemy. It was all there – I'm telling you, the story checks out!"

"Look," suggested Bex, "no one doubts that – after all, he is a professor, isn't he!"

"And Cassiterite." Alex was getting a bit too excited, pushing too hard. "Did you know that was an ancient Phoenician name for tin ore and that Britain had been a major source of tin in pre-history – so it was most probably one of the fabled Cassiterides!"

"Yes... well, no ...look, that's not the point," Bex tried to reason. "No one's saying that that historical part of the story won't check out."

Conna instinctively backed her up: "Yeah, I suppose so, and with a bit of research I suppose anyone could tell a story like that.

And like Bex says, he is a professor after all. Anyway," he argued, "this isn't a TV programme or a movie, this is happening to all of us. Right here – right now in Tynemouth – England – planet Earth!"

"That's not what I meant," Bex tried to clear up the misunderstanding. "What I meant was, that's not the difficult part to believe."

"Really, then what is?" asked Conna sarcastically.

"Look," continued Bex, getting suddenly exasperated herself. "Let's just get this out in the open. Tom's saying that it was he who rescued the boy on this... time–spacebubble–crackpot-chaser-machine-type-thing."

"Chrono-Cosmological-Fissure-Tracking-Machine," corrected Alex unhelpfully. "And by the way, I don't think he's saying that at all..."

"Anyway, whatever," she continued unabated. "The thing is, time-travel's just not possible, is it?"

"I don't know," said Alex truthfully. "What if it is?"

As the others listened stone-faced, Alex outlined everything he had recently found out about the subject of time travel. From the many popular fictional stories that he had read or at least found out about during the past couple of weeks, going back to possibly the very first proper 'time travel' story ever written in 1838. It was about a Tyneside pilgrim falling asleep under a tree and waking up in the time of the venerable St. Bede, the earliest chronicler of England's past, who, coincidentally lived his life within the walls of the monastery just across the south bank of the Tyne at Jarrow. He went on to H G Wells' *The Time Machine* and various other Hollywood and TV blockbusters. From there he told his friends about the many and various scientific theories he'd read recently – some bizarre, some less so. "Try looking on the web for a start," he told them. Scientific institutions from all over the world, even NASA, have looked at various theories about the possibility of travelling through time – and there are loads!"

Maddie had been trying to defend Alex's point of view but even she couldn't accept that readily. "Alex, please. It's just impossible, everyone knows that."

"No, not everyone," he countered, "not everyone at all. Even scientists and professors; for instance Albert Einstein, Stephen Hawking and Michio Kaku couldn't dismiss the idea scientifically."

"Mickey O'Who?" asked Conna.

"Okay," admitted Maddie, "even if it's scientifically possible, you're not saying you believe that kind of nonsense are you?" She raised her eyebrows, remembering Alex's comments about ghost stories.

Alex cringed at the rebuke. However, he thought, *if some of the greatest thinkers in the world thought it might be theoretically possible, do I, a fourteen year old boy, think any of it might work? Why not – in theory of course!* But, instead of committing himself, he changed tack. "And another thing – you saw those weird sparks too, didn't you!"

"Yes," admitted Maddie, "but what's that got to do with it?"

"I don't know," admitted Alex. "It's just…"

"Look," interjected Conna, swilling his teacake down with the orange juice. "We're not getting anywhere like this. Let's just go and hear the rest of the tale," he proposed, "that's the only way anyone's going to finally see sense."

"And by anyone, you mean me?" Alex guessed, raising his eyebrows.

"At this time?" said Maddie. "Yes!" She arched her own eyebrows pointedly at Alex. "Sorry, Alex, I'd love to believe it all but at this moment in time I just can't." Then she borrowed a phrase from Tom: "It's a harsh truth – live with it!" When her hackles were up, even Maddie could get prickly.

The kitchen fell silent. Realistically, Alex wasn't bothered that much by their negativity. He had expected it from the beginning and he realised that Maddie was trying to be an ally. No matter, surely by the end of the week they would all have to come to the same conclusion one way or another. He looked up at the clock on the kitchen wall. "We'll have to go soon – if you still want to?"

"Okay," they conceded jointly, there was no use getting this far only to quit. So, not wishing to fall out, they all agreed to disagree for various reasons and finished the pile of toasted teacakes in the usual ratio: two for Alex, one for each of the girls, and four for Conna – rather than let them go to waste – who, to raised eyebrows, declared he'd never had the 'expensive' marmalade before then.

After clearing up, to get the dog out of his mum's hair, Alex shouted into the dining room where she was now catching up with the ironing, "Bye Mam, we're off. I'm taking Boris with me." At the mention of his name, the dog came skittering in from his basket in the living room, almost slipping over on the tiled kitchen floor to stand on his back legs pawing at the air like a meerkat.

"Come on then boy," said Maddie, clapping her hands twice – chancing her luck. Then they all smiled at each other and gave Boris a pat in turn, each in their usual way, before leaving for next door. Boris had a way of repairing strained friendships.

Knocking politely before letting themselves into Tom's house again, the girls went straight into the laboratory. Conna and Boris joined them within minutes. Before coming in himself, Alex went to seek Tom to make sure he was ready, or at least to see if he needed any assistance. Stupidly though, although he knocked on the half opened bathroom door, he didn't wait for a reply. Instead, he popped his head around the door to see if Tom was okay. Tom stood in a pair of boxer shorts, looking in the mirror, propping himself over the washbasin and breathing deeply. A clean crepe bandage was wound around his chest from high up under his arms and continuing down to just below his ribcage. Startled, he swivelled around to face Alex, nearly knocking the opened bottle of pills onto the floor. He looked at the boy uncomfortably and picked up a towel to throw around his neck. "I'll be there shortly," he said, then held his finger to his lips.

Alex nodded his agreement. "Okay, sorry..." he replied, bowing out quietly. "I'll just wait with the others." The fleeting glimpse he'd had of Tom's back in the mirror shocked him. Both above and below the crepe bandage, the skin looked badly scarred.

Returning to the main room, even if he wished to, Alex didn't have time to discuss what he had seen. Within moments, he was followed by Tom, who greeted them all cheerily and in the same way as yesterday. All, that is, except for Conna, who raised his hand in greeting – from the opposite side of the sofa.

The old man sat down in his chair, looking a little fitter today. The girls sat back on the sofa, also happier that it appeared things had returned to the previously enjoyed cheerful status-quo. The boys returned to their own places and Boris jumped back onto Alex's lap.

"To continue the story of how the disastrous paradox was begun then..." Tom started abruptly, "the first Lio knew of what had happened, was when he came around from his coma fourteen days later...

The boy lay on his stomach, in the most comfortable, though somewhat firm bed that he had ever slept in: a plain, warm, Egyptian cotton mattress stuffed with new smelling hay. His eyes covered with a cloth bandage of some kind, he was awoken by the sensation of a woman bathing the nape of his neck and his shoulders with a damp cloth. At first he was filled with a literally blind panic. Presumably caused by the extreme trauma from the grave situation he had escaped, all recollection of it, even his own name, had been temporarily blotted from his memory. In time, these memories would return, but only in stages. However, for now, a kind voice with a foreign tongue that he recognised as Hebrew comforted him.

She told him her name was Miriam, and between the boy's understanding of foreign languages and Miriam's own efforts – she spoke some Greek, although not his own ancient Rhodos dialect – she managed to communicate with him. Miriam reassured him that all danger was now been left behind – whatever danger that was – and that he was now in safe hands. Her work colleague Kyrros, she said, had examined his eyes when he'd been unconscious – he'd screamed out a couple of times that he couldn't see – and as a precaution he'd bandaged them. The boy sensed that his new surroundings, even the hot, dry, earthy smell, were different to the

246

cool, damp, sea air that he had been used to. He was told only that he was safe on a farm on the edge of a desert, at a place known then, for some unexplained reason, as the hill of Drodos.

Miriam also assured the boy that in time his memory would in all probability return, although secretly she was not so certain. Nevertheless, in the meantime she asked him if it would be acceptable to call him simply 'Boy', until it did return. It was a request to which he readily acceded. In fact, throughout that period of his life, Miriam became the closest the boy had ever had to a real mother and, as he later came to appreciate, a pleasant looking one at that. It turned out that they would grow close and that he would remember her with affection for all of his days."

Alex looked at Conna who, at Tom's emotional description of the boy's new mother, had rolled his eyes upward and given a "Huh!"

Miriam had been there to see him arrive at the Mouseion in Alexandria in a dreadful state. Even though the machine had arrived exactly twenty-three hours later than designated, and although some had already begun to give up hope, she had waited dutifully, but worriedly with most of the others. As the machine banged down heavily, she had caught the boy from Kyrros as he dismounted. Then she listened briefly to the man's account of what he had witnessed happening to him in the temple square.

She had listened further while he attempted to explain to everyone who had now hurriedly re-assembled in the chamber why he had flouted all of the rules rather than commit an even greater moral wrong by letting his barbaric sacrifice continue. However, it was instantly decided that rather than risk compromising the secret project entirely, the boy would immediately be smuggled out of the Mouseion and the Royal Palace grounds to be taken to the private inland residence of Kyrros himself.

Kyrros had been given the message that the patient was awake, and in turn the message came back that this mysterious figure, whom the boy could not at that time remotely recall, would visit as soon as he could. For weeks then, he awaited the man whom he had only been told had been his rescuer from a 'bad situation'. His subconscious had taken care of the trauma by blocking it from him – preventing him from returning there. In the meantime, his new-found mother pampered him as only a mother could. Unmarried and approaching an age where she could no longer expect to have children of her own, she almost perpetually fussed over him for the next few weeks – something the boy had previously been entirely unused to."

Again, Conna punctuated the story with a very personal snort, this time causing the girls in particular to look at him impatiently.

Tom continued. "Lio relished this new found attention, not that he was physically recovered by any means. His back was still very sore, and although he had slept through most of the pain and it had largely healed, in some respects the tight sensation of the newly growing skin on his back, stretching as it healed itself, worried him. This sensation was more disturbing than painful, in that it seemed to threaten that the new skin may split open again if he was not very careful, and lead to a recurrence of the unbearable pain that was the only memory that he could clearly recall.

In order to treat that damage then, being aware that his extremely light coloured skin would be likely to burn at any other time, both early in the morning and late in the afternoon, when the sun was just warm, the boy, still with his eyes bandaged, was led by the hand by Miriam. Outside the house, she encouraged him to lie face down on a pile of soft blankets, simply to bask in the healing warmth of the sun's rays. There, he enjoyed the free, luxurious and sensual gift from above, allowing it to repair his naked back. Then afterwards, he would be led by Miriam to sit inside while she waited on him hand and foot.

She delighted in bringing him the favourite food that he gradually, dimly recalled: fruit, as well as some most exotic and highly spiced Egyptian dishes, not unlike some of the Persian dishes that at that time he could not recall properly but for some reason knew he liked.

Life at that time then was truly sensational. But even after several weeks, other than the fact that Miriam had told him that he was now in Egypt, the boy was still quite oblivious to anything that had previously happened to him."

CHAPTER 27:

A Clean Slate

"After weeks of recovery, finally, one afternoon, Miriam awakened Lio from the nap that he had now become used to taking after lunch. She brought him the news that Kyrros, his 'saviour' had at long last arrived. He still had no real recollection of the events – or the man – other than as the dream-like figure in white that he had begun to vaguely recall scooping him up and carrying him off on horseback. Sitting on his bed and still wearing the bandages across his eyes, the boy listened intently to the soft footsteps entering the room. Still standing some distance away, Kyrros called out a greeting to the boy.

'How are you feeling?' he enquired sympathetically. His voice, even though he meant it to be soft, was still booming and commanding. Although at that time he could not recall it, he would later have no doubts that if Kyrros had called out during 'the rescue', it really would have sounded like the voice of Zeus himself.

'I am very well, thank you. Much better now,' the boy answered the voice respectfully.

The voice spoke to Miriam as the man lightly examined the back of the boy's neck. 'I am quite amazed that he has recovered. When I last saw him, I would have sworn that he would not last much longer. How did you manage to help him through?'

'I performed only the surgical procedures that I have been taught at the Mouseion,' she answered: 'To relieve the pressure in his cranium, using the twist drill. And I kept him sedated with some of the medicines that I learned to prepare. Everything else was brought about naturally: warmth; rest; and a little care and attention – something we all need in our lives occasionally.'

'Indeed...' said the voice readily, 'indeed it is. And your back,' he spoke to the rescued boy, 'does it still pain you?'

'A little,' he answered truthfully, adding, 'sometimes it hurts more at night.'

'Yes,' the man considered, 'Miriam has told me you sometimes cry out during the night.'

'Do I?' he asked. This was news to the boy; no one had mentioned it to him.

'Boy,' Kyrros said, following Miriam's example, 'you have had a dramatic escape from a great danger.'

'Yes,' he said, 'I know – I have been told.'

Kyrros continued as levelly as he could, 'There is no simple way of telling you this, so I will just have to say it. I myself carried you off from Rhodos and brought you here to Egypt on a machine that transported you...' he paused to emphasise the fact, '...through time itself!'

Still not thinking particularly clearly, the idea baffled the boy slightly. However, as he had no reason to disbelieve the voice, he was immediately comfortable with the idea. He was ten years old and, as any child of that time, quite unsophisticated in many ways. All he knew, or at that time cared about, was that at that moment he was warm and comfortable – although he had the pain from his back to remind him that something bad had happened to him. Miriam had pampered him for weeks, and, although the boy could not see him, he knew no reason not to trust the new voice of the man that he had been told had rescued him. Not remembering anything about his past life, he thought simply, *yes, I am entirely happy with the concept of travelling through time.* Why wouldn't he be? There was no denying the boy's simple logic – he was, after all, *here and now.*

'Now,' Kyrros continued, 'when I remove your bandages, your eyes will look upon a world over five hundred years after you were born. Do you understand?'

'Yes,' he answered simply, more eager to know whether he could see properly again than what he might see. So Kyrros moved toward him and unwound the bandages from around his head. It took a while for his eyes to grow accustomed to the dim light reflected off the plain, whitewashed walls. He blinked a few times attempting to clear their lenses. He could see – although hazily – the tall figure of a man in his 'older prime'. Behind him, he could make out the more rounded silhouette of a woman standing in the doorway. Trying to focus, he rubbed his eyes gently with the backs of his loose fists.

'What can you see, boy?' Kyrros asked.

Lio was surprised, not to say a little disappointed, to finally come face-to-face with his 'hero'. He was not at all the god-like being he had expected. He was dressed in a white cotton garment from head to foot, a jubbah.'

'I can see you,' said Lio, 'and Miriam, though not well.' Kyrros tipped his head back and looked down his nose at him, examining his eyes, though neither of them knew how they had been hurt.

'Do not be concerned,' he reassured him, 'there are no obvious signs of injury. I had worried that the priest had blinded you in some way but it seems that he did not. He has remarkable eyes, does he not?' He said over his shoulder.

'As remarkable as yours,' commented Miriam.

Kyrros coughed modestly before continuing, 'With a little luck your eyesight should return fully in time, though perhaps it might always be weak.'

The boy went on blinking a few times, as his focus briefly returned then left again. He wondered about Kyrros' reference to a priest but decided not to ask any more. However, he did pose one question: 'Sir, how old am I now – am I more than five hundred years?'

Kyrros laughed: a booming laugh. 'The boy asks intelligent questions – he cannot be that damaged. I suppose you are still the same age that you were on Rhodos, whatever that was?'

Lio tried to remember. 'I don't know,' he admitted disappointedly.

'Not to worry, boy,' continued Kyrros, 'we will see what time returns to you. Rest,' he said. 'I will leave you now. I have many tasks ahead of me.' The philosopher saw the boy's lost look. After all, here he was, alone, without either a past or a future. In an effort to cheer the boy up, Kyrros offered, 'Someday you may even wish to help me – work with me.'

Lio sensed rather than saw the man's smile. 'Yes,' the boy smiled broadly back at him, 'I would like that.' Although what he thought he could help with or show his rescuer he did not know.

As he turned to leave, Kyrros mumbled something to Miriam; something about the boy staying there for a few months. Then she came toward him, and for the first time Lio saw her blurred but smiling face properly as she dried her hands on her long apron. She wrapped her arms around him and kissed him on both cheeks before hugging him intensely.

Those first few weeks of warmth, rest and caring passed so quickly. It took only a few days more before Lio could see much more clearly, and by the time Kyrros had arrived the following month, the blurring had gone altogether. However, as for the boy's permanent eyesight, his sensitivity to light never did change. In fact, from that day forward, his eyes were *always* more sensitive. As a result, Lio always had to wear something to protect his eyes against strong sunlight.

The sunlight had always been strong in that region of Egypt, hence the reason that most people adopted the ancient practice of painting dark pigment – charcoal – around their eyes. Of course, this had over the years become more and more stylised, with blues, reds and greens – and gold, by the pharaohs and priests – being added for dramatic effect. But its initial purpose, simply to cut down the reflected glare around the eye sockets, still worked. Unfortunately, for Lio however, this low level of protection was not sufficient. Kyrros realised this of course. And, ever the designer, he had a pair of 'solar-glare protection-shields' – or 'sun-protectors' made for him at once. They were possibly the first ever sunglasses!

He designed for the boy a pair of plain, round, bronze frames which were incorporated into two leather eyepieces. Each held two flat discs of polished green glass, fixed in with tiny bolts. The frames were tied onto the bridge of his nose by a leather thong that passed over his ears and around the back of his head. Air slits were punched through their sides to prevent them fogging up. Their optical clarity was not wonderful; they were not anything like as clear as modern sunglasses. They were not very comfortable and certainly not flattering to behold. Frankly, they were rather strange looking. However, when they arrived, they did allow the boy to go outside in the strong midday sunlight for the first time in months. And for that, the boy was eternally grateful.

Curiously, by that time, although his memory had still not returned, the boy was nevertheless mystifyingly drawn to watch the sun rise and set each day. But until his 'glasses' had arrived, he had not been able to watch these phenomena for more than a few minutes before his eyes would start to stream with tears, and before his head would pulse with blinding pain. Gradually, his eyes would get used to the sunlight again, but in future he would always be wary of walking out into the strong light unprotected. For a long time he would not be parted from his sun-protectors. In fact, they became almost a permanent feature and could constantly be found at least hanging around his neck.

Over the next period of the boy's life, Kyrros visited at the start of each month to check on his patient. There was perhaps, though, another reason for the long journeys from Alexandria. Lio noticed that Kyrros always stayed a day or two, taking the opportunity to chat with Miriam.

The house was part of an old walled farm which sat atop a small hill, surrounded by vast fields of cotton plants. Beyond this area was the ever expanding desert. Other than the odd looking geometric hills far in the distance, it was an almost flat, barren landscape. The farm was comfortable and had its own deep well, a well that Kyrros had bored out himself years ago. It was also more than adequately supplied with many chickens which ran freely in the yard. Those living at the farm had a ready supply of milk from the two cows held in the byre at one corner of the yard, and next to that was a sizeable general workshop with many hand tools. Lastly in the other corner, the furthest from the house, was a pigsty, complete with several pigs, though Miriam never strayed toward it. There were also two ponies and four camels, animals which Lio had never heard of before and after the extraordinary description that Miriam gave him, only believed existed when the bandages were removed. For all the time that his eyes had been covered, he had been convinced that the sound of distant burping was the few farm workers and paid servants trying to lead him on. When he finally got to see these 'ships of the desert', he couldn't believe his eyes. They were though, he thought, at least friendly; if rather ugly.

In all of the time that Lio spent there, no strangers ever approached the house, but everyone was always relaxed and happy in each other's own company. The same servants were always pulling his leg about one thing or another. Frequently, in the evenings they would sing and play much the same musical instruments that he seemed to remember somehow, but never could properly. One of them even started to teach him how to play the flute and even the bagpipes. As soon as he was able, the boy began to help Miriam and the other servants around the farm. By the third month, he'd even decided to build a sundial in the workshop, a copy of one he could vaguely recall seeing somewhere before. For no particular reason, just in order to do something with his time.

His version of the sundial, though, would be smaller than the one he could recall, and carved from a solid block of wood, the pointer or 'style' being made from a piece of a recycled bronze plough. In a little under a month he had achieved his goal. And, if the truth be known, he was quite proud of it. When it was as finished as he could make it, Lio sited it in front of the house. This was much to the satisfaction of the servants, who – with a little instruction from the boy – could use it to divide their work schedules and co-ordinate themselves more readily.

On Kyrros' next visit, Lio proudly showed him what he had been up to. Kyrros narrowed his eyes at the object, trying to recall where he'd also seen something similar, obviously both curious and impressed. He studied it in detail while the boy tried to explain that he had not invented it, merely copied it from somewhere. Noticing that it was slightly inaccurate, Kyrros at once tilted it forward on its base, until both he and the boy were happier with it. Still, Kyrros himself was very pleased at its apparent level of sophistication, although the boy could still not explain where those elements came from. There was one rumoured to have been on Rhodos many centuries ago, Kyrros told the boy. And possibly, come to think – now that he'd seen this one – he might have even glimpsed it briefly himself. Though in those long past primitive days, surely it would not have been nearly as sophisticated nor as accurate as the one the boy had just produced in this 'modern' age, would it? After all, the style or 'gnomon', had not been invented until the time of Aristarchus of Samos: around two hundred years before Kyrros' own time. It was therefore much later than the boy could have known, he assured the boy – warily.

By the time of his next visit, Lio would readily have confessed to have been getting bored. His back had now healed fully, and to all intents and purposes he was as fit as he ever would be. He had by now made many things. He carved toys for no one in particular, animals which he had never seen but somehow remembered: lions, crocodiles – of which he was told there were many in the river Nile just half a day away to their east – and a curious, quite squat and heavy looking unicorn that he'd 'imagined'.

During that same period, the boy had also made a device to help Miriam dry the washing. She had complained a few times that she could never seem to hang out the washing in the right place. The wind direction it seemed, would change deliberately to catch her out, scattering the clean washing around the yard so that it would have to be washed again. Also, it scared the chickens away, and they would have to be dutifully rounded-up again. If only she could 'see' where the wind was coming from and how strong it was, then she would at least have a chance to keep an eye on it and collect it in before the wind had a chance to blow it away. With that in mind, the boy designed and made her a wind direction indicator, a flat sided wooden sail and a pointer that was fixed to a pole. Caught by the wind, it rotated to point the direction it was blowing from. Also, if the wind got stronger, it waved about, signalling that it was time to collect the washing. As soon as it was finished, he had fixed it to the top of the byre opposite the house. Then, just for fun, he painted a picture on each side of it: one of the chickens that scattered each time the washing blew into them.

Over that whole period, Lio had begun to look increasingly forward to Kyrros' visits, but not only because of his boredom. Neither was it because his visitor would bring little treats with him for the boy. Instead, it was because, although the boy genuinely liked the down to earth attitude of the servants, deep inside him he craved the more learned pleasure of Kyrros' company.

Each time he visited, Kyrros would tell him of many strange devices and machines that he knew of and had experimented with. For his own part, the boy would tell Kyrros of how it used to be 'in the old days' with the temple machines; quite a turn around for a young boy to be telling an older man tales like this. Kyrros listened intently and made notes, especially if Lio described something that he'd remember out of the blue, of which he had not been previously aware. And so, in this very limited way, tiny memories began to return to him. Not of people or places, but of things – gadgets, safe subjects for the boy's mind to allow him to remember. And then one day, Lio's life changed again. Kyrros' next visit was expected at the end of the month, a few days away.

It was early evening. The boy had been standing a while outside the farm wall, looking at the sun sinking over the horizon in its yellow, almost green sky. He returned to the house to take a little supper with the servants and Miriam. Afterwards, as usual, she sent him to his own room for the night. As silly or as perhaps conceited as it may sound to others, Lio had never been mischievous or had wilfully disobeyed anyone as a small child. Perhaps this was because he didn't have to of course, although, as it came to pass, he would – and spectacularly so. But that evening, as usual, he obeyed Miriam, his mother, as she had encouraged him to call her.

That night in particular, he climbed into his comfortable bed, before falling straight to sleep. It was then that, entirely against his will, Lio was transported back in time!"

CHAPTER 28:

The Night-Mare

"In one sweeping, sickeningly vicious dream that left him panic-stricken and screaming at the top of his voice, the past that Lio had escaped suddenly caught up with him.

Hearing his terrified shouts, Miriam burst into the boy's room to find him clawing at the closed wooden window shutters. She ran to him as the other servants, who had similarly raced to his aid, looked on. Miriam held him tightly as he awakened, still shivering with fear. His nightshirt was almost entirely saturated in sweat as she tried to calm him down.

As he was able to recall it, Lio's dream had begun pleasantly enough. The wonderful, familiar face of his grandfather appeared to the boy as they sat in their private chamber together, talking. 'Helio' his grandfather called over to him, 'are you well?'

'Yes,' he assured him and they sat and talked a few moments longer, although what about he could never recall. Then, there came a thud outside and it seemed as if he was suddenly transported spiritually above the temple. Hovering, detached from his body, he looked down at the extraordinary scene below. From this bizarre perspective, a man clad in purple and gold appeared to limp to and fro with an outstretched metal stick, hitting a boy and a girl who sat cowering together for protection beside a sundial. Lio's grandfather tried to intervene and was cut down by him. Then, amongst them on the ground, there Lio was himself.

Suddenly, the figure turned his attention toward him, beating him all over viciously with the stick. Lio was powerless to protect himself. Even though it was dark, somehow the sun streamed into his eyes as he looked up at the faceless silhouette.

Now drums began to beat and dancers streamed all around them. Then came the rest of what had actually happened at that time: Zeus, his bolt of lightning, the leaping figure of Pegasus, the bright lights and the noises. Everything came colliding into the short but powerful nightmare that had nearly terrified the very life out of him.

His heart still pounding, racing as he sobbed, the boy clutched his mother tightly, as he realised instantly that he had seen a vision of something that had really happened to him. And, in a way, as horrifying as it was, this began the healing sequence that was necessary to him.

'I remember my name,' he cried, still sobbing but relieved. 'It is Lio! I am ten years old. My grandfather was the High Priest of the Temple of Helios. And the wicked man that I dreamt of was the High Priest of the Temple of Zeus.'

'Then the process has begun,' comforted Miriam. After all, it is only after confronting one's demons that it becomes possible to move on.

By the time Kyrros next arrived, Lio had had at least two more dreams. These were much less intense though. The boy saw familiar sights around Rhodos and many familiar faces, including the smiling face of his friend the food stallholder, whom he clearly remembered. He also saw and spoke to his friend Marduk.

There was, however, one other face that would not emerge. It was the outline of a girl's face, preferring to stay in silhouette. As he spoke to her, she listened, but she would not answer him. Instead, she simply nodded or shook her head. On both occasions, and a few after that, whenever he held out his hand to her, she would fade away. She would zoom out slowly into the distance before disappearing, leaving him no closer to solving the mystery of who she was or what she might be to him. He knew only that she seemed sad – and this haunted him. Later, whenever he spoke of this to his mother or Kyrros, neither could help him out with whom or what this vision might represent. However, both seemed happy that he had at least seen these things.

'Your memory has begun to return,' boomed Kyrros, 'good.'

'Yes,' the boy answered him, 'although I do not like many of the things that I see.'

'Mmm...' he mused at length, 'but perhaps that is necessary for your own good.'

'Perhaps,' Lio agreed reluctantly, 'although I still do not like it.'

Kyrros spoke next to Miriam. 'And is the patient now physically fit, have all of his scars healed properly?'

'Yes,' she assured him.

'And the swelling on the back of his skull that caused the coma, is that well and truly gone.'

'It is,' she confirmed.

'Good,' he said, beckoning Lio over so that he could make a final check on his health. He examined his back, gently stroking the exposed scars with the back of his hand. 'Is it sore?'

'No, not now,' Lio was able to say. 'Though I still cannot remember what caused it.'

Kyrros chose his words carefully. 'Lio, there are many wicked men – and women – in this world: people who quite wilfully hurt and torture others. Invariably, they blame a higher or lower power for their actions. But of all those wicked people, it is the adults who persistently mistreat and take advantage of those children who are not able to support or defend themselves; that I cannot accept.

Lio, I am a man who has never in my life beaten or struck anyone at all, even in fun – much as Miriam has told me you have described your own grandfather to her – but sometimes I wonder if the world would not be better off if these people had not been born. It seems, from what I saw with my own eyes, that this 'High Priest of Zeus' had thrashed you within a moment of your life, and it also seemed that he was about to do much worse to you.' At that point he stopped, shielding the boy from the full details of his rescue.

In the conversation that immediately followed, Kyrros relayed a toned down version of what he thought may have happened, helping Lio piece together the remembered snippets that he had told Miriam. He also told him something of the mysterious Hippo-Chronos machine that had been the rescue device that had carried him off.

As to why he had arrived at that precise moment in time and not as planned, twenty-four hours later than he was supposed to, he guessed simply that when he had counted the days back to the night of the eclipse from the present date, he had miscounted by one full day, and he was quite satisfied therefore that the accuracy of the machine was adequate. But as for the fact that the machine had landed on the square outside the Temple of Zeus, fifty paces from the square outside the Temple of Helios, where it was supposed to land, Kyrros admitted simply that, in that respect, the machine was not as accurate as the Chronology Society had hoped it to be.

It was simply an 'accident of fate' then, he explained, never considering for one moment that it could have ever been directed by a higher power. Nor was it, as Lio later asked pointedly, a result of the market trader's curse on the high priest!

Science and logic were all that existed in Kyrros' universe, and the boy could not help wondering whether in some way this would always be to his detriment. But Kyrros was absolutely, unshakably certain that this was the way of the world. It was a standpoint which the boy, in the main, learned to follow, and yet a tiny part of him would always share his grandfather's part-scientific, part-spiritual view of the universe. After all, what harm could personal belief do?

Miriam handed him his glasses as they stood up to leave the room together. He had become quite adept at tying them behind his head, to the approval of Kyrros who had not until now seen the object of his own design. He smiled at Lio and then all three of them strolled into the yard amongst the clucking chickens and toward the sundial so that the boy could show Kyrros his latest invention, the wind indicator.

He was now unashamedly showing off, behaviour of which I

am sure Kyrros was familiar himself, although unlike Lio, I am also sure that he would never publicly admit to it. Miriam and Kyrros strolled closely together as, walking in front, the boy excitedly talked him through how and why it worked... and how he had built it... and what he had made it from, and... Although looking back occasionally, he could see Kyrros was far more interested in talking to Miriam, laughing and joking with her, as she swung her apron in front of her while they walked.

Of course the elementary principle of his wind device was entirely self-evident to a man like Kyrros. In retrospect it was quite obvious, but as the pair stood and pretended to listen to the boy, Kyrros was at least encouraging and paid the boy a compliment. That compliment, more than any other that he received after, defined who Lio was and who in some ways he would wish to become more and more – although he never did quite make it.

'Lio,' Kyrros said impressively, 'you have realised something that many people do not in their whole lifetime realise. You have seized upon a simple idea, an idea that has eluded many men over the centuries. Many have held a wetted finger in the air to see which way the wind blows,' he demonstrated, 'but I cannot recall having seen anyone make a 'wind-direction indicator', and none till now have sited it on the tallest part of a building for maximum effect. Lio, you have not only become a craftsman in putting it together and installing it, you have taken something that existed before and improved it. As young as you are, you have moved forward the understanding of mankind: you have become a young designer.'

For the hundred pace walk back to the dining room, Lio floated a foot above the ground, riding on the satisfaction that that praise had given to him – a feeling which he would never forget. Those few days really were the start of a new life and one that should have taken him in a direction that would last forever. That is, if the boy had not later been so wilful and so reckless.

Later that evening, at dinner, Miriam and Kyrros sat together around the plain round wooden table. The other five servants and

263

Lio spread out equally around its circumference. This was a change especially for Miriam, as it was her who usually served the others. In deference to Miriam whose own faith forbade her to eat pork, Kyrros decided that the meat that was usually on the menu for his visits would be substituted for chicken. He even prepared, cooked and served the entire meal himself, using the spices and dried fruits he'd brought with him. It was a meal polished off with gusto by everyone around the table, laughing and joking as they did. At the end of the meal, he suddenly tapped the table politely, stood up and called for silence.

'I wish to ask someone at this table,' he announced, 'a question that first entered my head a few weeks ago.' The servants looked around quizzically. 'For years I have dedicated my life to my work, forgetting sometimes who I was. I am not getting any younger and so I ask you all to bear witness to a proposition I have.' He turned directly to Miriam. 'For some years now, I have worked with you, and I confess, I have taken you for granted. However, during these past few months I have finally realised, because of your absence from me, that I miss your company very much. For that reason, it would much please me if you would consider being a partner in my life!'

There was a frosty silence as everyone looked around uneasily. If it was intended to sound like anything other than a business proposition, it did not. Miriam's face gave nothing away. Confused by her less than enthusiastic reaction, Kyrros sat down again. After a moment he stood back up and continued. 'I mean... move your belongings... into my house.'

Miriam looked innocently back at him. 'But they are already here,' she explained.

'No, I mean... all of them,' he stumbled, 'and into my quarters in Alexandria.'

'Why?' she asked coolly.

Kyrros' eyes pleaded. 'But I thought... well I thought that... we get on well together, don't we?'

'Perhaps,' she conceded, 'but why would I move into your

quarters in Alexandria? I would rather go back to work in the Mouseion workshops than be a servant in your quarters.'

Lio looked at her, wondering if she might leave him here alone, but then smiled, sensing that she was playing a game.

Kyrros was shaken: his proposal had turned into his own worst nightmare. 'I thought that we might...'

'What?' she teased, straight-faced.

He shifted tack. 'Marry?'

She looked at the table in thought. 'But why would you wish to marry yourself to me?' She looked back up at him.

'Because...' he was about to list all of the logical reasons why, then realising the object of the game himself, he immediately conceded. 'Because,' he laughed, 'Miriam, I have fallen in love with you!'

She smiled at him, one of the soft gentle smiles that Lio was used to receiving. 'Oh!' she said, 'then in that case I will accept your "proposition" because it just so happens that I have fallen in love with you too. But,' she cautioned, 'I'll only marry you if we can take my new son Lio with us!'

The servants and Lio cheered and clapped as, without further delay, the newly betrothed couple hugged tightly for the first time. The table and its contents were moved immediately and the musical instruments were quickly retrieved from the servants' rooms. Although they played most evenings for a while, on this occasion the music was much brighter and the dancing began to the sounds of the tambourine and the symbols, the lyre, the flute and the bagpipes. The merriment lasted well into the evening. It was a wonderful night, and afterwards the boy stood briefly on his own in the courtyard. There, he listened to the chirruping of the surrounding frogs, and pondered how lucky he was to have found himself here, as he looked up at the stars.

It was one of the clearest, starriest nights that Lio would ever remember, full of millions of pinpricks of light in the heavens, miles from the rest of civilisation. Once again remembering the names taught to him five hundred years before, he followed the two pointing stars of Merak and Dubhe, which guided his eye and his imagination to Polaris. As illogical as it was even to him then, it seemed that his grandfather was looking down on him as countless other fathers and grandfathers, mothers and grandmothers, sons and daughters, had no doubt for many generations looked down on their families before. *Perhaps in some way never to be explained*, thought Lio, *my grandfather made it to his star after all.*

Despite the continuing merriment across the wall of the farm behind him, the boy was suddenly consumed with a feeling of deep loss. All he now knew was that, although he felt safe and loved once more, he suddenly missed his grandfather terribly. For one of the last times as a child, that night Lio climbed into his bed and sobbed himself to sleep."

Tom became suddenly quiet.

Alex stopped scribbling: "Bolts?" he looked up at him.

"What?" Tom asked distractedly.

"You said the glasses were held together with tiny bolts?"

"Archytas of Tarentum: fifth century BC," Tom explained before drifting off again.

Alex dutifully wrote it down.

Maddie also tried to snap Tom out of his dream world. "And they had invented bagpipes in Egypt... back then too?"

"Eh...? Oh, strictly speaking I'm not sure," he replied. "Those particular bagpipes belonged to one of the Greeks, from Macedon, where they were well known and used.

"What, like Scottish bagpipes?" challenged Conna.

"No, smaller, look over there," Tom nodded towards the coffee table. "Try them if you like."

Conna uncrossed his legs and got up painfully to bring them over. He blew into them and they made a discordant but quaint noise. Not at all like the loud Scottish bagpipes that he had heard before – more like a squeak. Thankfully, he didn't try again. He handed them to Tom who, after a little prompting from the others, stood up and blew into them inflating the goatskin. Tom then performed a short tune, which to the unfamiliar and untrained ear sounded frankly dreadful, though all four clapped along politely and kept their opinions to themselves.

"Now *that* is *my* Greek music – *real* Greek music," he said proudly, stopping himself before he inadvertently insulted Conna's chosen present of the bouzouki music CD. The four looked briefly at each other and Tom, all thinking more or less the same. They all preferred the bouzouki music to that cacophony.

"So they were like these bagpipes then?" asked Alex.

"Virtually identical," confirmed Tom.

"Well they don't look ancient," said Conna.

"That's because they are only my age – although from your younger point of view you might of course consider *me* ancient."

"No, no, not at all," came a brief chorus in return.

"Yes," smirked Tom, his eyes crinkling at the corners, "and I believe you!"

Tom sat down again and put the bagpipes down on the floor beside him, about to begin where he'd left off.

CHAPTER 29:

Sphinxes And Crocodiles!

"After a few more days on the farm, it was time for Kyrros to return to Alexandria, leaving Miriam with the boy. Both she and Kyrros had decided that to make the marriage work properly, Kyrros would now have to concentrate all of his efforts on making enough money to allow him to retire. If not in luxury, at least in comfort, if ever he wished to; he could not promise. And although he had the farm, he could not contemplate quitting Alexandria, or – more especially – the Mouseion! Living part of the year in each place seemed the best solution. Nevertheless, he did not have a house of his own in Alexandria, and neither of them especially liked the idea of sharing the tiny house Kyrros had been allocated in the Mouseion grounds. They would wait perhaps a year or so then, buy a house in Alexandria and only then get married.

When Kyrros returned to Alexandria, it was with the promise that he would come back for Miriam and the boy the next month to take them with him back to the city. There, he would introduce Lio as his 'long lost son' from Rhodos. Although tongues might wag, it would hopefully at least explain his Rhodian accent, why he was there and deflect attention away from who he really was. By that token, when they were married, Miriam would then properly become the boy's mother. Until then, Lio would continue to call her mother as a courtesy title. Kyrros was pleased with the simplicity of the necessary deception.

When the month had dragged past, it was with mixed emotions

that, late in the afternoon, to avoid the heat, Lio finally got to leave the farm. Ultimately, his return visit would be under much different circumstances than the time they had previously left Alexandria. Lio, Miriam and Kyrros said their goodbyes to four of the servants, their Macedonian bagpipe player coming with them to drive the donkey cart to the Nile. There, they would pick up Kyrros' pre-arranged boat, at which point the Macedonian would return to the farm. Sitting cross-legged in the back, Lio hitched-up the eye-protectors, and the donkey-cart trundled off along the rough farm track, leaving a trail of dust to blow across the tall cotton plants. In the back of the cart he played the borrowed bagpipes, if not well, at least softly and without complaint.

For months Lio had not known where the farm lay, and if someone had told him its location he would have been none the wiser anyway. But now, on their way to the great river, he began to marvel at the hitherto distant sights that grew near to him, sights that had previously been known to the boy only as the geometrically shaped hills on the horizon. As they approached them, his new father explained to Lio what they were, and he realised that these were some of the very structures that his grandfather had told him about as a very young boy. They were none other than the three Pyramids of Giza, plus, as they neared them, something the boy immediately recognised: the Great Sphinx.

As his father began to speak of their unknown origin, Lio remembered something of the tale his grandfather had told him as a small child. Built as tombs and as monuments to the once Great Kings of Egypt, in the most ancient of times, now no one remembered their names. Kyrros himself wondered aloud, 'Who knows how long they all took to build, or what happened to the people that had toiled over their construction? In particular, it is said that since the Sphinx was built, its head and face have been changed several times to represent successive pharaohs. And who knows what it originally looked like? Perhaps,' he suggested, 'that was the true riddle of the Sphinx!' Lio on the other hand simply marvelled at its sight.

The Sphinx grew larger and larger as they approached its base from the rear, its height was ten or even more times taller than Kyrros even. The cart drew along its haunches, to stop a while in its shade. The huge sculpted blocks that made up the monuments' construction seemed to reach into the sky. Once the small party had cooled down, a few moments later, they moved on. Passing its outstretched front paws, they stopped again. Lio marvelled at the huge head, wearing the long sided 'Nemes': the lightweight headdress reserved for royalty. Its carved twin Vulture and Asp, or Cobra, emblems above the brow towered over the cart. The boy had never known anything built by man to be as huge as these pyramids and their guardian. Now directly beneath it, the Sphinx appeared to threaten to stretch down its head and pounce on the boy; a most disquieting thought. Lio felt a chill run through him, partly of course as a result of the sun going down further, making it physically colder, but also as a reaction to the primeval architecture. As ancient as it was, and as primitive, it really was one of the most awe-inspiring sights that he had ever beheld in his life.

As they started off again toward their destination, now both Kyrros and Miriam barely giving it a second glance – they'd seen it many times before – Lio couldn't take his eyes off the splendid sight. Of course, he noticed that the Sphinx faced toward the east and therefore the rising sun, and it was that fact which prompted him to remember the legend that his grandfather had told him as a boy:

The fire-breathing Sphinx, he had told him, would wait in the desert facing the dawn. He would ask a riddle of the people who came too near – always the same riddle. And what riddle was that? The young boy had asked. No one knew, answered his grandfather. For everyone whom the Sphinx had asked the question, had failed to answer correctly, and as a result had been consumed by it. It was 'a great paradox' he had said, a riddle which no one could ever know or solve.

Slowly they trundled on, the boy not being able to take his eyes off the sculpture – just in case it moved!

It was growing cold as the small party approached the river, and Lio was immediately struck with the reason why it was always referred to as the 'Great River'. Although he had presumably travelled down it to get to the farm, he had been unconscious and therefore previously unaware of its vastness. This huge, wide, dirty brown river, the life-blood of Egypt, moved steadily north toward Lower Egypt, bringing silt from the southern uplands. Eventually the river would fan out into the vast, wide delta before reaching its final destination, the great Mediterranean, or middle Sea. Their small boat would follow the river and before reaching the delta, then it would turn into the great Alexandrian canal, which would bring them to the city. Once more, Lio was in awe. However, his father, Kyrros, assured him that it was not as impressive as it was normally, either in power or depth. The river had not risen that season and as a result, the surrounding farmland had become parched and unproductive. Next year perhaps, it would flood again and fertilise the fields. But for now, crop failure looked likely. Only the country's vast stores of grain would prevent famine.

The private 'felucca' that awaited them, the small flat-bottomed water taxi with its distinctive triangular sail was moored by the side of the river. Its master waited for them patiently in the stern. He had known Kyrros for years and therefore trusted the tall Greek he had brought down here two days before, quite happy to trust him to return as he said he would. More importantly, he knew that he would be well paid: probably in Roman coins. The party of three clambered onto the craft, and between them, the master and the cart driver then manhandled the various large items of baggage onto it behind them. Lio bade farewell to the Macedonian and handed him back the bagpipes. 'Hang onto them for me,' the man insisted, 'practice. And when you come back,' the servant assured him, 'I will help you make a set of your own.' Lio thanked him enthusiastically and promised to do so – every day. Miriam and Kyrros were less enthusiastic about the gift. The journey successfully accomplished, they all waved the servant goodbye and set off out into the river.

Not long afterwards, sitting in the stern, swathed in a blanket but still watching the outline of the Pyramids against the sunset, Lio fell asleep. Only now, to everyone's relief, did his music stop. Keeping to the centre of the river, the felucca sailed steadily with the wind behind it, twice as fast as the pace set by the little cart through the arid landscape. At that rate it would only take a day or so. It was twenty-four leagues to Alexandria, along the easternmost part of the Nile and the Great Alexandrian Canal. Travelling steadily through the moonless night, by morning, the master had completed more than ten leagues; fourteen more to go.

Lio was awoken hastily by his mother to look over to the distant riverbanks. On both sides they were lined by apparently sleeping crocodiles. In fact, the animals were only sunning their cold-blooded bodies in order to store enough of the sun's energy to slip into the river when an opportunity presented itself. *To make a meal of something – or someone*! thought the boy. Although he had often seen their skins in the market of Rhodos, Lio had never before seen one of the reptiles alive, but now he was fascinated and not to say a little intimidated by them. The Nile crocodiles had a most vicious reputation.

'Educationally' of course, Miriam began to tell him the tale of the distant bloodbath that had reputedly taken place on this very spot, many years before.

She began, 'As Alexander the Great continued his campaign in Persia, he died in mysterious circumstances. In the vacuum of power that was left, his most trusted general and childhood friend Ptolemy, immediately took Egypt for himself while the other successors squabbled. Another of the generals, Perdiccas, who had been alone with Alexander at his death, claimed that from his deathbed Alexander had given his signet ring and his sword to him. He then laid claim to the whole of the empire for himself. He also claimed Alexander's body. At that time, the possession of the mortal remains was important: the new ruler always laid to rest the old one. By this act especially, it demonstrated that power had been successfully transferred.

It was also claimed that after his death, Alexander's body had lain for ten days in his tent while his generals continued to argue: over who was the rightful successor; whether the empire should stay intact or whether it should be divided; and how they planned to get their huge army home to Greece. Thus began the long Wars of the "Diadochi" – the claimed successors of Alexander.

During this time, the body had "miraculously" not shown any signs of decay. Therefore, despite Alexander's own last wish – that his body be thrown into the nearby Euphrates river to be consumed – to perpetuate his own myth that he had indeed been a god and had not died but had been taken up to mount Olympus – his body was kept intact. After some time, a special ornamental carriage was constructed to carry the miraculous relic to Memphis in Egypt, to be embalmed by the priests of Amon. It was they who had earlier proclaimed Alexander to be the god Amon himself. Alexander had marched there with his vast army to "ask" if they thought he might be! Well, what would you tell him?' asked Miriam. 'From there, Perdiccas planned that the body would be returned to Macedonia and placed in the specially built mausoleum.

However, once the body had been taken to Egypt, in order to deprive Perdiccas of his excuse to take over, Ptolemy stole the body himself and took it to Memphis. The act both infuriated and prompted Perdiccas to attempt to invade Egypt with what was left of Alexander's army. And so it was that in the dead of night, Perdiccas had stood on the opposite side of the Nile, on the eastern bank, right here, at the area known as the Fort of Camels.' Lio looked across at the reptiles stretched out around the few remaining building stones, unmoving, waiting to be tempted, as Miriam continued the gory tale.

'Despite an earlier attempt to cross further downstream, which Ptolemy had thwarted, Perdiccas ordered his troops to wade into the deeper, crocodile infested waters, so that they could then outflank his enemy. The result, though, was both disastrous and shocking. Of the ten thousand troops that entered into the river that night, two thousand were killed: one thousand attacked by crocodiles and a further thousand drowned. In the ensuing panic and the anger of his own generals, Perdiccas was himself run through – doubtless by Alexander's own sword!

'The rest,' said Miriam, 'is history. Ptolemy rescued what was left of Alexander's troops and cared for them as his own. For this, he was himself rewarded. His own reputation as a commander in the style of Alexander himself was established throughout the world. He was left to rule Egypt in peace, building a new mausoleum for Alexander in Memphis, and later keeping the embalmed body there for safety.

If it had not been for the Nile Crocodiles,' said Miriam, 'perhaps the whole of history might have been changed. Perdiccas and not Ptolemy might have held the throne of Egypt. There might not have been the Mouseion, and without that, there would have been no library or scholars. Furthermore,' Miriam hitched the boy's glasses onto his head and looked into his wide eyes, 'Kyrros here would not have been able to construct the Hippo-Chronos – and none of us would now be sitting together in this boat!'

Lio shuddered at the tale, looking back at the crocodiles that were now, he was certain, sizing him up. Miriam leant forward and hugged him to her, driving out any fearful thoughts that he might be having.

'But what happened to Alexander's body?' Lio asked distractedly.

'Ah, no one truly knows. Throughout the years it was argued and fought over and moved successively from mausoleum to mausoleum, temple to temple. Strangely, more than one body came to light. After all, many had reason to lay claim to it. Popping up in several places, each one was claimed as 'the true relic'. Finally, most were content to believe that one, heavily bejewelled and crowned relic was the true body. It was housed in the building known as the Sema, in Alexandria. Another similarly prepared body was laid out in the huge temple known as the Serapeion. It was rumoured that both of these relics were false, but this suited Alexander's guardians. The real body was supposedly laid properly to rest in a secret tomb, its whereabouts known only by the direct descendants of Ptolemy himself. Whatever happened to it since then, the true body was never seen again. Perhaps,' said Miriam, 'the myth and the legend that is "Alexander the Great" was indeed perpetuated by all of this, but perhaps, just perhaps, he was transformed into a god after all – and taken up to live with them.'

Now Lio knew she was kidding. He snorted.

Kyrros chuckled at the way she had told the tale, 'Well done,' he said, 'I could not have brought the short history lesson to life better myself. Remember though, hero or not, that he was a man – just like all of us – and that Alexander had an unseemly side too. For instance, in one famous drunken rage, he killed his childhood friend Cleitus, a man who had saved his own life in battle. Later, when he invaded Asia Minor, despite begging forgiveness, he cruelly treated those Greeks who had settled in the city of Tyre. They were, after all, supposed to be the distant descendants of those who had earlier abandoned the battlefield of Troy! Accordingly, all males were killed, and females and children sold into slavery. It was not the first time he had treated the vanquished so. After this and many other incidents, many of the Greeks began to question his motives: was it to remove the Persian threat once and for all, or to become tyrant of the world? Perhaps that might explain why Alexander met an untimely death.'

As Kyrros ended the lesson, the small boat sailed on and the reptiles began to slide expertly into the water at its approach; although thankfully no one ever saw as much as one crocodile even approach them closely. Perhaps it was that their cold-blooded bodies were not yet warmed by the sun enough to produce enough energy for an attack.

The rest of that day was spent gazing around at the ever changing landscape and at the many workers trying to scratch a living out of the poorly irrigated surrounding farmlands. Both Kyrros and Miriam especially looked on concernedly as the boat passed them all. Food stocks must be getting low by now, the bulk of the reserve kept in the vast granaries of Alexandria looked likely to be exported to Rome whether or not Egypt could afford to feed its own population. Until now, the precious commodity was what had made the country, and especially the city of Alexandria great. Grain wealth was the oil wealth of that age: it was what fed not only the country's population, but what fuelled armies. Unfortunately though, this wealth, provided by the sun, would also be Egypt's downfall. It had for years made Rome attempt to dominate more and more, the country for itself. It could only be hoped that after the recent death of their father, Ptolemy XII, the new young king and queen, Ptolemy XIII and Cleopatra VII, would now begin to show unity – despite the vicious squabbling they'd engaged in since childhood. Hopefully they would be able to persuade their 'ally', Rome, that it would be in everyone's long term interests for Egypt to keep enough grain back to feed their own population. Now, at thirteen and nineteen years of age respectively, the brother and sister were married to each other in the Egyptian tradition: to prevent any possible rivalry!"

Both Maddie and Bex let out a distinct "Iwww...wuh!" at the distasteful revelation.

Tom continued. "Steadily, the boat approached the entrance of the canal itself: the man-made waterway that served to help make the city one of the greatest in the world. The canal would take them around and past the Great Walled City and the Great Harbour of Alexandria toward the smaller Royal, or Eunostos, dock inside the palace enclosure. From there, it was only a short distance to their own destination: the Great Mouseion and the Great Library of Alexandria. Everything in Egypt, it seemed to Lio at the time, was 'Great'."

Tom stopped as if suddenly remembering his own manners. "I am sorry, I forgot myself, would you like something to eat, a piece of fruit perhaps? My family and I have always placed great store in fruit: they described it as natural food, without fat or any of the other 'problem ingredients' that often accompany other foods." They all got up and crossed to the large fruit bowl on the coffee table. Bex and Alex took an apple, Maddie a huge orange and Conna whose stomach rumbling had, he suspected, prompted Tom to offer the snack, desperately grabbed both bananas. "Should we stop now or continue?" asked Tom.

"No, please go on," said Conna, "we can wait till later to eat." The boy hoped desperately there'd be something substantial prepared for him at home for a change, whether or not their maid was back yet.

"Alright," agreed Tom, "then I will."

CHAPTER 30:

The Mouseion

"Although the city was pitch black, as they passed along the canal and past its high walls, Lio was able to sense the vastness of a city much larger and greater than he could ever have imagined for himself, dwarfing his memory of Rhodos. Alexander's Great City was now firmly established as the Roman Empire's grain store, the powerhouse behind their great capital, Rome, and the fuel tank of many of its armies. Because of this, the capital of the North African continent had expanded more and more, stretching out far and wide.

Above the vast walls to their right, the boy could see huge buildings made of mud brick, some that were more than five stories high, towering way above the boat. He could also see the silhouette of the decorative finials at the corners of the rooftops of the temples which must have been much bigger even than the Temple of Zeus on Rhodos. Curving their way north, Kyrros pointed out the top of an especially huge temple that he told him was the Temple of Serapis – the 'Serapeion' – beloved of many Egyptians, Romans, Greeks and Persians – and supposedly one of the repositories of Alexander's body. It was, Kyrros said, the largest in the city; much larger, he assured the boy, than anything that Lio had ever seen before. Most who saw it took it to be a huge monument to the gods. Kyrros though, described it not only as a testament to the ingenuity of man's architectural and constructional skills, but more accusingly of his unending folly at constantly feeling obliged to invent new and ever more ridiculous gods, which were blatantly fictional excuses to cover man's own lack of searching for a proper scientific explanation into the workings of the universe. 'It was,' said Kyrros, 'as silly as the claim that the both the Sema and the Temple of the Serapeion each held the true body of Alexander.' Finally, after a full day on the water, their boat slid quietly and respectfully past the city and into their destination at the royal dock of Eunostos.

It did not take long for Lio to install himself successfully in the Mouseion complex, especially with the introduction of Kyrros – more formally known as Andronikos in that place. Not that he was able to have the run of the grounds – and especially not when playing the bagpipes. To begin with, fairly obviously, the huge and dominating Royal Palace, with its solid surrounding inner walls, was firmly out of bounds. But having seen the number of muscular Egyptian guards that surrounded the place, let alone their size and fierce bearing, the boy had no intention of ever going near. For some reason, they reminded him of someone.

Nor was he allowed through the tall and ornately decorated east and west bronze gates to either side of the large complex, each of which led respectively back to the smaller Eunostos dock and to the Great Dock. The waterfront of this massive dock was lined both with hundreds of boathouses and enormous granaries. Although obscured by the many buildings, there was also a huge tower which stood at the port entrance. Lio was disappointed as although he could see part of it from his bedroom window, it was the one thing that he wished to see closer, but never could. Nevertheless, sometimes when there was fog around, he could certainly hear it!

Kyrros assured him that although already two hundred years old, the tower was regarded as one of the marvels of the modern world. Someday soon, his father promised, he would take him to see it.

The boy did, however, have more or less free reign of the living quarters of the many philosophers who studied and worked at the

Mouseion, a long series of flat roofed houses which had been added to the Mouseion as the years went by. More importantly, he was occasionally allowed to accompany his father into the massive, long and high-roofed library itself and the lower store, or museum, which stood together with it, next to the Royal Palace.

As I have previously said, the Mouseion was divided in two. Firstly was the library proper – the repository of books – and secondly, the museum proper – the place where this knowledge was used. The repository of books, and the place where this knowledge was used practically. The Great Library of Alexandria was surrounded on all sides by stone columns in the Classical Greek temple style. Like the temples, it was also highly decorated with bas-reliefs carved into the lower walls. They reached around the whole of the visible perimeter, painted in rich colours: red, deep yellow-ochre and blue. Rows of statues lined its front facade and entrance. The hundreds of images on this building, however, were not gods. They were, categorically, all men: depictions of past philosophers, artists and engineers ranging through history. This included the largest statue – Ptolemy I Soter, founder of the Great Library, which stood to the centre of the square in front. He was surrounded on both sides by statues of other great men. To his right, the most ancient of them, which included the poets and political thinkers:

Aesop; Pindar; Solon of Athens; Chilon of Sparta; Periander of Corinth; and Cleobulus of Rhodos.

On the other side were those who had contemplated the universe:

Plato; Aristotle; Aristarchos of Samos; Eratosthenes of Cyrene; Hipparchos of Rhodos; and Seleucus of Seleucia – not forgetting *Demokritos and Leukippos,* who had expostulated the 'Atomos Theory' to name but a few.

The whole of the exterior of the Great Library was a wondrous sight and for many reasons, a tribute to rational man. No gods would ever be displayed here.

It did not stop there however. The interior was just as

spectacular to see. The entrance hall stretched right up to the intricately decorated ceilings. Painted throughout in more bright colour and displaying more statues – bronzes of those thought of as especially worthy to be represented in this way, but only a few:

Homer, author of both of the classics: the *Iliad* and the *Odyssey; Socrates,* one of the first philosophers who had questioned the unscientific principle that it was 'the gods' who ruled the world and everything in it, and who was subsequently sentenced to death by drinking hemlock – for corrupting the youth of Athens in this way; *Pythagoras* and *Archimedes,* both acclaimed engineers and mathematicians. And last but not least – *Sappho of Lesvos,* the acclaimed female poet, who set her beautiful 'lyrics' to music.

Moving into the main body of the library itself, there were two levels. Each was lit from natural sunlight streaming in from all sides. Ingeniously constructed 'ancient lights', or windows, were set high up in the walls, whilst the walls themselves were painted white to reflect the light's intensity all around the interior. So it was that the many scholars who sat at the many tables with their young helpers – the 'eyes' of those whose own had begun to grow dim – could see throughout the long days.

Each of the two levels of the library were filled with box-shaped shelves that lined the walls high up, to just below the windows, and those in the middle climbed right up to the ceiling. These divided the room north to south, standing back to back, so as to let the uninterrupted light illuminate the whole of the building. Rails were fixed to the tops of the shelves, holding long sturdy ladders on runners. These allowed the many librarian workers to slide them along in safety, in order to retrieve the scrolls carefully on behalf of the scholars. However, not even the greatest of scholars were allowed to perform this task, lest a single work should be misplaced and effectively lost amongst the half million papyri.

In those works was the accumulated knowledge, not to say the genius, which the greatest philosophers and engineers of all time had mused upon and had compiled over the centuries. Lio could not imagine what the scrolls in there contained. Everything presumably: the sum total of knowledge of the combined world. Mainly Greek works, of course, or at least works written in Greek by authors from all of the countries of the known earth; those who had lived and died in the five hundred years missing from Lio's personal experience. But these works included others even more ancient: works from Egypt, Persia, Israel, Libya, Phoenicia and Carthage. And new works from the Roman provinces, or those about to be: all of the Gauls, Hispania, Britannia, and many more places. There were works in Greek, Latin, Coptic, Hebrew and far more languages than even Lio was aware of. It was the most incredibly precious – though sadly, ultimately the most volatile – treasure in the world!

Behind the library was a single storey museum attached to it. This was accessible from the lower level only. It began with another entrance hall, although not as large or spectacular. It led to the main room. Lined similarly around the walls but this time with heavy benches that carried the 'exhibits': collections of curiosities which had been thought worthy of further study. There were collections of bronze and pottery-ware from around the world, mummified or preserved animals, birds and insects of various types, but the most fascinating things to Lio were the strange machines that lined the walls at the back of the building. Machines which were not dissimilar to these around us," Tom indicated the machines on his bench tops.

"Better still to Lio, as he settled in, whilst he was forbidden to visit the library unaccompanied, he was allowed to roam freely in and out of the many workshops surrounding the museum and its enclosed yards to both sides. It was there that he often helped the others with whatever they were working on at the time. In this way, the boy started to get a more practical education for himself. Within the Mouseion then, the whole library and museum complex, with even more offices and meeting rooms dotted around and within it, was vast. If not the biggest, it was at least the single most important seat of learning that the world would ever know.

As the son of the great man, Lio was welcomed almost

everywhere – by the Chronology Society members especially – for they were the only ones who knew his true identity and origin. Poseidonios, the colourful old athlete and world traveller, was particularly taken with him, fascinated as he was with Lio's open descriptions from another era. The old philosopher even let the boy glimpse the worn old map that he had constructed – a rare treat! Lio also met other scholars, from all areas: philosophers of life, engineers and scientists, all eager to meet him and ask questions, although with them, unlike in the presence of Kyrros or Poseidonios, he was always more guarded with his answers. To outsiders his father had openly spoken of his son only as a young scholar whose work, he'd told them grandly, included 'improvements in the field of chronology' – sundials. And 'atmospheric turbulence indication devices' – weather vanes. The boy was known both as Lio and as the little Kyrros or... what would be an appropriate modern name?" asked Tom aloud. "Yes, I have it, the 'whizz-kid', not least because he had 'whizzed through time.'

There was one thing that he was warned by his father never to talk about however, not unless Kyrros himself was there – even to the society members. That was the combined subject of his past and the machine that had rescued him. Still very much herkoose odonton, his father explained to him that – especially because he'd flouted the jointly agreed rules of the horse's use so outrageously – while he had been on the farm, there had been an enquiry as to the exact circumstances of the affair. The outcome of this meeting was that some even demanded that Kyrros' machine be immediately dismantled to prevent any further breaches of its use. Arguing against this, Kyrros had again apologised profusely for the situation he had created by bringing the boy back. But again he repeated the dilemma he had had to face alone at that instant: to either leave him to his certain death, or, as the boy's life was about to end there anyway, to bring him along with him. It could hardly be considered simply an 'interference' to save someone all but already dead, when one actually had the chance to save him, could it? 'And perhaps...' Kyrros argued philosophically, 'just perhaps... rescuing the boy was actually meant to be. Perhaps that was why the Hippo-Chronos had been invented? Maybe the boy had some higher achievement to accomplish in his own life. After all, it was a strange coincidence that he should arrive in the nick of time, to rescue him!' Others were far more sceptical.

Nevertheless, after much thought, it was decided by the Society that the three key parts would in future be separated. The two smaller and more manageable literal keys – the Cosmos-key, and the Chrono-key – would be stored separately in future, away from the Hippo-Chronos machine, which would be kept hidden indefinitely within the windowless room that it was now stored in. As first envisaged, the two keys were now actual keys to prevent its further use while they considered its eventual fate.

When Kyrros had later explained that, for reasons of security, Lio would never again be allowed to see the Hippo-Chronos, it became a matter of great sadness and regret to the boy. Not least because from then on he grew ever more curious to see what he could only dimly recall in a dream.

And even at that time, it was curiosity, it was said, that had killed the cat!

But there," prompted Tom, "I think we should stop for a while. Please take a piece of fruit if you wish and then we'll continue with cleaning the various component parts of the time-horse."

CHAPTER 31:

The Great Towers

Although none of them had done anything remotely mechanical before, Alex, Conna, Maddie and Bex again enjoyed the task before them: cleaning, polishing and learning what each of the bits did. As they helped, each of the four also talked about other things in their past, though nothing too private. And as they talked, each began to pull more closely together. Until, after two hours of fussing over and cleaning the complicated contraptions, on Tom's instruction, they all placed the parts of the horse carefully aside. Then they covered them against further contamination he continued the story from where he'd left off.

Now, once more in their regular places, Tom began: "Out of curiosity, it was not long after the boy had settled into his new surroundings at the Mouseion that Kyrros asked Lio to again draw out the design of the ingenious sundial. Lio was now fully able to explain that it was his grandfather's design.

The philosopher was taken aback with what the boy had now convinced him was an ancient design after all, but he had no other choice than to believe it. This truly was a revelation to him of how clever the ancients had been. However, he was still more than a little critical of their moral values in persecuting children for sacrifice to their gods. Then, an idea struck him. Despite his fairly recent re-visit to Tinos, he had still not begun the commission for the island's own sundial. Kyrros spotted an opportunity.

The sundial that Lio had now shown him represented a radical departure from all others that he had known, but with the boy's help, Kyrros was sure that he could improve the object even further. To do this he added a second, almost vertically, dished-out feature which would then allow not only the time of day to be read, but also the days and months of the year. What Kyrros had deduced from the boy's inaccurate wooden version, was that the face of the sundial had to be angled precisely in line with its position of longitude on earth. The change of its physical location by relocating it from Rhodos, to the south – the farm at Drodos – had been enough to throw out its accuracy. However, these required angles of longitude had already been calculated many years earlier by Hipparchos of Rhodos, and deposited right there at the library. So, between the work of Hipparchos, Kyrros, Lio and his grandfather, an exceptionally accurate and ingenious sundial could at last be made.

With Lio's enthusiastic approval, Kyrros began work on the long overdue project. But such was his high work rate, that within only a month, the sundial was almost finished and on its way to the port of Tinos. Lio was allowed to accompany him. And, on the way, realising that the sundial was not marked with the name of its designer, Lio successfully persuaded his father, though reluctantly, to let him inscribe it with his own hands. Unfortunately, in doing so, the boy managed to crack the marble rim, but by the time they reached the island Kyros had managed to repair it.

As I have said previously, at its formal unveiling – by chance, in front of the Roman Governor of Athens – the great man, Kyrros, instantly picked up a second, much larger and far more profitable commission on the strength of it. This commission alone would finally allow Kyrros to retire and marry Miriam. Although the Tower of the Winds – the Horologion of Athens – would take nearly another eighteen months to complete, this alone would reserve the name of Andronikos of Kyrros – or Andronicus of Cyrrhus – for future posterity.

For months, work on the Horologion had been under way, now taking full precedence within the museum. Kyrros designed almost all of it himself, though never did he worry that it was becoming too complicated. Even Lio himself sometimes got to help make some of those features he considered at the time to be extremely intricate.

The principle of the 'klepsydra', or water clock – from the Greek: 'hydra', or water, and 'klepsis', or thief – was well known and simple enough. It was a container with a constantly flowing water supply which kept it topped up to the brim, by allowing any excess water to overflow from its sides. This kept the water pressure in the bowl consistent. The flow from a spout which led from the bottom of the bowl could then be measured accurately. This, then, was also the principle of the Horologion – though on a massive scale.

Firstly, Kyrros proposed that the natural spring which occurred further up on the Acropolis of Athens be diverted. It would run across a small, purpose built aqueduct or bridge and into a constantly topped up water storage vessel. The constant jet of water from it, and therefore its ability to deliver a constant high pressure, would be used to power amazing mechanisms inside a small, purpose designed building, all of which Kyrros now proposed. Each of these mechanisms showed a different aspect of the man's genius. First and foremost, a simple, single-handed indicator that projected from the centre of a dial, marked around the edge in hours and minutes. It was designed to keep the public more easily in touch with time."

"A town clock!" Conna blurted out uncontrollably.

"Indeed, Conna, it was what would be the forerunner of the town clock," confirmed Tom.

Conna looked around him, clearly 'chuffed' with himself.

"Further to this, of course, was the fact that the same power source that moved the time indicator, or clock, could also be used to astound the Athenians by powering several other devices. One of which, currently under construction at the museum, was a machine, or computer, which divided the years into months, days and hours – displaying the result via an automated moving armillary.

This in turn showed the earth and the other planets spinning around the sun. Not forgetting the moon, which rotated around the earth.

Once the work on the various mechanisms was under way, Kyrros next turned his attention to the mechanism's housing. Realising that time was running out if they were to reach their accepted latest target of eighteen months – the Romans had already begun to redevelop the whole site and had brought in both the water-supply and the drains that Kyrros had previously designed for them – he was determined to use any means at his disposal to achieve the tight work schedule. So, in order to save himself many days of valuable drawing time, and also get the drawings as quickly as possible to the fabricators in Athens, the King's Engineer therefore sensibly adapted the unrealised and unused drawings that he had years before pored over as a potential vehicle for his secret work.

Accordingly, he dusted off his drawings of the eight-sided wooden cabinet originally intended to house the workings of the Hippo-Chronos machine, and adapted it for use as the housing of the Horologion. Of course, the housing was quadrupled in size and scale, and instead of wood, was to be carved in Athens from the locally quarried white marble. But it would make an admirable and most appropriate housing for this similarly time-related project. From the quarries, it would then be transported and assembled at the site of the Agora, ready to accept the many finished workings when they were shipped there from Alexandria.

Throughout that year, work on the Horologion continued unabated. Not that Kyrros had to push hard. The various teams that worked on different aspects of the project were as committed and hard working on this as they had been when they had worked on the Hippo-Chronos. Time seemed to fly past as Lio helped just as hard in the workshops. Indeed, he proved especially talented in designing the small parts of the mechanism given over to him. Better still, his confidence grew along with him, as he discovered a sensible and practical use for the talents that had been nurtured in him since he was a small child. He was eleven years old now and looking forward to each of the two days marked on the calendar that loomed ahead. The first was the target date that had been set for the completion of the project. He was excited, not least because Kyrros had promised to take the boy to Athens with him for the final installation and unveiling. The second was the wedding day of Miriam and Kyrros.

As the project was driven forward, for the first time in his life, Kyrros began to slow down and let some of the younger ones take over the tasks that, until a few months ago, he would never have considered letting go. Letting his favoured technician take his place had been a good move though – and as he did, he realised that the man's own enthusiasm leapt. It was good to see.

Kyross realised that although his whole life had been heavily caught up in the academic work of the Mouseion – since the 'success' of the Hippo-Chronos and the Tinos sundial – now, since his head had at last been turned by a woman, his enthusiasm in his work had at long last begun to wane. He found himself less driven, less able to put in the long hours he had previously done. He had also come to the conclusion that after the completion of the Horologion, he might indeed effectively retire, or at least slow down and more fully enjoy those new relationships with Miriam, and of course, Lio. He had realised reluctantly that although the boy was no absolute genius himself, there was the spark of something in him. If properly nurtured and educated, one day, he thought, he could become a much valued member of the Mouseion himself and perhaps, at least, follow partly in his own footsteps. The Horologion of Athens would, then, be Kyrros' swan-song: the greatest, but last of his public achievements. The great man would go out on a high note and then disappear, turning his full attention to family life.

The second date in Lio's calendar was ten days after their return from Athens, when the wedding would finally take place.

However, as the Horologion project neared completion, there was another date and event that occurred, and despite its apparent remoteness from Egypt, it was nevertheless critical. That previous January, mainly fuelled by the massive corruption in the capital of

289

the world, civil unrest had broken out in Rome. This unrest worsened until an unlikely saviour was found in the form of Julius Caesar. Seizing the day, he crossed the River Rubicon with his troops, an act forbidden by the elected Senate. This immediately triggered a civil war between them. For now though, the war was largely contained within Italy.

Duly, when the time came for Kyrros and many others to complete the whole project in Athens, it was only because of the war's remoteness that Miriam and Lio were allowed to still accompany them. Although Lio would not be allowed to work on the project on site – the finished result was to be a surprise."

Tom smiled. "The boy would remember every detail of that trip for the rest of his life." He dropped his head back, especially relaxed as he told the four faces now gazing at him in complete wonderment.

"It was late in the summer season, almost autumn, when the small party was led through the tall gates that led to the Great Harbour of Alexandria. Lio, who had still never been able to visit the dock, was excited at the prospect. The harbour, because of its sheer size, was the safest on the African coast – the others being constantly plagued by pirates. It was massive, even more so than Lio had expected. Certainly he had seen it often – almost every day. From his own upstairs bedroom in their house between the library and the Royal Palace he could see at least part of it, but the view from that distance did not give a true indication or feeling of the sheer scale of it all. Nor did it betray anything of its true nature. The working docks buzzed with the sounds and smells of people manhandling the various loads along the quayside, moving them into and out of the various sized and shaped haulers: boats from all over the world. Huge wooden hoists lined the waterside, in Lio's imagination, like giants. Cargoes of all sorts of raw materials, cotton, wool, and timber, were being swung into place. There were finished goods: furniture, marble sculptures – mostly being exported en-route to Rome – but conspicuously absent was the vast trade in grain. For the second year running, the Nile had failed to rise. Many sacrifices had been made by many priests, to many gods, to try to win back their favour for some imagined transgression or sin. But it was to no avail. Stocks were running out, and all exports had been cut drastically on the order of Ptolemy XIII.

There were also many warships: the galleys favoured by the Romans and larger triremes, with their single and three banks of oars respectively. No larger ships though. It was rumoured that the biggest of the navy ships, the quadriremes and quinquiremes, had now been stationed along the Nile Delta to prevent anyone attempting to export directly to the Mediterranean. Nevertheless, all of the ships present looked impressive to the boy as they made their way past and on toward the mole – the short pier that jutted out northward at the eastern end of the harbour. There, a robust cargo ship – a round nosed old Roman corbita, successor to the ancient haulers and now the true workhorse of the entire Mediterranean – lay tethered, already loaded and waiting.

Passing one of the war vessels, which had been dragged up the wooden slipway and out of the water, Kyrros couldn't help but point out the construction of it, towering as it did above them. Although he abhorred the use of any violence and could not contemplate their use in war, the designer in Kyrros could not help but admire the machines for their ingenuity, and he explained precisely how they worked as he picked up the boy to let him see from his own eye level, even coaxing him to lift up the eye-protectors in the bright sunlight. Of course, Lio had seen smaller warships before as a child on Rhodos – in those days they were penteconters. Modern galleys looked much similar but were lighter and more manoeuvrable. But these biremes and triremes were hugely different, as his father the engineer explained:

'Essentially, these galleys rely on three types of attack: ramming the side of the other vessel with their solid, extended bronze prows, drawing alongside it to smash its oars, or boarding it with their marines – soldiers especially trained in sea combat techniques who were carried on board for that specific purpose.

The larger and wider ships – biremes, triremes, quadriremes and quinquiremes – were,' Kyrros told him, 'tactically much different. Yes, they are capable of the same methods of attack as the galleys; unlike a pure sailing ship, they can accelerate even to half speed within a few seconds and can achieve short ramming speeds of up to ten or twelve nautical miles per hour. But their main advantage lies in their width and stability. These large ships hold catapults and ballistae on their wide decks, huge machines that were developed hundreds of years ago especially by the army of Alexander the Great. They were key weapons in his own arsenal! Now they have been developed into more powerful and accurate versions by the Egyptians, their idea has also been taken and copied by the Romans. In my youth, I myself studied their design in the large collection of ancient war machines that is kept in the Great Library. These weapons are capable of delivering heavy, ship-destroying boulders and bolts – like bolts of lightning – massive arrows that can be the size of small tree trunks. There is also the dreaded 'Greek fire' – a sticky, tar-like incendiary which is catapulted in breakable jars, or coated on cloth covered rocks at their target.'

Kyrros lowered Lio to the ground. As they moved on, in sharp contrast, the engineer's grudging admiration for the ship was more than could be said for the large painted eye on the bow. Lio recognised it instantly from his own childhood. The symbol of good luck drew a loud 'humpf' of disapproval from Kyrros as he shook his head at the superstition.

However, all of this paled into insignificance at the sight that had firmly caught the boy's own personal attention on the long island of Pharos. The island, which formed the sea wall of the natural safe haven, was connected to the mainland by a long, high, multi-arched bridge. As he looked at it, a large ship passed below it. With the possible exception of the Pyramids of Giza that he had seen nearly two years previously, never before had he seen such a tall structure. There, standing on the furthest point overlooking the sea, stood the enormous square tower that had become known erroneously as the 'Pharos of Alexandria'.

It was a tall marker beacon," explained Tom, "a building that pointed out from afar the location of Alexandria's harbour against the otherwise featureless North African coastline. It was also the forerunner of the lighthouse, built in part to guide ships safely into the harbour, even at night and in poor visibility. But one of the main reasons it was built so tall, was from a need for security. Not necessarily in the physical sense, but to bear witness to the great power and culture that was Egypt, and to frighten and intimidate anyone who sailed within its gaze. It was no accident that pirates steered clear of Alexandria.

Built by the architect Sostratos between 285-247 BC on the orders of Ptolemy Soter – Alexander's friend and the same ruler responsible for the building of The Great Library – the Pharos was perhaps one hundred times taller than even Kyrros. It dwarfed everything in the area.

As Lio looked up, at the top of the square tower stood a rounded, temple-like structure made up of tall slender columns, which in turn held a small metal cage atop. Kyrros explained to the boy, 'A fire is burned throughout the night in this,' he said. 'And, within this structure, also powered by the fire, is a steam powered "fog-horn".'

Tom paused and looked at the mouths that had dropped not so wide open this time at the mention of this last device. "In truth it was more of a huge trumpet," he admitted, "Ktesibios – first head librarian of Alexandria!"

This time, no one argued.

The storyteller continued distractedly. "How anyone could have dared to build such a breathtakingly high, elegant and useful structure, to this day baffles everyone. It was to stand for more than fifteen hundred years; perhaps the tallest structure in the world until its collapse in the middle ages. "Earthquake!" He explained shortly, before returning to the main narrative.

"One by one, everyone, including the many technicians, boarded their ship and sailed without delay through the harbour mouth, flanked by their two escorting galleys – the cargo was both valuable and important to the Romans. Lio looked firstly back at the city, then more closely at the seaward side of the tower and a huge carved dedication to mariners from the architect himself, and his father, born in Cnidia. He read it out:

'*Sostratus of Dexiphanes the Cnidian, to saviour gods, for the seafaring ones.*

'Father,' Lio asked, 'why is that inscription on the tower?'

Kyrros smiled broadly. 'That – is Sostratus' revenge on Ptolemy! Following a dispute, the tower's architect was forbidden to inscribe his name on his work. So, he cleverly inscribed his name on the seaward side and had it covered over with plaster. The plaster was then inscribed in honour of Ptolemy, the king. In time however, well after both of their deaths, the plaster began to rot – and Sostratus' own name and dedication became visible – only in the interests of posterity of course!' The boy smiled, appreciating the clever trick for what it really was. The architect had got the last word over his patron.

Now, Lio turned his head to the northwest, looking forward to his first trip to Athens. That five and a half day journey was calm and uneventful, especially thankfully to the boy's father, who was ill almost from the point of leaving the flat calm water in the harbour. Since then, he clung to the wooden hand rails, green faced: if not in terror, at least a close approximation of it. Lio and his mother tried not to smile at his constant look of dread."

Now, Tom grinned, "Andronikos of Kyrros was not super-human after all!"

CHAPTER 32

The Other 'Time-Machine'

NB a more detailed version of this chapter is posted on the Time-Horse website.

Tom stroked back his main of white hair as he continued. "On the hot, mid-morning of the sixth day at sea, Lio stood, hooded, and alone on deck with only a few of the ship's company. He watched as they prepared to sail into the harbour of Piraeus, the Port of Athens. Distantly, as they approached the mainland, although Kyrros was not on deck to point it out, Lio correctly guessed that the tall square-sided crag that stood out from the other, more rounded, mountains in the background was indeed the Acropolis. Furthermore, from his father's earlier description of it, he immediately recognised what was the Temple of Athena Parthenos – the Parthenon.

Standing in front of it, Lio could also make out the smaller Temple of Athena 'Nike', or Victory. But although he had been told that it had long since gone, he was still disappointed not to see the huge statue that had once stood to its fore, overlooking the whole panorama which had greeted the past Athenian warriors as they returned home from various wars. All the same, he could still imagine the impact that the patron god of the city would have had: the sun gleaming on the tip of her golden spear and on her decorated helmet, her ivory face and body glowing with warmth, and her richly painted clothes a vision of opulence. She would have been one of the first sights afforded to countless exhausted soldiers returning home.

Now growing nearer the small-ish circular harbour, what greeted

Lio was not at all what the boy had expected from Kyrros' less than glowing description of it. In contrast, it seemed quite picturesque, its interior neatly encircled by hundreds of tidily laid out galley sheds. Three 'T' shaped timber jetties ran from its harbour wall to its centre, where not more than a dozen ships were moored. In a way it reminded Lio of Rhodos, small and friendly. Now he was looking forward all the more to this, his first ever trip to the Greek mainland. Then, as he watched, the master turned slightly westward, and made to continue in the opposite direction around the headland.

It was the smell of Piraeus' main Kantharos Port that hit him first, the Athenian drains pouring their effluent into the huge but narrow mouthed harbour. As they sailed in, avoiding the many other vessels, mostly luggers waiting to dock, one of their escorts sailed ahead. Someone on board called out a warning to anyone who appeared to get too near. Next came the clamour of the crowds of people on the dockside itself, though once they realised that this was Roman business, most moved on.

Lio had made an innocent mistake. Like many before him, he had confused the ancient, now relatively small and recently renamed harbour of Zea, with the much larger Kantharos port. Zea was now the exclusive Roman military port on the opposite side of the headland, whereas it was Kantharos that had the dubious privilege of being the main port of Piraeus. Never mind though, his father was clambering on deck now, and by the way he was holding his nose, it would not be long before they were out of there! Indeed, it took them only that morning to get to the rather stuffy Roman governor's palace. There, they would all stay as guests for the duration of the installation of the mechanisms in the Horologion.

The Roman agora of Athens was a true revelation, nestled as it was beneath the high Acropolis and to the western edge of the far older and more historical Ancient Greek agora. The whole place was not just another city of great wonder to Lio as he had expected it to be, but through *his* eyes, it was far more beautiful in many ways than the exciting but sprawling business capital of Alexandria.

Athens was built not only in stone or, as most of Alexandria was, mud brick. It was, in addition, studded at regular intervals by many public buildings built in both the local Pentellic and imported Parian marble. Both of which were prized for their natural pristine white colour and strength. The whole area, as far as the eye could see, seemed built upon. Yet, somehow, it was still lush and green; the natural spring that flowed from the Acropolis and ran gradually downhill had for countless years, naturally irrigated the whole area. As a result, wonderful and exotically coloured plants and flowers of every description grew from between and around many of the buildings, giving the perfect impression of being both a long established literal and cultural oasis.

In the Roman agora alone, this impression had been furthered by the recent construction of the public bathing area – a series of deep, mosaic lined pools interspersed with dressing rooms, massage rooms, laundry rooms and last, but certainly not least, the public mixed, male and female lavatorium – or toilet."

The four friends variously smirked and wrinkled their noses.

"All of these buildings were linked by a Roman colonnade that ran in an elongated 'C' configuration around a central paved area. And to the eastern end, the end nearest the source of the spring itself, stood the short, narrow and as yet unused aqueduct. This in turn would carry the constant supply of water from the Acropolis to the open-topped water tank built into the rear of the now completed, but as yet empty, octagonal shell of Kyrros' Horologion. The King's Engineer could not have been given a better stage – a more prime site to make his mark on the world. Work on the installation would begin at first light in the morning."

"Shared toilets!" Maddie had waited for a suitable gap in the Tom's story to register her disgust at the concept. The looks on the faces of the others registered the same discomfort at the idea. Only Conna seemed to find the idea even slightly amusing, not that he would have said so aloud.

Tom simply shrugged in reply. He said casually, "Things were different then, it was even a place to socialise!" Then he carried on regardless.

"That morning, as Kyrros and his co-workers started work, Lio and his mother took the opportunity to discover the rest of the city: beginning with the Acropolis. In what now seemed to Lio to be his distant childhood, the pathway up the ramp to the Acropolis of Rhodos had been steep but thankfully short. By contrast, it looked as if the route to the Athens Acropolis was both very long and fairly steep. However, as a place of worship for the Athenians, the gods represented there held no interest for either of them. Instead, Miriam led the pair away from it and the Roman agora. Climbing up to briefly stand on the already worn dais that was the speaking platform on the hill of the Pnyx, mother and son stood and looked out over the city and at the Ancient gathering place directly below.

Miriam and Lio gazed down at what four hundred years earlier had been the cradle of democracy. 'This was the place,' she explained, 'where the early orators, or speakers, used to come to address the crowds on something that they wished to make happen. Together, they made real decisions: whether they needed to make or change a law; whether to ostracise, or banish a citizen or politician for the good of the city. True democracy: where the people decided directly – not through elected leaders who might betray their wishes through corruption. Each citizen's direct right to vote was taken seriously and never squandered. Battles were fought to defend their rights. Each of the assembled crowd was given a small pressed piece of pottery, a clay coin called an "Idikon", which he placed in one of two pots to register a *for* or an *against*. Anyone not using that precious Idikon was open to ridicule and became known as... an "Idiot"!'

Lio smiled at the origin of the word he knew to mean generally stupid.

Miriam continued. 'This, and the nearby Areios Pagos, or rock of Ares – also known as the rock of Mars, the god of war – was where other laws were also made – for instance, how to stop family vendetta. For hundreds – perhaps thousands of years – if someone was killed, it became the duty of the victim's family to take the life of the killer. It then became the duty of the other family to kill that killer, and so on, sometimes for many generations, all to attempt to satisfy so called "family honour!" Finally, it was decided right here, in this very place, that to break the circle of violence, the people would take the responsibility to hold a killer, or any other suspected criminal, to trial. Justice would be meted out by society. In this way, the vendetta had been broken – and replaced with law and order.' Lio watched Miriam standing there, drinking-in the atmosphere of that historic place.

Now he understood why Miriam had wished to head there instead of the spectacular temples of the Acropolis. This place was where true, *intelligent* people-power had started to replace brute force and ignorance! It was another place and lesson that the young boy would never forget.

Three short weeks later, Kyrros' Tower of the Winds – the Horologion of Athens – was duly completed. To Lio, this was the most incredible of all of the buildings in the city. At its ceremonial unveiling, Lio watched with pride as his father topped off the tower with an ornate version of Lio's wind indicator, a figure of Poseidon which indicated the wind direction with his trident. But it was the mechanisms that were to be found inside the tower which would astound the public.

The tall internal space was dominated by an enormous, stylised bronze Oak tree. On its trunk, mounted vertically, there were three clock faces. The first was a single handed clock, divided into twenty-four hours of the day – each hour subdivided into halves only. This was considered accurate enough for the Athenians' purposes – Kyrros did not wish their lives to be dominated by clock-watching. Oddly enough though, the Roman hour was not constant. Instead, the Roman day was divided into periods of light and darkness. Both of these periods were then divided into twelve equal hours. Therefore, daylight working hours became longer toward the summer solstice, and shorter again toward the winter solstice. Kyrros, of course, geared the movement of the pointer to reflect this.

The second clock face indicated the 365 days of the year, pointing out especially the important religious festivals. The third was divided into 223 lunar months – the Saros cycle. With this, Kyrros would point out to the entire population that eclipses were both entirely predictable and natural. There would be no more opportunity for priests to manipulate the crowds. No more reasons for sacrifices to appease the gods!

There was also another important device situated high around the trunk: a mechanical armillary, which showed the sun at the centre of the universe, and the known planets in orbit around it. Additionally, there were hundreds of other mechanical features mounted in and around the tree and perched on its branches, including moving animals and chirping birds. What was more, all of these were powered either by water power or steam from a small boiler inside the tower!

While those in attendance were captivated with its ingenuity and beauty, there was, however, one dissenting voice – that of the High Priest of Jupiter. Predictably, he had decided that Kyrros was undermining the tale of Jupiter's creation of the world. 'SACRILEGE!' was the one word he shouted before he stormed out in mock disgust. Kyrros instantly dismissed the childish fit of pique.

And one last thing: as everyone gazed on, Kyrros led Miriam behind the tree to point out one last and very personal feature – an engraving. There, high up on the trunk, a tiny Cupid had fired an arrow through an equally tiny heart inscribed with three words: 'Kyrros Eros Miriam'. It was a sentimental gesture that he had contemplated long and hard, wondering if at their late ages whether Miriam might not find it too silly. Lio watched his mother smile and then weep silently. Tears of joy ran down her face, before she buried her head in the folds of Kyrros' clothes, a little embarrassed but entirely happy with the courtly gesture and the public declaration of love.

After that official opening, the very next day, the whole party of Greeks returned swiftly home to Alexandria, though notably without either of their escorting galleys. They had delivered their cargo safely and now the Greeks were of no more interest to Rome. Those galleys were also far more needed nearer home; the Roman civil war was expanding."

As Tom finished this part of the tale, as amazing as it had all sounded to them, not one of the four had any doubt in their minds about the feasibility of the technology included in Kyrros' Horologion. Alex, in particular, now breathed in with satisfaction.

CHAPTER 33:

The Face Of Ashur

"Once back in Alexandria, now that the work on the Horologion had been completed and everyone had been paid, Miriam began to focus on her wedding. She and Kyrros would be married in ten days, just long enough to 'make a few small plans'. Although Kyrros was not normally disposed to celebration or fuss, he did not mind this at all. However, being a natural ascetic, he could not help rolling his eyes at the small extravagances his betrothed wished to include in their wedding feast. Lio's father now had more than enough money to both retire comfortably and buy a small villa by the sea. In preference, they would find somewhere not too far from the museum and library. This would allow him to live in the city and go on working there without living in the sometimes cloying atmosphere of the royal quarter. To the delight of Lio, it was also, promised Kyrros, enough to begin the boy's education at the Mouseion. Lio could not wait for his new life and his future to begin properly.

Like Kyrros, Miriam had no surviving close family, so the guest list was composed entirely of their friends and colleagues at the library. And since she had been accepted intellectually by the Chronology Society as a result of her earlier 'advances in metallurgy', they had all effectively become her surrogate family. The only 'real' family she had was Lio!

Only one further task remained before then. Intended as an honour, and a rare one at that, Kyrros, or to give him his proper, birth name, Andronicus of Cyrrhus, was to have a bronze sculpture made of him – although he himself thought the whole thing both ridiculous and tedious. Nevertheless, within days of the wedding, Lio accompanied him along to one of the workshop studios where he would be obliged to sit for days while a talented student sculpted his image in wax. However he would only agree to sit for the bust of his head to be made. Someone else, he insisted, would have to stand in for his body. On the second boring day, out of the blue, Kyrros suggested that the sculptor make a second likeness – of Lio. It was he who had inspired him in many aspects of his recent work – and had privately been the catalyst between Miriam and himself. In fact, he insisted acidly, as a comment on the 'hideously long time it was taking', that after the sculptor had finished his own bust, he'd best get straight on with the sculpture of the boy – before he had time to grow into manhood!

It was two days later that Lio himself stood in front of the sculptor to have his own bust made. Though, in agreement with the boy, the sculptor had decided to portray him 'a few years older': indeed, as a rather magnificent young man. The finished twinned bronze sculptures would stand side by side in the entrance hall of the Great Library: Andronicus of Cyrrhus, the scientist, philosopher and engineer – portraying expertise and achievement; and his learned assistant Helio of Rhodos – portraying both ambition and male beauty. Lio would forever reach out to grasp a symbol of the world in his fingertips – a small, delicate, golden globe – whilst Kyrros represented all that the youth might someday accomplish. Within a further few weeks, both wax sculptures would be finished, and within another couple of months, they would be cast in bronze. Then their images would be captured forever.

As time hurried along toward the big day, everyone busied themselves one way or another with the wedding plans. Lio was left quite happily on his own, and since there was nothing to be getting on with, his father encouraged the boy to see if he could find something or someone, perhaps nearer his own age, to amuse himself. So he took it literally: he had been given a licence to roam. In those few days, buoyed up by his newfound confidence, Lio began to explore the grounds, farther and wider.

Early one morning, despite the strict rules against it, Lio decided that it was high time for him to go alone to see the many hundreds of thousands of texts rolled up and deposited in what was the Great Library. He felt that he had earned the privilege. And after all, he was, he considered, as the sculptor had said, almost a man – twelve and a half years old. The boy walked boldly in through the great doors.

The head librarian, together with the colourfully dressed Poseidonios, was speaking to someone at the time: a small, slightly chubby youth, plainly dressed and with a clean shaven head. He was perhaps a few years older than Lio. Oddly enough though, he didn't look nearly as mature as Lio. The librarian especially stood attentively as the boy spoke; he didn't notice Lio pass by, so Lio was able to wander around freely in the first chamber which contained the written texts.

Inside, everything was silent; to assist concentration in the library, talking was not permitted. In the library, then as now, the golden rule was silence. Unfortunately for Lio, perhaps because he was reading a particularly dusty old script, he began to sneeze uncontrollably. The other occupants glared. Within a minute, the librarian walked up to him and immediately reprimanded him for daring to enter without the guidance of Kyrros. The other, shaven-headed, young boy smiled broadly as, despite Lio's protestations that he was nearly as old as he, he was unceremoniously ejected from the premises. There was some more general smirking from those that knew the librarian's attitude to protecting *his* books, and from those who knew the identity of the other boy. Nevertheless, emboldened by this small victory, Lio next decided to look further afield, which was completely uncharacteristic of him – but still quite fun.

The next day, he determined to see whether he could bluff his way past the guards around the palace itself – frankly just to see if he could. Although it would have been impossible for anyone to approach the Royal Palace from any other direction, from the direction of the gateway that led directly into the palace from the grounds of the Mouseion, it was not so difficult. As Lio neared the huge guard who still somehow reminded him of someone he didn't wish to remember, he took a deep breath and delivered the excuse that he'd previously rehearsed: He'd been sent on an errand from his father, Kyrros, the King's Engineer, to meet the young king himself. It was a near blatant, but harmless lie, although Kyrros had in fact told him to find someone nearer his own age to spend some time with. Not that he expected to get anywhere near the king. He had just thought that it would be a good enough excuse for him to get inside the palace grounds so that he could wander round for a while exploring. After that, he would leave again.

At first he was pleasantly surprised when the bluff worked, however he was then horrified that the guard turned and escorted him directly into the royal chambers, followed by a second guard. Unable to change his mind, but not exactly scared, now inside, he was determined to brazen the act out. Perhaps because he had approached from the Mouseion, he was not led into the formal throne room, but instead into what was obviously the private royal living quarters. Lio stood and waited patiently, looking around the richly painted and decorated surroundings in which the royals lived. It simply took his breath away, such was its sheer opulence. There were golden chairs in the form of animals, couches and a huge bed covered with exotic animal skins. Multi-layered curtains and fabrics covered the walls, swaying gently in the breeze from the many windows in this, the top level of the palace. Even the floor was covered with woollen and silk hand-woven rugs – just to walk on!

To his surprise, when the king arrived, he all was alone. Lio had by now almost expected a fanfare – but this was not an official visit. Instead, Ptolemy XIII, the boy king and co-ruler of Upper and Lower Egypt, casually walked in alone, stroking his shaven head.

He wore only a tight golden kilt and a pair of golden sandals. From each hand hung a white cotton sack; one containing something round, the other something rectangular. He placed them carefully down before turning his attention toward Lio.

Whomever Lio had expected the king to be, it was not this boy; though Lio recognised him at once. However, today he looked different – extremely confident, even arrogant – but unlike yesterday in the library, now quite sad. Sad in a way that Lio later realised could only be brought about by carrying the weight of the country's affairs on his own young shoulders – and by the subterfuge that was going on all around him.

Although he recognised Lio, now that he was once more dressed and wearing the persona of 'The King', Ptolemy looked blankly at his visitor, glancing at the sun-protectors hanging around his neck. 'Yes,' he asked, 'what is it?'

Taken aback by his harshness and his loud, if not mature voice, Lio replied. 'I thought you might like some company – of your own age, I mean. Someone to talk to... or play games with,' he suggested, clearly out of his depth.

The young king blinked at him trying to understand, though obviously completely uncomprehending of the alien concept. He was not used to 'talking' or 'playing'.

'If not, I can go...' Lio blundered-on, suddenly feeling ridiculous.

The boy in front of him, it seemed, had lost all of his youthfulness as a result of being treated solely as an adult and as the future king from the earliest age. For the rest of his own short life he would struggle against being manipulated by those around him – until his eventual defeat at the Battle of the Nile. Although he was vastly wealthy, one of the wealthiest rulers in the world, and although he shared command of power over Egypt with his sister Lio did not in the slightest envy him or this place.

Perhaps suddenly disarmed at being confronted by Lio, a boy of his own physical size, the expression on the king's face changed momentarily. In place of the imperious look, Lio caught, perhaps only for a few seconds, a haunted look of silent pleading in his eyes. The rare expression reminded him distantly of someone that he once knew – although he could not recall whom or where the memory came from.

The short moment was broken by a brash shout from a plain-looking, much older girl who strutted into the room shortly behind the king. Elegantly clad in a flowing purple silk gown, she wore the thick black wig that Lio immediately recognised from the newly struck Egyptian coins he'd seen: Queen Cleopatra VII, co-ruler of Egypt, Queen of the Nile, amongst many other grand titles she had assumed to date. 'Who's this?' she demanded of her younger brother and husband.

'My name is Helio,' Lio introduced himself formally, answering for him. 'I am the grandson of Kyrros.'

'Who?' She looked critically at Lio, obviously not recognising the man's name.

'Andronikos of Kyrros – the scientist and philosopher – the Engineer of the Mouseion,' Ptolemy attempted to prompt her, but she remained unaware.

The queen shot him a poisoned glance and sneered at Lio. 'Is he a king? Is he a ruler? A god like us?' She indicated with her hand. 'My husband, the God-King Ptolemy,' she sniggered, 'or myself: the Goddess-Queen Cleopatra?'

'No,' Lio answered flatly, unimpressed by her performance.

She walked toward him, looking at his hair. 'Is that real?' she asked.

'Yes,' answered Lio.

She put up her hand to touch it, stroking her fingers through it gently, testing it. 'Really?' she quizzed.

'Yes,' he stated, 'it is.'

'It's a pity it isn't longer. It might make a marvellous hairpiece.' Abruptly changing the subject she asked, 'How old are you?'

'I am twelve years old,' he replied.

'Not a man yet then, like my husband...' she sneered at Ptolemy '...nearly is. Shame!' She turned on her heel, losing interest. 'Then go,' she said, 'we do not wish to see you.' She clapped her hands twice: the royal command.

The boy king shot her a sideways glance that looked equally poisonous. The humiliated Ptolemy brushed his subject away with the back of his hand. But as he did, the king again looked almost pleadingly at him as Lio dutifully copied the bowing guard in front of him. He backed out of the room, and once out of the palace made a run for the gate.

From that short audience, it was plain that both king and queen hated each other. However, little did Lio know that, within a few weeks, their venom would spill out into a very public rift. A rift which would not only spell the end for the Ptolemaic dynasty, but one that would bring the end of greatness for Egypt and its significance as a world power. For Lio's part, he was glad to get out. Disturbed as he was by the experience, he went back home but made a point of not telling either his mother or father where he'd been or what he'd been up to.

That night, Lio went to bed very early. Again he drifted into a deep dream-sleep; this time, after two years, his mind finally repairing itself after being prompted by the Egyptian guard and the haunted look on the face of the boy king. Now, a dream filled-in the sketchy outlines with the missing details which his own defence mechanism had previously blotted-out:

Lio dreamed of a sun-filled, happy day that he had spent playing between two temples. He clearly remembered his friend Marduk smiling at him, as they competed to see who could pitch a pebble nearest a rock that had been placed in the middle. They giggled and laughed together, successively knocking each other's out of the way. Someone else, a slightly older girl, played in the dirt beside them with a toy: a squat wooden unicorn. Lio could still not see her face, though like themselves, she was happy. Then the mood changed. The sound of thunder approached overhead and both the boy and girl cowered from it as Lio tried to reassure them that it was all perfectly natural. But they were still afraid. Out of the angry sky, a zigzag bolt of lightning struck the boy, instantly leaving him lying still beside the temple wall. For all he appeared dead, Lio still heard his echoing voice say, 'You promised to take care of her.' Then the girl got up slowly and walked towards Lio, her hands and arms outstretched as if she wished him to hug her. At that, her face came into full view – a beautiful face that he at once recognised.

Lio sat bolt upright in his sleep and shouted her name aloud: 'Ashur!'

In an instant, Miriam was there beside him. She sat on the side of the boy's bed, hugging him as he rocked back and forth, his head full of other recalled images: the broken body of his friend Marduk; the High Priest of Zeus; his stick lashing across Lio's back in one of the rooms in the labyrinthine cellar; his huge servant; the total eclipse; and the green eyes of Helios looking down on him – everything hit him at once.

But the image that haunted Lio most, long after he had again settled and his mother had gone back to bed, was the face of Ashur. As he struggled to go back to sleep, big tears rolled onto his pillow. The boy could not forget her face, nor the story that he now remembered from over five hundred years earlier. Whatever had become of her, he wondered – the girl he had promised to protect? He began to fret. Had she survived the clutches of the self-styled Zeus? And what had happened to the same high priest, for that matter?

For the first time since his rescue, it hit him: no matter how much he wished to change the past, after five hundred years had elapsed, he was now powerless to help her.

Unless of course... Lio began to wonder."

CHAPTER 34:

Noughts And Crosses

"At daybreak, Lio once again crept into the library, this time with a purpose. Although no one had ever mentioned where the mysterious machine had been stored away, he had always assumed that it was buried somewhere deep inside the library or the museum – although he didn't know for sure. However, it seemed to him the most logical place to start looking. He waited until a small group approached the doors of the library and got on their blind side, away from the librarian, who was as always seated at the small desk to the side of the vast, open entrance hall.

Once inside, the boy crept stealthily from pillar to pillar, amongst the statues and past many scholars who stood in quiet private discussion. From there he went into the library proper: the vast book store. On this particular day, the main room was already busy; the precious early sunlight helped the scholars see more easily than in artificial light. Many were reading or writing texts – making notes or copying them. In this area there were too many people to sneak past unnoticed. So again Lio stood boldly upright and pretended to himself that he had been sent on a message to find his father, or so he would say if anyone asked him. It was another lie of course, although, he convinced himself, a white lie: possibly even a truth of sorts. After all, his mother had asked before he left that morning that if he bumped into Kyrros, to tell him not to forget his appointment to have his hair and beard trimmed!

Strolling through the main room of the library on his own, Lio now realised how vast the area was. He walked through all of the stored papers and into the next hall, to the one area where he had never been before. It was an area where more *solid writings* were stored – a library of ancient works. Some were carved in stone and wood, some written on fragile slabs of clay imprinted with symbols so ancient that he couldn't even begin to recognise it. As he strolled past them all, he was filled with renewed wonderment for the place.

Next he went through another set of doors and into a third vast area, a room full of other ancient artefacts. He had entered the display room of the museum. Egyptian statues from the Old Kingdom, similar to those he had known to stand outside the Egyptian temple on Rhodos. There were painted wooden guardians of tombs, wearing golden kilts. Old water jugs and amphorae, decorated with well known scenes from antiquity. There was a huge cast bronze pot, brought from Gaul, possibly big enough for him to fit inside, with ornate handles and decorations covering the rim and top half of it. Primitive stone statues like ones he had heard of, copies of the giant statue on the sacred island of Delos, the supposed birthplace of Zeus' son Apollo. Each exhibit was vastly different in style to the next, each a representative sample of any given style or culture. All had been brought here to this safe repository, a place to rest. Lio slipped past the working scholars and technicians transferring the designs onto papyrus to be dutifully filed away for posterity. From there, he went out through another set of doors and into an empty area, a large room filled only with benches. It was the speaking, or lecture room, he supposed, with a raised dais at the far end, from which one could stand and address scholars. Again he walked straight through it.

On he went, through another set of doors behind the dais which led him to a long, wide and well lit corridor, polished metal tubes in the ceiling letting in light from mirrored hatches in the roof. The corridor was studded with closed doors on each side. He had by now ceased to creep around; he was exploring, he told himself as he opened each door in turn. If the boy had expected to see anything exciting though, he was sadly disappointed: most of the dozen or so small rooms he entered, or at least opened the door of, were entirely empty apart from a table and one or two benches in each of them. Presumably the rooms were all for private study. He was about to give up his casual search and move off somewhere else, when he was drawn to the doorway directly at the end of the corridor. It was a much wider, double door that looked more grand than the others. Although he had never been superstitious, and neither had he believed in supernatural powers of any sort, if the term we now know as extra-sensory-perception had been used at that time, perhaps that would have best described what the boy most felt at that moment. It seemed to him that something behind that furthest door beckoned him toward it.

Lio walked slowly up the corridor and, as gently and as noiselessly as he could, pushed at the doors, testing them to see if they would open, but they were locked. He stood and looked at them a while, considering how to gain entry, when the strange sensation came over him again. Although the corridor was warm, he experienced a shivering sensation and the hairs on the back of his neck began to stand up. He imagined, rather than heard, a faint breathing noise coming from behind it. Then, as he pushed them again, there was a soft click and one of the doors opened: the lock was already broken. He opened it wide, however, to his disappointment, it was only an empty cupboard. But then the sensation overtook Lio again. He walked into it and tentatively pushed at the back of the cupboard. And at that, it moved!

Softly, in trepidation, Lio pushed the concealed inner door of the chamber half open, though sadly only to be disappointed by another dark and apparently empty room. However, this one was much larger than the others and, oddly, without windows. The boy stood for a few seconds and let his eyes get accustomed to the sparse light. He picked out the edge of something in the corner opposite and stepped forward to take a closer look, but it was only a large wooden crate lying open on its side. He looked around fleetingly, but there appeared to be nothing else there, so he turned to leave.

Once more, he could have sworn he heard something breathing. He stood at the door a while longer, watching and listening, but it was nothing. He made to leave, and without checking behind it, started to close the door behind him. As he left, this time he would have sworn he'd heard the same single, light breath. Yet again gripped by the strange feeling, he reopened the door but this time chanced leaving it wide open. Stepping back fully inside, he absolutely *felt* the presence of something else within the room. Lio squinted, his eyes finally getting accustomed to the scant light reflected from the white walls; still nothing. On impulse, he now peered behind the door. And there, in the corner, stood a large object covered in a dustsheet. It was taller than himself and as bulky as one of the ponies on the farm back at Drodos. The boy cautiously peeled back the sheet and it let it slip to the floor. Then, he came face to face with the object of his search: the Hippo-Chronos.

Strangely, he began to remember it as it had first appeared in front of him. At first he did nothing but stand and stare at the sculpture. Although it had no eyes, only dark, dead holes instead, the Time-Horse appeared to be looking back at him. Lio gazed in marvel at its outline, remembering now, in detail, what he had, in the main, previously blocked out. In flashbacks, he recalled steam pouring from its nostrils and how it appeared to rear into the air. His father, Kyrros, dressed in white, looking for all the world like Zeus with his bolt of lightning held high. Lio took a long sobbing breath deep into his lungs. Although he was not especially wary of the machine, it nevertheless held him in awe. He still could not bring himself to step too near. However, he did gently stretch out his hand toward it, careful not to spook the animal. He stroked the deliciously cool bronze head, as if finding a long lost childhood toy, marvelling at what he could now just about see, exploring its shape in the dark. Looking closely through the delicate metal tracery of its external skeleton, he could just begin to make out all sorts of variously complicated looking mechanisms packed tightly within it. They looked far more intricate than those he had helped build and had seen finally installed in the Horologion. These were mechanisms

313

so complicated that he could not in a million years begin to fathom how it worked. No wonder Kyrros had never been worried by the much less complicated Roman commission – the Horologion. Lio heard the soft breathing sound again, accompanied by a regular tink... tink... tink... every ten seconds. He looked for a sign of where the sounds might be coming from; but despite his search, he couldn't find a clue of what caused it, other than it seemed to be coming from deep inside the horse's chest. He thought it best not to probe physically in case he damaged something inside it. Then, just where one would expect to find the brain there was a gap where part of the mechanism had been removed.

He looked again at the rest of the animal, its saddle and at the opened hatch on top of its buttocks. There, was another gap where something else had been removed. Now Lio remembered the security measures the two keys to its unauthorised use. He could see they were missing! The horse was dead! They had killed it! And Lio had forgotten all about it.

His heart sank, he could not help feeling regret at what, to his gradually returning detailed memory had seemed a living, breathing animal. He absent-mindedly stroked its neck and flanks caringly, trying to work out how to get his hands on the two keys. It would not be easy.

His curiosity satisfied for now, he patted its saddle and covered it with the dustsheet again. He made his way to the door, closing it softly, subconsciously trying not to disturb the machine. Then he stepped back into the corridor. Halfway down it, the boy thought he heard footsteps approaching, but as the sound echoed around the space, he couldn't tell from which direction. He sprinted down the rest of the corridor and into the museum display room. As it was now midday and lunchtime, it was completely empty. As he hid, listening intently, eventually the footsteps reached the room. They stopped briefly, and then retreated. He waited about five more minutes before popping his head out of the bronze pot to check that the coast was clear. Thankfully, it had been large enough to take him after all.

As the head librarian padded back down the corridor to check inside the Hippo-Chronos room, he convinced himself that the room had not been discovered. However, he made a conscious note to himself to let Kyrros know that his grandson had been snooping around the library again. He would ask the man to ask the boy not to play in there again. Even if it was not in the librarian's nature, and even if it was he who was ultimately charged with the safety of the library, he secretly liked the intelligent boy, and he was not overly worried about the incident. After all, ultimately, what harm could a small boy do to the Great Library of Alexandria? Anyway, tomorrow, the machine would be crated up and taken away.

However, the writing was finally on the wall for Lio when he 'borrowed' the keys; although, in a way, he would never wish to turn the clock back on the incident. That night, over dinner, he asked casually about the Hippo-Chronos machine and how it worked, softening Kyrros up, as Lio thought; eager to learn, as Kyrros thought.

Kyrros explained some of the theory, trying to describe the various mechanisms that controlled it through time and distance; Lio could not understand much of it at all. To the boy, Kyrros was the world's greatest genius – Lio, on the other hand, was an ordinary twelve year old! Lio pretended to be fascinated at the idea of the Cosmos-key – the armillary, asking Kyrros to explain more.

Kyrros patiently obliged. 'Small, relatively light and quite portable,' as Kyrros said, 'it is fitted via a hatch on top of the horse's buttocks. It also works completely automatically – controlled by the settings on the Chrono-key.'

That much was all Lio could really take in – but Kyrros went on to explain it all in detail anyway.

'So what about the other key: the Chrono-key – the brains of the machine?' Lio asked

'That key,' explained Kyrros, 'is much different: it is far more portable: lighter again and less bulky than the Cosmos-key. But both are easily replaced within minutes. It is the programming that takes the time and expertise. Everything has to be pre-programmed well in advance of the machine's use – it is no easy task to change the time and location settings quickly. As a result, no one has so much as looked at, let alone touched the settings since its last use nearly two years ago.'

'So where are the missing keys kept?' the boy asked casually.

'That,' Kyrros said, 'was a secret known only to their keeper, the head librarian himself.'

Lio's heart sank; how could he get around the head librarian, he wondered. Every time he saw him he grimaced at him, there was no way he could.

And then his father let slip a secret. Unbeknown to the librarian, Kyrros still had the prototype keys, much simpler in many ways but still functional – though properly untested within the machine.

'And where are they?' Lio enquired innocently.

'Wait here,' Kyrros said, and moments later returned with two cloth wrapped packages.

Unfolding each of the cloths before setting them gently aside, he revealed two wooden boxes: the first, a perfect cube, about a foot and a half along each side; the second, over two feet long, about half as wide and about a third deep. Unlocking a small bronze clasp on each of the boxes, he opened them to reveal each mechanism. The first was the incredibly intricate, working bronze armillary sphere. Its settings were controlled from the second key, however.

This second mechanism was programmed via rows and rows of tiny thumbwheels, incorporated into the top of the device using a code that Kyrros had himself devised using only noughts and crosses – a kind of ancient binary code. Starting at the far right, the first digit represented one. Reading to its left, the second digit was doubled to two, the third doubled to four, the fourth to eight, and so on... Lio grappled with it all, trying to take it all in. Kyrros then continued the lesson of how all the other parts of the horse worked until late into the night, while the boy listened intently, if not

316

always understanding. But then he inadvertently gave Lio another way around the whole problem. Notwithstanding all of what he had already explained, both of the prototype keys had been set exactly the same as the missing keys which were held by the librarian! 'Which is just as well,' cautioned Kyrros, 'because if anyone ever rides the horse again – without knowing exactly how to program the device – they could disappear forever into the future!'

Nevertheless, the librarian's keys were meant to be kept in reserve, in case of last minute hitches. Both were though, he reminded the boy, made to lesser tolerances – and were possibly a little less accurate and prone to mechanical problems.

Now, way after his bed-time, and way after Miriam had gone to her own bed, Lio began to nod off. He had been up since dawn and was dog-tired, but now at least, he did have enough information for his purposes.

Without further ado, his father packed the equipment away into their boxes, leaving the keys in the centre of the table, then he physically carried the boy to bed. The next day would be the eve of the wedding and everyone except Lio had plenty of things to do. That night, as he slept, Lio's head was filled only with images of noughts and crosses."

CHAPTER 35:

Wilful Disobedience

Tom stopped abruptly. "Forgive me, Maddie, Bex, Conna, Alex, but I must take a short break – stretch my legs – and drinking all of this water..." Tom left the room swiftly.

"Well, what do you think now?" Alex asked the girls.

"He's very convincing, isn't he?" suggested Maddie non-committally, "but meeting Cleopatra? And combing her fingers through his hair?"

"He'll be bumping into Julius Caesar next," joked Conna.

Bex considered her own single comment: "Disgusting!" She shook her head, scunnering at the thought she could not remove since Tom had mentioned it. "Nineteen! Marrying your own thirteen year old brother – that's sick!"

"And dangerous," added Maddie helpfully.

Conna mused openly, "I saw a documentary once, about ancient Egypt – mummies and stuff. They were always doing things like that, marrying their own family. Some parents even married their own sons or daughters. 'Course there were loads of deformed kids born to them. But most died – or were even done away with at birth."

"Yecch! I still can't believe it," said Bex, turning down the corners of her mouth in disgust. Some things didn't bear thinking about.

Devilishly, Conna narrowed his eyes. "Oh, I don't know, Freddie's not that bad looking, is he?"

Maddie and Bex were horrified. "Our dad – yeeach!"

Despite themselves, the boys smirked at the girls' reactions to one of the world's ultimate taboos.

Noticing the looks on the boys' faces, Bex returned the idea. "And what about your mums, or should I say mummies?"

Alex's face was instantly straightened.

Conna's looked like it had been slapped. "Whoaa! Let's not even think about going there," he said, suddenly folding his arms tightly across his stomach.

"Noo!" "Nah!" "Yecch!" "No, no, no!" they all cringed. Then sat and waited silently.

Tom was amused at the stone faces on the four as he re-entered the room. It was as if they hadn't spoken since he'd got up, but had waited attentively for his return. Letting out another gasp, he sat down to resume where he'd left off. "I do wish I could remember where I left my old walking stick," he mumbled.

He now began to set the scene of the eve of Kyrros and Miriam's wedding. "Somewhere over the city of Alexandria a cockerel crowed, ushering in the dawn. Lio had overslept. Getting quickly washed, dressed and breakfasted, he laid out his wedding tunic on the bed, ready for tomorrow. As a last minute thought, he found another of his own clean garments and laid that also on the bed. It was of course a boy's garment, but in truth there was little difference between the dress of boys and girls apart from a few accessories, and he was sure that in the circumstances it would be acceptable as an emergency wedding outfit. Only Miriam was in the house. Lio looked casually around the place, calling out for his father before deciding it was safe to do what he had planned.

He went outside for a few minutes, only to return quickly. Next, quickly picking up the heavy packages containing the keys, he ran outside with them. Then he placed them carefully in one of the wooden hand-carts that were used to move various things around the workshops. The bright sunlight prompted him to remember his sun-protectors just in time, so he went back in to retrieve them, tying them around his neck. Finally, as he went out of the door for the last time, his mother asked where he was going. He said simply, 'To fetch a surprise – don't worry, I'll be back soon.' With both packages safely in the cart, the boy picked up the handles and set off over to the library to await an opportunity to get inside unnoticed. As he hung around outside, it did not take long before the opportunity presented itself.

The impressively large and overweight philosopher Lio knew only by his nickname – 'Bacchus the Epicurean' – waddled uncomfortably toward the door. Seizing on the event, the boy walked purposely behind and to the side of him furthest away from the librarian. He trailed the cart with its packages tightly beside him. As Bacchus moved past the librarian's desk, the boy slowly overtook him, careful to keep out of the line of sight. It worked! Once inside, no one so much as batted an eyelid as he walked purposefully through the library and on into the section which contained the ancient writings. It was only when he entered the museum of ancient artefacts and strolled past the bronze pot that Lio was recognised briefly by one of the Chronology Society members. However, apart from a curious frown at the cart, he just waved his hand in greeting as the boy passed through the room and then the door at the opposite end. Lio almost ran along the passage and barged into the thankfully still unlocked and unoccupied room. Today though, something was different. He walked in warily. All of the lamps had been lit around the room. In panic, he looked at the packing case and then behind him to the corner, dropping the handle of the cart as he did. The machine had gone! No, this couldn't be, surely. Had he been found out yesterday after all? Lio's plan had not so much changed as had evaporated. He couldn't believe it.

Then, as quickly as his plan had disappeared, it came back again. He simply hadn't looked properly: the packing crate was now upright and in it, just visible through a gap in the slats, was the polished figure of the Hippo-Chronos. The crate lid lay beside it on the floor. Lio breathed a deep sigh of relief. Fearing that he might be caught by whoever was packaging it up, without further ado he carefully unwrapped and un-boxed the first of the two keys: the Cosmos-key – the armillary.

He clambered onto one of the two stools that had been placed beside the Hippo-Chronos, then, holding the key against his chest with one hand, he climbed up the side of the case. Opening the hatch on top of the horse's buttocks and installing the key was simple, everything about the machine had been fabricated to great precision. He slipped the key into the cradle that was designed to accept it, and by the miracle of precision engineering, it clicked down. Then, as he closed the hatch, the necessary linkages automatically locked themselves into place.

Next, he brought out the second key: the Chrono-key – the time computer. Similarly, he opened the hatch in the back of the horse's neck, almost disastrously dropping the delicate equipment as he manoeuvred it into place onto its guide rails. This time the task was a bit more difficult, but eventually it slid easily along the rails and clicked into place. Now it locked itself into position and connected itself to the many linkages which would control the rest of the machine.

Only after closing the hatch, and after pausing with some apprehension, did Lio climb up gently onto the horse. For the first time, he sat alone on its back. He took a breath, trying to remember what he had to do next, but his mind went completely blank.

After what felt like an age, the code system slowly began to come back to him. Bit by bit he adjusted it in accordance with what Kyrros had explained. Confident that he now understood, he rotated the first few rows of thumbwheels, the destination distance, attempting to put right the tiny discrepancy between the square in front of the Temple of Zeus and the Temple of Helios, to ensure that this time the machine would arrive where it had been originally intended. In turn, he programmed the return time and place, but this time unfortunately not as accurately.

He would arrive, he calculated, at his destination at exactly eight o'clock in the evening, twenty hours after the night that Kyrros had rescued him. Satisfied that he had programmed everything safely, he got on with the next, more strenuous task.

Although the space in the packing case was tight, for the next hour he managed to wind up the spring motors using the retractable pedals that he'd identified. His confidence grew as he did. This task, however, was physically exhausting to the boy, and he had to rest several times. In time, the ready indicator on the control panel on the back of the horse's head clicked down and into place.

Now fearful again of being caught, Lio began to pluck up the courage to actually use the machine. He wondered, not for the first time, what both Kyrros and Miriam would say. In his own mind, naïvely, he hoped somehow that his father would be pleased with him – for managing to master his creation. *Surely*, he thought, *they would not object if I turn up to the wedding with just one extra guest*. Lio's own rescue mission would be completed well in time for him to bear witness to the wedding ceremony of Miriam and Kyrros, and everything would be fine!

Taking a last look around him, Lio slid his sun-protectors over his eyes and pushed the right hand lever forward; then, as the noise slowly grew higher and higher, he felt the horse rock back. The noise of the machine masked the urgently approaching footsteps, so it was only as he was surrounded by the flash of light that Lio caught a glimpse of the librarian's astonished face.

The horse hovered weightlessly, and in next to no time there was a bump. But the machine's arrival was not quite as planned – he was not outside on the square. Instead, he was within the very familiar territory of the inner sanctum of his grandfather's own temple – on the exact spot where his mother had given birth to him. And, while he had arrived safely, the event was once again not un-witnessed.

Pulling his glasses down around his neck, Lio climbed down from its back to see the astonished look on the face of the person he instantly recognised. However, it was not the one he had come to rescue: it was his friend the market trader.

The trader had fallen silently to his knees, eyes closed, gathering his thoughts. After a moment he opened them and said aghast, 'It's you!'

'Yes,' the boy answered him happily, pleased to see him once more.

'Are you dead?' the trader's astonishment continued.

'No,' Lio confirmed, as if it was necessary.

'Then it was not the gods who...'

'Rescued me? No – it was technology,' he looked directly at the trader as he stood up.

The Persian stepped toward him, his hand automatically reaching for the boy's head. 'Is it still permitted?' he asked.

'Yes,' Lio smiled, 'I am still the same, just a little older.'

He rubbed the boy's red hair, this time more in greeting than for luck. 'And I was going to ask the gods if I could take over the temple...' he said breathlessly, 'continue in your grandfather's good work.'

Lio laughed shortly, not realising until now what a profound effect his dramatic rescue must have made on those witnessing the spectacle.

The trader studied his face and the strange glass objects at his neck. 'You look much older, taller – more grown up.'

'I'm twelve years old now...'

The trader's face didn't flicker.

'I know – it's difficult to explain.'

'Oh?' the trader looked bemused but decided not to ask for an explanation. He simply continued. 'And your poor back?'

'Healed,' Lio said, hitching around his garments to let him see.

'In one day?' the trader asked. 'Then indeed it was a miracle!'

Lio could of course have tried to explain, but he was sure that whatever he'd said, the trader would have declared it a miracle. None of it was remotely explainable, after all.

'May I?' he held up his hand to stroke the horse's strange muzzle.

'Certainly,' answered Lio.

'So smooth... and beautiful,' the trader muttered under his breath.

The boy asked him the one question that he hoped he'd be able to answer, and the trader did so, smiling. 'The girl is outside,' he said, 'sitting on the square.'

'And is she alright?'

'Certainly, she's made of stern stuff, and all the better for that coward of a priest running off. Though how he escaped with that crowd after him I don't know – he must be halfway back to Sicilia by now.'

Lio snorted in relief, happy to trust that things might return to normal now that he had gone.

'Helio,' the trader advised softly, 'we buried your grandfather this morning, beside your friend Marduk, I am sorry.'

'Yes,' he thanked him. He had had almost two years to come to terms with his loss but now the suddenness of the memory caught him by surprise. Here, it was only yesterday that he had died after all. He felt suddenly choked. 'I am not aggrieved, and I know my grandfather was not. After all, it was an honourable way to depart this Earth – saving the life of another.'

The trader nodded and then continued: 'I read your grandfather's speech to the crowd who came to mourn him – a vast crowd, even bigger than the one which stood outside here yesterday. It was a fine speech; it made us all proud of who we are. Here,' he said, 'please read it for yourself.'

Suddenly overcome, Lio could not. Instead he folded the papyrus neatly and this time made sure he would not lose it. 'Thank you,' he said, 'I will read it when I get home.'

'Home! You're going away again?'

'I have a new home now... with a mother and a father,' he answered happily. 'Besides, what is left here for me now?'

The trader looked bemused, but accepted what he'd said. None of it was remotely understandable after all. Then he asked. 'So why did you return here?'

Something of the expression on the boy's face must have answered for him. The trader knew, although Lio still attempted to justify his journey back there to him with an excuse. 'I promised my friend Marduk, her brother.'

'Ah, yes,' the trader said, plainly understanding what the boy still failed to grasp.

'Then go to her, out there. She will go with you, I am certain. And a damaged girl needs a friend like you, Helio.'

With that, Lio nodded to him and walked through the opened doors, and into the main body of the temple. As he made his way across the marble floor to the main door, he remembered in detail the small journey that he had made a thousand times before in the company of his grandfather. As chance would have it, as he opened the main temple door and looked into the evening sky, the first thing he saw in front and of him was the North Star. Now he was forced back out of the temporary gloom that the short conversation had pushed him into, and into a smile. Not the same half-smile that he'd worn for the past two years but this time a deeply happy smile, the smile one can only have when one returns to the home of one's birth. And it was made all the happier by seeing Ashur.

The girl sat crouched over, cross-legged on the marble, her back towards him, now washed and wrapped loosely in the trader's bright robe. Absent-mindedly she pitched pebbles toward the foot of the sundial. A small pebble lay at Lio's feet. He bent to pick it up and, taking careful aim, he tossed it toward the bottom of the sundial, knocking hers aside.

The girl stiffened.

'Ashur,' he called her name softly, but she remained frozen. 'Ashur,' he called out a second time, and this time she stood up slowly and turned to face him.

The shocked look at the sight of him, her now much bigger and older friend, changed to a trembling smile as tears of joy welled up in her eyes. He had not forgotten her. He had come back for her after all.

Lio held out his hand. 'Come, Ashur,' he said simply, 'it is time to leave this place – forever!'

The girl frowned deeply and turned her head to glare darkly once more at the Temple of Zeus. Then she stepped forward toward the boy, holding out her hand to take his. In silence they returned to the Temple of Helios to say their last goodbyes to the trader.

After a short exchange, the trader patted them both very gently on the arm, still careful of the damage that they'd both suffered – yesterday. 'Will you ever come back?' he asked. 'To visit.'

'No,' Lio answered him, 'I don't think that would be wise.'

The man nodded acceptingly.

'And what will you do?' Lio asked.

'Who knows,' he said. 'Maybe I'll go on trading in the market place... or perhaps I might become a priest and serve in this temple after all... if it is still here tomorrow. After yesterday's events, who is to say what will happen to the Temple of Helios – and all of the temples here for that matter? I suspect they will either be burned to the ground – or rebuilt bigger – who knows. Whatever happens though, no children will ever be used, or misused in the temples again – I am determined to stop it!'

With that, Lio climbed back onto his horse, as he now thought of it, and the trader carefully picked up Ashur to sit her behind him, briefly kissing her twice on each cheek as he did. With a final wave of his hand to his Persian friend, Lio pulled up his glasses again, calling out to Ashur to close her eyes tightly. Then he pushed forward the second release lever, preparing to return to Alexandria.

As before, it did not take long before the noise began to pick up, and Ashur squeezed her arms tightly around him. He saw the trader cover his ears with his hands as the whirring continued to build, and then he looked down at the control panel. By the time he looked back, the Persian had gone, probably outside to avoid the noise and flash of light again. It was then, however, that the Hippo-Chronos gave a brief but dramatic lurch. The horse suddenly seemed heavier – something was making it unsteady.

Lio looked around uneasily to see what had caused it. And there, behind Ashur, desperately trying to push the girl out of the way, was the missing high priest!

'You're not getting away that easily,' he growled.

Ashur opened her eyes and turned her head to see the vicious snarl of the man only a breath away from her. She screamed, a terrified scream, squeezing Lio tighter.

Zeus gripped her painfully by the shoulder, trying to knock her to the ground – trying to get to Lio. The horse bucked wildly as the struggle continued for those few precious seconds. The boy held the lever tight with one hand and flailed around with the other arm, trying frantically to dislodge the interloper, but he couldn't quite reach... and now the priest had Ashur pushed almost off. She squeezed her eyes shut again and clung to Lio for dear life as her tormentor shuffled his way forward. He raised his stick to strike her. Then the boy suddenly found his mark, and his right elbow connected with the high priest's face. It was only a single blow, but it was a good one!

There came a muffled yell, and from the limited vision of the corner of his eye-protectors, Lio saw the man's body slide over the side of the machine head first. Zeus put out his hands to break his fall and as they hit the ground, his left hand, still clutching the cane, he gave a blood-curdling scream. At that, the horse gave one last lurch. Then, mercifully, there came the flash of light. A moment later, they landed with a hard bump, not in the library as intended, but outside on the steps of the square, just as the wedding feast was being laid out in front of the gathering guests.

The uneven ground immediately threw the machine out of kilter and sent it pitching to one side, the whirring gyroscopic mass of the flywheel forcing it further off-centre. There was a cry and several of the small crowd jumped for their own safety as the machine was thrust heavily over onto its side. Then it catapulted both Lio and Ashur across the smooth marble paving in one direction, tearing off his glasses, whilst the horse shot into the crowd before coming to an abrupt halt.

Lio jumped up immediately to see if Ashur appeared safe, then, picking her up, he checked around him to make sure that there was no sign of Zeus – thank goodness there was not. He put away the disturbing thought that somehow he might still have made it.

'Ashur,' he whispered to the girl. 'We mustn't let anyone know of Zeus. Let's just keep it to ourselves and never look back!'

Ashur nodded her head readily. She had no problem in consigning the man's memory to the back of her mind forever.

Lio checked around him again.

Only then was he relieved.

CHAPTER 36:

The Uninvited Guest

"As the commotion died down, shock, is the word that best describes the looks on the faces on many of the onlookers. Some looked nervously around to see who else might have been watching and there were a few faces that looked justifiably annoyed. However, it was a while before anyone spoke. All the boy could do now was stand there with Ashur. He again looked around the dozens of familiar faces, all astounded by him. He searched the crowd for his father, now fully expecting Kyrros to be furious with him, finally realising the potential danger of the machine. For all sorts of reasons, all Lio wanted to do was simply apologise to him.

On hearing the unmistakeable noise of the machine depart the day before, Kyrros had rushed to the darkened chamber only to see the librarian standing aghast in the room. It didn't take long to establish what had happened.

Firstly, unbeknown to Kyrros – the machine's designer and builder – the Chronology Society had finally, after almost two years, come to a decision as to what should be done with the Hippo-Chronos. The head librarian had taken it upon himself to keep it from Kyrros that it would be crated up and dispatched to a more suitable and secure store. His excuse was that the secret location of the horse had been discovered – the outside cupboard door had been breached. However, he had not considered that it had perhaps simply jammed and that it had been prised open for someone to get into the cupboard. In short, using this as a flimsy excuse, he had demanded the machine be taken off *his* premises. The 'failed' experiment was too dangerous to leave lying around in there.

Kyrros had been furious. That, he said, would be like himself clearing the most valuable books from the library without asking the librarian's permission. Kyrros rightly wouldn't stand for it. Outwardly he blamed the librarian for the whole fiasco, although inwardly he part accepted the fault himself. Returning to the house, he attempted to placate Miriam. Seeing the clothes laid out on the bed, he now knew that the boy intended to return in time for the wedding ,though why he couldn't choose between the two garments and had left both out, he, at first, couldn't begin to understand. He only hoped that he had taught the boy well enough to programme the machine to get back. At first, Miriam panicked, but then realised that Kyrros was probably right. Still, she didn't sleep properly that night, only finally drifting off before dawn. She had only woken up an hour or so before they heard the machine arrive in the square.

Hearing the commotion outside, Kyrros ran toward the source of it. Immediately sizing up the situation for himself as the scene turned to deathly silence on his own approach, he realised that now was neither the time nor the place to lecture the boy on his foolishness. Lio knew he had done wrong, just as Kyrros knew he had – even if it was with the best intent. Seeing the girl holding the boy's hand, he immediately guessed who she was. He had been right to trust the boy after all. Lio had something that should never be undervalued: he had a good heart. Whatever had happened, there was no use getting excited about it, it would, he reasoned, not have any benefit. Sensing Lio's anguish, and trying to calm the disastrous situation just a few hours before his wedding, he knew that the only option open to him was to make light of the situation.

Kyrros looked straight into the boy's squinting eyes – Lio held his retrieved glasses, one of the lenses now cracked. In his booming voice, the philosopher enquired dryly, 'And how was your trip?'

Gathering his wits, all Lio could do was join in the pretence of normality. He returned the answer equally dryly, 'Fine thank you father. Father... I'd like you to meet my friend Ashur.' The boy then turned to Ashur and introduced her formally. 'Ashur, this is my new father.'

Kyrros looked down his nose at Lio, knowing that he was indeed truly sorry. Then he looked at the little girl who was clearly in a distressed state. Bending toward her as she sloped around to hide behind Lio, he whispered, 'I'm very pleased to meet you at long last, Ashur, welcome.' Then to the boy, he said, 'Well, hurry along; go and clean yourself up. We all have a wedding to attend!'

The explosive situation diffused, the guests started to smile and laugh, although whether out of sympathy for the boy or embarrassment for Kyrros' wayward son, he would never know. Lio would forever recall only that at that point his worried mother ran through the small crowd and smiled broadly at him as she also gathered who the girl was. She took Lio's face in both hands, kissed him high on each cheek, then carefully, but immediately, swept up Ashur's emaciated body into her arms. She carried her off to be comforted and cleaned up and otherwise given proper attention for the first time in years. Lio, on the other hand, walked off contritely, to quickly clean himself up.

Several of the men stepped forward to pick up the 'experimental child's toy', as Kyrros attempted to explain it away: 'It was a self-propelled machine-sculpture that must have shot out of control from around the corner of the library.' Few of course believed him: the idea of a machine that could move under its own power was simply preposterous – whether Kyrros was a genius or not!

The horse was, as quickly as possible, transported back to the workshops before anyone else could see it – that is, if there was anyone left from the Mouseion who hadn't. The women stayed to help clear up the other mess. The wedding might now have been delayed, but it would not now be cancelled.

A few hundred feet away, now watching the aftermath, a short, solitary figure noted the direction that the mysterious machine was being taken in. content to just look – for now!

At five o'clock the wedding got back under way, and the couple were duly married. Kyrros and Miriam had almost agreed on the form it would take, given that he did not wish to be married in a temple. That, he said would be both ridiculous and dishonest, given also that he believed in no gods. Science alone would one day bear him out, he was steadfastly confident. The couple would then, they agreed, publicly exchange simple vows in a small canopy that had been set up within the library square – without anyone to officially witness or record the ceremony. By this token, the only ones who might suffer as a result of either of them breaking these vows, would be themselves. Simple gold bands were exchanged, that was all. In deference to Miriam's faith though, afterwards, one of the members of the Chronology Society read a shortened prayer in Hebrew, a blessing on the marriage from their friends.

However, there was, after all, one last surprise. Kyrros suddenly produced a gift for Miriam: an antique item of jewellery. It was something that he had bought for no reason other than he had immediately liked its design when he had seen it a while ago on his last solo visit to Rhodos. Perhaps, Lio wondered, it had been bought even before his marriage proposal. It was a gold Torc, an ancient design; who knew how old it was or where it came from? Possibly, he had been told, it had been made by the Keltes, from lands far away to the north. Whatever the truth, the exquisite knotted rope design had caught the designer's eye and now he placed it around Miriam's neck as she smiled serenely, knowing that she truly did have the man's heart.

The wedding feast and merriment started immediately afterward and continued until mid-evening, while Ashur, now looking much brighter, stayed close to Lio. Throughout, she gripped his hand tightly, perhaps out of fear that if she let go of it, this dream might pass and she would wake up back on Rhodos. For his part, Lio was content to take the place of her brother, to protect her against any more hurt. And so, the boy tried to help her fit in with the kind people around her.

She refused to eat, however, and though undoubtedly hungry, drank only milk all that night, frequently spilling it down the clean

– or now not-so-clean, dress. Lio guessed that her mouth was still in too much pain and that she didn't want to eat in front of the others out of humiliation; she didn't want to let them see what had been done to her. But as long as she was happy, no one cared, certainly not Lio. For his own part, the boy was happy to tuck into the variously flavoured foods that were served; when the spiced dishes arrived, he spared a thought for his old friends the Persian trader and Marduk.

As everyone took it in turn to make speeches about the newly married couple, Lio also decided to make his own, if that was the right description. And as it turned out, he stole the evening. Although, as he was quick to point out, the words he used were not his own: they were those of a wise man who had lived long, long ago. But which Lio thought entirely appropriate to that day.

Banging loudly but politely on the table, as everyone before him had done in turn, the boy got to his feet – before he was urged to stand on the bench so that he could be seen and heard properly. For the second time that day, Lio read the words of his grandfather, this time aloud.

'These words were written for me by the wisest man I have ever known,' Lio began. 'Though they were not written for a wedding, I hope that you will accept them as a wedding gift, from my grandfather and myself. Perhaps they can be another blessing on this day. He cleared his throat and began slowly and confidently. My grandfather entitled it:

'On the Mystery of Time, Space and Life.'

'I have lived many years, here on this small part of the earth, in peace and at least toleration of the mixed beliefs of the entire world. In my time, I have sought to understand many things and yet, nearly everything is still a mystery to me:

What lies beyond the nothingness of space? When did it begin to exist? What existed before it? When will time end – and what will come after it?

And if the gods exist, how can we explain where the first of them came

333

from – without deluding ourselves with trite answers? I do not know. I have tried to serve here only as an interpreter for the universe, attempting to help you open your own eyes to the infinite mysteries and beauties of the world – that is all.

No one, but no one, despite their own or jointly agreed extravagant claims, can tell you that the gods either exist or do not exist. That must be your own very personal choice; that is the basis of true faith, though even that does not have to be blind. Questioning these things is entirely natural. It is neither the work of demons – nor is it blasphemous as some insist. Furthermore, it does not follow that a man or woman who cannot believe in the existence of any gods is immoral, dangerous or stupid; at least, no more so than anyone else.

For myself, I choose to believe that someday man will find that the whole universe and everything in it is constructed on a rational, scientific basis – though perhaps that knowledge will not be for all of us to understand. I am myself satisfied that the mysteries of this universe, eternity and creation should always remain just that – mysteries. I am both happy and content at having been allowed only the tiniest glimpse of the world's vastness, and of the mechanics of how it all might work. Though, when the day comes that this is all at last revealed, I still doubt very much that it will either prove or disprove godly existence. Whilst we are alive, it is simply not ours to know!

Proven or not, however, the quest for scientific knowledge does not undermine our society or morality. With or without gods, man's behaviour should be based on the love of goodness, truth and sharing with each other – everyone and everything in this world. After all, the human pursuit of goodness is in essence, the basis of all worthwhile beliefs, is it not? These ideals may be hard for a selfish being like man to accept, but we must all try – and we must especially cease making excuses for why we can't, or rather won't, share! I have met many disbelievers who would give their last, and many believers who would use their gods as an excuse to cheat others 'less worthy' out of their last!

Mankind can never succeed if we are forever bound by superstition – if the only way we can be persuaded to do good is by us being manipulated by those who would supposedly teach us. By being coaxed with the hope of eternal reward, or bullied by the threat of eternal and painful damnation after

*death – only after wasting the opportunities afforded to us to do good in life –
or worse, by carrying out wickedness in the name of any god.*

*Ultimately, however, if we do not listen to our own consciences, it will
not be religion, but intolerance of each others' honestly held faiths and other
scientific beliefs, that will bring about the destruction of us all. The choice that
remains to us is simply this: to care for each other and the earth itself or to
destroy each other. And to prove what? Who is the true god? Who has the
strongest faith? Which is it to be? It would be a strange and vengeful god
indeed that would wish the 'zenith' of his creations to wipe each other out in
his name!*

*As difficult and as unpalatable as it is to accept, that everything we might
achieve in our own short lifetimes might eventually be lost in the vastness of
space and time, it is perhaps for that reason alone that we should respect each
and every man, woman and, not least, child living on this planet – no matter
how humble their circumstances.*

*The pursuit of knowledge, justice, peace and friendship, have carried me
in my own time on this earth. I implore you all to strive toward this difficult
goal – no matter how long it takes. And, to treat each other only as you
yourself would wish to be treated. Life is really that simple.*

*Strive for true knowledge, true peace and tolerance – true love and
forgiveness. Follow your own conscience – and your heart!'*

As the young boy finished, the absolute silence was broken only by
the sound of Kyrros and Miriam's footsteps crossing toward him.
Then, in turn, each of the guests called out in admiration for the
well delivered sentiment that they could all appreciate honestly.
Something they could all believe in individually and collectively –
whatever their religious beliefs or the lack of them. Together with
the little girl he had brought home to them, the new family
embraced each other silently.

Kyrros looked down at Lio and said, 'I could not have put it
better myself.'

'And neither could I have wished for a finer wedding speech,'
added Miriam.

As the thunderous applause continued, Lio realised now that

everyone knew why he'd had to take Kyrros' machine. Because in his own right, he had taken his grandfather's advice: he had simply followed his conscience and his heart!

Later that evening both he and Ashur, had grown very tired. So before turning to leave with his father, Lio said his goodbyes – and some apologies for his earlier performance of that morning. The old athlete, Poseidonios, tapped his spiral stick toward the boy, insistent on seeing him. He wore his best, brightest, chequered robe of red yellow, black and green – an ancient design. Kyrros nodded to his senior and stood back from him, giving them space to talk privately. 'Helio,' said Poseidonios solemnly, 'in a short while, I intend to retire at home on Rhodos. Therefore I would like you to take a small, but meaningful gift from me – my "sun-wheel".' He took a thin leather thong from around his neck; from its end hung a strange, almost circular symbol. Fabricated from twisted and bent silvery wire, it looked like a moving four-legged cross, the fourth leg of which had been cleverly re-fashioned into a head and arm. In all, it resembled a running matchstick man. 'I made it in my youth, from electrum,' he explained, 'after I returned from visiting the lands of Asia – to the east of the great river Hydaspes. It is based on an ancient religious symbol – a peace and good luck charm which I saw there. Over the years, it has become a personal symbol of my curiosity and my endless thirst for travel. But now, sadly, this athlete has run his last race. In any case, Lio, in some respects you have already travelled further than myself. I would like you to take it now, in anticipation of your own long and successful life's journey, and, hopefully, as a token of lasting friendship.' He handed it to the boy. Lio grasped the treasured token with a polite nod, then immediately placed the thong around his neck. When he grew up, he resolved, he would travel the world – just like Poseidonios!

'Now, one other thing,' added the senior philosopher. 'After the events of this morning, I have discussed the subject with Kyrros and the other members, and we are happy that after all of the many, many years of work and dedication of the Chronology

Society, something positive finally came of it. We have decided amongst us that you truly do deserve to join our membership – forever! Even in my retirement, I hope that we will all go on looking out for each other for a long time to come.' He held a forefinger to his lips: 'herkoose odonton!' He patted the boy on the shoulder in confirmation of the boy's secret membership. Lio smiled proudly, then he solemnly repeated the sign, elated to have been accepted as a member of that most secret and exclusive society. Though ultimately, that membership would cause him much sorrow.

Miriam carried Ashur the short distance to their quarters; still desperate not to close her eyes. Kyrros followed on with Lio. He could not get near enough to carry Ashur; she was still no doubt traumatized by him as the apparition of Zeus. In the house, Ashur finally succumbed to the fatigue she'd been through in the past week of her own life. She slept soundly on Lio's bed as Miriam prepared a second mattress on the opposite side of the room, then she picked up and tucked up the still sleeping girl safely in it.

By the time Lio had got into his own bed, still with the athlete symbol around his neck, both his father and mother came into the room to check briefly on both of them. 'Lio,' Kyrros said, 'thank you again for the excellent speech you made. It filled my heart with pride that I have been given the chance to continue where your grandfather left off. I now know who you truly are and why you acted in bringing your friend to us; and for what it is worth, I understand and forgive you completely. I have seen the wounds on the girl's back, so I am absolutely convinced that what you did was with the best intent. In any case, you did only what I did myself in rescuing you – except you did it more purposefully. However, the secret of the machine is much more likely to be out in the open now. And therefore, reluctantly, I think we will have to put your formal education at the library on hold. It would be best for all of us to return to the farm at Drodos rather than stay here – at least until we know what danger has been brought here today.'

Lio, though bitterly disappointed, nodded his acceptance of the terms – and the cost of keeping his word to Marduk. The boy looked at the girl's sleeping face and breathed in contently.

Miriam kissed Lio lightly on the forehead and whispered, 'And thank you for my surprise wedding gift, I've always wanted a little girl of my own.' She smiled and went over to kiss Ashur's forehead before blowing out the oil lamp by her bed. Immediately a squawk of distress sounded and Ashur sat bolt upright, so Miriam exchanged it for Lio's own lamp, still lit. As she settled once more, the door was closed as the newly married couple retired to their own room. But as it shut, without making a sound, Ashur crept quickly out of her bed in her nightgown and clambered into Lio's bed, snuggling herself into his back – her protector. The boy smiled warmly and closed his eyes, drifting immediately off to the most untroubled sleep he'd had in years."

Tom smiled himself and got up to stretch his legs. In silence, he crossed to the window and began to look out at the evening's darkness approaching. While he did so, the others sat patiently, sensing that something else was coming. The old man didn't turn around, but instead began to speak toward the sea. "Sadly, however, while that may be the end of the story of young Lio and Ashur so far, in many ways it was only the beginning." He turned back wearing a pained expression. "Indeed, while that may have been how the paradox was first caused, that paradox triggered more and more in turn, and there is one in particular which continues even today."

"What paradox is that?" Maddie asked warily.

"Perhaps I should have told you earlier," Tom confessed. "It is something which is poised to be used against the whole world – a most extraordinary weapon."

"A weapon!" Bex said incredulously, now shocked.

"What kind of weapon?" Conna joined in.

"A weapon of great stealth," Tom answered simply. "Normally, I do not believe in such things, but somehow, on this occasion, *the future seems written*. It is the weapon which you must help me remove from the world!"

"Us?" The four looked at each other and at Alex in particular. "Did you know about this?" Conna almost accused.

Tom spoke up: "Please do not blame Alex, I told him that he must keep all of what I am about to tell you all in great confidence."

"Like about his dad," Conna blurted out.

The girls began to stare, "What about his dad?" asked Maddie. She looked disappointedly at the boys and at Alex in particular.

Bex said more forcefully, "What other secrets are you all keeping?"

"Sorry," answered Alex contritely.

Tom thought for a moment then said, "We have only a short while left before the girls' father will arrive to pick them up: shall we continue?"

"Might as well," suggested Alex. "If you're all alright about it?"

"Okay then," agreed the girls tersely, wondering what they were getting into now.

Alex nodded. "I think we'd better."

Conna's stomach started to churn, but this time it was not solely for the want of food.

PART V:

THE EXODUS

EVERY MAN'S LIFE LIES WITHIN THE PRESENT;
FOR THE PAST IS SPENT AND DONE WITH,
AND THE FUTURE IS UNCERTAIN.

Marcus Aurelius 2rd Cent AD

CHAPTER 37:

A Scouring Wind Approaches

Tom sat back down and began again: "Over the next two days, as Ashur began to settle in and as she got used to Kyrros, he finally got to examine her mouth, but not before she had bitten him twice in trying. Eventually Miriam and Lio each held her hand gently, while Kyrros carefully coaxed her to 'open wide'.

To his great satisfaction, it seemed that they had all been wrong. Despite never uttering a word since Lio had seen her crying in the underground passage of the Temple of Zeus, Ashur's tongue was still perfectly intact. As Kyrros finished his examination though, her mouth snapped tight shut again – just in case he tried to take it. Together they realised that whatever the problem was with Ashur, it was not physical and no doubt had been caused by the terrible ordeal that she and her brother had been made to suffer. Remembering back a long time ago but still with the mutilated body of Marduk fresh in his mind, only then did the penny begin to drop with Lio. Someday, they *all* prayed, Ashur might be able to speak again.

Gradually, the new family started again to pack up the belongings that eighteen months ago had been brought to Alexandria – now they would be transported back. That, however, did not seem a bad idea to the boy, as winter was now well and truly here and by that token the drier heat of the farm at Giza would be welcome. By the second evening, two carts had been loaded. This included, noticeably to Lio at least, two decoratively cloth-wrapped parcels; even now Kyrros could not be parted from his prototype keys. The family were ready to take their things to the Eunostos dock, though for reasons of security, they would leave unannounced, not even telling their friends. The journey would again take a day and a half, even against the current of the further depleted Nile. But then they would hopefully be secure.

For the next few months, Lio's small family began to settle down to a slow, restful life on the farm. Exile is a strange word to use: admittedly they had little choice but to leave Alexandria. But at the same time this was, in effect, not so much a forced retirement for his father as much as a long earned rest after a hard working career. Lio was happy on the farm and Lio's mother was happy to have a worthy husband. Now, at forty years old herself, Miriam delighted Ashur constantly, showering her with small gifts and toys, the like of which she had been denied in her previous life: woollen dolls, which Ashur quickly learned to make for herself, along with carved animals. Miriam grew more and more close to the girl, the daughter that she thought she might be too old to have herself. Ashur and Lio also revelled in the farm life and although Lio was a little disappointed to have to forego his education in Alexandria for now, his father made himself the boy's personal tutor. On the other hand, it was still too early for Ashur; she needed to try to come to terms with what had happened to her. Like Lio had done years before, she needed to relax and soak up the healing rays of the sun.

Whilst nursing Lio back to health had originally rekindled Miriam's interest in practical medicine, now caring for Ashur in the same way brought out her interest at doctoring treatments and medicines. Gradually, after settling in around the farm, Ashur then became Miriam's assistant as well as her adopted daughter. She had her own natural curiosity for the subject. Every now and again, people from the surrounding population visited them for that purpose – news of the woman healer travelled fast. So it did not take long before Ashur came to relish the position of assistant or nurse to the unofficial doctor. Over that short period, Ashur started to build up her confidence. Within only a short time she had changed almost completely from the ragamuffin that Lio remembered, into quite normal a young girl. And the girl's prettiness grew along with her hair and her self-esteem.

Although she couldn't speak, that did not mean that she was silent. Firstly, she was capable of making plenty of noise, banging and clattering around if she did not agree with anyone – over anything at all! And secondly, Lio's father – now also Ashur's father – devised a limited sign language using their fingers to describe set questions and answers. This was not particularly sophisticated, but clear enough and simple enough for all of them to learn and understand. And, of course, the boy still continued to teach her to write.

They still played children's games together too; for instance, how to ride the various animals. Initially, it was the Macedonian servant who started them off, teaching them how to mount the donkey that was kept in the yard. Also, in time, they were shown how to get the camels to kneel, while they clambered aboard these ships of the desert – not always successfully, but eventually they mastered it. They also taught each other many useful things that their parents could not conceive of, for instance, how to saddle and ride a pig. Yes," Tom smiled to himself, "they did that – I can imagine her even now," he closed his eyes tightly, "galloping around the courtyard. Until in time, Ashur learned to laugh once more.

Their time back at the farm was to be brief though. A scouring wind was fast approaching – fanning the flames of war!

To begin with, the Nile had not risen that year either, making, in total, three long years of drought. Even the farm began to suffer, the desert encroaching steadily into what had not long ago been cotton fields. For two of those years, the ordinary population of Egypt had survived only due to strict rationing. But now, the country's grain supplies were running out completely, making it not just difficult for a lot of people but almost impossible for them to live. Famine stalked the country. People began to ask, 'Where are the king and queen, what are they doing to displease the gods in this way?' In many ways it was a fair question, but the people would very shortly know the answer for themselves, and would not be pleased with it.

King Ptolemy and Queen Cleopatra had been open enemies for some time now, the queen scheming to become sole ruler of Egypt. Their respective advisors, quick to take sides, had exploited this rift. Since shortly after Lio's ill-timed visit, Cleopatra had been ousted from the palace – though perhaps with good reason. More and more she had attempted to treat Ptolemy as a child and had begun to take many opportunities to undermine him whenever and wherever possible. But the most obvious clue as to her true ambition was that she had not long since commissioned coins to be struck with her face alone on them – not hers and the king's, as had always been the case before! Theirs was now an open power struggle.

Also, importantly, with Egypt's own reserves of grain now all but gone, gone too was its wealth. The country was almost on its knees. And this year again, there was little prospect of the harvest being brought in or the grain stores being refilled. Without the agreement of their powerful trading partner Rome, they would face certain ruin.

And from the Roman point of view, although the fire of their civil war had now raged for nearly a year, such was its vast wealth, that it was not itself substantially weakened. From their standpoint, whichever side eventually won, Caesar or the Senate would need to secure any future Egyptian harvest to replenish their own stores. This was imperative: to feed both the Roman citizens and their ever expanding army. It would simply be easier for Rome to keep that supply intact by treaty, rather than start another potentially lengthy war with Egypt. At least, until it suited!

Ptolemy knew that a treaty *must* be entered into quickly, but with which side? He favoured Caesar over the corrupt Senate; he hoped he would be able to conduct this treaty as a simple business transaction with the self-proclaimed Emperor, and somehow maintain his country's independence through these troubled times. Messages exchanged between Caesar and he seemed to confirm that this would be acceptable. However, alas, Ptolemy was new to the throne, inexperienced, and surrounded by corrupt advisors eager to fill their own coffers.

Cleopatra also knew that a treaty must be entered soon, although she had a far more direct approach: she would throw herself at whomsoever the eventual victor was, sell out her brother and family one by one, then the country, and then live in luxury – in Rome!

However, the problem of who would become eventual ruler then settled itself.

Until earlier that year, the battle between Caesar and Pompey, leader of the armies of the Senate had still seemed remote. Pompey the Great, consul, hero of Rome – and the husband of Caesar's own daughter – had now finally lost a decisive battle. After that battle, fought in central Greece, he had fled to Egypt where he had secretly negotiated refuge with Ptolemy's generals. When the king found out, however, he had ordered Pompey's arrest. But, to prevent him revealing the extent of the corrupt deal, one of Ptolemy's generals had then instantly had Pompey stabbed to death as he waded ashore. Pompey was then beheaded and his head pickled in vinegar. King Ptolemy was furious, though it had at least handed victory to his favourite – Caesar. He sent word to the Emperor, ensuring him of his allegiance.

Caesar duly arrived four days later with a small contingent of troops. He was preceded by one of his men carrying the 'faces', a ceremonial axe surrounded by sticks – which symbolised a strong leader protected by his followers – and the origin of the word fascist. Despite earlier recognising the king as the rightful leader, he immediately seized on Pompey's supposed refuge deal with Ptolemy to justify grasping power. Taking up residence in the palace, while he waited for Ptolemy's arrival, he had reportedly been further horrified at being presented with the head of his rival. He immediately declared against Ptolemy for the outrage, leading the boy king to declare to his country that he and Egypt had been betrayed. However, this change of Caesar's allegiance was perhaps more simply explained through Caesar's previously received 'better offer' from the ambitious queen. Had he also decided that he would be far more likely to be able to manipulate and control her over the king?

Certainly, just before his decision was announced, Cleopatra had had herself famously smuggled back into the palace and literally thrown at Caesar's feet. Concealed in a rolled up mattress – not a carpet, as is often said – she emerged naked to beg him to take her side and protect the country – the grain store of Rome – against her brother. The victorious dictator, now in his fifties, declared his undying love, or infatuation, and his full support in the royal dispute, unsurprisingly, for his new partner, the young Cleopatra. Within hours, Ptolemy and the rest of the Ptolemaic family – Cleopatra's own sisters and brothers – had in turn been ousted permanently from the palace in Alexandria, to be replaced by Cleopatra and Caesar alone.

Then, to consolidate his position, Caesar's troops had immediately occupied the older royal sector, a fifth of Alexandria, including the Mouseion, abandoning the rest of the city for now. Ptolemy's massive Egyptian fleet still held the docks, but with Caesar's mercenary fleet on its way from Syria and Rhodos, who knew what would happen next? The Great Library, the museum and its workshops, were now 'under Rome's protection'. The only seemingly good news in all of this was that the Romans had not immediately disrupted the Mouseion itself. But this was to be short lived. Eventually, the situation would also bring about the end of the Great Library.

With all of these disastrous events, as with many good things in life, Lio's new family life on the farm came to an abrupt end. Now in deep mid-winter, news was brought to Kyrros by one of the Society members, a man whom he had barely recognised after his long and tiring gallop on horseback: Kyrros' most trusted technician. He was exhausted and gaunt with hunger and thirst, having cut across the desert in the hope of reaching them in time. The Royal sector of Alexandria, he told them, was now in chaos!

The family sat around the table, waiting for the technician to deliver the latest news.

'Kyrros, for the past month, the Romans have been strengthening their position. More troops are due to arrive, along with Caesar's engineers. Their siege machines, including many catapults and ballistae, have already arrived, ready to take the entire city. Ptolemy's troops – most of the Egyptian armies have sided with the king, against the queen – still occupy the vast majority of the city. They have also brought in their own siege engines and towers. Their own engineers have even "somehow" it seems, copied – even bettered – those newer designs that the Romans have brought. Even now, they are holding the royal sector to siege. The technology of war,' he warned, 'is now playing an increasingly more important role.'

Kyrros and his family listened on intently.

'Yesterday morning, the library was visited by the Romans, demanding to know about the construction plans of ancient weapons, guessing that it is still, somehow, the source of Egyptian know-how.'

'And is it?' asked Kyrros.

'Quite probably,' the technician confirmed. 'Many have secretly declared *for* the boy king. Though, even now, the designs for machines long forgotten are being pored over by the Romans, seeking an edge over their opponents. In particular, the various ingenious war machines of Archimedes of Syracuse are being scrutinised...' He looked at Lio and Ashur in particular. 'The same Archimedes that, hundreds of years ago, was so feared by the Romans that he long ago become a legend. Through his many inventions he kept the Roman invasion of his own distant city at bay for years – until the city's betrayal and his own senseless death by Roman sword even as he worked.' He turned back to Kyrros and Miriam. 'Now, some of the oldest scholars of the Mouseion have already tried to flee; but the Romans allow only the eldest to do so, believing them senile.' He raised his eyebrows. 'And there has already occurred one other tragic loss,' he looked from Kyrros to Miriam. 'When they rounded up the others, we tried to protect Pelos and his mother. We told them he was important to us, but still they were taken away. Kyrros... both of them were summarily executed on Caesar's orders. The Romans said that they would not tolerate such ugliness!'

Miriam broke down and wept at the callousness and stupidity of the act.

As he listened, Kyrros felt sick to the stomach. The Great Library had unwittingly but absolutely been caught literally in the crossfire, to its own potential downfall. However, the main reason for the technician chancing his life in breaking through the siege to visit Kyrros was far more urgent and personal than even that.

'Kyrros, I have been sent at the behest of the librarian. He is in panic! Someone, one of Caesar's elite Praetorian Guard, has been probing about a rumour of a far more subtle, though ultimately decisive weapon – he was particularly inquisitive – as if he already knew something. 'So great is it,' quoted the technician, 'that whoever holds it must surely be victorious: a weapon that can turn back the tide of a battle. A machine,' he described worriedly, 'which could be used, perhaps by an assassin: to slip back in time and remove a rival's parents or grandparents even before he had been born.'

Now there was no question in Kyrros' mind as to why the librarian was in panic. The technician concluded: 'To date, although most of the younger scholars have been rounded up – forced to help the Romans – thankfully, of those that remain, only myself and the librarian are members of the Chronology Society. You can trust me not to speak – but I am worried about the librarian... he is not himself, he is sick with worry for his precious books. Kyrros...' he almost pleaded, 'he has asked me to seek your permission to destroy the Time-Horse!'

Kyrros had guessed what was coming, though by the look of shock on the faces of Miriam, Lio and Ashur, they had clearly not.

The engineer knew that if the machine was betrayed, it was

entirely possible that it would be only a matter of time before troops from one faction or another turned up to seize it for their own ends. Almost inevitably, they would then come for him, its designer and the one person who could show the faction who had captured it exactly how programme it. More urgent though was the further news that the many navigable mouths of the Nile Delta were being actively patrolled by both the Egyptians and the Romans to stop anyone or anything leaving Egypt, except by their permission. He discussed the situation further with the technician. Ptolemy still held the main docks in Alexandria, the technician advised, although he had now lost the smaller Eunostos dock. And, for now, the smaller surrounding Roman fleet was tied up with other work! In an attempt to squeeze Caesar out, Ptolemy had somehow managed to poison the entire water supply of the royal sector with seawater. Caesar was holding on only by rationing, and by sending his ships to secure fresh water from along the coast, though he only had to hold out a few days more for his promised fleet to arrive. In all, it looked like Rome would finally get its way and completely take over not just Alexandria but all of Egypt.

What to do? Kyrros wondered to himself. *Stay and risk capture, or attempt to flee?* Once the existence of the machine was discovered, destroying or disposing of it would surely put everyone in more danger. Either faction would force everyone to rebuild it. If he refused, they would undoubtedly have them all killed – from spite, if nothing else. It was not an easy dilemma to solve. After much discussion between them all, Kyrros spelt out his plan:

'Firstly, I have decided that the machine cannot be destroyed. Instead, however, it must be disabled. To that end,' the King's Engineer instructed the technician, 'return with all due haste to Alexandria and tell the head librarian to go into the sculpture workshops. There you must collect enough of the hard modelling wax that is used for making the bronzes and melt it down. Then, you must fill the entire Hippo-Chronos with it. This will at least seal it and prevent its use – with or without the two keys being present. Sometime, at a later date, when we can do so without threat of betrayal or reprisal, it can then be properly dismantled.'

'And put it to rest properly,' added Miriam.

'Next, to be absolutely safe, both of the other keys should be sealed likewise with wax before being hidden. Better still, the keys should be separated – as far away from each other as is humanly possible.' He looked at Miriam and the children. 'At the same time, to avoid the risk of being captured, we will flee the country immediately and contact the librarian at a later date.' No one argued against the sensible plan.

The decision taken, the rider joined them in a small meal, then at once headed back across the desert to relay the message, this time more safely, on one of the camels.

As for fleeing Egypt, this was far more fraught with danger for his family than for Kyrros himself, but the thought of leaving them behind to await possible capture and ransom was far worse. Tomorrow then, they would take just enough belongings, together with Kyrros' entire stash of gold coins, and head for the Nile.

'Perhaps,' said Kyrros, 'it is not too late to gain access to the sea. Surely the many outlets of the Nile Delta cannot all be patrolled. Once in the Mediterranean, we will head for Rhodos or Athens; then we will be safe. After all, I still have plenty of contacts in both places, and all of the other islands in the Cyclades. Delos, Mykonos, Tinos, any island will do, as long as we are all safe together. Perhaps after the hostilities have ceased, we will even be able to return to Alexandria or the farm.' For now, though, his only goal was his family's safety.

In conclusion then, it was agreed that the servants would only be told that they had decided to return to Alexandria and if the worst came to the worst, they would take whatever they needed and abandon the farm. They would only return when it was safe to do so – if ever!

The next morning, just before dawn, from the kitchen window, Lio curiously witnessed Kyrros climbing out of the well. He was alone and carrying a few small packages. When the man saw Lio watching, he shushed the boy with a single finger to his lips. Lio nodded his understanding. Kyrros went into the workshop and returned after a few minutes, whereupon he helped Miriam put on the gold Torc. She wrapped a heavy scarf around her neck and asked if it could be seen; it was, after all, too much of a temptation to would-be thieves.

In the cart there were only a few things: bags of clothes and a small chest filled with the best of Kyrros' tools from the workshop, which he consciously placed in the cart himself and which sat nearest him. There was also a compact leather bag containing Miriam's medical equipment and medicines and, predictably, the two still unwrapped 'wedding gifts'. Without further ado, tearful goodbyes were exchanged with the servants and, unexpectedly, the Macedonian gave a small gift to Lio. Overnight, he had alone finished off a set of bagpipes they had been making together, in the hope that one day the boy might learn to play them properly. Lio gratefully accepted the token of friendship. It was a thoughtful gift that would always remind him of his carefree days at the farm.

Once again then, the boy and his family were on the move. They sat in the donkey cart, Lio and Ashur dangling their legs down over the back. Lio attempted to play a simple tune on his bagpipes, until after a long while, Miriam asked him if he could not practise some other time. Thankfully, he took the hint. As they approached the Pyramids, he put the bagpipes away and immediately his young mind began to quiz himself about their situation.

Whilst he had always previously enjoyed these journeys with his father, this time he did not, uncertain as he was where they would end up or what would happen to them if they were caught. Lio was worried, for all their sakes but especially for his new personal responsibility – Ashur. The same worry that showed on Miriam's and Kyrros' faces was now reflected in the girl's.

Hitherto, the boy had begun to think of the Hippo-Chronos – his horse – only as a blessing, despite his father's occasional comments on the subject. It had, after all, rescued him from certain death and had also rescued Ashur from a life of undeserved misery. And yet, this

353

new situation, the threat of all of their lives being taken away from them, couldn't help but cause him to reflect on how, perhaps, none of it was meant to be. They were in great danger, all because of the machine. Now Lio began to realise that the Hippo-Chronos had also clearly become a curse. Only much later, however, did he eventually realise how great a curse it was: that without its keys, the machine could now only be used to move forward through time – never to return!

Within a short while, they passed the pyramids. Looking back from the cart, the boy once more studied the stone face of the Sphinx, triggering again the tale of the riddle, 'The Great Paradox'. But Lio now, at last, realised that it was he himself that was the great paradox: someone whom should not now exist – a disquieting thought. *And*, he wondered, *what might be the eventual outcome of it.* He was aware only that he was one of two people in the whole world in the same position. Looking across the small pile of things that separated him from Ashur, he smiled at her bravely and held out his hand toward her – the sister of his friend. He was entirely happy that he had done the right thing, both for Marduk and Ashur's sake. Truth be known, he was now also entirely happy and relaxed in her company. In fact, he had become quite fond of her in a way. *Perhaps in some ways,* he thought, *even though she was a girl, she was even as good a companion as Marduk* – not that he would have admitted it to anyone of course.

The girl, who had been lost in her own thoughts again, tried to smile back but couldn't quite manage, so it turned into a flat, worried smile instead. Nevertheless, Ashur gratefully took Lio's hand in hers, happy to have him, her friend and protector, beside her. As if to check that he had not lost it, with his other hand, Lio grasped the treasured athlete symbol that still hung around his neck. And together, the small family trailed toward the great River Nile and back towards danger. Not an ordinary danger, but one that would eventually engulf the whole world and its entire future!"

CHAPTER 38:

Questions!

As Tom concluded the tale, he stopped and stared out of the window. There followed a long, long silence...

It was Conna who eventually spoke up: "Is that it?... Is that how the story ends?"

"Only so far," mumbled Tom.

Alex also decided to speak out: "Tom, can I ask you something? Why *is* this story called the *Tale of Eos*? What does it mean, anyway?"

Tom didn't answer, now seemingly lost again in a world of his own.

"Yeah, and what happened to the Hippo-Chronos?" asked Connor. "What's it doing here and now?"

Still Tom didn't answer.

"Anyway, what's any of this got to do with Alex's dad?" asked Maddie. She once more looked pointedly at Alex.

Alex looked ruefully at her, but didn't speak.

"Oh..." said Tom, not quite snapping out of his daze, "Alex's father agreed to help me in my task. Trust me, I will reveal all in time..."

"So what about the keys?" added Bex. "What happened to them?"

"Hmm? Oh, the keys..." Tom said almost inconsequentially, "regarding those – and the horse: as soon as the technician arrived back in Alexandria, the task to preserve them in wax was duly carried out. They were then separated just as Kyrros commanded and one of the keys was even sent to the end of the world –

carried by a trusted courier. In fact, the Chrono-key – the computer – was immediately dispatched on an Arab vessel, sailing to the dark, far northern reaches of the globe – the Scotos Lands. The ship was to have only one port of call – to pick up a precious phial of purple dye from the island of Porphyrusa, or Kythera. In a shortcut, it would pass between the far western tip of the island of Crete, and the deep waters surrounding its neighbour, Aegilia, or Antikythera."

"And the ship sank there," concluded Bex.

Tom took a sharp intake of breath. "Oh no..." he scratched his head, returning properly from his wandering thoughts. "No, it passed by there safely. That was not how the so-called Antikythera device came to languish at the bottom of the sea. That would be an entirely different story!"

The four friends looked from one to another, now entirely intrigued.

"You still haven't told us about this weapon," Alex said frustratedly.

Tom nodded in acceptance of the rebuke. "Then I will tell you now...

In the streets of the royal sector of Alexandria, those of the population who were still left ran around in panic as fear mounted. Martial law had been imposed from the outset of the Romans taking up position there. Now, as the population looked on, Caesar's troops, who were there to supposedly rescue the queen and country from the king, were preparing for the oncoming battle with the king's steadily amassing armies. With Cleopatra once more ensconced within the old city palace, and more of Ptolemy's troops arriving outside the walls by the hour, it was time for those of the population who were able, to flee.

The king had granted one day for those who wished to leave, to go before battle commenced. As a result, the streets heaved with people, donkeys, mules and other domestic animals, carts and other wheeled transport, all piled high with belongings. The young, old and infirm jostled to get out of the place before they were locked in. The dreadful clamour of angry cries of frustration, animals braying and babies crying grew steadily as the streets became jammed. Slowly, the traffic began to move again, past the massive temple of the Serapeion and through the mile long streets that converged on the Mouseion square. It would not be long before Alexandria would face the onslaught.

Within a few hours, the old city was virtually deserted. Only a few remained: a few of the scholars, philosophers and technicians who had not already been corralled by the Romans; a few of the old retainers and slaves, suddenly with nowhere to go. The eerie silence, broken only by the distant barking of a tethered dog, was in some ways worse than the previous noise. It conveyed the feeling of impending doom.

Opposite the Great Library, standing back from an upper storey window, was a solitary figure. He was dressed in the black uniform of Caesar's Praetorian Guard, though wearing a colourful extra layer against the cold. Not that there was now anyone left to notice, he had been waiting there for days – in fact, since he had spotted the technician he had quizzed on that previous morning in the library. He had watched him gallop off on a horse, only to return next day by camel. Now his suspicions were confirmed.

In the cold air, the soldier rocked back and forth, stroking his hands and wrists, trying to cope with the pains from his aching, aged limbs. Alone, the third, unwelcome time-traveller, who had hitched a ride from ancient Rhodos, pulled his purple cloak tighter around his shoulders and settled down to his vigil, hoping that it would not be in vain. Zeus, the self-proclaimed representative of the gods, marked time, tapping his thin cane on the floor. Once everything was in place, he would, he decided, steal the Hippo-Chronos. He would then adapt the Greeks' enlightened technology to one more fitting to the challenges of the Latin world. He had some time ago resolved to build the greatest weapon the world would ever see, and with it begin to change the history of the future. And, he decided, he had even

357

devised an appropriate name for the superweapon. He would call the half Greek – half Latin machine – The Hippo-Tempus!"

Tom took a deep breath and sighed before he looked up. "But now," he said, "I think that this is a convenient place to finish the story for today – and, if I am not mistaken, I think I can hear a car approaching. Perhaps," he suggested, "you might come back a little later tomorrow – it is school holiday after all. Maybe," he proposed, "if you come back at around eleven o'clock, you might even take proper lunch with me – but only if you wish? I will prepare something appropriate." That much was agreed then: tomorrow at eleven-ish – after which, they would continue with *The Tale of Eos.*

As Maddie and Bex got ready to leave that evening, each of them wondered again what they were doing there, except to say that they were quite happy to be helping out an old man living on his own. Though in truth, neither of them could decide where his strange but engaging story was taking them. Maybe as the story continued, they hoped, each in her own way would be able to decide what was to be done about it – and Tom himself! Now that the disappearance of Alex's dad seemed to be involved worried them a little, but that was another reason to trawl though his story – for their new friend's sake.

"You will be coming back tomorrow, won't you?" Alex checked again.

"Of course we will, Alex," reassured Maddie, "we wouldn't dream of missing it, would we Bex? All for one..." she smiled.

Bex nodded, though a little more tersely "...and one for all. We'll be here," she agreed.

"Thanks," he said a little sheepishly. "It means a lot..."

"We know..." Maddie reassured. "Don't worry – you can rely on us... promise!"

Alex smiled into the girl's eyes, knowing that he could.

When the knock came at the door, Conna thanked the twins and their dad for the offer of a lift home, but decided to hang back. Then, outside, when the car had gone, Conna asked, "Alex, I know you think this is something to do with your dad, and I know it's meant to be hypothingummy, but are we still meant to believe all of this? I mean, what happens next and what's it all got to do with us anyway?"

Alex looked on as Boris shot after one of the rabbits by the side of the cliff, then he looked as his dad's watch. He smiled – a wry smile. "Conna," he admitted, "I really don't know whether to believe him myself, I only hope some of it's true. If it is, it will mean an awful lot to us all – especially me."

Conna turned to his friend, trusting his judgement. "Okay then mate... if you say so. Like Maddie and Bex said: three musketeers... and that other bloke."

"And Boris." Alex laughed at the dog, now chasing another rabbit around, glad to know that his friends were happy to stick with him to the last.

Together, as the weather began to change for the worse, Conna and Alex looked out around the landscape – to the silhouette of the ruined priory on Pen Bal Crag, then back toward the black middens, each lost in his own thoughts. Whether Tom actually knew anything about Alex's father's disappearance, only time would tell.

In the early hours of that same morning, Tom stood unsteadily beside the covered lump that was the Hippo-Chronos. He peeled back the sheet that covered the strange, battered sculpture and stood gazing at its painted smile. "Not long now," the old man said to it, patting the tuft that was the remnant of its mane.

He crossed over to stand alone at the opened window of the laboratory, the house now in pitch darkness. Like the boys before him, he scanned the silhouetted views of the priory and castle walls to his left, then all the way to the black rocks to his right. Then, closing his eyes, he inhaled the cold night air deeply into his lungs. The effort caught his breath a little and he began to cough, clutching his chest against the pain. The bandage felt damp under his hand. He took the pill that he held in his hand and placed it under his tongue. Not for the first time, he wondered whether he would be able to carry on to the end of his story.

His eyes now closed, in his mind he saw the familiar, broad shouldered figure of a young man standing beside the rocks. Tom immediately recognised the shoulders as his own. Then he almost felt a huge blast of warm air, as the whole world burst into a ball of black and orange flame. Tom's mouth dropped open at the disturbing thought, not knowing where it had come from. He staggered back to his chair and sat down heavily, covering his face with his free hand. The memory had taken him to a place uneasy to revisit.

For the rest of the night he sat in his chair, suddenly terrified to go to sleep in case the image returned to haunt him. It was only just after watching the dawn come up that he finally drifted off.

EPILOGUE

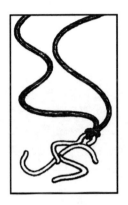

I KNOW THAT I KNOW NOTHING

Socrates 5th century BC

Estam!

The Nile Delta:
13ᵗʰ January 47 BC – only weeks after the eventual fall of Alexandria

Cloaked in the grey light of dawn, Ptolemy, the boy king of Egypt, stood with his two companions at the edge of the low river island. Somewhere behind him sprawled the camp of almost his entire army: 15,000 well armed but underfed soldiers. All around him was unnaturally silent. At fifteen years of age, the fate of the entire world rested on his shoulders. Today would be the battle that would define all of future history. Ptolemy XIII knew this and it was not a responsibility which he took lightly. It was something he'd had to learn to cope with in the last few months in almost a baptism of fire. He had been ousted from the Royal Palace by his sister Cleopatra and her new lover Julius Caesar, and following the siege, due to the corruption and incompetence of his generals, he'd finally lost the city of Alexandria. This battle would be his last stand. If the grain store that was Egypt fell completely into Roman hands, there would be dire consequences for the future of civilization.

Again he screwed up his eyes, attempting to peer through the thick sea fret that hung doggedly over the river, obscuring its muddy banks. Only a few untrodden bulrushes and the tops of a few clumps of reeds now betrayed its edge. Since crossing the thin crust of dried silt to make camp here yesterday, the river had swollen overnight and although only shallow, it had cut them off. As titular commander of his armies, he had not approved of the plan to cross to this supposed safe haven. However, the powerful generals had got there before him and, as always, had decided in his absence. Now, as a result, everything had been jeopardised.

He had awoken earlier to both the slowly increasing sound of the encroaching river and the sound of troops moving on the opposite bank. The long-awaited rains had finally come, but now only to the detriment of the boy king. Of course, his own cavalry and chariots had been left over there to guard the camp – not least because the thin crust across to the island could not have supported the weight of the horses – but the earlier noise had betrayed the fact that his cavalry had already fled. Now there was only the sound of massive numbers of foot soldiers – the Romans had arrived.

Yet, although only a hundred feet away across the water, Ptolemy still could not establish the weight of numbers of his adversary. With the absence of wind to disperse the mist, and without the heat of the sun's rays to evaporate it, he could not evaluate how bad things were. Neither of his two spies had returned. It seemed to him, though, that the situation had changed dramatically overnight.

Only days before, Caesar's ally and Egypt's arch enemy King Mithridates of Pergamum, had marched his own sizeable army into Egypt. Ptolemy had watched his own generals marching 10,000 of his troops out to stop them while he stayed with the main force, but since then, news had not returned of the outcome. Now, despite his remaining generals' optimism, Ptolemy grew uneasy. In these changed conditions, it would be difficult to mobilise, difficult to see the terrain on which the battle would commence, let alone get to it. Nevertheless, Ptolemy's generals still decided that this would be to their own troops' advantage. After all, they were safe here. To attack, the Romans would have to wade knee deep before getting to them. And, of course, the river was, as always, protected by the god: Sobek!

Regardless of anyone's opinion though, it was now too late to do anything but wait for the mist to settle. Now, at long last, the generals and their own advisors arrived with good news – or so they claimed. Three high priests approached the twin figures dressed in gold, and the solitary, quite ordinary-looking man standing behind the king. Ptolemy took the queen's hand to comfort her while they listened. Feigning obeisance, one of the three priests stooped over before the royal couple, his hands smeared with blood from a recently sacrificed bird. The fresh smelling contents of the stomach of the sacred Ibis confirmed the good omens, he assured. "And, your majesties..." the high priest reassured, "in addition to this, both vultures and snakes have been spotted by the shores this morning. These symbols of your rule over both upper and lower Egypt are most portentous. The gods have let it be known that this day a great victory will be had."

Ptolemy XIII looked at the fawning priest and wondered how anyone could take these omens for anything other than the stupidity and superstition that they were. Of course there were vultures and snakes here – this was the Nile! And as for the contents of the guts of a dead wading-bird... He brushed the corrupt fool away with his hand, turned to his sister and murmured to her solemnly, "But for *whom* are these signs portentous of victory?"

Arsinoë IV, the newly self-declared *rightful* Queen of Egypt, didn't answer. She had recently arrived with her own troops to bolster up those of her brother, determined to drive out the Romans and her ruthless elder sister Cleopatra from the country. She looked worriedly back at him, knowing that in reality the situation was less optimistic. The generals gazed at them unconcerned, entirely happy with the prediction. "Pass the word to the troops," was their only command, "we must make ready."

Forget reality. Forget tactics: choosing the battlefield that would best suit their troops and weapons; or even simply counting numbers. After all the books he had read in the Great Library of Alexandria, all of those rational, logical observations about the world and how it worked, it seemed ironic to Ptolemy that both his own people and Caesar himself were still only impressed by myth and superstition. He wondered fleetingly how long it would be before these adults finally grew up – like him. He was tempted to ask the pink-faced man behind him if the world would ever change.

Resignedly, instead, he turned and shook his head ruefully at him. His older friend of only a few weeks did not speak, but fully understood and shared his feelings. Then, from the southeast, the Euros wind began to pick up briefly.

Within no more than a few minutes, each of the generals' faces dropped. As the mist finally cleared, there, opposite them, stood a vast, assembled Roman force. It took only a short while to establish their number – 25,000 strong. Now, instead of the Egyptians' massive advantage in numbers, only last night they had predicted that their 15,000 troops would face only 3000 Romans, it appeared that they had themselves been outnumbered. Obviously the bulk of the soldiers now on the opposite riverbank were those of Mithridates. He had destroyed Ptolemy's other body of troops and had now arrived to join Caesar. Now at last, it dawned on the Egyptians that they had simply stranded themselves on a muddy island facing a combined superior force!

As the king watched, a lone felucca crossed the wide river toward them. In it, a single unarmed messenger, a slave, held up a smaller copy of the red banner of Rome, its gold eagle spreading its wings before it. But this was not the usual 'SPQR' standard. It did not seek to declare that the Emperor represented both the government and the people: 'Senatus et Populus Que Romanus'. This was Caesar's own new black, red and white standard, one which depicted the fascist symbol of the axe surrounded by the bundle of sticks. Additionally, below the eagle, there was a gold disc. On it was depicted a curious good luck symbol: a four-legged running cross. It was not unlike the eastern symbol – the sun-wheel – given by Poseidonios to Lio, but this one stood out ominously.

Once landed, the messenger was brought before the royal couple. "You may speak," Ptolemy said looking directly at him. The Roman cleared his dry throat and duly delivered the message he'd been given. "Your majesty," Arsinoë noticed the singular term "it is the earnest request of Emperor Julius Caesar that no more blood is spilt in the dispute for the throne of Egypt. Therefore, he extends to you a generous offer: that both yourself and your royal sister relinquish your claim to the throne of Egypt, and stand down your armies. If this is acceptable, it is the proposition of Caesar that you be given the titles of King and Queen of Cyprus. Furthermore, Caesar guarantees your safe passage there."

"And what of my country?" returned the king. "What will become of those loyal to me? Am I to believe that the usurper and traitoress Cleopatra (Arsinoë appreciated the insults) will allow the country to avoid this bloodshed. Or is it that if I stand down, she and your Emperor will decimate my troops in the Roman manner?"

The messenger did not answer. He had witnessed the way the Emperor had previously executed one in ten of his own troops as a punishment for failure. It was exceedingly likely that Caesar, or more likely, Cleopatra would at least do the same or worse to the Egyptians who had remained loyal to her brother. How many would she slaughter, and by what method?
Arsinoë considered the offer silently, while her brother spoke for her.

"Tell Caesar that I will stand here," continued Ptolemy. "Tell him that if he wishes to take the throne of Egypt from me, he will have to fight for it. I may be but a boy to him, but I would rather die here than betray the responsibility handed to me by my forbears. This is the word of the true and rightful king."

Arsinoë confirmed the decision, "That is the loyal queen's decision also."

The messenger respectfully saluted with the flat of his hand against his white tunic. He bowed and turned to leave. One of the king's generals whispered to the soldier beside him, who clutched his machete-axe, grinned and followed the messenger back to the boat.

Ptolemy turned again and walked the few paces to the man standing behind him. He looked at the strangely familiar pendant that hung around his neck. "Have I done right, Estam?" He mispronounced the tricky name as always. Since only his second meeting with the king a short while ago, when he'd been picked up making his way toward the Egyptian camp, he had for many reasons been taken immediately into Ptolemy's confidence. Since then, the two had talked of many amazing things, but nothing that might be allowed to affect the inevitable outcome of the battle. Though in truth, even though the king knew exactly where the stranger had come from, and how he had arrived, he had not probed – he knew not to. Over that short period, the man had got to know the young king well. He liked him and was happy to accompany him till what he knew would be the end. "Yes, your majesty," he said finally, placing his hand on the king's shoulder as he would his own son. "I am certain that your decision was both a brave and an honest one."

Ptolemy smiled: a knowing, half-smile. He inhaled suddenly: "Then you should go now, you must not get caught up in this. Your own son will be waiting for you, and I also wish you to tell Helio that I died with honour!"

The man raked back his gingery-grey hair with his fingers and nodded, choked and unable to say any more. To do so would, he knew, cause another massive time paradox, one so fundamental that it would change the entire future of world events – and no doubt prevent him from being there. Instead, he nodded once, squeezed the young man's shoulder and walked away.

Julius Caesar stood on the opposite bank of the Nile and watched the apparently empty felucca drift toward him. He was entirely confident that his own sayers had read the omens well – that the vultures and snakes spotted by the shores assured him of victory over upper and lower Egypt. He strapped-on his purple plumed helmet and breastplate, then folded his arms confidently. As the boat got to within a few feet, he looked down at the mutilated body of the messenger and sighed resignedly; there had been little doubt in his mind what the answer would be. For the past few weeks, each time he had sent a message, the outcome had always been the same. The Egyptian generals were entirely predictable. So be it.

He gazed over the now clearing mist and at the island, choosing where to start, satisfied with his decision to leave the majority of his cavalry to guard Cleopatra in Alexandria. "Are the nets in place upriver?" he checked.

One of his generals saluted the emperor with his right palm outstretched toward him. "Yes, Emperor," came the confirmation.

"Then we will attack here. I will not risk the few horses we have; instead we will march into the shallows and surround the island on three sides. The enemy will be forced to retreat from it and attempt to regroup on the opposite riverbank, where they will fall into panic. The river runs deep there – and they will have more than us to deal with," he smirked sardonically. His generals snorted at the dark joke. "But before we commence, let the messenger here help us one last time. Tow his body upriver and let it drift back down on my signal, the scent of blood should be enough to get our other friends to follow – and don't forget his head!"

Ptolemy turned to Arsinoë and prompted her to pass the message to make ready her royal barge. If the battle did indeed go the wrong way, it would provide an escape route for her. "ESTAM!" Ptolemy called out one last time to his guest. "Stay in the boat and out of trouble. Someday you may wish to report this – that the Egyptian peoples did not readily hand over the fuel supply to the armies of fascism!"

The man held up his hand in silent reply and in final salute.

In fleeing the gunmen on the back of the Hippo-Chronos, Alex's archaeologist dad had trapped himself in the past. However, what had started as an accident was now about to present him with the opportunity of a lifetime; the chance to witness one of the most important, but forgotten battles of the ancient world.

Though afterwards, if he was ever going to make it back home to his own family safely, Stan would have to first make it to the allotted rendezvous point. And in that task, he could not afford to waste time!

Acknowledgements

I'm afraid I have a confession to make regarding the sources of the material I have used for this book, which I suppose I've inadvertently researched for many years. That confession being, those sources are so many and various, I cannot justifiably single out any one of them. Nevertheless, I will attempt to at least group them into seven.

Firstly, as a youth at school and as a student of ancient history, I often found my mind wandering away from the curriculum (much to the consternation of my teachers). Instead of concentrating my efforts on what happened, when and why, I began to imagine myself there. However, I did not imagine myself as one of the main historical figures, but instead as one of the ordinary people. It was then that I began to wonder how the big events I was studying would have impacted on the general world population. That thought process in turn made me more curious as to what direct effect it all had on today's society. I wanted to know how the relatively enlightened world of the Greeks had succumbed to the oppressive Roman world. Obviously, the answer to this second question was Roman might. But more than that, I began to form the opinion that because the Romans absorbed the Greek world rather than conquered it, it was much easier and less threatening to the Greeks. Gradually their more learned, though admittedly still sometimes brutal attitudes were waylaid by the far more openly corrupt Roman ones. I personally do not blame the Romans for this so much as the Greeks in the period after Alexander the Great, for rolling over and almost letting them take over. Nevertheless, I

370

would like to pay tribute to the schoolteachers who opened my eyes to this whole subject all those years ago – and to schoolteaching as a profession.

Secondly, throughout my life, my career and my travels, I seem to have inadvertently absorbed much. I have listened to many on-site lectures, especially by the excellent accredited Greek tourist guides. These are learned and passionate people who have not only given me the official historical story, but quite often, the less well known and admittedly more controversial, line. Whilst I would hesitate to suggest that this is a serious history book, but instead a thought provoking lay-historian's introduction to it and other subjects, I can't help wondering at what point speculation actually becomes accepted as history. (I am certain that Prof. Derek DeSolla-Price must have faced the same resistance to his outlandish beliefs regarding the Antikythera device.) This is especially true of the very helpful staff of both the Acropolis archaeological site and the Athens Museum of Ancient Antiquities. Thankyou then, to the many professional guides who have shared with me the benefits of their considerable collective expertise.

Thirdly, there are many ordinary local people who I have bumped into on my recent travels in particular. Some of those I met, by what I will only permit myself to call the most incredible coincidence, have been able to lead me down new avenues of research. The information and local colour which I was able to glean from these private, sometimes personal conversations have been invaluable to me. These kind locals include the many helpful people I met on the islands of Rhodes, Tinos and Antikythera especially. Individuals who got me into a seasonally closed museum, and others who took me to see the well of Andronicus, the underground water spring (although I have changed its location slightly), as well as take me to where the true wreck site lay (as opposed to the official tourist guide). Also, in this respect, I would like to thank a certain Athenian sculptor and designer, who after only one short, straight conversation – during which he was astounded by the repeated coincidences I outlined to him – helped

371

reconfirm my own view: that somehow, this book was meant to be!

Fourthly, to all of the librarians and archivists who have helped me enthusiastically, without knowing the reason why, I extend my warm thanks. This of course includes the local people of my native North East England.

Fifthly, I would like to thank my family and friends, who have unselfishly contributed in a very real sense, spending many hours of their time in getting personally involved, and not least, poring through the many early drafts. Without being trite, their input really was invaluable.

Sixthly, penultimately, without the wise and considered words of Albert Einstein, I would have struggled to write Lio's grandfather's speech. In his lifetime Einstein was repeatedly 'accused' of being an atheist, although he denied this, preferring to take a more open view of whether there was, or was not, a God. As a man in tune with the scientific universe, I guess Lio's grandfather's thoughts might be similarly in tune with the words of Einstein. I have added to these sentiments, using likely thoughts that were around from at least the time of Socrates, 470 BC, an idealist and prophet of the sun who was condemned to death for his intellectual, though 'heretical' teachings.

And finally, I am certain that I have, over the years, absorbed much from books and TV, and the *BBC, The History Channel* and *National Geographic* channels in particular. Through them, I began years ago to connect seemingly unrelated events as I have. Years later, I am delighted to learn that the same private theories that I would not have dared to make public at the time are now quite well accepted by professionals. No doubt there will be many who will recognise something of the themes of their own work in these pages. In some cases I have borrowed from these shared themes, in others, some details and learned explanations. I trust that I have not overstepped the mark. If I have, I hope that interest in these fascinating previous documentary works and theories will be rekindled as a result, but they are, again, too numerous to list.

On second thoughts, if I could, after all, pick out one single source of both information and especially verification, there is one selfless, learned body to whom I would like to pay particular homage. This truly exceptional organisation advocates the freely accessible and uncensored education of the whole planet. Eventually, I, for one, believe that this enlightenment may very well be the saviour of us all. I refer of course to *Wikipedia*. Please then, accept my heartfelt thanks – to all of its contributors.